A
BEAUTIFUL
POISON

A BEAUTIFUL POISON

LYDIA KANG

LAKE UNION
PUBLISHING

Text copyright © 2017 by Lydia Kang

Excerpt from "Two Fusiliers" by Robert Graves, from *The Complete Poems Volume I*, edited by Beryl Graves and Dunstan Ward.

Published by Lake Union Publishing, Seattle

www.apub.com

Amazon, the Amazon logo, and Lake Union Publishing are trademarks of Amazon.com, Inc., or its affiliates.

ISBN-13: 9781477848876
ISBN-10: 1477848878

Cover design by PEPE *Nymi*

Printed in the United States of America

For Alice

Show me the two so closely bound
As we, by the wet bond of blood,
By friendship, blossoming from mud,
By Death: we faced him, and we found
Beauty in Death,
In dead men breath.

—"Two Fusiliers," 1918, Robert Graves

CHAPTER 1

August 17, 1918

At the bottom of the oak staircase at the stately Cutter house on Fifth Avenue, Florence Waxworth—tedious busybody and recent debutante—lay askew, shapely legs draped over the last step. One silk slipper perched on the top landing, where it had been violently kicked off at the start of her fall. The other was still buckled chastely onto her left foot.

The skirt of her gilt dress had ridden up, revealing satin garters above her knees. Her face was turned to the wall as if Florence herself couldn't bear such an embarrassing predicament. Her hair was a tumbled mess, and a smear of blood marked where her cheekbone had collided with a stair edge during the descent. An odd darkness mottled her skin. The broken remnants of a Baccarat wineglass reflected light—an earthbound chandelier scattered on the floor.

All the while, the fiancée of the hour, Allene Cutter, simply stared. Electric happiness mixed in with the horrific, like when you saw a broken robin's egg on the ground in spring, full of smashed baby bird, and still thought—what a *splendid* blue color of eggshell.

She had dreaded this party. Dreaded being engaged to Andrew. And yet she wanted both with an equal, opposite volume of craving. Such a match ought to be nothing but wonderful. Shouldn't it be grand to be *Mrs. Andrew Smythe Biddle III*? And at the enviable age of eighteen? But Florence's death brought splendor to Allene's cheeks not because of the snuffing out of a certain needle-nosed, irritating socialite, but because of whom it drew to her side.

Jasper Jones and Birdie Dreyer.

"Turn her over—gently!" Jasper cautioned. He was the closest thing to a doctor at the party, though he worked at Bellevue Hospital, and his official métier was janitor and he had yet to begin his medical studies. Father had been awfully foul when he discovered that Allene had invited him. But at least *someone* was doing *something*, and it wasn't one of his prized guests. "Bring some smelling salts. Quickly!" Jasper ordered. He was damned handsome when he yelled like that.

Servants crowded Florence's body, uncorking bottles of ammonium salts. A slim hand slipped into Allene's and squeezed gently. Forgivingly.

Birdie.

She was Allene's height but lacked her breadth. She was, as always, like her name—something you desperately wanted to keep caged for the sheer greed of possessing it. After being absent from the Cutter house for four long years, Birdie was still slender and fragile, as if snipped off a piece of cloud. Her golden hair was loosely knotted above the nape of her neck. Her skin had that translucent quality of milk glass and moonstones.

Next to Birdie, Allene felt gaudy and overdrawn, even though Birdie wore the borrowed feathers of an ill-fitting peach silk dress from Allene's own armoire. Allene wished she hadn't painted so much lipstick and rouge on herself.

But something had changed about Birdie during her absence from the Cutter house. She'd always been this fairy girl, but now she had a bosom and hips and—oh! That face! She had the sort of beauty that left you bleeding internally after gazing for too long. Throughout the party, Andrew had barely been able to stop staring.

"The smelling salts aren't working," Jasper said. He withdrew his fingers from Florence's neck, which was now swollen and purpling under the warm electric lights. "By God, Allene. Florence is most certainly dead."

Of course she is, Allene nearly said, before biting her tongue.

"Oh my gosh!" Ernie added uselessly.

Ernest Fielding was all chubby face and blond hair and too much awkward elbow. He was the one who was invited to all the parties but to whom no one wished to speak. In the last hour, he'd already retold the same joke, laughed the same laugh, and discussed the price of gold bullion twice, as if anyone truly cared. His father was a banker and a bore, and Ernie was dutifully following in his footsteps. As usual, everyone ignored his exclamation, which came approximately ten minutes too late.

Birdie caught the almost-mischievous look in Allene's eyes, and she surreptitiously leaned in, as if keenly remarking, I know what you are. You and your schemes, always trying to knit us together, always leaving poor Ernie behind and laughing about it, always playing people like they were chess pieces underfoot. Don't think I forgot. It's only been four years.

Meanwhile, Jasper went to speak with Andrew by the enormous fireplace with its white marble mantel, burdened with a cloche-covered clock and crystal vases stuffed to choking with roses. Dark hair fell roguishly into Jasper's hazel eyes. He wore a proper sack suit in nut brown, but it looked wrinkled next to Andrew's impeccable silk tuxedo. Allene could see the fraying of the trouser cuffs, but Jasper sported a straightness to his spine. Even in the midst of the tragedy, he caught her glance and winked at her in a challenge. Tell me I'm wrinkled, and I'll wrestle you in the mud. Just try me.

My, but he'd grown. His shoulders were wider, and he was far taller than before—almost a head taller. Thank goodness he was too young for the draft. Oh, that war. That terrible, bloody war. And yet Jasper had gone through something himself these last four years. Hard labor and time away from the Upper East Side had stolen the boyish roundness of his cheeks, replacing them with angles that simply hadn't been there before. Here he was—a man. He'd grown without Allene's permission. She wanted to stamp the floor with her Louis heels.

Andrew came to her side. Together, the Almost Mr. and Mrs. Biddle. Wonderful.

"Darling. You must be so upset," he murmured. "Do you need to retire upstairs? I can explain your absence. It would be most understandable."

By all accounts, Andrew was handsome, with that perfectly trimmed chestnut hair slicked with pomade and his waistcoat shining with a gold fob. And like any gentleman of breeding, he kept his emotions well concealed. He wasn't like Birdie, whose emotions swirled like oil on water in her eyes, or Jasper, who blurted out his feelings with a quick smirk or frown, unable to hide anything. But did Andrew not care that their party was ruined? Or was he thrilled? Perhaps he was waiting for another opportunity for a surreptitious glance at Birdie's breasts. Allene had an unnatural urge to prick him with a brooch pin, just to see if he actually bled. But the Biddles didn't bleed. Like the Fieldings, they were bankers; they bled other people.

"I'm fine. I want to make sure my guests are well. Please attend to Father. I'd be so grateful."

"Of course." He leaned down to kiss her cheek, and she stiffened so as not to cringe. Unconsciously, she squeezed Birdie's hand, and Birdie squeezed back. They were a united front against . . . what, exactly? She wasn't sure.

By now, the servants had turned Florence onto her back, laying her flat on the polished floor. Lucy stepped smartly forward. She wore her usual uniform of black with apron tied crisply around her narrow waist, with thick cream stockings that, bless her, only a maid or old lady would wear, though she was only thirtysomething years old. Her capable hands carried a blanket, which she draped over Florence from neck to ankles. Allene stifled an urge to laugh. Florence hadn't shown so little ankle since her debut two years ago.

Florence's eyes were half open, with a telltale gaze that stared at oblivion. Allene's father stepped into the circle that surrounded Florence. He was full of beard and belly and ensconced in his too-tight tuxedo and white spats.

"For God's sake!" Mr. Cutter exclaimed. "What sort of person dies from tripping on steps?" As if Florence's family lineage were at fault for the mess of an evening.

"But it wasn't a simple trip. She fell. She didn't look right," Lucy remarked.

Allene paled. "What do you mean, Lucy?"

"Excuse me, Miss Allene," Lucy said. The excitement of the evening was wearing on Lucy; her Italian accent, usually well buttoned down, was evident. "But I saw her coming up the stairs, and I asked if she needed anything. All the guests were in the parlor. I thought it was odd she wanted to come to the chambers on the second floor."

Here, Birdie stared at her feet. Jasper exchanged guilty glances with Allene. They knew why Florence had gone upstairs. She wanted to find out why the three of them had quietly escaped the party. They'd disappeared about an hour before the accident—when Allene should have been entertaining her guests with Andrew, enjoying the unpatriotic, decadent food that wasn't wheatless, meatless, and sweetless, like the posters said it should be. When Jasper should not have been shamefully lounging on Allene's bed. When Birdie had been naked behind Allene's silk dressing screen. When they all had been doing something rather wrong. Rather scandalously wrong.

"What then?" Mr. Cutter asked, and Birdie's, Jasper's, and Allene's eyes snapped up to attention. They all wore their guilt like wet raincoats.

Lucy continued. "She paused on the top step. She couldn't speak! Oh, she had a terrible color to her face! I thought she was going to be sick. I said, 'Miss! Miss!' but she didn't seem to hear me. And then she fell back, back, back. Twisted around on those heels of hers."

"An accident," Mr. Cutter announced, businesslike. "Terrible. She must have had too many glasses of champagne." He wrung his hands. "I . . . need to take care of my guests." He stepped into the throng of questioning friends, who covered their mouths as if death could be caught by inhaling the air surrounding the corpse.

Andrew stood by, wanting to be helpful. "Someone needs to find her family and notify the police." He went to speak to Lucy and the other servants, who began ushering the guests away from Florence's body.

Allene's hand grew limp in Birdie's. She must have seen Allene's little color drain away. Jasper noticed it too and grasped her other hand.

"Allene!" he whispered. "Are you going to faint?"

She closed her eyes and clasped their hands tightly with a strength that surprised her. Ah, this was what she'd missed: Jasper and Birdie at her side, always at her side, stealing jam from the cook, leaning sleepy heads on each other as they drowsed beneath the summer sun on the shore, their parents drinking cold champagne elsewhere while they were all sticky hands and mischievous smiles.

"No. I'm fine," Allene said. She opened her eyes and met theirs. "Please don't leave. I beg you. Both of you."

Florence's death was the perfect excuse to keep Birdie and Jasper in her life now that they were back. She would do whatever it took to keep them there. Anything. This time, she would fight. This time, she would lie.

Four years ago, Father had the power to say that Jasper wasn't good enough to set foot in the house anymore after his family's scandal. Father had the power to say that the Dreyers were no longer welcomed, and Allene was forbidden from contacting both friends. Letters were torn up before they left the Cutter household; incoming ones were seized before Allene could lay eyes upon them.

But she was on the cusp of being the mistress of her own estate now. Father had relented when she had said Jasper and Birdie would come to the party. It was her particular wish. Perhaps enough time had passed that he believed Allene was far beyond their influence. He'd no idea that she worried it was the other way around.

"Please," Allene begged.

Neither of them answered. They didn't need to. Someone approached their group, and Jasper withdrew his hand just in time. Allene's hand felt far too empty.

Jasper backed away as guests said their good-byes. Motorcars rumbled to the curb, their Klaxons adding noise to the hive of nervous, bustling activity in the foyer. The chaos of it all would have made anyone dizzy. Allene wasn't dizzy, and she wasn't faint. She felt more alive than she had in ages.

Within the hour, police were everywhere. Andrew was bringing Allene a glass of water she didn't care for. Darkly uniformed officers swarmed like ants over the house, over Florence's body. Allene was half fascinated, half horrified by the spindly, three-legged camera stand they set up. Like a crippled metal spider, it towered almost eight feet above the body. A young man propped up a ladder to capture photographs of the scene, yawning afterward. Death in Manhattan must be a rather boring affair, even when it happened to the rich and beautiful.

Two other officers quarreled with Mr. Cutter, and Jasper was clearly leaning in to listen. Allene touched his elbow.

"What are they saying?" she whispered.

"They're wondering if they should call Norris's office."

"Who?"

"Dr. Norris, the chief medical examiner. To see if it's a suspicious death."

"Why? Is it?" Birdie looked shocked. "I thought she simply fell!"

"So did I. But—"

Jasper quieted further when Mr. Cutter placed his hands heavily on two of the senior officers' shoulders. He ushered them into his study down the hallway. Allene left Jasper and Birdie to casually follow her father. She saw him open a cherrywood humidor on his desk and hand each officer a cigar. Mr. Cutter turned to close the doors, briefly frowning at Allene.

She knew that frown all too well. He'd grimace like that when she used to entertain evening guests with her parlor tricks. She'd had an unwomanly habit of loving chemistry since she was a girl. Her mother thought it a charming entertainment, but ever since Mother had taken herself to a health spa in Saratoga, chemistry had been all but outlawed in the Cutter house. At parties, Allene used to light a tiny ball of cotton soaked in naphtha and hidden in her ungloved palm. She'd give the illusion of conjuring fire with her bare hands. With all eyes on her, she felt a spark of something that amounted to more than just one dull life. Something dangerous and unquenchable. But then her father's frown would land on her like a thousand pounds of wet wool, and the good feeling would flee.

Just as the door to her father's study closed, she noticed that one of the officers wasn't holding a cigar; it was a small roll of money. She hurried back to Jasper and Birdie, then whispered what she'd seen.

"Well, of all the . . . ," Jasper began.

"Why would he do such a thing?" Birdie asked.

Jasper stared at the closed oak doors. "Probably just to clean up the mess quicker. He doesn't want a drawn-out investigation. If they ask the medical examiner to come, the case will be open for weeks. There would be an autopsy."

Birdie stared at him, eyebrows lifted. "How on earth do you know this?"

Jasper shrugged. "I'm in and out of Dr. Norris's office and labs all the time. I keep my eyes and ears open." Unlike the other boys at the party, Jasper didn't brashly boast of wanting to fight the Krauts in

France as soon as he was old enough to register. His brother, Oscar, had gone to Camp Upton to train and had died of peritonitis the previous winter. Jasper was ambitious, but not when it came to dying for his country. "Besides. People who empty the trash see more than just the garbage," he said, winking at Birdie. It was Jasper's second wink of the night, and Allene was jealous that she hadn't owned them both.

The evening ended quickly after that. The police scribbled notes as they listened to Lucy's account. They briefly spoke to Birdie, Jasper, and Allene, but since they'd all been in Allene's bedroom at the time, there wasn't much information to gather.

"We've spoken to Mr. Biddle. Anyone else who spoke to Miss Waxworth tonight? We'll need to take a statement from them."

"What about Ernie?" Birdie asked.

They looked around, but Ernie was gone. He must have left with the rest of the guests. The irony made Allene smile. Their childhoods were full of stories of distracting Ernie to escape him, so they could have each other to themselves.

"I'll take his name, and we'll obtain a statement tomorrow," the lieutenant said.

It was past midnight when the police took Florence's body away. Her stockinged foot peeped out from the shroud they'd covered her with, and something about the sight made Birdie start crying. Allene handed her a French lace handkerchief, but she wouldn't take it, instead smearing her eyes on a palm. Even now, after Allene had ignored Birdie so abominably for so long, Birdie refused to rumple the nice things in Allene's life.

Allene thought, I don't deserve her. But on second consideration, she decided, Why yes, I do.

Mr. Cutter said a few last words to the officers. Florence's parents were at their tobacco estate in North Carolina for the week, soon to return. A telegram would be sent. With the war, telegrams never held anything good.

Lucy approached the group. Her lace cap was a little crooked, her normally smoothly combed ebony hair falling out in loose tendrils. "Miss Birdie, I've turned down the guest room bed and laid out some sleeping things for you. Mr. Jones, I believe Mr. Biddle is arranging for the motor to take both you gentlemen home."

"Thank you, Lucy," Allene said. She caught Jasper's eye and smiled, even though death was in the air, even though there was a door about to close on the evening. She smiled her best, most perfect smile, and waited.

Like a slow sunrise on Christmas morning, Jasper smiled back. Her heart knocked inside her rib cage. She knew she would see him again, and soon.

She and Birdie walked Jasper to the door. By necessity, they had to pass the stairs. No one wanted to look; a splotch of blood darkened the polished oak, and the remnants of the champagne glass had yet to be cleaned up.

"Do you smell that?" Jasper asked, sniffing.

"What? You mean that perfume?" Allene asked. Without the crowd of guests, it was quite noticeable now.

Birdie's eyebrows pinched together. "I smell it too. Like Christmas cookies that got baked too long."

Jasper stooped and picked up a shard of glass, one that still cradled a little liquid. "Almonds."

"Almonds?" Allene and Birdie asked at the same time.

"Bitter almonds." Jasper turned to them with a grim expression on his face. "I would know that smell anywhere, because my parents reeked of it when they died." He dropped the shard before wiping his hands on his trousers. The glass clinked as it bounced.

"What is it?" Allene asked.

"Florence Waxworth didn't just break her neck from tripping on the stairs," Jasper said. "Someone poisoned her."

CHAPTER 2

Almonds, sweetish but almost burnt, like overcooked nut brittle. The scent was one he'd never forget.

It spiraled Jasper into memories of his parents' Fifth Avenue bedroom. He could see his mother's paper-white hand hanging over the bed, nails perfectly filed into ovals. His father's mouth sagged open, as if his last word had gagged him. Both were neatly dressed for church, though it wasn't a Sunday. Their hands were far apart in death, and they faced opposite walls, their bodies sinking into the goose down of the coverlet. They had chosen to die, and to die together, but not amicably.

Young Jasper had crawled onto the bed, put his mother's hand in his father's stiff one, and then rung for the police.

He should have seen the symptoms of the cataclysm. Only in retrospect had he realized that over the past six months, Mother's neck and earlobes had grown less and less ornamented with gold and pearls. There were nervous whispers behind closed doors, wrung hands, arguments. Oscar had taken to leaving for weeks at a time for the company of college chums on Long Island. The servants had been sent away. The townhouse was being sold.

Jasper had been too distracted to notice. He spent his spare hours at the Cutter house with his Birdie and Allene, whose boyish, twig-like figures were rounding out, much to his fascination. Birdie, in particular, was blooming with an almost unearthly beauty. He'd see her in his mind's eye when he slept at night. The sight of her new breasts affected his own growing body in ways that were terrifically strange and inconvenient.

He had dismissed the new, relentless changes at home. After all, his parents were probably packing up for another summer trip to the shore. Instead, they'd left for a different destination.

They'd left him and Oscar behind. They'd left them penniless.

And they'd left them with that smell.

God, *this* smell.

"Are you . . . absolutely sure?" Allene whispered, glancing at the servants only a few feet away. Behind her, Mr. Cutter was escorting the last police officers out the door.

"I think so," Jasper whispered back.

"Well, that's exciting!" Allene blurted, then covered her mouth.

Jasper took a step closer. "For God's sake. Someone *died*, Allene!"

"Someone whom none of us is that sad about!" she reminded him.

"Shhh!" said Birdie, scandalized. "It isn't Christian to speak of the dead."

"What you smelled?" he told them. "It's poison. Cyanide. I would bet my life on it."

They looked at him and knew he was right. Everyone knew about Jasper's parents. Four years ago, he lost them, lost his money, and gained a scandal. He went to live with his alcoholic uncle in the Bowery. Mr. Cutter had instructed his servants not to answer the door when Mr. Jones called at the house. He'd forbidden Allene from finding him. Birdie, unaware she was about to be cast out, lived in Allene's shadow. And her shadow had shunned him too.

Allene took a huge breath. "Well, if you're sure, Jasper Jones, then you're about to turn my life inside out." She somehow didn't look upset by this possibility.

He took a step back, trying to clear his head of the cobweb of memories that threatened to ensnare him again. His mother's face on the pillow, her lifeless hazel eyes wide open. Jasper had inherited those eyes. God. "Look. I could be wrong. I'll be at the Bellevue morgue tomorrow for work. I'm assigned to that wing of the building. Maybe I can . . . take another look at Florence. To be sure."

Allene's eyes sparkled with curiosity. "You could do that?"

Jasper nodded. He tried damn hard not to grin. After working every shift he could squeeze in and sleeping a scant five hours a day, he had finished his two years of college at age seventeen. There wasn't enough money for medical school, not yet. But he'd read all about Dr. Norris. The medical examiner's office at Bellevue had opened only a few months before and already was eschewing bribes from the Tammany Hall politicians. The forensics department was rapidly but quietly gaining fame for scientifically and systematically finding murderers, no matter how inconvenient. The murder-suicide that turned out to be a double murder by a jealous police sergeant. The twin babies that died "naturally" in their sleep from a purposeful overdose of teething medicine given by the wife of a Tammany Hall regular who "didn't want to be bothered by their screeching anymore."

If he could get his foot in the door of the medical examiner's office, it would be his ticket out of obscurity. He wouldn't follow his brother's listless path, finding direction only once he'd been drafted, then dying soon after. In the last few years, he'd snubbed offers of friendship, girlfriends, and he even dispensed smiles with tightfisted, calculated effort. He was too busy to be friendly to strangers, and most people burnt time he didn't have. At eighteen, he felt it running thin through his hands.

No, Jasper would be in charge of the fate of the most notorious and the most powerful people in New York, the ones who thought they had the right to decide who lived or died in this world. He looked well bred, had himself a good brain and loads of ambition—and now he had a corpse.

13

Alive, Florence was a snooty socialite who'd thrown snide remarks at him countless times, including last evening.

Dead, she was his salvation.

"Jasper." Allene was watching him as carefully as Birdie was. "Thank you. I'll speak to Father about all this. Right now, you need to go home. But promise to see me again. Soon."

Something in her expression made him pause. It wasn't just excitement; it was the brightness and energy you see in a bird behind gilded cage wires. So pretty, so alive, but trapped all the same. He saw how Allene had reacted to Andrew's kiss before. She could care less about that lucky bum.

Jasper donned a brilliant smile. "Oh, I'll see you soon. Even if you're going to be married, doesn't mean I can't get my share of your time before then. Thank Florence for that." He leaned forward and gave her a slow kiss on the cheek. When he pulled away, he squeezed her waist. Allene was blushing. Excellent.

"You're a cad," she said.

He winked. "Of course I am."

Allene was a piece of a puzzle in a plan he was still working out. No doubt he was resentful of her for snubbing him these past years, but she would make it up to him. He would make sure of that. When he'd received the invitation, he had thought of torching it in the sink, but then considered. Allene had everything he no longer did—connections and money. There were smart ways to get both without begging. Some of the most eminent physicians were friends of the Cutters—perhaps they would cross his path now. If he wanted to find Florence's murderer and rise beyond being a janitor forever, he would need Allene.

She led him reluctantly to the large double doors. Andrew was waiting for him, looking clean worn out. "Aren't they something?" he murmured, watching Allene's and Birdie's mesmerizing feminine silhouettes recede to the drawing room.

"Mmm." Jasper wasn't sure how to respond. Andrew seemed like a friendly chap, never once looking down his nose at him, unlike everyone else at the party. If things had been different, Jasper would have been the one in the tuxedo, marrying into the Cutter family. He wouldn't have to wake up tomorrow morning on Eldridge Street and scrub urine stains off Bellevue's tiled floors.

Actually, Jasper despised Andrew, now that he thought of it.

"You're very lucky," Andrew said, filling the silence.

Jasper twitched out of his resentful torpor. "Excuse me?"

"Birdie. What a patootie. She's your girl, isn't she?"

"I thought I was the one who was supposed to be doing the congratulating tonight," Jasper replied.

This time, it was Andrew's turn to say, "Mmm." He abruptly faced Jasper, just as the motorcar rumbled up to the curb. Lowering his voice, he asked, "Say. When Florence fell down the stairs . . . where were you, really? You weren't actually in Allene's room, were you?"

Where was he? Where he shouldn't have been, of course.

"Just kiss her!" Allene had teased.

Jasper had been lounging on her bed, surrounded by an overabundance of lace pillows.

It was a dare and a test. He knew it. Birdie had scorched her cheap dress by standing too close to the fireplace. She'd always done that, trying to escape notice by backing against a wall. He'd followed them to Allene's room, past the party guests, and Allene had permitted him to enter. Just like when they were children.

It was all innocent. Birdie had changed behind a silk screen, damn it. So much for seeing more of Birdie Dreyer. But Allene had caught him staring and wouldn't let it go.

"I'll bet she's never been kissed," Allene went on. "Have you, Birdie?"

Birdie shook her head. The blush now extended down to the top of her bosom, peeping out from the borrowed dress.

"If you're such an expert," Jasper challenged Allene, "then show me how it's done. I'm just a poor student, you see."

She laughed and waggled her large sapphire ring at him. "I'm getting married! This is my engagement party, if you haven't noticed." But she took a timid step closer to him anyway.

"You're not married yet. Consider it an early present." His hubris was irresistible; Allene stepped another inch closer.

"No."

"Yes!"

"Jasper Jones!" But now she was laughing less. "Fine. You can kiss me if you kiss Birdie too. That will make it all very equitable and innocent," she said, as if trying to convince herself. Her fingers fiddled with the beads on her dress. After being so keen on the idea, she seemed awfully nervous now. Jasper had hardly moved. "This is a terrible idea."

"Don't you just love those?" Jasper said, smirking. Birdie tittered in agreement. He stood and reached for Allene's waist and closed the final distance between them. "Just remember, Allene. You invited us here, not the other way around." The lace of her dress caught his rough fingertips. He looked down on her perfectly coiffed hair, and she lifted her chin.

"Don't you dare tell a soul," she whispered, her voice shaking a little. The giggles and bravado had dissolved away.

"Not by a darn sight," he said. "Cross my heart."

She was so close that their bellies touched, and her hip bones tapped against his. Her lips were smudged with a coralline salve that smelled of roses. The tiniest sound escaped her mouth when he leaned in. A whimper, almost.

The kiss was long and short, soft and firm at the same time. She tasted like sugar and flowers. Much better than the Bowery girls he'd meet in the cheap dance hall on Third Street, the ones who fell victim to his rather effective, crookedly roguish smile. They'd let him dispense his heated frustrations between their welcoming thighs for an evening and wonder why he didn't call on them afterward. Like sticks of chewing gum, their sweetness lasted for only so long before he no longer wanted them.

When Jasper's lips pulled away from Allene's, he realized his eyes had been closed. Allene blinked a few times and put her fingertips to her lips.

"Oh. Well." She turned away, red faced. "Birdie, now you."

Birdie shook her head. "Oh, I don't think so."

"Come now! It's only fair."

"Well . . ."

"I'll show you how harmless it all is," said Allene. She gaily swept over to rest her hands on Birdie's shoulders, barely covered by the silk gauze of her dress. She looked to make sure Jasper was watching. Of course he was.

"Now you put your hands here, on my hips," Allene instructed. "Close your eyes."

Birdie obeyed, and Allene leaned forward. Her eyelids drooped as her lips captured Birdie's under her own. Allene leaned in a little more, and Birdie's mouth yielded to the pressure. The kiss might have lasted a thousand years, or a second. Jasper couldn't tell.

"Golly" was all he could manage to say, after swallowing hard. "Golly," he said again.

The girls parted and swayed drunkenly, though neither had sipped any champagne that evening.

"Oh," Birdie murmured.

"Nothing to it," Allene said, trying to smile but failing. She seemed desperate to look at anything that wasn't Birdie or Jasper. "Well? What are you waiting for, Mr. Jones?"

This time, Jasper didn't hesitate. He stepped over the ottoman by Allene's vanity and slid his hand around Birdie's silk-bedecked waist. She was thinner and more delicate than Allene. He could break her in two if he wanted.

"One kiss." Birdie held up a cautionary finger. She seemed slightly out of breath, still recovering. "Between old friends."

"Between old friends," Jasper repeated. Birdie's lips were slightly parted, and he tasted the tiniest bit of sweet tongue and a bit of rose salve from Allene, which confused him. Warmth rose in his body like a humid July day. His hands squeezed her waist harder before he abruptly stepped back.

"Why, Jasper Jones, you're red as a beet!" Allene hooted. Her own face had already cooled, and her eyes were neutral, watching.

He had the sudden urge to escape the two of them. He didn't feel like he knew what he was doing anymore.

A series of thumps and crashes shook the floor below them.

"What was that?" Allene wiped her mouth hastily and straightened her dress and hair. Footsteps pounded toward the bedroom door, and the dark-haired maid, Lucy, burst inside.

"Oh, Miss Allene! I do believe Miss Florence Waxworth has fallen down dead!"

A Klaxon sounded obnoxiously from the waiting car, and Jasper jolted back to the curb, where the August evening warmed him in his suit. Andrew had been studying the various emotions playing over his face.

"So where were you when Florence died?" Andrew asked again.

Ruining my life.

Jasper slapped on a quick grin. "I was in the bathroom. Champagne went right through me. I'm more of a suds downer myself."

Andrew looked dissatisfied, but the lie had slid off Jasper as easily as water on oiled paper.

Somehow he knew the lying would get easier from here on out.

CHAPTER 3

Florence had stared at the three of them just before they ascended the stairs so Birdie could change her burnt gown.

"Look at you all," she had drawled, after a sip of champagne. "Trying so damn hard not to be yourselves."

Something dug sharply into Birdie's hand, and the memory of Florence's acid comment disappeared. She looked down. Allene's sapphire ring was enormous and the new platinum prongs were sharp. Birdie wished it was gone, like all the other guests that had fled the Cutter house minutes ago.

"You'll stay tonight, won't you?" Allene's face was expectant, but not desperate. She knew Birdie's answer even before Birdie did.

"Of course," she said. "But I need to telephone my mother first, to let her know."

Allene squeezed her hand again. It pained Birdie's fingers, but she swallowed the discomfort.

Allene looked over her shoulder. "Lucy? Show Birdie to the study, will you?"

The gesture was unnecessary. Birdie knew her way around the Cutter house in the dark. She had been born here, after all—her mother too. The Dreyer women had always been lady's companions to the Cutters, with their own rooms and allowances and personal maids. For three generations, they'd been a part of the Cutter family, until they weren't. Until Mrs. Cutter decided that her case of consumption should be blamed on the prettier Hazel Dreyer—and the scourge and her daughter should leave the Cutter house forever.

And here Birdie was again, after all these years. She didn't want to go back home to Brooklyn. Their life there was a cancer that was slowly eating away at their worth, and women like the Dreyers—with no money and no patrician blood running through their veins—had precious little to begin with.

It was too late for her mother. Maybe even for Birdie herself. But when Allene's engagement invitation showed up encased in its cream linen envelope, Birdie's heart had fluttered with hope. It was the first correspondence she'd received since she'd left. Allene never replied to Birdie's letters, so she had stopped sending them. There was no pleasure in writing to a void.

Allene didn't even know Holly existed. But the invitation nudged her optimism. With Birdie's toe in the door, maybe Allene could meet Holly. Maybe she could help them, somehow, before it was too late. Birdie would swallow her pride for Holly's sake. She would swallow her fear too. The Cutter house had spit her and her mother out. There was a good chance she'd tear those scarred memories wide open again.

Lucy led her to the study before curtsying. Her dark eyes seemed judging, and she'd been tight on smiles ever since Birdie had arrived that evening. It was no surprise. Lucy had gone from playing chambermaid to filling Birdie's shoes after she was disinvited from the Cutter house. The way Allene whispered and leaned toward Lucy—it wasn't the ordering around of any ordinary servant. Allene would have needed someone the way she'd needed Birdie all those years. Lucy was even the same height as Birdie, but with staunch hips and shoulders, used to hard work. But now that Birdie was growing closer in Allene's heart as the minutes ticked by, Lucy no doubt imagined that her position was already changing. Ranks were falling.

"Thank you, Lucy," Birdie said. But the maid had already turned her back. Birdie shrugged and picked up the candlestick phone on the desk. When the switch operator answered, Birdie told her it was an emergency. Casual telephone calls were frowned upon due to the war.

The operator rang the apartment, and the landlady—the only tenant in the building with a telephone—answered and went to fetch her mother. Minutes ticked by.

"This is Hazel Dreyer speaking."

"Mother, it's me, Birdie," she said in a low voice, hoping to keep the conversation quiet. "I'm staying over at the Cutter house tonight. There's been a terrible accident."

Usually, there was a telltale click of telephones hanging up on the party line, but this time, everyone near Birdie's building listened. The Bradleys across the street; the Salzki sisters in the building next door. So much for privacy.

"At the Cutter house," her mother repeated through a crackle of static.

God, yes. Here, of all places. "Yes, Mother. It's very important. Allene asked me to stay."

"I see."

There were a thousand statements in those two words, but the worst was the implication that she was abandoning her family for the Cutters, who'd become monsters in her and her mother's eyes.

Her mother released a long sigh. "Are you quite sure?"

"Yes."

Another long sigh. "Well, if you must."

"Thank you. And Mother? Please stay with Holly tonight." She bit her lip. "Just Holly."

"Birdie. You know I can't. Rent is due soon."

"I'm asking you. Please stay with Holly. She'll be frightened without me. I'll make up for it. I'll work extra hours at the factory."

"Very well." Her mother's voice sounded ironed out. Birdie hoped there was some room for affection in there, something left over for Holly. As for herself, she didn't care. It had been a long time since she'd expected anything of that sort for herself. So she was surprised when her mother asked, "How is your tooth?"

"Fine, Mother." Birdie reached with her other hand to cradle her left jaw. She'd had a sore molar for weeks now, and it was on the verge of falling out. Thank goodness the swelling had calmed enough to go unnoticed at the party, but it hurt to chew. She hadn't eaten a morsel all day. But her tooth wasn't the only thing wrong. She hadn't told Mother or Holly about her aching joints, the pain in her thigh bone, the chronic tiredness that made her cry for more sleep, or the other loose teeth.

In bits and pieces, Birdie was falling apart. She was running out of time. She thought of Allene, and Jasper's coffee-warm kiss, and Florence's dead gaze. But mostly, she thought of Holly.

Oh God, Birdie thought. Please give me more time.

The switch operator interrupted. "I am getting another caller on the line."

"It's all right. We're done here," Birdie said.

Immediately, she heard the click of no less than four other households hanging up.

"Good-bye. I'll see you—"

Her mother hung up before she finished her sentence. Outside in the corridor, Lucy waited, expressionless, those large black eyes watching everything. The main floor was deserted of servants and guests. An eerie quiet had settled into the bones of the house. Lucy led her down the hallway, and Mr. Cutter bumped into them at the base of the staircase. Birdie shrank from the contact.

"Oh. Miss Dreyer. You look quite like your mother now." It should have been a compliment, but his voice was flat. There was a curl of a sneer at the corner of his bulbous nose. Unlike most of the men at the party that night, her beauty held no magic for him. He seemed to be waiting for her to say something bitter. But Birdie knew her place.

"Thank you," Birdie replied. She dropped her eyes and waited for him to order her out of the house. After all, she reminded him of scandals and gossip, and of her mother and his wife.

But he didn't throw her out. The butler called to Mr. Cutter, and he turned on his heel without another word. And Birdie was grateful.

She followed Lucy to one of the spare bedrooms—Birdie's old room. Gone were the bits of pink and red ribbon she used to collect, or the playbills she'd acquired and trapped in the edges of the dressing mirror. The room was sterile and simple now, with a woven white spread, white pillows, and white brocade-covered chair. Birdie had been bleached right out of the room.

"I've laid out a nightgown for you," Lucy said, matter-of-factly. She didn't offer to help her undress. It was no surprise, but it was a snub no less. Like her mother, Birdie had once been used to the maids' attention. But she didn't deserve that kind of care anymore.

When the door shut, she peeled off her showy, borrowed dress; unhooked her confining brassiere and underthings; and slipped on the lawn nightgown. She'd only just dropped the hem to her ankles when Allene walked right in, wearing a frilly nightgown and a rose-colored robe cinched about her waist. She didn't bother to knock. Birdie's privacy seemed to belong to Allene once again.

Good.

"Look what I've got." Allene held out a loosely balled handkerchief, then carefully unwrapped it in her palm. Inside, a triangle of broken glass shone under the lamplight. "It's from Florence's drinking glass. Evidence!" She pulled Birdie's hand, and they skipped down the hall to Allene's frilled bedroom. "We'll hide it in here," she announced, pulling open the vanity drawer. She placed the parcel inside and locked it, pocketing the brass key. "I'll be back in a bit. I'm going to have a word with Father." Her eyes blazed. "It's all so exciting, really. We have a mystery in our midst, don't we?"

"Shall I come with you?" Birdie asked, though she was terrified at the prospect of speaking to Mr. Cutter again.

"No. You go to sleep."

Birdie at first turned toward the guest room, Allene's slippered feet padding away, but she couldn't resist following Allene to Mr. Cutter's bedroom. Her heart pounded. She hated the very walls of this house, and her body reminded her of that truth. She hid behind the half-opened door, hovering in the shadows of the hallway that had been dimmed for the night.

Mr. Cutter, his beard slightly disheveled, sat on the edge of his enormous four-poster bed. Swathes of satin lashed the bed curtains to the carved bedposts, and Allene fiddled with tying and untying them. Mr. Cutter had changed into a striped robe of gray and white that was too small to wrap about his stately belly, and the room smelled of warm tobacco. It used to smell of Mrs. Cutter's jasmine perfume, but that scent was long since gone.

"What a terrible, terrible evening. It will be in all the papers tomorrow, whether we like it or not. I'm so sorry your party should end in such a way, my dear." When he looked up at his daughter, his face seemed weary. Life ought to have been easy for him. Inheriting money from the railroads and making sure that people turned that money into more money was his only job, if that could be called a job. But for that well-fed stomach, he looked as if he'd just come off laying down railroad ties himself. Shadows magnified the sagging skin beneath his eyes. The past few years had made him ancient.

Allene took a deep breath. "Father." She tied the bed-curtain sash tightly, as if attempting to strangle the bedpost. "I believe that Florence may have been . . . murdered."

His face darkened. "Do not say such things, Allene."

"But we smelled a chemical on her. It might be poison."

"Don't be ridiculous!" Mr. Cutter's forehead went lobster red. "You have far too fanciful an imagination when it comes to chemicals. I should have thrown those old books of yours out. They aren't healthy for the female mind. In any case, the officer himself said she broke her neck in the fall."

"But we think she *fell* because she'd been poisoned."

"We? *We?* And who is this *we?*"

"Jasper said—"

"It was a mistake to invite him. I never should have permitted it."

Allene opened her mouth to argue, but Mr. Cutter stood up. He was immense next to his daughter, a bear overshadowing a fawn.

"I told the police to close the case, for your sake. For everyone's sake. There's no good that will come about from an investigation."

"But Father!"

Mr. Cutter grabbed her upper arms and squeezed so tightly that she gasped with pain.

"The Waxworths have always spoken ill of our family and our circle of friends, always looking for a reason to bring us down. I've heard Florence was as ruthless as her mother. If you and those . . . guests of yours hadn't disappeared upstairs, then Florence would never have had a reason to follow, digging for gossip. She wouldn't have tripped on the stairs, and she wouldn't have died. This was your doing, and I am making this go away for you and for us. Do you understand?" He shook her so hard, a loose hairpin fell from Allene's knot and clinked to the floor. "It ends here, Allene. I'll hear no more of this, never again."

He released her, and Allene stumbled. Birdie hastily backed away, padding silently back to the guest room. She switched off the light and dove under the covers, thinking, *I should have never been allowed to come either, but here I am.*

One silent minute passed, then another. The door quietly opened and Allene's dark figure entered, sniffling. She paused before the little table by the door and plucked out the rest of her hairpins, dropping them into a china dish. She shed her slippers and robe before climbing into bed. Birdie moved over to make room, but Allene didn't let her get far; she captured Birdie's thin torso in her arms and snuggled close until their foreheads were almost touching.

Birdie didn't ask how the conversation went. She knew better.

"This is like old times, isn't it?" Allene whispered. "You don't mind, do you?"

"Of course not." Birdie's bones betrayed her with a deep ache, but she ignored it.

After a few minutes, Allene sagged into the mattress. Birdie thought she'd fallen asleep, when Allene sharply inhaled.

"Why, Birdie Dreyer. You're glowing like a lamp!"

Birdie looked down at herself. Indeed, her hands and forearms possessed a faint greenish, yellowy glow. She had taken her hair down and braided it, and the braid running over her shoulder held a halo of light that illuminated the space about it.

"It's the radium dust," Birdie whispered. "We paint it onto the watch dials at the clock factory, so our boys can see them in the dark trenches. I get covered with it after a day's work."

Allene went slack jawed for a moment. "You . . . work in a clock factory?"

Birdie could have said, Yes, and it's your family's fault. But she didn't. She was in the Cutter house again with Allene, and wasn't that all that mattered? "Yes."

Allene's expression of surprise softened. "Radium, huh? Lovely element. I hear that Madame Curie used to carry radium around in her pocket, like a glowing little pet of hers. I have a copy of her doctoral thesis. It's wonderful reading."

"You do?"

"Yes. It's under my bed." Allene yawned. She was so peculiar sometimes. Birdie remembered the time she ignited some elements in the garden in a spectacular fireworks display that set an expensive ornamental maple tree on fire. Mr. Cutter had been far from happy about that. "Well, don't let the boys see you in the dark. They'll try to catch you and never let you go." She hugged Birdie closer. "You don't belong here on earth with the rest of us, Birdie Dreyer."

Birdie watched her fall asleep, fighting to keep her eyes open as long as possible.

She saw unwanted fiancés, and Mr. Cutter shaking Allene like a rat. She saw her mother undulating beneath the shadows of countless men, and Holly covering her ears. She saw terrible things that should never, ever happen.

And she saw her own death approaching with a momentum that terrified her.

Tomorrow, she and Allene would deal with pleasanter things in life.

Like finding Florence's killer.

CHAPTER 4

Allene awoke in a tangle.

Somehow in the middle of the night, she and Birdie had managed to twist their legs together, as if unconsciously attempting to wrestle, conquer, and give in simultaneously. The hems of their cool, cotton nightgowns had ridden up beneath the covers, and now Allene's bare thigh was clasped by Birdie's bent knees. She held her breath, afraid to move.

Birdie was dead asleep on the pillow next to her, unmoving save for the tidal rise and fall of her chest and the zigzag of her eyeballs beneath pink satin eyelids. Her hand was a warm weight on Allene's hip. Allene had no inclination to remove it.

What does she dream of? Allene wondered. Something delicious and wonderful. Maybe she dreams of me and Jasper, she mused. Maybe not.

Birdie stirred and her lips parted. She murmured, "No. No, I don't." Her eyes crinkled with sleepy concern.

Well, maybe those dreams weren't something to covet, after all.

"Birdie. Dear, wake up," Allene whispered, patting her shoulder.

Birdie's face struggled, shivering off whatever unpleasantries haunted her. She rubbed her eyes, yawning like an infant. When she blinked her eyes open, wonder filled them as they traveled from the intricate molding along the ceiling to the honeyed Sunday sunshine peeking through the curtains. She smiled at Allene, making no move to disentangle their legs or speak. For an eternal moment, they fed on each other's warmth and let the silence simmer about them.

But when Allene closed her eyes, she saw Florence's purpling, dead corpse. It demanded that she speak. Something must be done.

"Last night . . ." But as soon as she started, knuckles rapped smartly on the door. The girls unwound their legs in a mad scramble, sitting up in bed and smoothing the covers. Birdie pulled the duvet up to decently cover her chest. There was no time to cool down the heat that had risen to their cheeks.

Lucy entered with an armful of clean linens. She set them down on the end of the bed and lifted her chin.

"Look at you two. Like twins. Like you always were," she said. "All you're missing is Jasper."

Lucy was smiling at them, but it was a portrait smile—the kind designed to be held in place by sheer willpower. "Miss Birdie, I pressed your gown and mended the burn spot. We had tarlatan scraps that matched nicely. Miss Allene, your father left the house early for church. He said he would be back home for luncheon. I have your things ready in your room."

"Thank you," Birdie and Allene chimed together.

"I'll come to my room in a minute, Lucy," Allene said. She pretended to yawn but afterward wasn't sure why she pretended.

"Be quick, miss. Mr. Biddle arrived just a few minutes ago. He waits for you in the salon." Lucy left, and Allene's shoulders fell.

"What's the matter?" Birdie asked.

"I asked Andrew not to come. I wanted to have a day to myself."

Birdie seemed to shrink inwardly at the comment. "I'll be out of the house soon. I should get home anyway."

"No!"

The word came out so quickly she didn't have time to modulate her voice. A hollowness bored through her at the thought of Birdie leaving. Allene had grown accustomed to the gnawing, empty sensation, but it wasn't time to return to that. Not yet. "I just meant . . . I can't imagine having to spend a day with Andrew after last night. I'd much rather have you here."

"What about Andrew? You'll be married soon. What will he think?"

"He's not my husband yet."

Birdie opened her mouth at this audacity, but Allene adopted an expression that wouldn't take no for an answer.

"But I have to check on Holly. And Mother."

"Holly. Who's Holly?"

"Holly's my sister."

Allene sat back, as if the news were a dose of poisonous ptomaine. "What? You have a sister? When? How?"

"I think you know *how*, Allene." Birdie smiled. "Holly's nearly four years old."

Allene stared at her blankly. Of all the—so Hazel Dreyer had been banished from their home while she was in the family way? Vaguely, she remembered Hazel wearing looser, ill-fitting gowns around the time she'd left. She always thought her mother had been jealous of Hazel's arresting beauty and that perhaps Hazel had dressed more plainly to tone it down. Well. Allene had no idea it wasn't her beauty she had attempted to hide.

"You ought to meet her sometime soon. But I do have to go home and make sure she's all right."

"What about me?" A slight panic welled.

"You'll be fine, Allene."

"But what about *Florence*?"

"I don't need to check on Florence. She's dead," Birdie said. After the words came out, she clapped her hand over her mouth.

Allene was just as shocked, and for a minute, silence hung between them. Then they burst out laughing. It was too ridiculous, too morbid, too awful. Laughing at the dead. Somewhere, the dead were laughing back at them.

Finally, after they caught their breath, Birdie put her hand on Allene's shoulder.

"Oh goodness. We are terrible, aren't we?" asked Allene.

"We're the rottenest," Birdie agreed. "But anyway. Andrew is waiting for you, isn't he?"

Allene grabbed Birdie's arms, and desperation made her squeeze a little too hard. "Oh, Birdie. What if we just run away from everything and see if we can figure out who killed Florence Waxworth?"

"What do you mean?" Birdie whispered.

Allene gripped Birdie's arm, probably harder than she should have. "Look. I'm to be married soon. And . . . oh God, Birdie. I'm so young. I've barely had time to be me before I have to be Mrs. Andrew Biddle. This would give me a little adventure before I'm locked away in Andrew's house for endless salon parties and boring suppers. I need this." It was difficult to hide the desperation in her voice.

"I see."

"Well, you and I and Jasper know that Florence was probably poisoned. Father made sure that there wouldn't be an investigation. But why Florence? Everyone knows how mean she could be, but maybe someone got too mad this time. Let's see if we can figure it out. We'll be good as gold! We'll be heroes!"

"Is that what you want to be, Allene? A hero?"

"Oh, I don't know." She waved her hand carelessly. "I just . . . want this. Consider it an engagement gift. Help me figure it all out. One day I can tell my grandchildren that I solved a murder!"

"But I'm not qualified for any sort of investigating. I paint clocks and watches for a living," Birdie said.

"So you know details! I have the social connections. Jasper has access to the morgue. Why, he's probably investigating right now."

Birdie sighed in acquiescence. "All right. But I don't . . . how would we even begin?"

It was astonishing how easily the plan was coming together. Allene secretly thanked Florence for getting herself killed. She hadn't felt this alive in ages.

"We gather information. All three of us were upstairs when the deed was done. We need to find out what people saw. Maybe you can ask Andrew who else was with Florence last night." When Birdie hesitated, she added, "I can have Andrew escort you home. It'll get him out of my hair, and you can ask him what he might know about Florence. He spoke with her last night when we were, er, upstairs. Since you don't know each other, it will be more natural if you ask a million questions."

"All right."

"How about I drop by tomorrow and see what you've learned?"

"Tomorrow is Monday. I have to work, Allene."

"That's a fact." Allene furrowed her eyebrows and then snapped her fingers. "I'll go with you!"

"Excuse me?"

"To work! We can spend the day together."

Birdie stared at her like she was slightly mad. Which was appropriate. Allene felt slightly unhinged, and it was *wonderful*.

"For Pete's sake, Allene. It's a factory, not a carnival. What will I tell my boss?"

"We'll figure that part out later. I'll see you first thing in the morning. I need to get dressed." She hugged Birdie, who was so slight in her billowing nightgown, she almost seemed to wince at Allene's enthusiasm. But this was nothing new. She'd always dragged Birdie into her childhood scrapes and plans. Bending the rules wasn't fun unless her good sense told her that she was, in fact, being naughty. And Birdie had always been that good sense. Why, without Birdie, she'd been senseless!

She laughed quietly and washed up in the bathroom, splashing the porcelain that gleamed around her.

Lucy was waiting for her in her bedroom, her drawers, brassiere, and long corset laid out. The maid enveloped her in layer upon layer, lacing and tightening until Allene's soft, rounded figure was molded tightly under whalebone stays and silk ribbons. A frock of pale-green gauze over darker green went on over her head, and Allene perched straight spined in front of her vanity. Lucy clasped a beaded jet necklace around her throat (it was so funerary, but perhaps that was appropriate) and began brushing out her long hair. Allene watched in the mirror but looked down after being disappointed, once again, that she wasn't as beautiful as Mary Pickford and had none of the mysterious, arresting presence of Theda Bara. "Well looking" never seemed reasonable compensation for not being heartbreakingly beautiful.

"This silk poplin becomes you," Lucy said, smoothing out the seams of her dress. She always let her accent show more around Allene, who didn't correct her the way her father did.

"Hmm." Allene wasn't really listening, but she spoke to be polite. "Yes. Poplin. Such an odd word."

"It comes from *papeline*. The French used it to dress the pope in the fifteenth century." Lucy laughed a little, showing crooked but white teeth. "Pope or not, it washes well."

Allene stared at Lucy's reflection in the mirror. She rarely laughed; it was such a pleasant change. "How did you know that?"

"I know lots of things, Miss Allene." Lucy's smile faded. "I know you're happy to have your friends back," she said, braiding so swiftly it jerked Allene out of her thoughts. "I remember how you three were. I have a feeling I won't see you as much now. I miss you already."

"Oh, Lucy!" Allene turned to throw her arms around the maid, who smelled as she always did, like newly baked bread and honey. Her olive-brown cheek was soft and forgiving. "I don't know what I'd do without you. Don't talk like that."

She wanted to say that Birdie was more like a sister, only she wasn't. And she wanted to say that Lucy was like a mother, only Mother was in Saratoga and Father paid Lucy to be nice to her, so that didn't seem right either. Lucy was too young to be like her mother and too old to be a friend. She didn't know exactly what Lucy was, except that she needed her.

"I will take care of you," Lucy said. "I have since you were a child, and I will until I die—whether or not Miss Birdie is here."

Allene stiffened and pulled away. Her words sounded vaguely like a threat, though the maid's face was kindness itself. So she smiled.

"Thank you, Lucy. For everything."

"Yes ma'am."

"Tell Andrew I'll be down in a minute."

Lucy nodded and left. Allene spun around and checked herself in the mirror one last time, then opened up her vanity drawer. She pulled out a tiny cigarette lighter. It was a dandy little thing, a Ronson Wonderliter, ever so much nicer than a boring box of matches. The tiny silver case resembled a miniature flask. She unscrewed the little top and pulled out the metal wand, hollow but for a wick soaked in naphtha, and struck the wand against the rough ridge along the bottom of the flask.

And there was fire. The transformation of the ordinary into the extraordinary—light and energy and new molecules. She blew it out quickly, replaced the wand, and hid the contraption in a pocket she'd had Lucy sew into a seam of all of her dresses. Allene had once heard her mother say, "A woman's heart is full of secrets." If Father knew she'd bought the lighter, he'd have a fit. Andrew might too. She patted her pocket and smiled.

Allene swept through the door to meet her fate downstairs. Andrew was comfortably seated in one of the watered silk wing chairs of the salon, as if he belonged there. As if he already owned the furniture, the house, even the air. His legs were crossed, and he set his cigarette in a powder-blue Wedgwood ashtray when he saw her.

"Darling." He always said the word as if he were speaking of good wine or new spats. He reached out his hands.

Allene accepted them as she always did. "You shouldn't have come, Andrew. Really, it's quite unnecessary."

"You had quite a fright last night. I had to know you were well."

"There are such things as telephones," she said. It sounded peevish, almost saucy. She put on a smile to counter the tone of her voice. "But I am glad you've come. I need a favor. It's Birdie Dreyer."

"Birdie." Andrew let go of her hands. He turned to retrieve his cigarette, inhaling deeply.

"You remember her. My old friend, from the party last night? She spent the night, and she needs an escort home. Last night gave her quite a scare."

"Oh." He regarded her a little too long. Soon, his face was obscured in a cloud of smoke. "If you think it's best—"

Birdie's foot squeaked at the top of the stairs, and they exited the room to watch her descend. Andrew barely even acknowledged her. He picked a fleck of tobacco off his lip instead.

"Andrew will make sure you get home safely, Birdie. Won't you, dear?"

He finally looked up politely. "Of course. It would be my pleasure." A benign smile appeared on his face. Poor Andrew. It was a strain to be associating with her déclassé friends. What a sport he was.

Outside, one of the Cutters' motorcars stood idling by the curb. The driver opened the back door, and Birdie scuttled in, followed by Andrew. Before the driver shut the door, Allene mouthed "Thank you" to Andrew, who rolled his eyes at her.

As soon as the door shut, Allene all but galloped inside to the library.

With Birdie and Jasper gone, she felt herself wanting to tie herself in any way she could to last evening, even if it meant embracing the most morbid of thoughts. She would allow death to be a constant companion for as long as necessary.

Inside the library, books filled the oak shelves floor to ceiling. She took to the rolling ladder to access the top shelf of books, which were hers alone. She pulled out a thick leather tome and nestled it against her bosom as she descended the ladder one handed.

At the library desk, she ran her fingers over the embossed cover.

The Organic Chemistry of Nitrogen
by Nevil Vincent Sidgwick

She flipped with easy familiarity to the page she wanted. Chapter nine, "Cyanogen Compounds."

She sighed and let her fingertip run over the chemical formula for cyanide. By God, it was a thing of beauty and simplicity. One nitrogen and one carbon atom married together with three bonds. Not one, not two. Cyanide demanded a trifecta of irresistible gravities. Such a thing of dark beauty created from the basic matter of life present in all living creatures.

Her mother hadn't understood why Allene loved this book so, even though the attraction was her mother's fault. Allene was named after her maternal grandmother, but it was only at an evening party when she was a girl of eight that she had understood her namesake.

A wizened old German professor had been perusing the books in Father's library, brandy clutched in one arthritic hand. Elsewhere in the house, there were conversations over politics and vapid discussions on the business of railroads. Boredom had driven Allene to her safe place, but the old man clearly had the same intentions. He discovered her hiding beneath the library table when he nearly stepped on her fingertips. She was reading a book of nursery rhymes.

"What are you doing here?" he asked. "I am Professor Hoffman. What is your name?"

The questions were gently asked, but there were angles and points to his German accent that made her shrink deeper under the table, gathering her blue faille dress around her stockinged ankles.

"My name is Allene," she finally whispered.

"Allene, eh? Your name comes from chemistry. And I am a chemist, so we are already good friends. Come, I will show you."

He had spoken without fear—unlike the Germans around the city today, who might be dragged away by the American Protective League for their unpatriotic names and accents. Allene had been too curious to stay hidden. He pulled a stub of a pencil from his coat pocket and drew on a sheet of paper taken from her father's study.

"One carbon atom bound to two others, each with a double bond. That is you, Allene. You are a pretty thing in a chemist's world."

The drawing resembled an angular butterfly. After that party, she had learned everything she could about chemistry, and then in secret once her father had announced that it was unwomanly to study the sciences. He didn't want to raise a Marie Curie in the Cutter family. That was a decidedly *Polish* thing to do.

So when Allene now looked with longing over her chemistry book, she paused over words like *tautomeric* and *aromatic diamines* and *pyridinium*. Like jewels, there were rings and chains, and compounds broken and made anew with heat and pressure. It was a fairy dance of creation and destruction, wooing her.

She licked her lips. Cyanide. She knew little of its effect, only that it was a poison. But she knew precisely where cyanide was kept in the house. She would make a mental list of everyone who had access to it.

Which included herself, of course.

Allene was closing the book hastily when a rectangle of paper fluttered out from beneath the cover and fell in gentle arcs to the floor. She picked it up, frowning. She didn't recall putting any notes in this book. The paper was folded thrice, and she unfolded it only to find two words written in beautiful penmanship:

You're welcome.

What on earth did it mean?

CHAPTER 5

Jasper woke up in his room, the faint flavor of last night's champagne rancid on his tongue. He remembered the car and the wordless driver dropping him off in front of his tenement, all too happy to speed away from the Bowery.

His head pounded.

No—a fist pounded. On the door.

"Wake up! It's already seven o'clock, boy. You'll be late for work."

Jasper turned and groaned. Morning light squeezed around the edges of the curtains, weaker than whey but still stinging his eyes. Several piles of textbooks lay next to his floor mattress, acting as a nightstand. He'd accidentally toppled them to the floor when he flipped over on his bed. He cursed. Wasn't it a Sunday?

Oh, right. He worked on Sundays, rest be damned. His uncle pounded again. Jasper growled, "I'm up, I'm up."

He pulled on his trousers and rinsed the sleep from his face in the diminutive bathroom. Last night. Good God, last night. There was the scent of Allene's perfume and the look of gladness in her eyes that she couldn't hide when she saw him. Birdie and all her astounding beauty by his side; jealous glances from the gents at the party.

Lounging in Allene's room like they were careless children pretending to be older than they were.

But other thoughts flitted through his awakening mind as well: Florence's broken body; the scent of almonds; the flat, shocked looks on Allene's and Birdie's faces at the thought of murder.

What in the deuce happened last night?

Florence Waxworth was dead as dead. Right now, she'd be lying in the morgue at Bellevue. In the pathology building. The very building he was assigned to clean on Sundays.

Lord help him.

He peered down the hallway. The scrolled wallpaper was coming down from the ceiling, as if some unseen hand were dog-earing it bit by bit. The strong scent of paint thinner and whiskey permeated the air and worsened his nausea. Copies of the *Times* lay on the floor, where Jasper had dropped them after scanning them with dread, anxiously awaiting General Crowder's announcement of the next draft. Photographs of Oscar and their parents rested facedown on the bureau after he'd bumped them with an errant elbow and never bothered to right them.

These were the truths that existed in Jasper's world. Not champagne in cut crystal glasses or the whip-smart repartee he used to enjoy.

A clinking noise came from down the hallway. He followed the sound into the kitchen, where cans of paint thinner and solvents from the local hardware store lined the walls. Cases of Jamaica ginger were currently doubling as a kitchen chair, and a case of aftershave crowded the doorway. The long enameled sink was stacked to the brim with dirty dishes and bowls of uneaten oatmeal that were beginning to smell vaguely like cheap beer. Jars and bottles, filled to different levels and in shades from clear to amber to dark brown, covered the countertops to nearly overflowing.

Uncle Fred stood in the corner fiddling with a piece of glass piping. He was tall and spare, a specter of a man. Quiffs of wheat-colored strands barely covered his bald pate, and his eyes were so dark they appeared black. Jasper liked to think that God had added those inkblot eyes as an afterthought—an oddly unsettling shade to make up for the rest of his faded self.

And faded he was. He'd been the younger son in a family that had no money, whereas Jasper's mother had been quick witted and richly stylish (she had been a brilliant sewer) and had easily snagged herself a husband beyond her circle.

Embarrassingly, Uncle Fred had barely been able to keep a job for longer than a month at a time, driven to stay in his apartment for fear of falling into the sky. That was the only way Jasper could describe the anxiety that plagued his uncle. He'd step outside and put his hands out as if the fresh air were attempting to suffocate him, as if the sun and clouds were attempting to murder him where he stood. Booze helped, but not enough.

Oscar had stayed at home with Fred for months. Jasper's brother had never been able to pull himself out of the mire of his melancholy, which appeared after their colossal decline in consequence. Oscar had been terrified of life as much as Uncle Fred was of the open sky. So when Oscar died even before he stepped into a European trench, Jasper hadn't known whether to be surprised or relieved for his sake.

Uncle Fred was fitting a glass cylinder the width of his thumb to an elbow joint, smearing glycerin on the frosted edges to engage them smoothly. But his hands trembled, and he lay the cylinder down to drink from a small glass filled with amber liquid. When he swallowed, he closed his eyes, as if in prayer.

His undershirt was stained yellow beneath the armpits, and suspenders kept his loose pants from hitting the ground, though Jasper knew that his uncle couldn't care less about scandal. When your most common companions were the four walls of a room, not much else mattered. Jasper was impressed he was even wearing trousers.

"How's the search for cheap intoxicants going?" Jasper asked, after a huge yawn. He rolled up his sleeves and started washing the mountain of dishes.

"Swimmingly."

"Did you eat breakfast?"

His uncle shook his head.

"I left you dinner last night, and you didn't eat that either. What would you like, toast? I think we have some eggs." Jasper wiped his hands and opened the icebox, but it wasn't cold anymore. He eyed a bottle of milk suspiciously and sniffed the butter. It seemed all right.

His uncle hitched up his loose trousers. "Tell you what I need. A few more flasks to finish up my rig. Bring me a few from work today, will you?"

Jasper closed the icebox and sighed. His uncle liked to think of Bellevue as a pickpocket's grocery. The staff was too harried and the patients too numerous to notice a few missing pieces of glassware here or steel tongs there.

He immediately saw the hesitation on Jasper's face. "Now, Jasper. You know I can't buy these things. I have to be careful. Any day now, there won't be a blessed drop of legal stuff anywhere in Manhattan."

For him or for selling, Jasper wasn't exactly sure. Spirits seemed to ooze out of his uncle's pores. Fred was frantic at the idea of the dreaded prohibition amendment actually being fully ratified.

Jasper picked up a half-full box of Nabiscos but after two bites lost his appetite for the wafers that dried his mouth with their powdery sweetness. There was no chance of coffee because they'd used the last of it yesterday morning. If it wasn't for him, his uncle would be living off whiskey alone. It irritated him to run errands and grocery shop for two, but there was also something sacrilegious about his pale-skinned, indoor-dwelling uncle in the raw brightness of the sun. Uncle Fred seemed to know this; he hadn't left the building in eighteen months.

The last time was because the next-door apartment had a fire, and smoke had choked their rooms with darkness.

Jasper headed for the door, tucking in his shirttails. "Well, I'm off. Don't forget that there's half a loaf of bread in the bread box, and butter. You should eat that. Don't touch those eggs—I think they've gone bad."

"You worry too much."

"It's what I do best," he said, grimacing. Fred had a little cash to help with rent, but it was running out. He promised that his little alcoholic experiments would bring in money someday, but Jasper wondered if it would land them all in jail. He tried not to think too hard on that.

"Have a good day," Fred told him, waving the now-empty glass.

"Eat breakfast," Jasper nagged, pulling on his mackinaw.

"Good-bye."

"Eat breakfast." He pointed at Fred. "Don't die while I'm gone." It was both a joke and not a joke, but he said it often enough that Fred thought it was hilarious.

His uncle waved him away, chuckling as he began cramming pieces of sawdust into a large, stained flask. Soon, he'd cook it to coax out the alcoholic vapors. It would be a miracle if their whole apartment didn't go up in flames.

Jasper scuttled down the two flights of stairs and strode onto the sidewalk. The air was cool and brisk, and the city relatively quiet. The plain row houses and tenements held the morning sun at bay, and trash littered the gutters. In the distance, bells tolled for churchgoers. Jasper ignored the sound.

Florence was waiting, after all.

One of his favorite stores that sold him cigarettes had changed its name. Heppenheimer's Shoppe was now the Stars and Stripes, trying to convince its customers that the owners were patriots, begging them not to turn them in to the local APL. A restaurant advertised "liberty steak" instead of evil German hamburger. The world buffeted people in all directions, telling them how things should be. How he ought to be. There was no escaping any of it.

Good thing Bellevue was walking distance; it saved him five cents twice a day. As he walked under the El on First Avenue, the train rumbled by and the ground shuddered. He passed a grocery with exorbitant prices in the window. Fifty-seven cents for a dozen eggs? He shook his head. A few buildings had scrawny war gardens peeping out from their back lots, growing poorly in the city soil.

Soon, Bellevue and its stately buildings loomed before him. Glossy ivy covered the brick facades and Corinthian columns. Beneath the greenery, the ivy's wiry brown fingers insinuated themselves over whole buildings—clawing and clinging. He walked along the iron fence for a block before entering the arched gateway leading to the cobbled main courtyard. An old, giant elm tree stood guard over the incoming sick who were unloaded from the ambulances. Metal balconies jutted out from the main building, the old Almshouse, with its galleries running all the way around the courtyard. Occasionally, on clear days, Ringling Brothers would bring their circus to entertain the sick, who would watch from those balconies. But for now, the tuberculous slept quietly there on their cots, wrapped in blankets and breathing the unsullied morning air.

Jasper jogged up the curving stairs and tipped his head to a heavyset guard in the entranceway. "Morning, David."

"Hello, Jasper! Working on a Sunday?"

"Don't I always?" Jasper pulled a piece of wrapped candy from his pocket, a "Hooverite" of chocolate and corn syrup. Expensive, but worth every penny. David was a good old scout with a terrible sweet tooth. "Any news?"

David scooped up the candy, licking his lips. "They're going to post some new positions in two weeks. Better salary, for sure. I'll give you the scoop before they go up."

Jasper touched his cap. "Much obliged." He bounded up the interior steps and past the admitting office. To his left, one of the wards was sedate but busy enough. White-clad nurses carried trays that tinkled with the sounds of metal and glass. A sour scent, urine mixed with carbolic acid and old wood, issued from the wards. Rows of iron beds stood next to one another, the sick lying limply beneath the sheets. Jasper didn't look too closely.

After signing in at the office down the hallway, he exited the building and wound around the courtyard to the pathology building. Most people in the city knew it better as the city morgue and were ignorant of the living, breathing people within the brick walls—the doctors and chemists trying to tease out the what, the when, and the how of why the hospital patients were sick elsewhere on campus.

The pathology building was classic McKim, Mead & White (Lord, what odd bits of information he remembered from his Fifth Avenue days!), with white trim and fine windows. In a small ground-floor closet, he hung his mackinaw on a peg and replaced it with a stained cloth coat. Finally, he grabbed his lowly weapons—dust rags, a bucket filled with clean water and soap, and a sturdy mop stained deep gray from the endless dirt. He took down a circlet of keys and attached it to his belt.

Jasper hauled his equipment from lab to office, office to lab, dusting and mopping as he went. It wasn't long before he arrived at the double doors of the morgue.

It was quiet inside. Today, there would be no visitor tours, no entertaining of curious citizens with the macabre normalcy within those walls. Inside the clouded windows were the dead of New York who came after the heart attacks and dramatic falls off the Brooklyn Bridge. And the quieter passings too—the tiny still babies that emerged from their mothers never to issue that abrupt cry announcing themselves; the ancient, arthritic elderly who had forgotten to wake up in the morning. The metal drawers full of corpses, called the *bureau*, resided here.

Jasper didn't mind cleaning the morgue. When he first started working here, he had feared that he would be tainted afterward, polluted by the effluvia. But a job was a job, and the dead were dead. They couldn't hurt him, but they might help.

He twisted the key carefully in the lock. The room was long and spare. In the locked theater next door, there would be all the instruments for autopsy covered under clean linens, on rolling tables against the wall. The sinks against the walls were empty. Several metal tables stood in a row in the middle of the room, four of them holding bodies beneath white sheets. A ledger lay open to record the newest occupants.

On the nearest table, a thin, elegant hand drooped from under a sheet. The nails were curved and perfectly filed, and even from here he could see the half-moons at the nail bed. A few strands of strawberry-blonde hair had escaped as well.

Florence. It had to be. His heart thumped. He could almost hear her neck cracking on the stairs as she fell, though he hadn't witnessed the accident. Without thinking, he walked over to the table and stared at her hand, now stiffened from rigor mortis. The scent of perfume rose from her hair, and with it, the unmistakable odor of bitter almonds.

Jasper knew what he would see if he lifted the sheet. He'd seen it well enough when he'd found his parents in the bedroom that Sunday morning. Like Florence, they too were found mottled with a bluish-purple coloring—starved of oxygen in the telltale way that cyanide strangled its victims, one red blood cell at a time.

Jasper had always wondered—was it still murder if you murdered yourself?

He lifted the sheet, holding his breath.

They had taken down Florence's fancy hairdo, and the orangey-blonde waves rippled in a halo around her head. She was naked beneath the sheet, her jewelry and underthings removed. He blinked away the image of the nighttime morgue technician unceremoniously yanking off her rings and undergarments. It was degrading and utterly dehumanizing to be as bare as the next dead person, who likely lacked the grander lineage that the Waxworths possessed. So this was what happened when life chewed you up and spat you to the curb.

"What are you waiting for? An introduction?"

Jasper dropped the sheet and whirled around.

A dark-suited man stood in the door, frowning. His salt-and-pepper goatee came to a perfect point below his chin and thick, bushy eyebrows passed judgment. He was one of those men who exuded intimidation, a gift Jasper himself wished to own. When Jasper continued to stand openmouthed and frozen next to Florence's body, the man cocked his head.

"You could kiss her, but I promise you, she won't wake up."

Jasper finally found his voice. "I apologize, Dr. Norris. I was just . . . I was cleaning and . . ."

"I understand. You're curious. You've been working here for about two years and still curious. That's a good sign."

"Of what, sir?"

"Of giving a damn."

Jasper shut his mouth. He was surprised that Dr. Norris had even noticed him cleaning the garbage bins. But those dark, piercing eyes seemed to observe beyond the obvious.

"I see you have an interest in dead, pretty girls."

"Oh. No sir! I'm sorry, it's just that . . ." He turned back to the table and gazed at the flowing strawberry-blonde hair. Words formed and died on his lips.

"Ah. You knew this young lady?"

"Yes sir," Jasper admitted. "I saw her alive last night, actually, at my friend's engagement party uptown."

"Indeed. She came in after midnight." Dr. Norris examined the ledger on the nearest table. "Fall. An accident, apparently, after too much champagne. Probably fractured cervical vertebrae." Those eyes looked up and bored right into him again. "Is that correct? It's always convenient to have a fresh witness standing in my morgue for questioning."

"Yes sir. Er, no sir." Oh Lord, Jasper sounded like a simpleton. "I didn't see her fall, I only heard about it. And I saw her behavior beforehand. She was a bit gassed. But . . ."

"But what?"

"Look." Jasper pulled the sheet back, and the blueness of Florence's face and neck was a stark contrast to the cloth that covered her body. "This is not what someone should look like after a fall down the stairs. A few bruises, maybe, but not this."

Dr. Norris furrowed his considerable brows. He took a pencil from inside his jacket and used the blunt end to pull Florence's lower lip down. The inside of her mouth looked ragged from irritation.

"It's cyanide," Jasper said.

Dr. Norris removed the pencil and dropped it onto the table. "And how, my boy, would you know?"

"I just know." After a beat, Jasper's face went hot. "I could smell it on her." He felt silly because the odor was far fainter now, like he'd been imagining it all.

Dr. Norris waited for more, but Jasper kept his jaw shut. "Well, if you can't do better than that, I'd best return to my lab. Alexander wants me to examine a brain sample he's cooked down with sodium hydroxide."

He headed toward the door, his shoes shuffling with each footstep. Desperation filled Jasper. Since the party, he'd felt like, for the first time in four years, things could move in a direction he wanted. He had the attention of a person who could change his entire life, if he played it the right way. All that was needed was one more push.

Jasper blurted, "Sodium cyanide. Taken orally. We smelled it on her. I'll bet that her neck isn't even broken, just sprained, and that it was the poison that killed her."

Dr. Norris turned on his heel and surveyed Jasper with a new light in his eyes. "What's this? Are you a medical resident disguising yourself as a janitor?"

"No sir. I finished college this past spring. Going to apply to medical school once I've saved enough for tuition."

"Hence your dance partner there."

"Sir?"

"The mop."

"Oh. Yes sir."

He could tell that Dr. Norris was on the edge of some decision. As he swayed in his polished leather shoes, Jasper tried one more time. "Please, Dr. Norris. This was a murder. I'd bet my life on it."

After a long pause, the doctor lifted his chin. "Your life, eh? Well, that's worth a Sunday morning, isn't it?" He huffed without mirth, and Jasper replaced the sheet over Florence's corpse. Dr. Norris glanced at the ledger again. "Very well, let's take a look. Florence Waxworth. Oh! Of *the* Waxworths. For a mere cleaning boy, you have quite the social life." He gave Jasper a sidelong glance before returning to the paperwork. "The medical examiner's office was not contacted for this case. Nothing suspicious on the police report."

"Can't we investigate anyway?"

"Just because she's dead doesn't mean we can do whatever we want. Her family will have my head on a stick if the body is touched without permission, and I'd prefer to keep my head intact. I've no authority here. Slicing up dead socialites at the request of a janitor is not on my schedule." He headed toward the door, leaving Jasper in his wake. "I have three hundred cases to deal with, just this month. I only just opened my offices a few months ago, and I barely have enough equipment for my laboratories. I've been stealing new faculty from all the boroughs just to staff my department. Tammany Hall won't increase a cent of my budget right now, damn them."

In two seconds, he was through the doors, which slammed behind him with finality. Jasper's shoulders slumped.

So. That was the end of that.

The door opened again, and the goateed face reappeared. "Good God, boy," he growled. "If you learn anything from me and my department, it's never take no for an answer. Follow me."

Jasper fairly ran after Dr. Norris, leaving his mop and bucket behind him, along with Florence, who didn't seem to care one way or the other.

CHAPTER 6

Birdie had stayed silent throughout the motorcar ride, as had Andrew. His fists had clenched and unclenched, as if her very nearness irritated him. He must be furious, having to tend to his fiancée's whims. Well, it would only get worse after the wedding, knowing Allene.

Birdie barely noticed the fine houses of Fifth Avenue passing by, their small gardens green from mid-August warmth. She was thankful when the Brooklyn Bridge finally came into view. Dawlish shifted in the driver's seat. Looking just as she remembered him, he was the human version of overcooked cabbage. Pale, slouchy, and unable to make a decision without being told. His nose resembled a small potato. When the bridge came into view, he sighed, as if the very thought of Brooklyn pained his liver.

Birdie fingered the patched spot on her dress. How shameful that someone else's maid had darned her dress, but it was too late for pride now. She was sadly out of touch with the fashions. She hadn't read an issue of the *Delineator* in ages. It had taken energy at the party last night not to gape at the rising hemlines and the rich lace overlays.

A few sad horses pulled a rare carriage, not the least bit spooked by the automobiles that smoked and rolled along. Smocked women stood on street corners, asking for help in the war effort. A Liberty Bond rally would be held tomorrow. Birdie relaxed in the car's luxurious comfort. Today, there would be no crowding onto a subway or packed streetcar that stank of sweat.

She ought to begin asking Andrew questions about last night. They had only a few minutes before she arrived home. After steeling herself with a breath, she turned to face him and was surprised to find him sitting closer than before. His trousered thigh was only an inch away from hers now. He stared intensely back. It was an unsettling gaze, as if he was taking every bit of her in greedily but at the same time not really seeing her. "Andrew? Are you quite all right?"

"You're very beautiful, Birdie," he blurted.

Oh no.

No, no, no. Not this, not now. *Not him.*

He waited for the answer to a question he hadn't yet asked. Birdie knew the question. She'd heard it a thousand times—in the looks and glances of the managers at the clock factory, in the warm hands that brushed against her bodice on the cramped trolleys, in the whistles on the street when obscurity was impossible.

She tried to keep her voice calm, though her heart fluttered. "Allene is very beautiful," she countered. "And she's practically your wife."

"I'm not married yet."

"Andrew!" she whispered. She glanced forward to see if Dawlish noticed their conversation. As always, he hunched over the steering wheel, oblivious. Birdie had a sudden urge to jump out of the car and walk home.

Andrew lowered his voice. "You don't remember me, do you?"

"Of course I do! We met just last night."

"No, I meant before then," he said, his eyes searching her face. "Don't I look familiar?"

Birdie tried to shake the cobwebs that clouded her memories. Andrew Biddle. Did she know him? When she lived with the Cutters, she and Allene had frequented countless parties together. She vaguely remembered the Biddle family, but only his parents came to mind. Stately, handsome couple. She couldn't place Andrew at all.

"I don't think so," she admitted.

"At the factory? My father and I have put a good deal of money in the Ansonia Clock Company. We have part ownership now." When Birdie continued to look confused, he added, "I saw you there. Several times, in fact, when I toured the facility. You're on the second floor, on the north side."

Birdie was used to having the bosses walk about the girls' dial-painting stations. But she was a good worker who didn't get distracted. She kept her eyes on the tiny globules of paint dabbed just so onto the numbers and sweeps of the faces, dragging the camel-hair brush on her lower lip every so often to keep it pointed. She was efficient and fast. The last thing she wanted was her supervisors to see her daydreaming idly as random people strode through their factory. But Andrew? She had no memory of him.

Which meant that he'd watched her—several times, he said—without her knowing. And then a new thought sank into her consciousness, one that made her shiver.

Andrew Biddle partly owned the factory where she worked. He was her boss. He held her job in his hands, one of which now slipped over hers.

"Your hand is chilled," he said.

It wasn't the only part of Birdie that had gone icy. Forget Florence—she was as good as inside a satin-lined coffin, and here Birdie felt herself enclosed and unable to escape. This had to stop. She could find another job if she had to. Couldn't she? It was wartime. They needed people like her in all sorts of factories.

But there wouldn't be another position, not like this one. One where she could sit quietly all day and not exert herself. Birdie knew how weak she'd become. What else could she do that wouldn't exhaust her after a few minutes or make her bones ache? She needed her dial-painting job. So did Holly.

"Please," Birdie whispered, her eyes on her lap. She couldn't bear to meet his eyes or see his face. "Please. Allene is my friend."

"I know." He kept his hand over hers so she couldn't pull away. "I think Allene would enjoy it if you spent more time over at the Cutter house. I would too. Very much. I could talk to your boss and make your schedule more lenient. It would give me pleasure to do so."

Nausea filled her, swirling inside her stomach. The Cutter house was exactly where she needed to be. But oh God! Not like this.

The car was now traversing the Brooklyn Bridge. The dense cables whirred by, a crisscross pattern of lines and blue sky that was simultaneously pretty and shattered. Andrew cleared his throat. "Were you going to say something to me earlier?"

Birdie hesitated. Allene would be disappointed if she found out nothing about Florence.

"I had some . . . oh, odd things to ask you. About Florence. Last night was so very strange, I'm still trying to make sense of it. But I need to go home." She wanted nothing more than to crawl into that fluffy, comforting guest bed at the Cutter house and go back to her bad dreams, because reality wasn't a pleasant alternative right now.

"Ask me all the questions you want. I have all day."

"But I need to buy groceries . . ."

"I'll help you buy your groceries," Andrew insisted. "A whole month's worth. I'll buy your time, if you'll be gracious enough to donate some to me. I promise I'll be a gentleman. I'm your best friend's fiancé, after all."

His face was so darned earnest that Birdie's heart softened. She knew what he felt—that desperation of wanting something so much and knowing that you were this close to losing it. It was how Birdie felt about Holly, even about Jasper and Allene.

The car slowed, then stopped in front of a dingy four-story apartment building of darkening brownstone, as nondescript as its neighbors. Some windows had curtains blowing outward, some drawn together demurely, some missing. A few broken glass panes were patched with cardboard, as if the whole facade had suffered an apoplectic fit.

As the engine ticked away like a too-loud heart, Birdie put one hand on the door, ready to bolt. Dawlish rounded the motorcar to let her out, but he was slow as molasses. Andrew had yet to surrender her other hand.

"If you give me a little of your time, I'll answer any question you have," Andrew said. She shivered, and the near heat of his body warmed her—not an unpleasant sensation. God, he smelled delicious. Like crisp, new money.

Birdie turned her head quickly, her eyes locking onto Andrew's. She was caught. He smiled, knowing this, and nuzzled his lips almost against her ear.

"I know what you want, Birdie Abigail Dreyer."

Did he? Could he really know? She'd long been thinking of ways to ensure that Holly would escape from their drab apartment, from the shared toilet that stank in the summer, from the aching of hands after twelve hours of factory work. Allene was the answer. Mr. Cutter was aging, his power fading as Allene came of age, ready to unite two wealthy households in marriage. The Cutter house could be Holly's home and salvation if Birdie could figure out the pathway back. And now she might have Andrew to help.

So she didn't pull her hand away, just waited. His breath fluttered the tendrils of hair around her neck as he whispered:

"You want to know why Florence Waxworth was murdered."

CHAPTER 7

You're welcome.

Had the note come from the bookstore where Allene had ordered the chemistry tome? Or was it a leftover note to herself? She brought it to her nose and sniffed delicately. The ink smelled fresh and the paper was springy, as if it hadn't been folded for very long.

How odd.

She tucked the note back into the book and replaced it on the shelf. She didn't know what it meant, but now wasn't the time to think of such things. She was on a mission to visit the poisons in the Cutter house kitchen.

Esther, the cook, came in through the back kitchen door carrying a basket full of yellow wax beans. Her son had disembarked in Brest just a few months earlier, and she'd asked permission to plant a victory garden in the Cutters' back plot of land. Allene was sick to death of wax beans but propriety told her to say nothing—at least to Esther's face.

The scent of juicy chicken and tarragon roasting in the oven wafted throughout the kitchen. Allene eyed a cream sauce simmering on the stove. A rumbling stomach reminded her that she'd missed breakfast. A few servants were cleaning the large numbers of dirty glasses and dishes from the evening before.

They welcomed her with curtsies and bows before returning to their work. None seemed surprised at her being there. She had a funny habit of reading labels on all sorts of things that came through the house. She was an odd girl, always had been, and the staff knew it. Once or twice, she'd overheard Lucy schooling a new maid on humoring Miss Allene and her peculiar ways.

Even though her mother hadn't set foot in the house for years, Dorothy Cutter's signature was everywhere. The perfect marble inlay on the hallway tables matched the damask drapery; the silverware was polished weekly, no matter what. The servants snapped to attention whenever Allene or her father entered the room, though neither enforced such behavior. Mother's ghost (if a living person could have a ghost) watched everything.

And yet she was also numbingly far away. The last words Allene had exchanged with her in person had been to beg her mother to let Birdie return. She had been only thirteen then—nearly fourteen. Fourteen and so, so naive.

"But Birdie isn't sick! Surely she doesn't have consumption. She won't make me ill, Mother. I promise."

"Absolutely not. It's for your own good. And consider it a blessing not to have such a beautiful girl in your sphere. It's a dreadful vexation to be a shadow when you're supposed to be the sun."

Allene had said nothing more.

She'd received letters every other week the first year Mother had left to regain her health. The year after, they came every other month. As Mother's correspondence faded, so did the memories of her familiar clicking heels on the marble floors, the cadence of pearls at her throat when she fingered them, and that perfectly powdered aquiline nose. Andrew's marriage proposal was approved of and blessed by post. Of course, Mother never would have sanctioned Allene's renewed interest in Jasper and Birdie. Her ghost might whisper her disapproval, but she had become too quiet—not from declining health, but from neglect and declining consequence in her daughter's life.

Allene stooped down before a cabinet in the kitchen, ignoring the curious glances from the servants. She opened one cupboard, then another. Not every product displayed a list of chemicals. Companies could be secretive about their proprietary products. She was rummaging through the shelves when one of the chambermaids, Josephine, curtsied neatly. She was short, with bell-shaped hips that swung almost merrily when she walked. Her hands were large and capable; Allene could have worn them as gloves. At the thought of slipping on the warm, bloodied, and flayed skin of another person, she shivered. Why did she sometimes have such un-Christian thoughts?

"What may we be helpin' yeh with, miss?"

"Cyanide," she murmured under her breath, moving bottles aside.

"I'm sorry, Miss Allene? I didn't hear yeh."

Allene turned. "Uh. Yes. The silver polish. I know it's here somewhere."

"Why, Lucy used it yesterday to clean all the house silver. Would you like me to polish somethin' for yeh now?"

"No, no. I just wanted to check something."

She moved aside jars and bottles of every sort, for cleaning and scrubbing and such, but the metal can of polish was nowhere to be seen. It was always here, on the second shelf, next to the bottle of lemon oil and the box of bluing. A telltale ring of rust showed where it usually lived.

Allene furrowed her brow. "Where is Lucy?" she asked.

"Lucia?" The maid said her name with almost a sneer.

Amongst the servants, Lucy wasn't a favorite. Perhaps because she was a favorite of Allene's. Perhaps because lady's maids with Mediterranean complexions were not often seen on Fifth Avenue. Allene didn't spend too much time considering it. Every society had its own dramas, even within a single home, her mother had warned her. Here, Allene saw nothing but a household running well.

"Do you know where she is?" Allene asked again.

The cook walked by with a large dish of scalloped potatoes. "I believe she stepped out, Miss Allene. Said you sent her on an errand."

Allene planted a smile on her face before she could show her surprise. "Of course, I remember now."

But there was nothing to remember. She'd not sent Lucy on an errand. Granted, Lucy *did* run errands for her all the time, and Allene had been so preoccupied lately that maybe she'd simply forgotten.

But that wouldn't explain the missing silver polish.

She had vivid visions of a gloved finger swiping a smear of creamy silver polish along the inside of a champagne flute. It would need only a thin film, nothing that one would notice once the liquid was poured, for the champagne bubbles would obscure any signs of polish. That might be enough. She thought of the bruised coloring on Florence's skin and closed her eyes.

The slow and steady footsteps of her father's elderly butler, George—who had come out of retirement when their younger butler joined the war—echoed in the foyer. He welcomed someone before the front door was shut. Allene's heart began to dance within her chest. It couldn't be Birdie or Andrew. Which meant it must be Jasper. She calmed herself and pinched her cheeks, rubbing her lips together to make them cherry bright. Her fingers grazed over her loose light-brown curls, smoothing them as she walked to the foyer.

George stood stiffly at the ready, the outline of a gentleman behind his considerable frame.

"If you please, Miss Allene. You have a visitor."

Allene strode forward, smiling. But her smile disappeared as George stepped aside.

"Mr. Ernest Fielding."

Ernie must have seen her enthusiasm deflate; his own smile wilted. He seemed to understand his position as an ersatz Jasper, or Andrew, for that matter.

She wished she hadn't pinched her cheeks so. They were damned sore now. With as much energy as she could muster, she said, "How nice to see you, Ernie." Allene couldn't bear to be confined within four walls with Ernie, of all people. She motioned to the french doors at the other end of the salon. "Let's have a seat outside in the garden, shall we?"

It was a lovely walled garden with lush ivy climbing the brick on two sides. A single, locked ironwork gate opened onto Fifth Avenue, and the paved bluestone walkways were cleanly swept of debris. Even the moss and creeping thyme in the cracks behaved and grew only where allowed. Mother's rosebushes had long since bloomed and faded, and now the pink and purple dahlias were on display along the walls. A few birds chirped merrily, while the slower Sunday motorcar noise crept over the walls.

Allene sat on an iron bench, and Ernie leaned against a peach tree laden with ripe fruit. His clothes were neat and impeccably fine. And there was that hair—that dirty shade of blond with the slight curl that he'd combed into submission with goose grease. In a photo, he'd be considered handsome, but in reality, he oozed a milk-and-water personality.

"I came by to see if you were all right," Ernie said, eyes wide with concern. "Last night was quite a scare. You must be dead tired."

"I'm well, Ernie. Thanks for asking."

For a long stretch, neither of them said a word. Allene fussed with a thread at the hem of her emerald skirt while Ernie looked appraisingly around the garden, reminding her of a time when they were ten, and Ernie had come over while all the mothers had tea in the salon. Birdie and Jasper and Allene had been on the cusp of putting the last touches on a camera obscura they'd created from onionskin paper and nicked cigar boxes (the missing cigars, her father would be upset to find later, were piled in a handkerchief drawer). Soon, they might stare at ghostly images of each other within the box, because in reality they couldn't get enough of each other. Birdie especially would look so angelic and quizzical imprinted onto the thin onionskin paper within the camera obscura. Allene could imagine staring for hours. They needed to steal only one more box to make the top, when Ernie showed up.

"What are you doing? Can I play? Did you see *Oliver Twist* at the theater yet? I did! Splendid! Say, do you want to play Lasca? I brought the game with me. Are you hungry? Did you see those tea cakes? They looked jolly good!"

It was too much Ernie, in the way, all the time. Even now in the garden, Allene pitied him, but her pity didn't sink in very deep. She was too annoyed for that.

"It was good to see Jasper and Birdie after all these years," Ernie said at last. "They were a good-looking couple."

"They aren't a couple," Allene said. Perhaps too quickly. "Good looking, yes. Although Jasper could do with a nicer suit."

More silence. Good God, how long would this conversation last?

"How is your cousin?" he said after some time.

"Who?"

"The one in the war."

"Oh. Clarence. I don't know. I believe he's all right."

"Well, it'll be my turn soon," he said. His chest puffed out a bit.

"Ugh. Why are boys always in such a hurry to die?" Allene said, almost to herself. "You know, those trenches are full of filth. Lice and rats and such. And influenza has been killing the Germans all summer."

"Let it kill the Krauts. It won't get me," he said brightly.

Spoken like someone who knew nothing of suffering. Allene would know; she recognized the empty bravado in herself.

After a long pause, Ernie changed the subject. "I suppose Andrew is pretty upset. He seemed to be having a swell time chatting with Florence last night. A regular old gabfest."

His words had their desired effect.

"Yes, I suppose they did talk a bit last night." She remembered how Andrew had removed Florence from her vicinity. "What did they speak of, if I may ask?"

"Oh! A jolly good number of things." He ticked off a list, finger by finger. "The Petersons' wedding last month. How she hated everyone for being so damned artificial and they all hated her back for gossiping, when all she ever said was the truth."

"Really," Allene said. So she wasn't the only person who despised Florence.

Ernie forged on. "And Florence was annoyed that her European tour was on hold because of the war. And she hated the Kentucky Derby. In Kentucky, you know." Allene groaned inwardly. "They had me send for champagne, a few times actually."

"Oh. Did they?" Allene asked, disappointed. It all sounded rather undramatic. "Did . . . did Florence drink a lot?"

"Oh, yes. She's no bluenose, let me tell you. I think she was rather crocked by the third round. She had trouble walking. Andrew didn't though. Good thing too, since she was holding onto him."

"I see."

"And then they had a row."

"What?" Allene's voice rose in pitch.

"Yes. But I don't know what about. Florence was trying to go upstairs to find you three, and he was holding her back by the arm. Oh, she was really angry at your fiancé. She said, 'You have no idea what you want, Andrew!' That was all I heard, because when I told them the servant had brought more champagne, Florence excused herself."

Allene pursed her lips, feeling chilled. What on earth had Andrew and Florence been discussing? She took a breath. "And then?"

"And then, a little while later, she was falling down the stairs."

"Where was Andrew then?"

Just then, the french doors opened. Allene tempered a squeal of surprise. Her father stood in the doorway, still dressed in his overcoat from church. He frowned at her show of discomposure, then reached out a hand and shook Ernie's.

"Ernest. Good to see you. Got any new financial advice for me?"

"Oh, heaps! I'll bend your ear whenever you want."

"Did you arrive with Andrew?"

"He'll be back momentarily," Allene explained. She didn't mention Birdie. "How was church?"

"Abominable. Word's got round about poor Florence's accident." His brown eyes flicked to Allene, warning her to behave. Her sore arms reminded her of the previous night's conversation. "Her family cabled that they'll arrive tomorrow. The funeral is set for Friday."

The funeral. She'd be surrounded by Florence's family and a sea of too many people. There would be grieving, and gossip, and whispered questions beneath wide-brimmed, black-lace hats. Allene might go mad from the piercing stares that would come her way.

Footsteps approached behind them, and Allene's mouth dropped when Lucy curtsied at the doorway to the garden.

"Miss Allene. Mr. Cutter. Mr. Fielding. May I bring tea and biscuits?" Lucy asked.

"Lucy!" Allene squeaked. "You're back!"

"I'm sorry, miss. Did you ring for me? I went to pick up some of that powder you've been wanting."

Allene was utterly confused. She didn't recall asking Lucy to procure any powder. And now the silver polish was missing, and Florence had been arguing with Andrew last night. Father noticed her shocked expression, and he raised his eyebrows at her. If eyebrows could speak, they'd tell her to act like a normal Cutter woman.

Which she couldn't. How had she gotten out of her depth so quickly?

CHAPTER 8

Jasper followed Dr. Norris up the oak staircase. The odor in the stairwell was a familiar one—a mix of musty wood, soapsuds, and nose-stinging formaldehyde. Vaguely, he remembered that he was supposed to be cleaning this building top to bottom. He would get in trouble if he didn't finish. And then, as if aware that Jasper's mind was wandering, Dr. Norris barked at him.

"It's only one flight, boy. Keep up!"

So he did. Jasper stepped closely behind Norris's black, polished shoes as they swept into a chemistry laboratory on the second floor. Jasper had seen it dozens of times while working, but on every visit it changed. More and more equipment crowded the tables. The supply closet had gone from being haphazardly strewn with labeled brown bottles to being organized within an inch of its life.

In the center of the room, under milky ceiling lamps, a table was crowded with gas burners, flasks, and glass-stoppered bottles. The scent of biting preservative was far stronger in here. Jasper wrinkled his nose. As soon as he saw Norris observing him, he smoothed his face into an expression of benign calm.

An oddly shaped package wrapped in butcher paper lay on a table by the tall windows, red-and-white-striped twine hanging over the edge.

Jasper peered beneath the paper covering and saw several pounds of fresh cow liver oozing burgundy blood.

"Hungry?"

He tried not to jump back. What was it with these fellows and sneaking up on you? He turned to see another man at the doorway, staring at him with pale, calculating eyes. The beginnings of a double chin and peaked eyebrows added to an expression that was anything but friendly. Wearing a lab coat with frayed holes in the sleeves, the man motioned to Norris.

"Who's this? You stealing more staff from the Brooklyn coroner?" The man had a powerful Brooklyn accent that would make a sugar lump go bitter.

"No. Alexander, this is Mr. Jones. Surely you recognize him."

"You're the janitor." He was still staring. Jasper felt like he'd rather be back in the morgue, where the bodies weren't quite so rude.

"Perhaps. Perhaps not. Jasper Jones, this is Alexander Gettler. My chief forensic chemist."

"How do you do?" Jasper asked.

"I'd be better if my horses won at the tracks more often." He walked past Jasper to organize half a dozen bottles, making notes on a ledger.

"Alexander, Jasper believes that a young woman in the morgue was murdered."

"Does he now?"

"Indeed. With cyanide."

"Oh yeah?" Gettler turned around. "What makes you an expert in cyanide?" He had picked up a rather large knife the way a person might hold a book or a pen. Casually, as if it were the most normal thing in the world.

"I know what a cyanide death looks like," Jasper said, feeling more confident—the sight of the knife hadn't rattled him at all.

"What, are you a medical intern too?" Gettler twirled the knife, but Jasper didn't back away.

"No sir. But I'm applying to the school here. Next year."

"So you're not even a medical student?"

"No sir. But I will be." He said the words with confidence. There would be no question of his studying here. He knew it.

"So that head"—Gettler pointed the knife at Jasper's forehead—"is still empty." Seeming already bored, he pushed up his sleeves and unwrapped the chunk of glistening liver. It quivered nauseatingly, as if entertained by the conversation. A deep fissure bisected the mass into two lobes. "What do you know about methyl alcohol poisoning?"

It was such an ordinary chemical, so terribly undramatic. Jasper's uncle certainly liked methyl alcohol. He was making bottles of it in the kitchen, after all. If Gettler was already preparing to detect poisonings, he knew what was coming with the upcoming laws. Smart fellow, he thought.

"I know a little. It's cheap booze, but poisonous," Jasper said. He pointed to the liver. "What's this for?"

"I'm mixing liver samples with methyl alcohol so I can determine how best to test for it in human tissue samples."

"Oh." Jasper crossed his arms. "So . . . you don't know much about methyl alcohol either."

Dr. Norris laughed heartily. Gettler turned, looking like he'd just swallowed a bad lemon. He pursed his lips.

"Well, the young squirt's got a tongue on him, eh? All right then. Tell me what you know about cyanide."

He spoke of cyanide as if it were a person, a formidable enemy that needed thorough and respectful discussion. Norris simply leaned against the doorjamb, watching the exchange. Which meant the burden was on Jasper. If he wanted to be part of this department, part of unraveling the mystery of Florence's death, part of something beyond last night's engagement party and his own failed past, then everything was up to him. He could mention his parents' death as the reason why he knew of cyanide. But no. He wouldn't ride on sympathy to boost him up. Pity would not create his successes. He lifted his chin to speak.

"A Prussian blue test could reveal a poisoning. That would be easy enough. All we'd need was a sample."

"From where?" Gettler had turned back to the jiggling hunk on the butcher paper, making a long slice in the liver. His blade hit no connective tissue, sliding through the organ as if it were warm butter.

"The stomach," Jasper guessed. He tried to sound more confident than he was. He heard Dr. Norris chuckling behind him but dared not turn around.

"And how would we extract it?" Gettler sank his blade into the liver again, but this time his slice was crooked. He was paying more attention to the conversation than the cutting.

"Cyanide salts would dissolve in water. I'd do an aqueous extraction after macerating a sample."

"Then what?"

"Then I'd distill it to separate out the particulates." Jasper waited for another challenge, but when it didn't come, he pressed further. "Friedrich Otto's textbook on the matter is very clear, though I think he is a bit too wordy."

At this, the two doctors gaped. Dr. Gettler rested the bloody knife on the counter and stared him straight in the eyes.

"And why do you care to know how this particular person died?"

"I knew her, sir."

"Doesn't matter. Let the office take care of that. We can't make things personal here."

"It's not just that," Jasper said, feeling like he was on the cusp of losing first place in a race. "Everyone thinks it was an accident. If that's not true, then there is a murderer out there who's getting away with it. Someone clever enough to know it would look like an accident."

"And you think you're cleverer than this killer?"

"Yes sir."

"You care about this woman."

"No, I don't." Gettler's eyes snapped onto him, and Jasper realized how callous he sounded. But it was true. Florence's smug stares and acid words were the only things about her that had ever touched him.

"It doesn't matter what I think of her. Isn't the truth worth fighting for?" The two men exchanged glances with each other. In the silence that followed, Jasper stepped up to Dr. Gettler and held out his hand. "And, truth or not, you need someone to slice up that liver for you, so you can do more important things. Don't you?"

Dr. Norris's bristled eyebrows rose in mirth. Even Dr. Gettler allowed a small smile.

"Well. It looks like Bellevue may have just lost a janitor," Dr. Norris said. He took a white laboratory coat down from a peg on the wall and threw it at Jasper, who pulled it over his arms and tried not to smile like a fool as he buttoned it. Gettler shook Jasper's hand with his own blood-sticky one (somehow, this seemed done on purpose). With the clean hand, he opened his palm, motioning to the small laboratory surrounding them.

"Welcome, Mr. Jones, to the chemistry of death."

⟨⟩

Jasper wasn't unhappy to leave his janitorial work behind. The only benefit had been having complete access to everything in the building. Which meant no more "borrowing" textbooks off the shelves on a Friday and returning them Sunday morning, before anyone noticed they'd been missing. No more sniffing around the locked chemical closets. But it didn't matter. Other doors were opening now. Better ones.

After about an hour's worth of chopping, mincing, and grinding, Jasper was an expert in the total annihilation of cow's liver. He was up to his forearms in blood, and he didn't care. He loved the wood paneling, the smoke-stained plaster walls, and Gettler's murmuring and brutal

Brooklynisms. Gettler would explain his techniques, saying things like "First of all . . . ," which sounded like *foist of all . . .* Good Lord, Jasper would hear that voice in his dreams tonight.

After he had washed off the blood and sinew, Dr. Norris came by to discuss his new position in the laboratory.

"I can pay you eight hundred dollars a year. That's all."

Jasper nodded, a little too quickly. It would be almost double what he'd made as a janitor, even though it was still not much. But he might finally afford medical school next year if he saved carefully, if his uncle could handle some of the bills at home. He would have a head start in the field of pathology. A life's career speckled with words like *leader in his field* and *forensics prodigy* was staring down at him. His heart did backflips.

"You'll work here full time as Dr. Gettler's assistant and help when the office is called to a crime scene. I need a stenographer, someone to run the chemistry labs and order equipment, someone to answer the phones . . ."

"I'll do it," Jasper answered, without a trace of hesitancy.

"And one more thing. How old are you?"

"I'm eighteen."

"Don't grow up any faster, young man."

"Sir?"

"I'll lose you to the next draft. They lower the age limit every time. I won't have my whole department turned into doughboys pushing up daisies."

"Yes sir! I'll do my very best not to age, sir."

"Excellent."

When Norris was done with him, Gettler dug in with his provisos.

"First, you keep up on the reading," he lectured. "You know some but not enough. You'll learn plenty in medical school but not fast enough for me." He took book after book off his shelves and patted them lovingly. Jasper glanced at the familiar bindings.

"But I already read those," Jasper protested.

"When?" Gettler asked, incredulous.

"I've been working here for over two years. I read them during my . . . erm . . . breaks."

"While you were in college? A bit early for someone your age, eh?"

Jasper shrugged. "I'm impatient."

"I see. And you're a terrible janitor, if you were spending all your time reading."

"Yes sir, I was."

Gettler laughed. "Well, I worked"—(*woiked*—Lord, that accent!)—"the night shift at the ferry while I finished my PhD. Who am I to talk?" He pushed the books aside and waggled his finger. "One other thing."

"Yes?"

"That dead girl."

The grin on Jasper's face melted away. "Yes?"

"Charles showed me the police file while you were dicing up that liver. Our office was not called for an autopsy. Dr. Norris can make a request to open the case, but it's the police that have the final say."

"Which means?"

"Which means our department can't touch that body. And since you're in our department now, you can't either."

Jasper wilted under his steady, icy gaze. What was the point of being here if he couldn't find out what really happened to Florence? Or show the world that a kid from the Bowery could solve a Fifth Avenue crime?

Gettler watched the different emotions transform his face. "We don't break rules here. We don't bend them, not even a smidge. Tammany Hall is chock full of shady deals and dirty handshakes. Norris put a kibosh on coroners for hire, and I agree with him a hundred percent. We do it right here, boy, or we don't do it at all. Got it?"

"Yes sir."

Jasper went back to his work and dutifully added different amounts of icy-clear methanol to a dozen samples of carefully weighed liver. In his mind, he couldn't stop hearing Dr. Gettler's disdain for rule breaking. And all the while he worked, Jasper had only one other thought that tumbled over and over again:

Gettler and Norris had just hired a liar.

CHAPTER 9

Andrew opened the car door and held out his hand to Birdie. She took it tentatively but appreciated the strength of his support as she stepped onto the uneven cobblestones. Her building had peeling paint along the windows and was dull, brown brick. Nothing to look at, but Andrew's watchful eyes took it in anyway.

Birdie was reaching for the building's front door when it swung inward on its own accord. A gentleman, short and mustachioed, pulled his hat lower over his eyes.

"S'cuse me, miss," he said, but wouldn't make eye contact with her or Andrew. Andrew didn't seem to be bothered by this, but Birdie frowned, poisoned by the man's proximity. She was grateful that the stranger was on his way out.

And then she remembered: *Holly.* She'd begged Mother to stay home with her. Alone. Anger quickened her pulse.

"Will you wait here?" she asked Andrew. "It'll just be a moment while I check on Holly and Mother."

"I'd rather not," he replied. He seemed too eager to be near her, even in this shabby Brooklyn apartment. She shrank from shame. She didn't want Andrew here, but she needed to hear what he knew about Florence and she needed to check on Holly. If she resisted, Andrew and his information would leave. Lately, the only resistance she possessed was in refusing to enter her mother's profession. She had no other energy otherwise.

"Very well," she said.

She led Andrew to the fourth floor. Their apartments were at the end of the hallway, two doors next to each other. One for her mother, and one for her and Holly, connected by a door between their living rooms. It cost a great deal more to rent two apartments, but Birdie was adamant about keeping Holly away from Mother's work, even if it meant more hours at the clock factory.

"Well. Here we are," Birdie said between labored breaths. She turned a key in the lock. Inside, a threadbare, patternless carpet lay beneath a rickety dining table and mismatched chairs. The tiny kitchen off to the side was scrupulously clean, but the enamel of the sink was worn down to its iron bones. Teacups were drying nearby, showing chinks and chips at their edges.

"Holly? Mother? I've got a visitor," she announced.

The pattering of feet preceded a spindly little girl who came running around the kitchen corner. She skidded to a halt when she saw Andrew and hung back, a finger in her mouth. Even now, though Holly's features were emblazoned in her mind, Birdie never tired of that face. Holly's cupid bow of a mouth was perpetually red, as if stained on strawberry ices. Her dress was faded yellow-and-white gingham that looked like a sunset smudged by smoke. She hadn't brushed her brown hair yet, and sleep still caked the corners of her eyes. No one had helped her wash that morning.

Birdie opened her arms—"Holly Berry!"—and the little girl ran into her embrace.

Holly was pretty in a brown-bird sort of way—lovely, but without the arresting beauty Birdie herself possessed, the kind that stopped men midstride. Thank goodness Holly was plainer. It was a blessing.

After a long embrace, Holly dropped down to hide behind Birdie's skirts.

"Who's that?" Holly pointed a raw-tipped finger at Andrew.

"Don't point, my dear. It's not polite. And stop biting your nails. This is Mr. Biddle. He's a friend of Miss Allene's, and he brought me home."

"Is he going to talk to Mama?" she asked. Andrew quirked his eyebrows, and Birdie shook her head.

"No, sweetie. He's going to help us get groceries. Is Mother out of her room yet?"

"No. She had a talker, but he's all gone away."

"Did you eat breakfast?"

"No. And I'm awful hungry. The milk is pinchy"—Holly's made-up word for sour milk—"and I'm all hollow inside. Lookee." She grabbed at her belly through her dress and squeezed the loose fabric around her waist.

"Well, we'll have to remedy that, won't we?" Birdie said, trying to be chipper. She tied an apron over her tarlatan dress and put water in the kettle. Ignoring Andrew for the moment, she was drawn to a stale smell emanating from the icebox. She opened it and found a pool of dirty water in the basin at the bottom. The ice had melted, and a small, rancid block of butter sat softening on a shelf within. The milk bottle held a curdled inch of thick whiteness.

There was half a crust of bread in the bread box and a nearly empty jar of huckleberry jam. A box of crackers was full of crumbs. There were some oats left in the oat crock, but no milk to make a decent porridge. Embarrassment flooded her, and she heard Andrew clear his throat.

"It's a beautiful day for August," he remarked. "Not too warm. Don't you think so, Holly? Maybe the jigger shop is open."

Holly frowned. "It's Sunday. God says: 'No chocolate phosphates on Sunday!'"

"Is that a fact? What else won't God let you do on a Sunday?"

"Oh, heaps! Heaps and heaps." Holly climbed onto a chair, growing comfortable. She kicked the chair rungs with her bare heels. "Chewing gum. Bad words. Go to school."

"All the fun things, eh?" He grinned down at her.

"And candy." Holly wasn't really listening. She was too busy listing. "And chewing gum, and . . ."

Andrew suppressed a chuckle.

Birdie's eyes flicked back and forth between the two. She covered her mouth with the back of her fingertips, hiding a smile. Andrew drew closer to her and smiled too, as if they were sharing a secret. Which, Birdie remembered—they were. None of this was supposed to be happening. Not quite. There was something wrong about Andrew being here, alongside the few tattered doilies decorating the furniture and the spare kitchen. Birdie felt naked, and there was no way to conceal herself. But she still didn't have the answers she wanted.

And then it got infinitely worse.

"Birdie? Is that you?" her mother's low voice intoned from the other side of the wall. The doorknob between the two apartments turned, the tumbler clicking with the twist of a key. Hazel Dreyer emerged, tying a blue satin robe tightly around her narrow waist, which hadn't thickened a single inch after childbearing. Her flaxen hair, just like Birdie's, was loose around her shoulders, but some of it clung in ropy locks. She needed a good shampooing. Faded silk slippers covered her feet, and her generous breasts were noticeable beneath the thin fabric of the robe.

Mother was still pretty. Her thinness had made her eyes larger in her face, big orbs of green that flitted from face to face, unwilling to rest peacefully on any one person. Her cheekbones were high and the skin of her neck had yet to sag. There was good breeding in the way she held herself, as if she wore an invisible corset. She pulled the edges of her mouth up when she saw Andrew, and crow's-feet sprouted from the edges of her smiling eyes.

"Oh. Is it already one o'clock? I'm sorry to have kept you waiting. Did I forget to say it was apartment 4B, not 4A?"

Birdie wanted to die of shame. She quickly stepped forward. "Mother, you misunderstand. This is Andrew Biddle. Allene's fiancé? He escorted me home this morning. As a favor to Allene."

"Oh! I see. Well! Andrew, please make yourself comfortable." She laughed and swept her hand through the air, an attempt to erase her mistake. "I haven't had my medicine yet. I'm afraid I'm a little fuzzy." She laughed again, and it sounded like tin cans tumbling down an alley.

"I'll get your medicine, Mama." Holly jumped onto the countertop like a little monkey, procured a small glass jar from a cupboard, and fetched a large brown bottle from the other apartment. Holly messily poured a few drams of dark liquid into the jar. She carefully delivered it to her mother, leaving a trail of sloshed liquid on the floor.

"Thank you, Holly. So, how was the party?"

"Good," Birdie said. She didn't want to talk about it.

"And James?" How odd to hear Mr. Cutter addressed as such. Mother fiddled with a stray thread on her robe, keeping her eyes downcast.

"He looked well, I suppose." Birdie shrugged. "We hardly spoke."

"I see." She was frowning now. When she looked up, Holly caught her eye, and she smiled, a little too brilliantly. "Come, Holly. I need to change. You may play the Victrola while I dress."

Holly squealed and followed her into the other apartment. Birdie had no words. She wished that Andrew would go away.

After a long minute, he said, "Where's your father?"

"He's dead. He was a salesman and traveled a lot overseas, but he drank too much and something happened with his liver." It all sounded so clinical, but Birdie hadn't much sadness for a father who'd barely stepped into her life. If anything, his absence had been a convenience. Hazel and Birdie had been happily situated at the Cutter house all the while he was gone. It was more convenient that he was nonexistent, even now.

"Your sister is something," he said, quick to change the subject.

Birdie smiled. "A little headstrong, though."

"I'd need more time to see if that's true." Their eyes met, and Birdie understood that he was asking a question. Before she could queue up her nonresponse, someone rapped on the door. It made them both jump.

If she ignored it, maybe the person would go away.

Please, please go away.

The person knocked again. Mother often forgot to tell her callers which door to knock on. The annoyance blossomed into a nightmare as Birdie stood there, afraid to move.

"Do you need to get that?" Andrew asked, but Birdie shook her head. A moment later her mother swept back into the living room, as if suspecting that Birdie would ignore the caller. Holly skipped at her heels. Hazel undid the three locks and opened the door.

"Geoffrey! Have a seat. Holly, be a dear and bring Mr. Geoffrey a glass of water."

"Yes, Mama."

The man was older, about the same age as Mr. Cutter. He wore a fine Sunday suit and held his wool hat in his hands. Silver dotted his temples, and he had a round stomach that spoke of regular steaks at Delmonico's and a fat wallet that paid no heed to the sky-high prices of meat and sugar. At the sight of Andrew, he nodded, as if acknowledging another member of the club. Andrew looked uncomfortably at Birdie, who was biting her lip. The man smiled.

"You're a pretty thing. Are you one of Hazel's sisters?"

"No. I'm her daughter." Birdie refused to introduce herself properly.

"Ah, well, she certainly fooled me," he said, winking at Hazel, who wasn't listening. She was looking past him through the window, blinking at the midmorning sunlight. The opium spirits worked quickly; Birdie could sense them easing the tension in Hazel's body already, and her cheeks were regaining their color. The man extended his arm to Holly, who skipped over with a half glass of water. The other half had splattered on the floor. "What a little doll you are! Come to Mr. Geoffrey. Let me take a look at you."

Birdie froze. She wanted to step forward and grab Holly, but something glued her shoes to the ground. Holly put the glass down on the side table and hesitated.

"It's all right, Holly dear," Hazel murmured. She waved her hand. "Sit down like a good girl."

"Maybe we should go out?" Andrew suggested, but no one seemed to hear him.

Her mother's words had worked. Holly approached Mr. Geoffrey without fear. God, to be fearless again! Birdie could hardly remember what that felt like.

Mr. Geoffrey took Holly's hand in his, then patted his knees. "Come, have a seat on my lap. Do as you're told." When Holly climbed onto his knees, Birdie felt a miasma rising in her throat. Her hands were hundred-pound weights at her sides. She couldn't move. Why couldn't she move?

Mr. Geoffrey touched the brown curls while his other hand slid onto Holly's knee. It was as if Birdie could feel the broad, heavy hand on her own knee, the stubby fingers tracing a path behind her ear, down the nape of her neck . . .

A voice cracked into the tomb that had momentarily swallowed her. "Holly. What do you say to finding that jigger shop now?" Andrew suggested.

"Oh yes, please!" Holly scrambled off Mr. Geoffrey's lap and ran almost full force into Andrew, grabbing his hand. Irritation snaked through Mr. Geoffrey's expression.

"Let's go," Birdie rasped, barely able to speak. She felt Andrew's warm palm on her low back, pushing her toward the door. Push harder, she thought. Throw us both out of here. For God's sake.

She barely remembered opening the door, Andrew grabbing her purse with the apartment keys, or the sound of her mother's voice coaxing Mr. Geoffrey toward the opened inner door. "Darling, I'm all yours," she said. All the way down the bowing steps, Andrew chatted gamely, keeping Holly occupied while Birdie collected herself. When the light of the Sunday afternoon hit her face as they exited the building, she found that once again she could breathe. But she felt spoiled and soured.

"Are you all right?" Andrew asked her.

"I'm sorry. I'm so sorry," she repeated.

"For what?"

She wrung her hands. "I don't know. I wish you hadn't come."

Andrew didn't answer. Regret didn't stain his features; in fact, he appeared rather contented.

"You enjoy this, don't you?" she murmured. "As with Florence. You like knowing things."

"I do and I don't. It's not enjoyable, understanding what pains people so."

"What about Florence?" she pressed.

Holly ran forward to investigate Dawlish's motorcar parked by the sidewalk. The chauffeur looked bleakly at the little girl and sighed, as if the world's problems were the fault of adorable children. Birdie took that moment to face Andrew.

He lowered his voice. "I spent a while with Florence last night, while you three were upstairs. She wouldn't stop talking. It's amazing how much a person will talk if you give them the time and patience to fill up a conversation. Spent a good amount gossiping about you, Allene, and Jasper. I didn't know you all when we were younger, but Florence did. Said you three were like peas in a pod, always thick as thieves. She said once at a picnic, you all went missing and they found you swimming in a pond hours later, almost a mile away. 'Glued to each other' is what she said. But she said it with so much jealousy and hate."

Birdie shook her head. She was poor now. She had nothing. Jasper was nearly as badly off. "Why on earth would she hate us?"

"I don't know. But she disparaged Allene's engagement to me, your dress, Jasper's job and station. She spoke of Jasper like he was a leper, and you like you were a . . ." Andrew looked elsewhere, not wanting to finish the sentence.

"Like my mother," Birdie finished his thought. Like a whore. Everyone in Allene's circle must know the truth, and the saying went, like mother, like daughter. Birdie flushed. One day, those thoughts might touch Holly, and she was livid at the possibility. "But Andrew. Why would anyone hurt her over idle gossip?"

"This wasn't so harmless, Birdie. You should have seen her eyes. You should have seen her face. There is dislike, and there is absolute hatred. I thought to myself, if she could, Florence would push any one of you off a cliff and not regret it one bit. I thought that I should keep a close eye on her. So when she died, I couldn't help but think—someone wanted her dead because of how vicious her feelings were. Someone who wanted to protect one or more of the three of you."

"Likely we weren't the only ones she spoke ill about. There was a whole party of people."

"True. I was with her for only a few minutes last night, after all."

"You know, I had no idea she felt this way. After all, the three of us haven't been an 'us' for years."

"Doesn't matter. You have that effect on people. Look at poor Ernie! He worships all of you. Like a dog."

"Yes, poor boy. He needs a wife!" she joked, then sobered.

"He was the one who was fetching her champagne all night," Andrew said. "After she went to the bathroom, I lost track of her. Until . . ."

Until they disappeared. Until she died.

"Hungry!" Holly yelped from their side. The motorcar forgotten, she scrabbled between them, searching until her small hands emerged triumphantly holding one of each of their hands. When Andrew warmly clasped Holly's hand, Birdie's heart fissured a little. The little girl dragged them both forward, and Andrew and Birdie laughed, as though they were being pulled by an energetic puppy. There were more people walking the streets, neatly folded into their Sunday best. A few people smiled sweetly at them—a well-dressed man, a lovely woman, the child bridging them with her own small body.

Why, they think we're a family, Birdie thought. Here we are, a bundle of innocence, shame, and lies. Some family. It wasn't that different from her real one, and her heart cracked a little further.

They'd walked almost all the way to Union Street when Andrew pointed out a small corner store that had a meager showing of produce in the windows. It was surprising that any vegetables were available at all—people tried to grow their own victory gardens, and the rest went toward the war effort. He pushed the door open and a tiny bell strung to the door jingled a twinkling welcome. They nodded to the clerk, who was reading a newspaper behind the countertop.

Andrew spoke low to Birdie. "Whatever you want, it's yours."

Birdie looked up at him. "Anything?"

"Anything."

"That's a lot to promise, Andrew. Not even the devil would make such a deal."

"Well then, I guess the devil's got nothing on me."

She was torn between her hunger and her bleeding pride, but hunger won out. Holly's hunger, at least. Andrew got the attention of the clerk, and one by one Birdie and Holly selected a wealth of groceries from the shelves. The prices were exorbitant, as they had been for some time now. One loaf of day-old rye bread, a pound of butter, four jars of jam, one of honey, a hunk of cured ham, a two-pound sack of oatmeal, three cans of corned beef, two tins of sardines, a jar of cucumber pickles, and one of pickled peaches. Holly received a striped bag of penny candy. Altogether, it cost more than Birdie earned in two weeks at the factory. The clerk couldn't hide his surprise when Andrew drew off several bills from a roll in his pocket.

As they carried the groceries back to the apartment, Birdie hesitated. She didn't want to ask, but Andrew had said "anything." In front of her door, the Cutters' motorcar still waited. Birdie shifted the smaller bag of groceries in her arms.

"I can help you bring them up," he said.

"No. I've got it from here. I can't thank you enough." She paused, then pushed the words out. "Andrew . . . there is one other thing."

"Anything, Birdie."

She looked into his eyes. They were a peculiar shade of blue, with brilliant flecks of copper and almost red at their centers. As she readied her question, Holly leaned into her, and Andrew smiled fondly. He really would do anything for them. Anything at all.

"Would you mind . . . Mother has had trouble procuring her medicine lately. We can't afford a doctor, and the war has driven up the price terribly. She's on her last bottle. She has . . . women's problems, you know. A lot of pain. When she doesn't have the medicine, she suffers so much."

"I can get her a prescription. No problem." Andrew smiled. As he withdrew to the car, Holly stepped forward and pointed at Birdie's face.

"Will you kiss Birdie?"

Birdie went crimson, and Dawlish frowned at the both of them. Aware of their audience, Andrew stepped forward and kissed Birdie chastely on the cheek.

"Thank you, Andrew," she breathed.

"No. It's me who should thank you," he whispered into her ear. His breath stirred the curls near her ear, and she shrugged away from the ticklish feeling. As he drove down the street, Birdie shivered with guilt. He was Allene's, not hers. Even if Andrew promised to buy her the world, nothing was really hers.

CHAPTER 10

Allene never knew that murder could make Monday mornings so wonderful.

It was a fresh new day, served with a glorious sunrise and of course Florence's untimely death to solve. There was brand-new information to gather from Jasper and Birdie, and her own suspicions about Lucy to investigate. There could be legions of others who might have had a grudge against Florence. So much to think about.

Allene had woken at half past five in the morning with purpose and a smile. Before the house had creaked its first yawn, she'd rung the bell for Lucy. Her groggy maid let out a faint groan when she entered Allene's room.

"Even roosters should be sleeping now, Miss Allene."

Allene grinned. "What a comparison. I'm not a fowl, and I'm not a boy."

"No, you are not," Lucy agreed. "You're like . . . a squirrel. A smart squirrel. Trouble." She soon tightened her lips and painted on a more proper expression. Allene loved it when Lucy let out these tidy bits of saltiness, but they were rare indeed. If Father heard her, she would be fired in an instant.

Lucy stayed silent as she helped Allene into a regular day dress of polished lavender cotton. As usual, Allene stowed her cigarette lighter into the hidden pocket. After a breakfast of poached eggs on toast and scalding tea, Allene rang for the motor. Lucy handed her a beige pair of gloves.

Allene cleared her throat and gathered her courage. "Lucy. Where . . . where is the silver polish?"

Lucy didn't blink. "Pardon me, miss?"

"The silver polish. The can in the kitchen is missing."

"Don't you worry about such things, Miss Allene. We keep the supplies well stocked, even if it is wartime."

"I don't mean that. It's just . . . gone."

"Well, it was empty. So I threw it away."

"Oh! Are you sure? I didn't think the can was so old—"

"It was." Lucy never interrupted; Allene stared at her. "When the lady of the house starts asking about missing things, people get fired. And during a time like this, it's impossible for someone like me to find a new position."

"I didn't mean that, Lucy." How did the conversation veer off to this place? Lucy tucked the last curl into the knot on Allene's head, but she was frowning with something between irritation and concern. Allene surrendered. "Very well. Tell Father I've gone out to the new hat shop on Seventh Avenue and am going to see a film with Andrew's sister. I'll be home by dinner."

Lucy nodded primly. When the driver asked for instructions, Allene didn't even have to look at the folded paper in her beaded reticule.

"Three-thirty Fifth Avenue, Brooklyn."

Dawlish was even more cabbage-like than usual; he likely hadn't yet had his morning tea. He frowned upon hearing the address. "Brooklyn? Why, I was just there—"

"Oh, Dawlish, just *go*, for heaven's sake."

He turned around in his seat and wordlessly drove. Wise man. A copy of the *Times* was on the seat next to her. Dawlish always kept a recent paper there for Father to read, as it was usually he who was chauffeured first thing in the morning. Allene perused the headlines. "Liner Had Five Deaths Due to Influenza: Big Passenger Steamship Reports Twenty-One Cases on Voyage to New York."

"Well. It's a good thing I'm not traveling," she said to no one in particular. Hmm. Could Florence have succumbed to a sudden illness? She doubted it. From what she knew, influenza wasn't so flagrantly ambitious as to suddenly kill off healthy young people like herself or Florence.

"Here we are, Miss Allene."

Allene looked out the window. She had barely noticed the streets and bridge whizzing past, and here she was. The brownstone building had bricks shadowed in black stains and a broken first step. The windows were darkened by curtains, and Allene immediately had the sense that the structure itself was trying its darnedest to shut her out.

"Shall I wait for you, miss?" Dawlish asked. He seemed more anxious than she.

"No. Come back for me around quarter to six. Good-bye."

Dawlish idled at the curb anyway. Up and down the street, men and women were walking to work. Mothers led children to the school yard down the street, where the little ones peeled off. Men walked with a telltale arthritic, stiffened gait and leaned on canes. There was something odd about the proportion of men to women. She narrowed her eyes.

Oh. So many young men had gone to war, of course.

Well, not all had gone. She thought of Jasper and Andrew—both yet too young for the draft, and Father was too old. Father occasionally wrote to the family of his former butler, Stephen, who was fighting in France. Her cousin was there too, but she never asked Father for news about Clarence—she didn't really want to know. All news was bad news.

Allene was thankful every day that she had been born a girl. She thought of Jasper and remembered hearing that his older brother, Oscar, had died—was it from some terrible training accident? She couldn't recall. Why, Jasper hadn't mentioned him one bit at the party. And what was worse, Allene hadn't asked how he fared as an only child like her, or as an orphan.

Across the street, two posters on a shop window glared at her. Uncle Sam pointed at her so rudely—Lord, she was tired of seeing that obnoxious finger—and the other showed a girl bedecked in stars and stripes, dozing on a chaise. "Wake up, America!" it yelled at Allene. Father bought plenty of Liberty Bonds to help with the war effort, and they'd drastically cut down on buying sugar lately. She drank her tea plain, didn't she? She allowed Esther to enforce Meatless Tuesdays and Wheatless Wednesdays.

After one last glance at the poster, Allene murmured under her breath, "No one with an ounce of sense would wear a scarf like that. How utterly gauche."

She stepped to the front door of Birdie's apartment building and knocked, but the door opened immediately. Birdie stood in the doorway, clad in a plain work dress of faded green, a satchel in hand. Allene looked over her shoulder and waved Dawlish away like he was an errant gnat, and the shining motorcar grumbled off.

Allene embraced Birdie and gave her a smacking kiss on the cheek. A waft of stale air oozed out from the building's stairwell. Allene tried not to make a face.

"Well, good morning! Aren't I to come up to your place first?"

Birdie stiffened. "Whatever for? Did you have breakfast yet?"

"Oh yes." Seeing Birdie's face, she realized Birdie didn't want her there. But she was curious, especially about Holly and Hazel. Her eye twitched, and disappointment pushed out her lower lip. "Well, I suppose we should get on. Anyway, the posters on the street are giving me the evil eye. Let's go."

"Is . . . is that what you're wearing?" Birdie pointed.

Allene spread her skirt with her gloved hands. Was it not sufficiently au courant? Had it creased on the drive over? "Well, yes. Should I be wearing something else?"

"You don't look like you're going to work. We're going to a factory. You look as if you *own* it." There was an inscrutable expression on her face. "Did you bring another dress to change into?"

"Oh dear, no. Well, must you go to work? Surely you can take the day off."

"I can't." Birdie hesitated. Finally, she mumbled, "We need the money."

"Well, what I have to tell you can't wait until Saturday."

"I have to work Saturday too."

"Good God, you do?" She bit her lip, thinking. "Very well then, maybe I can borrow a day dress from you?"

Birdie reddened. She seemed trapped. A streetcar rumbled by a few blocks over. Somewhere in the distance, a clock chimed.

"All right. Come on up. We don't have much time."

Birdie widened the door, and Allene slipped inside. The stale air turned into a stench. Somewhere, someone's toilet wasn't working; she covered her mouth, and Birdie's eyes flicked to the floor as she led her up the stairs.

"It's not always this bad. I'm sorry. We'll be out of here soon enough."

Allene nodded, paralyzed into silence by the odor. The stairwell had plaster stained brown here and there, and a few scraps of rubbish adorned the corners. The steps creaked with each footstep as they made their way up. On the second floor, Allene took her hand away so she could breathe more deeply despite the smell. By the fourth floor, she was panting with exertion. She'd never had to climb more than two flights at a time in her entire life, and not in such conditions. The Cutter house took up almost half a city block and was a three-story affair, but Allene hardly ever felt the need to run up those steps.

At the top of the stairwell, Birdie unlocked a door and quietly pushed it open, poking her head inside before letting Allene in. The room wasn't a sitting room or kitchen or bedroom chamber. It was everything at once. The sink and icebox were crammed into the space by the door, decently clean, though everything was old and tired. The upholstery on the sofa was worn and tattered at the edges. The space was mercilessly depressing.

In the corner under the sole window, a tiny mattress held a lump, tangled and covered by a thin sheet. "Is that . . ." Allene began.

"Let's not wake her up. Come with me. I have something you can change into." Birdie took Allene's hand and drew her past the kitchen and opened a door she hadn't seen before. There were two, actually—but one had a skeleton key in the lock. Birdie opened the lockless door. Inside was a plain, thin bed and a chiffonier that had seen better days, propped up with a pail where a leg was missing. Birdie pulled out a drab gray dress that was creased beyond cure.

"You want me to wear that?"

"If you want to pretend to be my cousin in need of a job and spend a day with me, then yes. Don't worry, it's clean."

Allene raised her eyebrows. Was it worth it? She felt in desperate need of a bath, and all she'd done was step inside Birdie's world. Part of her itched to uncover that mysterious, sleeping lump in the next room. Surely it was the little sister, right?

Birdie tapped her toe, waiting.

"Very well." Allene pulled off her gloves and laid them on the bed. "Do what you will with me," she intoned.

Birdie got to work. She slipped off Allene's perfectly trimmed hat and unpinned the silken, heavy knot in her hair, so well tamed into perfect curves and twists by Lucy's expert hands. Birdie let down the shining mass, nearly to Allene's waist, then braided it simply and knotted it at the base of her neck. A clean but rough handkerchief rubbed off the faint bit of rouge on her cheeks and the saucy pink lipstick that shone on her lips.

As always, Allene stood with her arms akimbo like a doll being dressed—or in this case, undressed. There was no Lucy here or other maid to undress her, so Birdie would have to do. And she did, patiently undoing the rows of covered buttons down her back and slipping the gown off. Allene stepped out of the ring of polished cotton and lace piled on the floor. Now she was in only her corset, tightly laced from hips to under her breasts, where a French brassiere kept her loosely cinched.

Birdie reached to loosen the laces. "You don't even need this. It's hard to bend over a bench wearing a corset."

"Really?"

"Really. No one will notice. And you're going incognito anyway, aren't you?"

"You're my maker today, Birdie, so whatever you choose."

Birdie carefully loosened the laces of her corset before unlatching the front. Allene took a deep breath and color filled her cheeks. Her cotton chemise still covered her decently, but it was a lovely feeling. She felt as she always did when released from her stays—like she was floating.

Birdie slipped the drab dress over Allene's head and buttoned her up. It took all of a minute. Shockingly quick. Finally, a pair of plain work shoes were switched for Allene's silk heels. Birdie looked with satisfaction at her deconstructed doll and pointed to a scratched mirror over the chiffonier.

"There we go. No fuss, no feathers."

Allene stared at her reflection. It was just her plain self, the one she woke up to alone in the mornings. No embellishments or lies. She peered closer, noticing how the dress hung limply on her shoulders and stray hairs frizzed out from her temples.

"Oh, for Pete's sake. I'm ugly," Allene announced.

"No." Birdie leaned over, her face next to Allene's as they regarded her reflection. "I think you're more beautiful like this, to be honest." She kissed Allene's cheek, and Allene kept staring at her reflection before shrugging. At least Jasper wouldn't see her like this.

"Oh, one moment." Allene fished the Wonderliter from her dress pocket.

"What is that?"

"A cigarette lighter. Isn't it something? I bought it only last year." She demonstrated with a flourish, and afterward Birdie smiled at the metal wand's tiny torch.

"That's rather adorable! How does it work? Is that flint on the bottom?"

"It's not flint. It's ferrocerium. An iron and cerium alloy. Works like flint, though. It has wonderful pyrophoricity."

"Interesting," Birdie said, but Allene could tell she was only being polite. Birdie gathered her satchel and Allene reached for her reticule, dropping the Wonderliter inside.

"You won't need your purse. I have lunch for both of us. You'll be my guest today. We'll come back to change you after the day's done."

"Just in case. I'd rather," Allene insisted, so Birdie acquiesced and placed the shining beaded bag inside her own plain satchel, which carried two wrapped sandwiches. Goodness, but they were tiny sandwiches. Was that all that Birdie was accustomed to eating? She literally ate like a bird.

They quietly crept through the main room and headed for the door. When Birdie opened it, a tiny voice broke the silence behind them.

"Whozzat?"

They both spun around. The little girl was sitting up in her cot, a thin chemise covering her spindly frame. Large round eyes of a muddy green color stared at them without a bit of tiredness. She was four, if Allene recalled correctly. For her, children generally fell into three age categories: infants, perpetually in the way, or debut ready. This one was certainly in the middle category.

"Holly." Birdie kneeled down next to the little girl. "This is my friend, Miss Allene Cutter."

Holly cocked her head to the side, and Allene had the distinct feeling she was being judged. The girl's eyes traveled from shopworn shoe up to her frazzled head, as if puzzling why the sky would be violet instead of blue today. Her eyes widened with recognition.

Without so much as a curtsy, she blurted, "Oh. You're *her*," and smiled, showing a gap-toothed grin. "But why are you wearing Birdie's dress?"

The little girl was less repelling than expected, as far as children went. And yet she managed to disappoint. Any progeny of Hazel Dreyer ought to be incandescently stunning, like Birdie. Holly was more like the species that Allene belonged to—pleasing to the eye, but nothing that kept one's gaze fixed for the sheer joy of just looking. She immediately felt a kinship to the little girl. After all, she knew what it was to fall in the shadows beside such a bright specimen as Birdie Dreyer.

"Hello, Holly. It's nice to meet you." She extended her hand, and Holly ambled forward.

"Where have you been?"

Allene paused. She was always uncomfortable with the non sequiturs of children. Did she mean in the last day? Or in the last four years? Either way, Allene didn't feel fit to answer. So she replied to a question Holly hadn't asked. It was what you did when children asked what you didn't want to answer.

"I'm spending the day with your sister."

"Will you come play later?"

Birdie interjected. "Never mind that, Holly. Don't forget we have new jam in the cupboard, and remind Ma to eat too, when she wakes up."

Holly nodded. That girl needed a good Mason Pearson brush to attack that tangle of brown hair, but there was no time for such things. Birdie pushed open the door, and soon, they were in the bowel-scented stairwell, then out into the sunlight of Monday morning.

Birdie led her silently up Brooklyn's Fifth Avenue, past all the stores that were opening up, and down Twelfth Street. Allene finally broke the silence.

"Holly seems like a nice girl. I suppose she looks a bit more like Mr. Dreyer."

"Yes," Birdie agreed, but her face clouded over. Allene had never met Birdie's absentee father. She was glad for that; life was easier with the menfolk out of the way. Allene was vastly happier when she hadn't seen her father or Andrew all day. Of course, they weren't dead, but perhaps that situation was the most convenient of all. Oh, stop it, Allene thought to herself. You're such a monster. "Well. We're here," Birdie announced.

Allene looked up to see a factory building taking up an entire block. It was plain brown brick, four stories high, with arched windows regularly breaking up the facade and a row of homely trees on the sidewalk. A smoking chimney climbed from somewhere in the back of the building, dirtying the morning sky with a smudge of smoke. Women clad similarly in muted colors entered through a front entrance before being swallowed by the factory.

Birdie perked up. "Good, we're not late."

They walked through the darkened entrance, and Birdie led Allene down a corridor. Left and right, they passed rooms with metal working equipment. The scent of unfamiliar chemicals assailed Allene's nose as she paused to stare at the contents of one particular room. Metal vats of liquid simmered, and above them hung metal armatures with countless hooks.

"Oh! What's that?"

"You and chemistry! I suppose you might spend the whole day in the electroplating room if I didn't—Allene! Where are you going?"

Allene had popped into the electroplating room, and Birdie stood at the doorway hissing at her to come back, like she was a puppy on the loose. Men in heavy aprons were tending to large industrial tanks. Wires and countless racks of watch cases hung over the vats. Allene ignored Birdie's pleas and gazed into a tank the way another woman might gaze at an emerald brooch in the window of Cartier.

"What are you electroplating? Silver? Gold?" Allene asked, brash as can be.

An older man, white of beard, ambled over. "You one of the painting girls?"

"Yes," Allene lied without hesitation. "What do you use for the solution? Silver nitrate?"

"Why yes. How did you know that?"

But Allene had already zipped over to a smaller assembly where gold clock hands had been freshly gilded, shining like molten sunlight. Before she could ask anything, Birdie appeared and hooked Allene's arm, dragging her out the door.

"I apologize for my . . . coworker. Sorry to bother!"

"Did you see that? All it takes is electricity. Electricity! And you can gild anything. The most boring bit of base metal covered in a rich layer of silver or gold or copper. Isn't it magic?"

"Oh, Allene. Only you would find magic in that chemical dungeon."

"Can I work there today?" she asked.

"Of course not! Come on, or we'll be late. We're on the third floor, where the light is best."

"Ugh, more stairs?"

Birdie ignored her. Before long, she showed her into a long, narrow room with a row of windows that brought in buttery morning light. A long table was sectioned on both sides into individual workstations. Tiny pots, bottles, and brushes lay at each station, and cases of watches and clock faces were stacked next to each stool. Birdie hung her satchel on a peg near the door, as did every other girl who followed. She led Allene to a station at the end of the table.

"Sit here. I'll get another stool. And don't touch a thing," Birdie instructed her in a low whisper.

At the front of the room, an older man stood marking up a sheaf of papers. Allene immediately began to look over the little pots on the desk while leaning closer to hear Birdie's conversation.

"Mr. Rizzoni? I'm sorry to bother you, but I would like permission to have my cousin work with me today. She wants to learn a little and apply for a job soon. I promise I'll make my quota as usual and be responsible for her."

The mustachioed man didn't seem at all happy with the prospect. In an office nearby, an even older gentleman with a bushy beard raised his eyes at the exchange.

"Miss Dreyer, we don't have the time to be anyone's nanny. She'll cost me even if she knocks over a bottle of radium. God forbid she breaks a clock."

"I understand. But—"

The older gentleman from within the office had scooted his chair back to stand up. Oh no. Allene feared that she'd just cost Birdie her job and began to touch her feet to the floor. She watched sideways as the white-headed gentleman spoke a few stern words to the gray-headed man with the mustache. Birdie seemed to quake in her shoes before them. And then she was dismissed and sent back to her station.

"I'm sorry, Birdie," Allene said. The other women were watching them from their stations. "I shouldn't have forced this on you."

"It's all right," Birdie whispered. "The manager said you may stay, so long as I keep up my quota."

"What's your quota?"

"Two hundred and fifty dials a day, six days a week. But I aim for two seventy-five."

Allene dropped her jaw, but Birdie ignored her surprise. Behind her, the two men were talking closely, occasionally glancing at the girls.

"Well," Allene said. "It looks like someone thinks highly of you. Maybe he wants to be your beau!"

"Don't be a goose. I'm just a good painter. Just watch."

So she did. Allene observed with fascination as Birdie's thin hands picked up a tiny porcelain dish. She tipped into it a small quantity of radium powder mixed with a zinc compound. In the daylight, it didn't glow one bit but had a greenish, yellowy cast to it that seemed altogether unnatural. Birdie mixed it carefully with paste so it would stick, then added a water-based thinner until she was satisfied it was just the right consistency—neither too runny nor too thick. Taking a camel-hair brush in hand, she drew the tip across the wet part of her bottom lip and twirled it until it came to a fine point. She lifted her chin at Allene.

"Hand me a tray of those watch faces next to you. Be careful!"

Allene picked up a wooden tray that was partitioned into a grid. She laid the tray on Birdie's workstation. Birdie took one watch face that already had the sweeps attached. She dipped the pointed brush into the radium paint, dotting it precisely on the hour markers, redipped it, then filled in the almost-heart-shaped ends of the sweeps. Allene's neck and back ached just watching her hunch over her work. Finally, Birdie handed the finished dial to Allene, who placed it back in the tray to dry.

Some of the girls painted larger clocks bound for someone's dark bedroom. The whole thing looked like a load of fun until you saw the faces of all the girls working. Crinkles of concentration drew lines between their eyebrows, and their mouths all turned down with determination. Some of the girls chatted quietly with their neighbors, some didn't. It almost looked as if Birdie didn't breathe. Allene scanned the hundreds of watches waiting for her attention. Every day Birdie did this. Every day.

The rough fabric of the work dress itched Allene's neck, but she ignored it. Birdie tipped the brush on her lower lip to keep it pointed and waved it over another watch face.

"Shouldn't I help more? I could—" Allene began.

"No."

"But maybe—"

"Oh, for heaven's sake, Allene." Birdie straightened from her work and raised her eyebrows. "Be quiet, watch me work, and tell me all you've learned about Florence's death already. And I'll tell you what I know."

She went back to her relentless painting, and Allene grinned. It was good to see Birdie with a little ginger for a change. So Allene did what she did best and chatted Birdie's ear off. She spoke of Lucy and the polish.

"Why, I had no idea silver polish was poisonous!" Birdie said.

"Oh, I did. But that's a dead end. Lucy said the can was empty."

"Was it? How can you be sure?"

"Well, she said so." Allene realized how stupid that sounded. "Lucy's never been anything but honest with me."

"Allene." Birdie took a precious few seconds to stop painting and stare at her. "She's not a friend or family. You're her employer. She could be lying to save her job. Is there any chance the polish could have been accidentally transferred to a glass?"

Allene bit her lip. Lucy had touched on the prospect of unemployment too. "I don't see how. But without the polish can, what can we do? And Lucy had no reason to hurt Florence. So what did you learn from Andrew?"

The way Birdie spoke, it had been a task getting the information.

"Andrew said that Florence was gossiping about us? That's not unusual," Allene said.

"But in more bitter terms than usual, I suppose. Think about it, though. Everyone we've ever known hasn't liked Florence. As children, we hid from her at parties! She was horrible then and is horrible now. Or was."

"Well, that means that my entire guest list is suspect. She bickered with Andrew. Ernie said so."

"So you suspect Andrew? What about your father?"

"Oh dear, no, neither of them. Andrew would be too concerned about scuffing his spats. He could care less about what Florence said about me." She sighed. "And Father's never had a grudge against anyone. He's too busy making money to kill off anyone."

Birdie lipped her brush, concentrating on a particularly small pocket watch. "Hmm. Andrew, Lucy, Ernie, your father . . . there must have been someone at the party who was angry at her. Don't you think?"

"There were over fifty guests. I don't remember her having a row with anyone."

"Neither do I. But poisoning someone isn't a spur-of-the-moment action."

"You're right." Allene sat up straight. "Someone planned this. Someone who wanted to kill Florence and make a scandal of my party."

"True. Or maybe they were looking to hide their actions amidst the confusion and busyness of a social event," Birdie added.

It would take a little time to try to find out who in the Cutters' social circle had a particular vendetta against Florence or her family. The funeral would be a good place to start asking some well-timed questions.

The noon bell sounded. It was hard to believe that they'd been chatting on and off for four hours. They gobbled down the sandwiches that Birdie had packed in her satchel (well, Allene gobbled; Birdie ate mincingly, like the fairy that she was) and whispered nonstop, while the other factory girls gossiped and knitted khaki wristlets and stump socks for the boys overseas. It wasn't until the end of the day that Birdie let Allene paint the last watch dial all by herself.

Allene botched it, of course—left dots of paint beyond her allowed boundaries and refused to put the brush in her mouth ("But it's the only way to get a good point!" Birdie chided her, to no avail). Birdie reached over to correct every spot that Allene painted too sloppily.

At five o'clock, they left the building along with all the other working girls. Allene was tired, though she'd barely done anything but talk. Gossip took a good deal of energy.

"I'm glad you came," Birdie admitted, and Allene hooked her arm in her own, patting her with contentment.

"Even if I look dreadful, it was worth it."

"You both look rather fetching to me," a voice spoke, almost under their noses. "Drab suits you both; it doesn't hide one jot."

A young man leaned beneath one of the trees, cigarette dying between his fingertips.

"Jasper Jones. What on earth are you doing here, larking about?" Allene smiled. When he glanced at Birdie, she stole a moment to bite her lips to bring some cherry color to her face. In this horrid outfit, she needed all the help she could get.

"Coming to find you two, of course. We gotta go, tout de suite." He let the cigarette stub loose and squashed it beneath his heel before grinning at them both. "It's time for us to visit poor Florence."

CHAPTER 11

"Come on," Jasper said. "We're going to the city morgue."

"What?" Allene exclaimed, with more excitement than fear.

He hadn't expected to find Allene here, especially dressed like this—hair in a frizzled bun; wearing drab, loose-fitting clothing that kept all her curved blessings in disguise. But she wore a brilliant smile, and without the rouge and trimmings, the snap in her eye was lively as ever. It was a look that said she was ready for anything.

Good.

"What on earth?" Birdie echoed Allene's admonishment, but she seemed more tired and weary than Allene.

It was obvious who'd done the lion's share of the work in the factory today. When he stepped out of the way, the girls could see that Allene's chauffeur waited behind him with the motorcar. Allene slapped Jasper on the arm.

"What is Dawlish doing here?"

"I went to see if Birdie could come, and this chap was waiting for you at her place. I figured you were both at the factory, so we came over to get you."

"I can't have him drive us to the morgue!" Allene whispered, well out of earshot of Dawlish. The driver was all goggle eyed at the three of them, particularly Allene's shabby clothing.

"Of course you can. He works for you, doesn't he?"

"He'll tell Father!"

Jasper crossed his arms. "Allene. You're the only heir to the Cutter fortune. Surely he's going to be loyal to his future employer, isn't he? If not, make him!"

He saw Birdie squeeze Allene's arm, and Allene calmed herself before striding forward. Dawlish opened the door, mouth still hanging open.

"Oh, for heaven's sake, stop catching flies, Dawlish," Allene said. "Take us to the city morgue, and don't you dare tell Father or . . . or . . . I'll tell him you've nicked a bottle of his best brandy."

"But I haven't, miss!"

"Exactly." She let Birdie slide into the backseat first before hissing at Jasper. "You're going to be the death of me, Jasper Jones!"

"I certainly hope not." He winked at her.

They crowded into the backseat, with Jasper squeezed between the two girls. Heaven. He reached his arms around their shoulders, and like a well-timed vaudeville act, the girls slapped his hands in synchrony. Rather hard too.

"Ow. I deserved that."

"Yes, you did," Allene chided, though he caught a drift of a smile on her lips. They quieted down as they departed Brooklyn, watching people headed home, listening to the trolley jangling its call on the street corners. As the sunlight weakened over the city skyline, they passed over the Brooklyn Bridge. Jasper whistled.

"Well, this is dandy. Been a while since I traveled in style." He regretted the words almost as soon as they had passed his lips; Allene gave him a pitying look, and Birdie turned toward her window. He wasn't begging for charity, after all. He ought not to let his inner thoughts out too briskly from now on. There was something about being in the midst of Birdie and Allene—he couldn't help but be himself. He'd attempted to wear a sheen of downtown worldliness, but it felt strange. With them, he was simply Jasper after all. And that wasn't good enough, not even for him.

The motorcar drew up to the gates of Bellevue Hospital. An ambulance rolled just ahead of them through the entrance, relieving itself of a stretcher burdened with an old, wheezing man. As they parked on the curb, Dawlish exited to let them out.

"Miss, Mr. Cutter is to dine with the Sandersons in one hour's time. I cannot be late."

"But I need you, Dawlish." Allene's voice sounded petulant, and it worked marvelously. Dawlish began to perspire. He pulled at his starched collar.

Jasper stepped forward. "We'll get you home, Allene. Let your driver go. We don't want your father wondering what's going on."

"He's right," Birdie agreed. "And we're wasting time."

With that, Dawlish was released, and the three of them entered the hospital campus, with Jasper speaking to the guard. They passed the ambulance and main buildings and hurried northward toward the daunting pathology building, with its large arches and iron railings.

The girls gripped each other's hands as Jasper led them inside. He watched them with something akin to merriment as their wide eyes wandered over the coffered ceilings and wood paneling. Their nostrils flared from the irritating scent of fixative and cleaning chemicals. Allene seemed more curious, but Birdie drew closer to her friend, as if fearing that the very walls might bite. Jasper led them down the stairs to the large double doors of the morgue. He tried the copper-handled door; it was locked.

"What are we going to do?" Birdie whispered. Footsteps sounded behind them, and she twirled around with a sharp inhale. A middle-aged man in a white coat, scuffed shoes, and a scowl approached them. When he saw the party, he grimaced, revealing a few missing teeth.

"It's about time. What're yeh bringing womenfolk down here for? We don't do the tours for the public after hours."

"Barston." Jasper took a step closer and raised his eyebrows. "Thank you *for not asking questions*. You promise to . . . clean up our mess?"

"Like we discussed. O'course."

"And the undertaker?"

"He'll get fifty percent and make 'er lovely as a bride. Promise."

Jasper stepped forward and handed him something from his palm. Barston counted the bills and stared hard at Jasper.

"Wot? This won't do."

"This is what we agreed on."

"Not if I'm to split it fifty-fifty like." Barston took out a ring of iron keys, jiggled them, and began to walk away. Jasper felt his insides smoldering with rage and shame. Barston had just walked off with this month's rent. And now he had no rent, no body, and no plan.

"Wait!" Allene yelled out. She grabbed at the deflated satchel that Birdie carried and clawed inside it. She withdrew her hand and held out a ten-dollar bill. "This is all I have. If you don't take it, then we'll leave and we won't be back."

Mr. Barston's eyes glittered at the sight of the money, and he walked back and snatched the crisp bill without a word, stuffing it into his pocket and picking out a key from the ring. The door was soon opened, and he tipped his head to Jasper.

"Lab'll be open too, but I'm locking the whole lot in four hours. A'right?"

"Outstanding. Thank you, Barston."

Jasper held the door open as Birdie and Allene entered, and he locked the doors behind him. The two girls wandered around the bureau where the bodies were stored for claiming or autopsy. Sometimes both, sometimes neither. They were careful not to touch the cold tables that held three bodies covered in sheets. Birdie walked over to a table by one of many sinks and began flipping through a large tome next to a stack of neat ledgers. Immediately, she put her hand to her mouth. Jasper quickly went to her side and shut the book.

"It's a book of the unknowns," he explained. "They photograph them and document everything before they're taken to the potter's field on Hart Island." He put his hand on hers and withdrew it from the book and found that her hand was shaking. The photos were full of indecencies and horrors—disfigured corpses, decapitations, battered babies that stared at oblivion, and some that quietly slipped out of this world without anyone caring one jot—soulless bodies that no decent person ought to lay eyes upon. Birdie would not soon unsee the pages of that book, and for that, Jasper regretted not having sheltered her in time.

And yet here all three of them were, and on his accord. He couldn't shelter her from Florence, not if they were going to get some answers. He turned Birdie away and walked her toward Allene. "We should get to work and do this."

"Do what exactly?" Allene's shoes made a crisp noise on the polished floor as she met him. "What did you mean by bringing us here?"

"Well, we think that Florence was poisoned. But we don't know for sure. And the medical examiner—Dr. Norris—won't have his people touch her because she's not slated for an autopsy. But we can find the truth."

"By desecrating her body? Jasper, are you out of your wits?" Birdie whispered.

"Why are you whispering? It's just us. The dead don't care," Jasper said.

Allene strode forward and pinched him on the ear.

"Ow."

"The dead may not care, but some of us do." She tipped her head toward Birdie. "Behave!" She placed a soft hand on Birdie's and turned her head to Jasper. "So. What did you have in mind?"

He took a deep breath. If he played this poorly, he would not be seeing Birdie or Allene ever again. But he needed them. Birdie was poor, sure, but that face could open doors. And Allene was a treasure chest of opportunity. They both owed him for kicking him out of their lives.

"I want to take a sample of tissue from Florence and test it for cyanide." He swallowed and saw Birdie squeeze Allene's hand. Funny, he'd thought it would be Allene, with her hoity-toity life, who would balk at the idea, but she was the one listening with calm regard. Her steady gaze chilled him.

She asked questions. Where the sample would come from, whether Barston could be trusted to make sure Florence's corpse would be perfectly presentable at the wake in two days, and if he and the mortician could be trusted to keep quiet. Jasper answered them one by one, and finally she nodded with satisfaction.

"The autopsy room is this way. Barston put Florence in there. Come on."

The autopsy room was large and clean. Shining copper taps rose at the head of each marble table. Each table owned its own hanging light, and a wheeled cart laid out with shining sharp instruments for dissection waited nearby. Florence's strawberry-blonde hair peeked out, once again, from the white sheet over her body.

Jasper took off his jacket and found a chair for Birdie to sit on, far away from the tables. He took down two waxed aprons and handed one to Allene.

"I'll need an assistant. You won't faint, will you?"

"The dead won't make me swoon and neither will you, Mr. Jones."

"Pity," Jasper said.

"A little respect, please!" Birdie chastised them from the far end of the room. Apparently she couldn't bear to watch and was facing the corner, like a misbehaving schoolchild.

"Let's start." He handed Allene some ill-fitting gloves and picked up a scalpel. They stood on either side of the table.

"The stomach?" Allene verified.

Jasper nodded.

"Have you done an autopsy before?"

"No. But I've watched about three today."

"I thought you were a janitor!" Allene said.

"I was. I got promoted only yesterday. I'm now an assistant in the medical examiner's office."

"You are? That's splendid!" Birdie chimed from her corner.

"That's awfully convenient, Jasper. Congratulations," Allene added, but she didn't sound as happy for him as Birdie was.

His limited experience would have to be good enough. Allene peeled back the sheet to Florence's bare waist. It was both shocking and ordinary to see her like this. She was a woman like half the people on God's earth, and yet she was Florence. Florence, with that terrible, biting wit that was a whip to the cheek whenever she wielded it. But then again, it wasn't her. Florence was gone. This was a body. This was clay. Or so he reminded himself.

"We'll make only a small incision. I just need a sample."

Jasper picked up a scalpel. It cut through the skin like it was supple kidskin leather, and the blade sliced muscle and fat that was already softening from death. He asked Allene to keep the incision open with a pair of retractors, which she did without complaining or turning green. When he flicked his eyes to her, he saw that she also kept her eyes fixed on the area at hand. Neither of them looked at Florence's face to see how *she* felt about the whole affair. From a distance, Birdie whimpered every time an instrument clanked on the tray.

Jasper pushed aside omental fat and slippery intestines before cutting higher up toward her rib cage to finally locate her stomach. He grasped its sagging mass with forceps and jabbed it with the scalpel. Black liquid bubbled out, smelling of sour rot and iron.

"Oh, God in heaven," Allene gasped, lifting one of her gloved hands to shield her mouth. "What on earth is that?"

"I don't know. I think it's old, curdled blood." Sweat beaded over his lip and forehead, and he tried to ignore the smell, but it was impossible. Jasper sawed and jabbed with the knife until he came away with a good-sized piece of raw, purplish stomach, with that same liquefied black ooze clinging to it. Black pudding-like liquid leaked out over the incision and pooled on the table. He put the sample in an enameled pan and draped a cloth over it. They withdrew their instruments and covered Florence up decently—as decently as one might do after stealing bits of someone's internal organs. That smell was still in the air. They washed their hands and hung up the aprons. Jasper took the pan and led them out the door.

"Are we going to the lab now?" Allene asked. She offered her arm to Birdie, who leaned on her gratefully and wiped away a tear.

"Yes."

They followed Jasper up the few flights of stairs, noting the shadow of Mr. Barston walking into the morgue to "fix up" Florence before shipping her off to the undertaker. Up in Dr. Gettler's laboratory, Jasper set the covered enamel pan down.

He looked to Allene and Birdie, the former who was hardly paying attention and already sniffing around the bottles of chemicals up on the shelf above the main table. The latter was gaining a little color and sat at Dr. Norris's desk and chair, folding her hands in her lap.

"Now," Jasper began. "We'll have to—"

"We'll have to do an extraction. The sample needs to be macerated first," Allene interrupted.

"Well, yes, and then—"

"You'll do a Prussian blue test, won't you?" she interrupted again. She was a trolley with no brakes, this girl.

"Good Lord. You'll run off and do this without me if I don't keep an eye on you. Take a look at this book. It's a beaut." He handed Allene a thick tome, and she smiled.

"*A Manual of the Detection of Poisons.* 1857. Splendid, though a bit outdated." She licked her fingertips to riffle through the pages. It was hard not to notice how incandescent her expression had become.

"Look at her, having a jazzy time!" Jasper teased. "You'd think that book was her beau instead of Andrew."

"Enough, you two." Birdie seemed to have recovered from their trip to the morgue and stood between them. "Now. What are we to do? We have to be quick about it. That chap said we had four hours tops."

Allene pointed and read aloud. "Chapter three. 'On the detection of hydrocyanic acid.' Let's see . . ." She instructed Jasper to cut the tissue sample into strips, add distilled water and a touch of sulfuric acid. "You need a retort."

"But he didn't say anything rude," Birdie commented.

"Not that kind of retort," Jasper said. "A retort is a flask with this long gooseneck—"

"Here you go." Allene had already fetched a clean one—a beautiful thing that looked like a pointed flask that had bowed a curtsy and stayed that way. "And you'll need to heat it up and gather the distillate. Then add some caustic potassium and a few drops of green vitriol, then cook it with some sulfuric acid to reveal the Prussian blue—"

"For God's sake, woman. Slow down!"

Allene smirked. She and Birdie fetched the chemicals from the storeroom while Jasper built the apparatus. Before long, they'd reached the final step. Allene was the one who dripped the acid into the flask. It darkened to the deep midnight blue of a winter's night.

"Oh, it's beautiful!" Allene breathed. "Absolutely beautiful."

"What is it?" Birdie asked.

Jasper suppressed a smile. "It's definitive proof that Florence was poisoned."

CHAPTER 12

Birdie felt transfixed by the intense opaque blue coloring in the flask. She imagined tipping the flask over, dipping a finger in, and smearing the cream-painted walls with it, like a child. Meanwhile, her left cheek thrummed with an incessant, blossoming pain. That damned toothache had come back with a fiery vengeance in the last twelve hours. She'd hid it well from Allene, but it was starting to demand her full attention. She bit her lip hard to focus and said, "Now what do we do?"

"Oh. What about the broken glass? We should test that too, right?" Allene asked.

Jasper thought for a moment. "We should. But we don't have time. Barston will be back soon to close up."

"Perhaps I could try to test it myself. But in any case, we can't keep this to ourselves. We know she didn't die naturally," Allene said.

"So we tell people. The police. Her family." Jasper ticked off a list as he began to clean up the equipment they'd used.

"And Father," Allene added doubtfully. She certainly didn't seem excited by the prospect.

"And we still don't know who could have killed her," Birdie said. "Florence certainly wasn't well liked."

"That's being kind. If her father weren't so rich and so well connected, she'd never have been invited anywhere. Florence was . . ."

"Not nice?" Jasper offered.

"Repellent," Allene said. "So everyone on the guest list is a suspect. But there are a few that feuded with her more often than not. Grace Howland is one. Oh, and Benjamin Winthrop! And—"

"So we have somewhere to start," Jasper said. "Maybe you can speak to them. When is the funeral?"

"Friday," Allene answered. "Maybe it won't be such a bore as I'd expected. Imagine the hurricane of gossip! I wonder what the Howlands and Winthrops will say if I suggest that someone purposely killed her off to ruin my party. I can read a guilty look like anybody, I'm sure."

Birdie clutched her throat. "Allene! How could you say such a thing in public?"

"Because I can!" Her eyes danced with merriment. "I'm a Cutter and I'm practically a Biddle. That is one powerful social brew, and everyone knows it. No one will be anything but obsequious. Besides, I might shock people into telling the truth."

Birdie and Jasper were left to nod in agreement. "Jasper and I ought to go as well," Birdie noted, rubbing her cheek. "Though I doubt anyone would care if we did. What do you think, Jasper?"

"I'll leave it to you, Birdie. I am your servant."

Birdie saw Allene's face tighten. She probably wished everyone were *her* servant, after all. After a breath, she asked, "Will you tell the people here?"

"I'll speak to Dr. Gettler first." He didn't sound enthusiastic.

"I'll speak to Father," Allene said. "Which will not go well, but we must figure out how best to bring it up with Florence's parents."

Birdie's footing felt unsteady, and the throbbing in her jaw was spreading upward to her temples. She felt a flush of fever.

The three of them exited the pathology building and quietly left the Bellevue campus. Another ambulance had driven up, and they walked away from its bright headlamps.

"I wonder if influenza has landed in Manhattan yet," Allene said absently, staring at the ambulance.

"Don't be silly. The grippe never hits until the fall. It's only August," Jasper said.

"But I read in the papers—"

Jasper shushed her, and in his expression, Birdie could see his own limited time telescoping in front of him. If the rumors were true, the next draft would lower the eligible age to eighteen. "There's only one little war right here that we need to pay attention to. With one casualty. Florence."

Birdie and Allene nodded. The streetlights cast yellow blobs that illuminated the cobblestones and sidewalk. Allene took her reticule back from Birdie and began pawing at the bottom of it. It reminded Birdie of a dog scratching for a buried bone.

"Father will be furious with me for coming home so late. I'll have to find a taxicab somehow." She jiggled the reticule, finding only a gilded tube of lipstick and her lighter. "Oh, for Pete's sake. I'm broke. I gave it all to that man in the morgue!"

Jasper held up his hands. "Don't look at me. He's got all my dough too."

Birdie sighed. She opened her satchel and procured two nickels. That was all she had. The rest of her money was kept in a crock in the kitchen cupboard, and there was still more hidden from her mother where Birdie had sewn it into her mattress. That was for Holly, and Holly alone. She handed one five-cent piece to Allene.

"Here, Allene. You can get home with this. Jasper, you'll have to walk. I'm taking the subway myself."

"What am I to do with one coin?" Allene demanded. Birdie couldn't answer because the question was so utterly stupid. Jasper raised an eyebrow at Allene and started pointing in directions. Allene turned in a circle, bewildered.

"You've got your luxurious choice of streetcar, subway, or the El. You can't afford a taxicab with five cents." He bowed in the darkness. "Ladies, thank you for a stirring evening. I'll see you both at the funeral." He shoved his hands deep into his trouser pockets and began walking down First Avenue. It was obvious, even in the dim light, that he was grinning ear to ear.

"Birdie!" Allene looked at her helplessly.

"I'm sorry, Allene. I must get home to Holly, and you and I are going in different directions. There'll be a trolley stop within a block or two."

"But my clothes! My shoes!"

"We'll exchange them soon enough. You have a spare outfit or two, I daresay. Good-bye. I'll see you at the funeral."

She gave Allene a helping smile, but that was all she could manage. She heard Allene start to speak—there was complaint and irritation and helplessness in that tiny squeak—but nothing followed. Allene looked this way and that before walking west, guided by the street lamps and the tepid half-moon.

Birdie's headache was pounding harder than a hammer beating out a sheet of tin. She'd even be tempted to take her mother's laudanum, it was that bad. The cresting fever began to draw perspiration to her upper lip. Wooziness occupied the inside of her skull and was growing worse. She had to get home soon. Every step filled her head with agonizing pain. When she finally found shelter beneath the glass-and-metal awning of the Twenty-Third Street elevated station, a train was rumbling to a stop above her, but she ignored it; she would catch the next one.

Her hand gripped the iron railing. Looking left and right and seeing no one, she forced a finger into her mouth, wiggling it between her cheek and teeth, and pressed at her gumline where the pain was most excruciating. There would be no dentist because there wasn't enough money. And she didn't have time to lie in bed, head bound with ice and a scarf, hoping for the pain to go away.

She pushed and pushed harder. She pulled her hand out and dried her fingers on a handkerchief, then went in to grip the offending tooth, which was surprisingly loose in the socket. The gum where it was embedded seemed spongy, all too willing to release the molar's roots. Tears squeezed out of the side of her eyes, and a crunching noise reverberated inside her skull. She pulled hard with a grunt and a strangled cry, and as the tooth came out, her mouth filled with the salty foulness of infection and the iron tang of blood. Birdie spat out a mouthful of blood and pus, along with the rotted molar. The tooth bounced onto the sidewalk and tumbled into the gutter.

She wiped her mouth on the last clean corner of handkerchief and went home.

⟞⟝

The swelling in her cheek went down in the next two days, to the point where it was only a slight rise. Birdie wondered how much Allene and Jasper had told everyone of their suspicions, but there was no use wondering. She would find out soon enough.

On Friday, the day of the funeral, the swelling was hardly noticeable. While Holly and her mother slept, Birdie dressed in her best stockings and shoes, a faded black velvet hat with a drooping brim, and a black dress of stiff silk that belonged to her mother and smelled vaguely of sweat and spirits.

The day after the morgue visit, she had informed the manager at the factory of the funeral and her coming absence. He'd frowned at her second indiscretion of the week, but Mr. Murphy, his supervisor, once again stepped in to quiet him. Birdie suspected that Andrew had influence here but didn't ask. Feigned ignorance was a friend.

But Andrew would be at the funeral with Allene by his side. Her tongue would go numb in their presence, and her burning cheeks would give away the generosity he'd shown her the other day. And the fact that he wanted more.

She remembered her promise to herself.

Get in Allene's good graces. Make a future for Holly, somehow, out of this mess of a situation.

And then she remembered: she'd left Allene, blue-blooded to the end, alone on the Lower East Side with nothing but a nickel.

She bit off a smile before it could form on her face. Sometimes Birdie was entirely stupid and stubborn.

She gave a good-bye kiss to her slumbering mother, in her syrupy, narcotic dream world. She woke Holly, washed and dressed her quickly, and dropped her off with the landlady, paid twenty-five cents to watch her for the day. Holly immediately went to play with a beloved collection of wooden trains belonging to the landlady's grandson.

Before long, Birdie was riding the subway, hardly noticing the scrubbed tile and mosaics that rushed by. By nine o'clock, she was walking up to the triple-portal facade of the new Saint Bartholomew's Church on Park Avenue and Fifty-First Street.

"It's sad, isn't it?"

The voice spoke almost in her ear. She turned to see Ernie Fielding. He looked grave in his mourning clothes. He looked odd. And then she realized: she hardly recognized him without the perpetual smile.

"Indeed, it is. She was so young."

"No, not that. It is sad, of course! But sad that no one's really upset that she's gone. Look."

He was right. People milled about, entering the church, but there were no tears. She even saw smiles between friends and family members. The lack of grief stunned her.

Ernie was soon drawn away by some relations who shooed him inside the church. Birdie shivered and looked around. Left and right, people in black hats and suits hovered by the grand bronze doors and Romanesque columns of swirling green and gray. Sprinkled amidst them were dabs of white handkerchiefs that were held but not used. Someone touched her sleeve.

"There you are. Isn't this a swell lot of fun? I feel stiffer than Florence right now," Jasper whispered. He wore a celluloid collar that endeavored to bite into his neck. He glanced about irritably, but when his eyes settled on Birdie, they softened, and one corner of his rakish mouth lifted. "Well, you make drab black look good as gold, don't you?"

Birdie ignored his words. "So have you seen Allene?"

"No."

"Did you tell that doctor fellow about the cyanide? About what we found the other night?"

Jasper's face fell. "No."

"Well, what the dickens—"

"I'll tell you later."

Somber organ music began to play from inside the church, and they strode forward, tight lipped. They were shown to a pew seat in the back. Good. Birdie had already spent far too much time in close proximity to Florence, dead and alive. Words swam in her head from their childhood, when Florence had taken every opportunity to put her in her place.

That cast-off Cutter dress looks splendid on you.

I ate all the cookies, Birdie. Why don't you be a good scullery maid and make some more?

Go fetch my new ermine coat, Birdie. You're so good at fetching things.

And yet she felt only sadness for the lack of generosity in Florence's heart. That would make her grave all the colder.

But as the program began, an isolated sob interrupted a pause in the prayer. She saw Florence's mother sitting stoically in the front pew, but on her right, Mr. Waxworth shamelessly wept into his handkerchief. He was the only one who did.

Birdie wondered: When she died, would her mother weep for her? She wasn't sure. Lately, Mother's heart seemed pickled by laudanum, with hardly any true sentiment to spare for Holly or herself. It was Holly whom Birdie's absence would wound, profoundly and permanently. She thought of how Holly crept into her bed every night and snuggled close to Birdie's center, wrapping her arms around her body, as if she could absorb all the goodness and warmth of the world in one night's sleep. That would be gone. All gone.

Birdie began to cry.

Her small sounds were enveloped by the quiet around her. She was almost angry at Florence for bringing her to this place.

"Funerals always make me happy," Jasper whispered to Birdie. He handed her his handkerchief because hers was already dampened through.

"You," Birdie whispered back through a sniffle, "are a monster."

"I'm not happy she's dead. Not by a darn sight. But a funeral reminds you to be alive, doesn't it? It slaps you across the face and points out that there's still warm blood doing a jig in your veins." Jasper's hand fell to Birdie's pale forearm, and he put his two fingers on her wrist, where her pulse was. It was a clinical gesture, cold, if not for the warmth of his fingertips. Oh, she was alive all right. Stubbornly living, despite everything. She withdrew her hand and bowed her head.

"Did you feel the same way at Oscar's funeral?"

"We didn't have one. No money," Jasper responded, tight lipped.

"I'm sorry." Birdie sighed. She patted his arm. "I'm so sorry. You haven't talked about your brother."

"What's the point?"

His cold words ended the conversation. The mourners all stood for a hymn, but neither Birdie nor Jasper sang a single note. Once the service had finished, Birdie shuffled with the rest of the crowd to the doors. A small cadre of family entered a string of motorcars for the funeral cortege. People clumped together to discuss the tragedy in hushed whispers. Birdie felt penned in, and Jasper led her out to the front of the church. In the fresher air, she took a huge breath, as if she hadn't breathed for hours.

"What now?" she asked, feeling lost amongst the dissipating crowd of mourners.

"I don't know," Jasper said.

At the curb, a dark burgundy Daimler purred. A gloved hand emerged from the window and waved at them, fluidly at first, then more frantically.

"Is that—" Birdie started.

"It is." Jasper shook his head. "Come on."

The Daimler was different from the car that Dawlish usually drove, longer and narrower, fit for a grander patriarch—Mr. Cutter. It was good enough for the British monarchy, and hence good enough for the Cutters. But Mr. Cutter wasn't inside. It was only Allene who peered at them, waving them forward. She was dressed in tailored black satin, and a mourning veil fell to her collarbone. For a moment, her aristocratic features seemed more like marble than warm-blooded human.

"Come inside. We'll follow the procession to the interment. They're going to the Evergreens Cemetery. We'll have time to talk."

Dawlish had come around already and opened the door. Allene moved to make room, as the back was narrower than the back of the other automobile. "We'll squeeze like sardines in an army can."

"Where is your father? And Andrew?" Jasper began.

"They went back to the house in the other car. Father was feeling tired and wanted Andrew to help him fend off the reporters. He let us use the Daimler. It has so much more presence."

Jasper rolled his eyes, but Allene didn't notice. Dawlish started the motor's engine, and the cortege began to move forward. Florence's casket must have already been transferred to the hearse.

The procession moved down Park Avenue, making a wide berth around the clamor and soot of Grand Central Station. Allene kept one window down, and the blowing air wreaked havoc on her hair but created enough noise that they could speak, close headed, with some amount of privacy.

"Did you speak to your father?" Jasper asked Allene.

She puckered her lips inward, as if she'd just sucked on a pickled lime. "No. I wanted to. Honestly. But he was so cross with me for coming home so late and unchaperoned that night. Ugh, and I was still in my factory clothes! He was livid. He said that if my behavior wasn't better, he'd tell Dawlish to stop driving me about and take away my walking-around money. I just . . . couldn't. Did you talk to anyone at Bellevue?"

Jasper shook his head. "I tried. I asked Gettler what would happen, theoretically, if someone tested Florence for cyanide anyway—wouldn't the truth be worth breaking the rules? And he said, 'Theoretically, yes, and theoretically, you'd be arrested and fired too.'" He opened his mouth but shut it quickly. Birdie understood. A murdered Florence was one thing; becoming a convict and losing a salary when you were already poor was entirely another. "Golly, it all seemed like such a good idea until it wasn't. Remember that time we made a cherry bomb—"

"Oh!" Allene popped up straight in her seat. "From magnesium and potassium nitrate? It was splendid!"

Birdie laughed, feeling light for the first time that day. "Except we set it off in the parlor and burnt the wallpaper. And the chaise. And the carpet. Oh, and part of my hair."

"Yes. Brilliant idea, not too well thought out, though, in execution," Jasper said.

"But who killed Florence? Allene, did you talk to the Winthrops? Or Grace Howland? Did they have a bad grudge against her?" Birdie asked.

"I did. Benjamin couldn't stop talking about buying a new Thoroughbred. He didn't seem like someone who cared about murder, one way or the other. And Grace Howland? Why, she used to bicker with Florence all the time this past season, so of course I chatted with her for a while. The girl is a stunner, but my Lord, she's dumber than a five-pound rock. I always thought her only crime was being a bore! She's just too stupid to commit a clever murder. Honestly, the only person who really stood out was—"

"Mr. Waxworth. He was the only person crying, wasn't he?" Jasper noted.

"He was. Crying like a baby," Allene agreed. "But her own father? He would have had to hire someone, and no one at the party was of that sort of class. And what an abominable thought! A parent! She was an heiress, like me. The only child."

"Money does strange things to people," Jasper said. "He might have had his reasons. Or maybe the next in line wanted the money."

"Money is always a good reason to be vicious," Allene agreed. "I don't know a thing about Florence's cousins, or if the line was entailed to men in the family. It's an old notion, but some families are still strict. I can look into it."

"Still, our suspects are drying up a bit fast," Birdie said. "So what are we going to do?"

"I hate to say it," Jasper said, "but even if we figure out who to accuse, the authorities will want to exhume the body to prove it, and then I'll still be in trouble. The only way to work around that is to get a confession."

Soon, the cars spilled onto Fourth Avenue, which led them down toward Lafayette and the Brooklyn Bridge. A war rally crowded the corner of Canal Street. Jasper eyed it warily, before Allene pulled his chin toward her, tsking at him.

"No, Jasper. Down, boy."

"There's talk of another draft," he said evenly. "How is Clarence doing?"

"My cousin is fine," she said quickly. Too quickly, Birdie thought. Lord, did she even know? She hardly spoke of him. "Now *you*—you're not going, Jasper."

He rolled his eyes. "You don't have power over that."

"I might. None of *my* boys are going to war, if I have my say."

"So I belong to you?" Jasper asked, rather seriously.

Allene looked out the window, where a worker was pasting up new war posters on a building front. She didn't seem to want to acknowledge the truth, that perhaps Jasper wasn't really hers to have. Maybe she felt that way about Birdie too. But Birdie would be willing to be owned. For Holly, she would do anything.

Birdie slipped her thin arm around Allene. "Never mind who belongs to whom. We're all in God's hands, aren't we?" Neither Allene nor Jasper seemed cheered by this. "I have an idea. After the interment, we'll meet again in a day or two," Birdie said.

"Yes, let's," Allene agreed.

Good. She didn't want Allene to forget her or Holly. She wished Jasper could meet Holly too. Holly needed a godfather, or any father, for that matter.

They rode in silence for half an hour until the rolling green hills rose before them and the arched metal gates of the Evergreens Cemetery passed above. The skies began to darken, and a pattering of rain fell gently. Black umbrellas bloomed like bruises over the green hillock where Florence was laid. Allene stood close to the Waxworth family, while Birdie and Jasper hung back quietly.

When it finally came time to leave, Allene began to hug and shake hands with the family. They would soon go to the gathering at the Waxworths' to chat consolingly with one another over cups of tea and plates of cold jellied chicken. And Allene would search out the details of Florence's inheritance.

Jasper and Birdie walked soundlessly to a small berm a distance away and watched the mourners enter their motorcars. The priest left as well, and soon, there was no one there but a single man. Birdie assumed that he was there to pitch the mound of soft soil onto Florence's casket, but he was too well dressed, and he never touched the shovel that was only a few feet away.

"Look, Jasper." Birdie pointed. Even from a distance, she could see the dusty blond hair, the hands clutching his hat, and the shoulders wet from the rain. The shoulders shook. The man was alone, weeping over the casket.

"Good God," Jasper whispered. "I do believe that's Ernie."

CHAPTER 13

By Monday morning, the August heat had cooked the refuse in the gutters, and the stench turned the Brooklyn air fetid. Birdie reached the front doors of the Ansonia Clock factory just before eight o'clock. When she saw a shining motorcar parked just outside the building, she was not surprised. She'd wondered if Allene would show up, dressed inappropriately and begging for a day's worth of sleuthing. Truth be told, Birdie was eager to share what she and Jasper had seen after the funeral. What would Allene have to say about whether Ernie and Florence had more than just a nodding acquaintance? Would she know anything about Florence's inheritance?

Then Andrew exited the vehicle.

Birdie paused while other workers funneled into the entrance. In her plain work dress and brown shoes, she was a smudge of dust like the rest of them, but Andrew's eyes searched her out immediately. At times like this, she wished her hair were more pigeon brown than flaxen. It was hard to hide even beneath her baggy knit hat. When Andrew walked up to her, with his crisp suit and well-bred air, she heard some of the other factory girls whisper to each other.

"What are you doing here?" Birdie asked.

"I've something for Holly." He led her to the car. In the backseat was a large wicker basket covered with a clean, flowered cloth. "It's a smoked ham, half a dozen jellies, some apples, peppermints—"

"Thank you." Birdie cut him off. "It looks heavy. If you could drop it off, I'd be obliged."

"And I've this too." He reached into the open window and pulled out a large, brown-paper-wrapped parcel. Birdie peeked under the coarse wrapper. It was an enormous bottle of opium tincture.

"You do know how to woo a girl," Birdie said dryly.

"Am I doing a good job?" Andrew asked. He attempted a roguish sort of air, but it ended up making him look somewhat frightened, if not dyspeptic. Birdie realized, Oh—he's nervous.

"Thank you. I need to go in or I'll be late for work. Mother is home and can accept the packages, I'm sure." She added, "Thank you," because she couldn't remember if she'd thanked him already.

"Oh, I already stopped by just after you left. The steam heat and rent are paid for this month. They're both having fresh eggs, applesauce, and toast for breakfast as we speak."

"Are they." Birdie watched him.

"Yes."

"I still have to go to work."

"Not today you don't." Andrew stepped aside as his driver opened the door. There was a glance exchanged between the driver and Andrew, and between Andrew and the guard who stood just inside the factory doors. A nodding of male chins. Complicity.

Birdie opened her mouth to refuse, then closed it. "Where are we going?"

"Wherever you wish. I'll take you to the park for a walk. Perhaps the museum. I could take you shopping for a new wardrobe. Or we could go to the Red Cross and knit wristlets all day, if you want to be heroic."

"I'm no hero," Birdie said. She walked past Andrew, and the driver opened the back door. She slid onto the seat beside the basket of groceries. When Andrew sat next to her, he picked up her hand the way one might a newly laid egg still warm from the nest.

"Where shall we go, Birdie?"

She tried to smile but failed. "Take me wherever you want, Andrew."

Andrew leaned forward to murmur to the driver, and the car hummed louder and pulled away from the factory.

"I've arranged it so that your hours are shorter than before," Andrew said, when the silence became too starched and stiff. "That way, you can always have a leisurely breakfast with Holly and be home before rush hour. And you need to work only three days instead of six."

"But—"

"And your salary won't change. In fact, it's gone up. For being such a hard worker all these years." He put his other hand on hers. "You deserve it. I reviewed your work logs. You've painted more dials per week than any other girl for the last four years. Your most unproductive month was the first one you ever worked in that dial-painting room."

Birdie turned to face him. Andrew had gone into her work records? It was an invasive gesture wrapped in the guise of consideration. She didn't know whether to be frightened, appalled, or both. His kindness was wearing her down like sandpaper. And lately Birdie had been feeling paper thin.

They crossed the Brooklyn Bridge, though she barely noticed. Streamers and banners in support of the soldiers abroad decorated several corners near Canal Street. And then she thought, why, it might be only a few weeks before Andrew was drafted and she might never see him again. Her pity expanded to allow her to squeeze his hand back. The motorcar stopped in front of the Hotel Martinique.

It was a lovely establishment. The doormen were in beautiful uniforms with bright, polished brass buttons that Holly would have coveted. There was a red carpet and polished glass windows and eyes—a few too many—on her drab work dress and clunky shoes. This was how she would remember the day later. A mix of blurred images and thoughts, as if her story were playing in grainy black and white at the Strand Theatre.

Andrew never checked in because he had planned everything beforehand with a good deal of hope and optimism. He'd no idea that Birdie would be so compliant. He turned a brass key on the fifth floor, and inside was a bed made with rich ruby-red damask and soft down-filled pillows fluffed within an inch of their lives. Nearby was an armoire filled with lacy pink-and-cream satin negligees; they probably would fit her figure flawlessly. She saw a claw-foot desk and fancy stationery, a silver platter with wine and water. The scent of roses mixed with the tang of lemon-oil polish, hiding the smells of whoever had slept in the room before. Soon, it would hide Birdie's presence too.

She stood at the foot of the bed, staring at the linens. They were worth more than she earned in a month. And when Andrew stood behind her, his heat penetrating the thin material of her dress, she shivered. Taking her shudder as encouragement, he began to slowly unbutton the back of her dress, slipping the frock off her shoulders. Off came her loosely laced brassiere and underthings, her stockings and shoes. He even relished taking the hairpins from her knot of hair, letting her hair tumble over her thin shoulders.

His hands were on her belly, her hips, her breasts. Lips on her neck. On her earlobes.

How did I get here? Birdie wondered, before she silenced herself. You're here. So *be* here.

Wordlessly, Andrew undressed himself and laid her on the bed, kissing her on the lips gently. Too gently. She pulled away and shook her head.

"No. Not there."

She let him puzzle out the rest. He would do his best, trying to kiss her body awake though she was dry as sawdust. And when he climbed on top of her, she cried out in pain from the weight of him on her fragile bones, her joints rebelling from the angles of her hips.

"Golly, I'm sorry!" Andrew exclaimed, face full of worry.

"I'm breakable," Birdie reminded him, breathless.

Gentleman to the end, Andrew held himself aloft with his arms. But he hurt her anyway, unknowingly, as he canted into her, the tempo of their bodies singing the same bitter song in her head.

She didn't remember how many times Andrew made love to her in that hotel room. She didn't remember how she got home that day, or how she ended up back at the hotel the following week, and the week after that.

She had tried so hard not to become Hazel, and it had happened anyway.

CHAPTER 14

September 11, 1918

Three weeks.

Well, two weeks and five days. Nearly three weeks, which was well-nigh unacceptable.

That's how long it had been since Florence's funeral, since Allene had been together with Jasper and Birdie alone. Far too long.

She perched at her vanity, readying herself to do something she absolutely shouldn't. She'd sat here since after breakfast, fiddling with the contents locked in the vanity drawer. The broken glass from the champagne flute Florence had been drinking from at the party was hidden in one of her father's empty cigar boxes, shoved to the back of the drawer. She had thought about purchasing the equipment and chemicals to test it for cyanide, but Father had found her perusing her favorite Central Scientific Company catalogue and forbidden it. Josephine, who was more afraid of Mr. Cutter than Allene, was charged with destroying any similar catalogues that entered the house.

At the reception after Florence's funeral, Allene had overheard Mr. Waxworth stating that he would bequeath the majority of their estate to a trust benefitting the arts or a hospital in North Carolina, near their tobacco estate. Clearly, there was no usurper in line to grab Florence's money. Allene had been waiting to meet with Jasper and Birdie to tell them so. Three weeks of waiting.

Knowing that Florence died of cyanide made everything worse—they knew the partial truth. But partials weren't good enough—the how and the why and the who, those were the truths she wanted to learn.

She refused to throw away the shard. Not yet. Lucy knocked on the door, and she hastily shut the drawer, turning the key.

"Are you ready, Miss Allene? Shall I call for the motor?"

"Oh. No, Lucy. That won't be necessary."

The door opened. Lucy's brown eyes quizzed her. "Are you quite sure, miss? All that shopping without a driver?"

"I'm quite sure." She smiled, but it felt painted on. Lucy stepped into the room, turned Allene to face the mirror, and picked up a tortoiseshell comb.

"You're just like your mother, you know." Lucy smoothed an errant strand on Allene's head, and Allene reflexively closed her eyes. Her hands were so gentle. "They say before she was married, she was . . . what is the word . . . *restless.*"

"Was she?"

"Mmm-hmm." Lucy picked up a pink silk ribbon and expertly wove it around the twist of her knot. "I was, too, when my mother brought me here from Sicily as a child. I wanted to be an actress." She laughed, another rare one. "Young and very restless."

Allene turned around. "You make it sound like it's all over. Like you're so old now!"

"No. I'm only thirty-five. But an old thirty-five."

"And I'm sweet eighteen!" Allene grinned. "I can't imagine you being anything but a saint, Lucy. What dramas did you have?"

"Never mind that. I am a saint now." She smiled. "I have to be." She said nothing for several moments, like she was seeing something inside herself. Then she shook off the memory and continued. "Your mother finally settled in after she married your father. It's too bad she's still ill."

Yes, too bad. For someone so stricken with consumption as to remove herself to a sanatorium for nearly four years, Mother sure seemed to die awful slow. Or, as Allene had begun to suspect lately, maybe it was just a convenient excuse not to be with her father. Or Allene.

Lucy drew away, but her eyes softened. Everyone, including Lucy, knew what manner of cage Allene was entering with marriage.

"You'll be all right, child. The Cutter women are always strong."

Allene fought the sting in her eyes and nodded. Lucy bent down and plucked a book from the floor, where it was peeking out from the ruffled bed skirt. Cohen's *Practical Organic Chemistry*, her recent night reading. The maid covered it in some discarded clothing, hugging it gently to her chest.

"You need to hide your secrets a little better, Miss Allene. I'll be sure your father doesn't see me put it back on the shelf."

Allene thought of the missing silver polish that Lucy had waved away with finality. "And you? Do you have secrets too, Lucy?"

"Don't be silly. I am an open book. You need only to look to find the answers." She withdrew, the hidden book cradled to her bosom.

What did Lucy mean by that? Allene remembered again how her mother had told her about secrets. "As you turn into a lady, you'll know which ones to bury forever." Allene hadn't understood then, but she did now.

She pulled two folded letters from her vanity drawer. The first piece of disappointment was a letter from Jasper, written two weeks ago. He'd been working almost sixteen-hour shifts at the medical examiner's office, accompanying the staff to crime scenes, keeping the log books organized, ordering supplies, and answering the telephone that never ceased to ring.

The Great Green Allene! My Spleen!

Ugh. Would he ever forget those dratted childish nicknames? They were so utterly unattractive.

> *I'm working like the deuce. Apparently I mean more to the ME than my own sleep, they keep me so blame busy. So our investigation of poor Florence shall have to wait. Let me know if you hear anything. Give my best to Birdie, and kiss that Andrew for me. He's so absogoldarn-lutely handsome, isn't he?*
>> *Exhaustedly yours,*
>> *Jasper*

Allene could practically hear him laughing at her. The fire that had brought them together had gone out. Not just gone out, but been buried six feet under in the Evergreens. And meanwhile, Birdie had sent her an altogether different kind of note. Short, but not so sweet.

> *Dearest Allene,*
> *Mother is ill again. I won't be able to make it. See you soon?*
>> *Love,*
>> *Birdie*

She had not received another letter from Birdie or from Jasper to follow up with their plans. Honestly, was it so hard to dip the so-called quill and send her another note? Allene had written notes to them both, and they'd gone unanswered.

And these last few days, Allene had met with her mother-in-law and spoken with florists, the dressmaker, the caterer, deciding on whether they should have the filet mignon or veal sweetbreads for their wedding supper. Mother would, of course, approve from afar. Her letters, however rare they were, lately were all by proxy, written by her nursemaids. She had little to say about anything at all. Allene tried to cry, but her eyes stayed dry.

The wedding invitations—thick cream cards with engraved script—had gone out days after Florence's funeral. Already, the majority of the handwritten replies had been received. There would be over three hundred guests.

Minus two.

Jasper and Birdie had yet to reply. Allene would have been ecstatic if they'd refused. It would have meant a confrontation, a row. And she'd have been a little perturbed if they'd accepted, because it wouldn't have been in person and because Jasper hadn't counteroffered with a proposal that promised high drama.

But no reply? Absolutely unforgivable.

Allene refused to be ignored. She had decided to do something about it without risking Dawlish reporting back to her father. Five minutes later, she had walked out the front door of the Cutter house and headed toward Third Avenue. Later, the wizened butler would read her note, in which she promised to be back in several hours, and rub his chin with puzzlement: How could Miss Cutter simply let herself out—did she even know how to unlock the great brass door? But Allene relished the small rebellion. She held it inside herself, a glowing coal that would singe if she wasn't careful. But she wouldn't mind the sting. Anything to penetrate the numbness of wedding preparations.

As she passed the avenues, the beautiful houses gave way to smaller, shabbier buildings and storefronts. Before long, the Third Avenue El loomed and crossed Eighty-Fourth Street, a familiar blemish on the low skyline. This was how she had come home alone all those nights ago after their illicit stint in the morgue.

She fished out five cents from her purse like everyone else around her and boarded the train, wearing a self-satisfied smile. That is, until she realized she'd accidentally gone uptown. She switched trains at Eighty-Ninth Street, the smug grin scrubbed clean off her face.

When Allene got off at Houston Street, her head felt rattled from the ride. The two Els hulked over the streets, casting shadows and making the buildings look dirtier than they were. A few groups of people—young men—were talking excitedly over the newspaper headlines. Allene only heard scraps of words—"Finally!" and "Sick and tired of bumming around . . ."—before she walked on.

Laundry was festooned between buildings, waving cheerfully, and plumes of smoke dirtied the air from the motorcars going east and west. A few seedy men walked a mite too close. Allene hurried along, clutching her purse. She wished she had worn her older coat. Without missing a step, she tugged the pink ribbon out of her hair and stuffed it into her pocket.

Eldridge Street was soon before her, thank goodness, since her shoes were rubbing a blister on her heel. Inside the entranceway of Jasper's tenement, a lady with a face like an overcooked dumpling was picking up old newspapers. She appraised Allene with bright, currant-like eyes.

"Is Mr. Jones in?"

"*Tak,*" she said, nodding, before grabbing a bundle of old *Youth's Companion* magazines. Allene sidled past her, trying her darnedest not to touch anything. The stairwell here didn't have the terrible outhouse stench of Birdie's home but instead smelled vaguely like a chemistry lab. She closed her eyes and inhaled deeply. Lovely.

At the top of the stairs, she knocked.

"Door's open," a muffled voice called.

She opened the door and stepped inside. It was one of those railroad apartments, where the rooms were strung like beads on a single thread. The sitting room was neat but spare. She noticed the peeling wallpaper and a pile of laundry on the couch that was carefully folded, recently pulled in from a window line. A brass receipt holder had impaled countless bills in what resembled a messy paper Christmas tree. She peered at it closely and saw repeating words on the edges.

Past Due. In Arrears. Third Notice.

She blinked and moved on, unwilling to touch a thing. This apartment wasn't anything like her world, and she felt foreign within it. The next room was a bedroom, but the door was only open a crack. She could see bottles and cups haphazardly strewn on the floor, and a dirty shirt carelessly tossed near them. Someone snored from within. Allene didn't dare to explore further.

The kitchen was unrecognizable as such. A glass chemistry apparatus took up most of the table space. Every inch of counter was crammed with bottles of various shapes and sizes. Crates of medicinals towered on the floor. It was utterly chaotic, yet Allene was warmed by the sight of so much glassware. Chemistry lived here, and it welcomed her as if she were finally home. She reached for one of the random brown bottles on the countertop and sniffed it delicately.

"I wouldn't do that, if I were you."

Jasper was leaning against the door frame with a newspaper tucked under his arm, watching her. She hadn't noticed him at all. She put the bottle down too fast, and it twirled on its bottom and tipped over.

"Oh! I'm so sorry." She watched the brown liquid spill over the surface, then drip onto the floor.

Merriment danced in Jasper's eyes as he pointed to a dirty rag hanging from the kitchen sink. "Over here, we clean up our own messes. No Lucy to help you this time."

"Oh! Of course! I'm so sorry." Allene grabbed the damp rag with two fingers, holding it like it harbored every rude and untoward germ in the nation, and mopped up the mess.

"I'll bet that's the first time you've cleaned anything, Miss Cutter."

"Don't be impertinent," Allene retorted, trying to regain her composure. "What is all this, anyway?"

"My uncle's project. He's a dandy entrepreneur, he is. In this kitchen, the best moonshine ever will be concocted before all alcohol is illegal. Someone's got to keep New Yorkers crocked if that law goes into effect."

"Well, that's ambitious, if not entirely legal."

"*Pfft*. He'll probably drink it down before it pays the bills, anyway." Jasper exited the kitchen, and Allene followed him to the very end of the hallway, her dirty hand forgotten. Inside Jasper's room, there was a neatly made mattress on the floor and towers of books everywhere. Jasper patted the seat of a rickety chair while he leaned against the wall. He lit a match and sucked on a small cigarette before tossing the match out the window.

"Look at all these books! Getting ready for medical school, are we?"

"Not this year. Maybe never." He handed the newspaper to Allene. "What is this?"

"Obviously it's the *New York Times*."

"I ought to pinch you."

"Just you try," he said, but his expression was anything but playful. "Read it."

Allene scanned the headline. "French Drive Pushes Closer to Saint-Quentin." And then her eyes fell to the smaller articles below. Her heart thumped harder. "Crowder Says Many Thousands Probably Will Be Needed at Camps in October."

"Registration tomorrow . . ." She dropped the newspaper to her lap and stared at Jasper. "Oh. The draft. Registration is tomorrow, isn't it?"

"Yes."

She bit her lip. "You're eighteen."

"Just like you. Our birthdays are both in June."

"Yes. When summer cherries go ripe, we always got our birthday cake." But she wasn't smiling at the memory. She pointed to a number in the newspaper. "And now, General Crowder wants to register thirteen million more boys."

"Including me."

"But it's not for sure, right? The lower age limit? And just because you register doesn't mean you'll get picked. Surely you can get an exemption!"

"I don't know if Norris has that power. He might, touch wood. Anyway"—he extinguished his cigarette—"the war is going to ruin my future illustrious career as New York's best-known medical examiner. At least I'll look good in olive drab wool, six feet under in a trench."

"Stop it." Allene's eyes were watering. "By God, sometimes you're awful, Jasper."

"You know, I spend so much time not thinking about what happened to Oscar, it's no surprise. The dead don't like being ignored." It was hard to read his expression. "Speaking of the dead, I suppose Florence's case has gone cold. Have you seen Ernie lately?"

"Ernie? What about Ernie?"

"I forgot to tell you. At the end of interment, he showed up, sad as a drowned kitten, crying his eyes out over her casket."

"He did? Really? He wasn't at the reception afterward." She frowned. "Do you think he felt guilty? Oh, but I don't believe Ernie could hurt a fly! Florence wasn't any meaner to him than anyone else. Less, actually, because you know how everyone ignores him all the time."

"Maybe he wanted more attention than that," Jasper suggested.

"To the point of committing a murder? This is Ernie we're speaking of."

"Maybe they were secretly lovers," Jasper said, but he and Allene both laughed at the thought.

"Completely unbelievable," Allene said. "Anyway, I've brought Florence up a few times, and Ernie acts appropriate enough. Not like a guilty killer."

"You've seen him?"

"Unlike you, Jasper, he still cares enough to visit," Allene said. She waited for a retort; there was none.

"So. What brings the illustrious Miss Cutter down to my neck of the woods? You're lucky you caught me. I only ran home for lunch, and here you are when I'm all set to leave."

"You haven't visited." Her voice was thin as a thread.

"Neither have you."

"Well, I only came to deliver this." She pulled out a slightly bent invitation from her purse and handed it to Jasper. He didn't take it.

"Oh. I already got one. Quite a tony invite too."

"Well, weren't you going to at least pay me the respect of responding?"

"What for?" He stared out the window and exhaled smoke from his nostrils.

Allene looked at her feet. What could she say that wasn't the wrong thing? Why was she even here?

She knew the answers. He didn't care. He was leaving her behind, as she'd left him behind years ago. She could tell him that she was lonely. She could say she'd missed him, but the words sounded childish and weak. Good God, Allene. What a mess you are.

Tears welled in her eyes. She wouldn't let him see them. Never. She stood up quickly and dropped the invitation to the floor. "Well, here it is, all the same," she said, and escaped into the hallway. She wanted to leave before he could see her swimming eyes. Why did the hallway have to be so damned long?

A strong hand hooked her arm when she neared the kitchen and, off balance, she nearly fell over. Jasper clasped her waist to keep her from falling. By God, he was strong. There was no jest in his face anymore. He looked contrite, and when he saw the tears streaking down her face and darkening her dress, the expression was replaced with shock.

"Oh jiminy! I'm sorry, Allene. Really sorry."

Allene freed an arm to blot her face with the back of her hand. "Never mind. I want to go home."

"Don't. Let me get you some water first." He walked her back to his bedroom, and she let him. It was such a relief to be led, to be placed gently in the chair, to be cared for. It was comforting, what Allene was used to. He kneeled in front of her, already forgetting to fetch the glass of water. "Look, Allene. I'm sorry. I'm the rottenest. I guess I figured that you sent the invitation to be nice, but you didn't really want me to be there."

"I do. I do want you there." She pulled out a handkerchief and blotted her face. She looked down to those hazel eyes. Those were the eyes she knew so well—the ones that weren't all jesting, all the time.

Her mind spun backward in time, remembering when those eyes would ignite with happiness when they'd write invisible-ink paper notes to each other. Oh, they had been no ordinary invisible inks, with the kinds of messages easily released with a wash of red cabbage water or a lightbulb. Theirs had been a far more refined technique. The words had been scribed with quills dipped in salt water—even tears would have worked—then developed with a wash of silver nitrate pilfered from the cook's bottle of stomach medicine. Together, they'd bring the paper into the morning sunlight and watch the words darken to black, to truth.

Secret puzzle for Allene, one note had read.

> *It isn't red,*
> *It isn't blue,*
> *It has one oxygen,*
> *And hydrogen—two.*
>   *Love, Jasper*

It was everything. In his eyes, and what they shared—this love of secrets, of chemicals, of each other. Perhaps the words meant something.

Love, Jasper

It was just childish innocence. They'd been only twelve then.

And all the while, Birdie would be mending one of Allene's dresses in the corner of the parlor, cautioning them to be careful. And they would spring on her, tugging on her stockings in a good tease and gazing at her fondly, as if she were their own personal wax doll.

Allene would keep the messages but always feared their discovery. They only ever lasted a day before she burnt them in a wisp of hearth smoke. They were for her and only her.

Jasper still crouched at her feet, worry altering the handsome lines of his face as he watched the memories play across her features.

"Good God, Jasper." She sighed. "I wish it were you I was going to marry."

Jasper froze, as did Allene. She couldn't believe she had spoken the words aloud. His face drained of color, before pinking up quickly.

"Allene," he began, "you know I would marry you in a minute."

Oh God. That tone, that face! Was he pitying her? It was worse than kindness. "Don't make fun of me." She turned her face and tried to stand.

Jasper captured her wrists in his hands. "I'm not making fun."

He pulled gently, bringing her closer. She could have twisted her arms and released herself, but she didn't. She could smell his heat rising from around his shirt collar. Warm and alluring. She imagined weaving a blanket out of it and sliding beneath it after a long, warm bath.

"Do you really want to marry me?" Jasper whispered. "Or are you just trying not to marry someone else?" His eyes went from teasing to something harder, more flintlike. As if he were sizing up her net worth, wondering if she was worth the task of marriage.

"Forget I said anything," Allene whispered.

Jasper let go of one of her hands to lift her chin. "Do you mean that? Let me at least give you a wedding gift, one way or another."

Before Allene could say a word, he leaned in and kissed her. It was firm and strong and ever so different from the night of the engagement party. His hand at her chin spread to clasp her jawline, snake around the back of her neck, preventing escape. His lips moved over hers, tongue slipping expertly between her lips, which parted in surrender. Jasper's other arm released her other wrist and spread over her bodice, just under her right breast.

He deepened the kiss, sending rings of pressure and electricity to everywhere that was forbidden, to the place that only her hands had probed in secret shame in bed or in the bath. When he released her, her jellied legs couldn't hold her up. She sat down weakly on his bed.

Jasper turned around quickly, blotting his lips. Allene covered her face.

"We shouldn't have . . . done that," Allene said.

"I think you're right." Jasper forced a laugh and turned around. "I guess you won't be marrying me after all, eh?"

"I suppose not." She didn't even know what she was saying, she was so discombobulated. She took a makeup compact out of her purse and powdered the flush off her face. "Anyway, could you imagine?" She said the words more to herself than to Jasper. "You'd be able to pay for tuition and go to medical school. Even better, you wouldn't have to work. And you might get a draft exemption, because we'd be married and I'd be dependent on you."

Jasper was quiet at this. She'd expected a tart comeback—something about pride and pulling up bootstraps and such. But instead, he seemed to take in everything she'd said, turning it over, examining the worth of each phrase. Allene didn't like how he regarded her—like a jeweler with a loupe, searching for flaws and weighing carats carefully. Without blinking, he said, "I appreciate the offer. But I don't think the terms are to my liking."

She snapped her compact closed. "The terms? Or me?" She looked around. "So you'd rather go on living here."

Jasper shrugged. "This place? The Taj Mahal? Why wouldn't I?"

The tension between them broke as they laughed, and laughed hard, but Jasper soon sobered.

"Anyway, my uncle needs me. Used to be the other way around, but . . ." He raked his fingers through his hair, making it almost stand on end. "I don't know how he's going to survive if I end up in the army. Besides," he said, tucking his hand into his pocket, "if you married me, I'd never know if it was because you didn't want to marry Andrew. And you'd never know if it was because I needed money."

They weren't the words she wanted to hear. She could sense Jasper watching her, and it felt like a heavy heat was bearing down on her.

"I really ought to go," she said finally.

"Dawlish waiting for you, huh?"

"Actually, I took the train."

He raised his eyebrows appraisingly. "I can call you a cab. Wait here. I'll be back in a moment."

Jasper went to the front door, and when he'd left, she touched her lips. They were still softened from the kiss and ever so slightly swollen. But her throat was searingly dry, as if all the fluid in her body had poured out of her eyes. She walked back to the kitchen, blinking at the glassware apparatus perched crookedly on the table. Erlenmeyer flasks, funnels, condensers, and tubes tangled together with small burners. Over the stovetop, another crude contraption was larger with metal drums and tubes that ended in a container over the icebox.

A bottle labeled "Apricot Brandy" cozied up against larger bottles of wine, whiskey, and gin on the countertop. The brandy, only a quarter full, was stoppered with a cork. A single empty glass sat nearby, as if anticipating her presence. She uncorked the squat brown bottle and sniffed it. The odor of apricot was fainter than she expected. Surely Jasper's uncle wouldn't miss a sip, and her throat was still so terribly dry. So she poured a small amount of the brown liquid.

She brought the glass to her lips, resting it against her bottom lip—cool and comforting. As she tipped the glass, a shadow flickered on the edge of her vision.

Before she could react, the glass was slapped out of her hand.

Allene jerked back in surprise as the glass flew to the wall, shattering on impact. Jasper's uncle stood next to her, eyes wide with anxiety. She would have recoiled if she wasn't in shock. She'd never met the man before, and the aggression of his action made her want to flee her very skin.

His skin was sallow, his jaw stubbled with gray, and he wore an undershirt stained yellow near the armpits. Old baggy trousers were tethered in place with brown suspenders, and his bald pate was scantily covered in wisps of greasy hair.

But his eyes—those eyes—deep set and staring with concern and intelligence. The irises may have been a different shade and ever so dark; they were also very much Jasper's eyes.

"What are you doing, young lady?"

"I'm sorry—I was thirsty and . . . I'm sorry!"

"No, *I'm* so sorry, miss. That boy should have told you so. You shouldn't be drinking that."

"Why?"

He started cleaning up the pieces of broken glass. "Because you could have died."

Allene crossed her arms, slowly regaining her composure. "Well, that's exaggerating. It's only apricot brandy."

"It *was* apricot brandy, before I drank it," he corrected her, before searching out a broom in the corner. "It's filled with mostly wood spirits now. I can make a dollar off of it someday, but it's not fit to drink now."

"Wood spirits? You mean methyl alcohol?"

Jasper's uncle stopped sweeping the glass shards into a dustpan to stare at her with those inkblot eyes. "You're Allene, aren't you?"

"That I am."

"You must be that girl in the photograph."

"What photograph?"

"The one Jasper keeps hidden in his textbooks. He never lets me get close enough, but I'm sure he looks at it every day."

Allene's face went crimson.

"It's kind of you to call on my nephew, but you shouldn't be here. A nice girl like you. The boy works so durned hard, and he don't know how to be a gentleman anymore. Neither of us do."

"Well," Allene said, "more reason to have some womenfolk around."

He straightened up and bent his head closer. "I don't know about that. Jasper said good-bye to your uptown kind years ago. You do yourself a favor and stay away, miss."

He may have resembled a common gutter tramp, but warmth glowed in the crinkle of his eyes despite his words, a warmth she wished Father possessed. If she didn't know better, Allene would think that Uncle Fred was protecting her from Jasper.

Somewhere in the apartment, a door slammed and footsteps came from down the hall. Jasper swung around the kitchen door and raised his eyebrows.

"Ready? Your cab is waiting." When he saw his uncle, his nose wrinkled. "Fred, you need to put a shirt on when company's over."

"I didn't know company was over until the company almost killed herself."

"Excuse me?"

Allene waved her hand. "Long story." She turned to Jasper's uncle and smiled brightly. She liked him, even if he didn't want her there. "But do put on a shirt. Then you can walk me to my cab."

Uncle Fred shrank away from her. "No, miss. The sun and I, we don't get along."

"But it's cloudy outside, with a lovely breeze," she insisted.

"No, miss," he said, and patted the doorway. "These walls are all I need. Even the windows, I don't like 'em. I might fall right out into the sky and never find my way back. Jasper, you walk her out and come right back now. Be quick."

"Very well." Allene and Jasper were headed to the front door, when Allene turned. "Oh. I left my purse in your room."

"I'll get it."

"Don't bother. I'll be back in a jiff."

She trotted down to Jasper's room and picked up her purse from the chair. She glanced quickly around at the piles of textbooks and saw a single book lying squarely in the middle of his mattress. A small paperish square stuck out from the page edges. A bookmark.

She cocked an ear toward the hallway and heard Jasper murmuring with his uncle from a distance. Quickly, she leaned over to open the book and pulled out a photograph. A fairylike girl sat in a chair, staring at the photographer with a small, delicate smile. It was Birdie.

"Birdie!" Jasper's voice sounded sharply from the hallway, and Allene dropped the photograph, her heart pounding with vexation and confusion. She scrambled to gather her purse and went to the hallway, where she was shocked to see Birdie gesticulating wildly at Jasper. Little Holly was cowering behind her sister, sobbing. Birdie turned to Allene, surprised only for a moment.

"What on earth is going on?" Allene demanded.

Birdie choked the words out, her eyes huge with terror. "Something's happened to Mother. I think she's dead."

CHAPTER 15

Jasper could hardly believe his ears.

"What do you mean, you think she's dead?" Allene asked.

Holly flapped her hands, howling. Jasper had never seen the girl before. In the midst of the chaos, he thought, Oh. Well, that explains a lot. That's why Hazel Dreyer got kicked to the curb from the Cutter house. He remembered she'd been wearing some frumpy dresses around the time that she left. Now he knew what she had been hiding. God, Hazel had been stunning in her day—beautiful enough to be a film star with that stunning figure and large, catlike eyes and cupid-bow lips, always perfectly rosy. Jasper hadn't been able to keep his eyes off her when he came to visit. Apparently, Mr. Cutter hadn't been able to keep more than his eyes off Hazel Dreyer.

Little Holly tried to jump into Birdie's arms, but Birdie looked too done in to hold Holly like an infant.

"Holly, hush," Birdie tried to console her, but she herself looked almost crazed with fright. Allene reached into her purse and pulled out a shiny wrapped peppermint. She offered it to the girl the way you'd give a peanut to a circus elephant, pinkie akimbo.

"Here. Take it," Allene offered.

Oddly, Allene's awkwardness shifted the girl's focus. She took the candy and stepped closer to Allene, who seemed worried that the child might spontaneously hug her.

Allene turned to Birdie. "Go on. Tell us what happened."

"She was fine this morning. Just a big headache last night, but it wasn't anything unusual. Holly and I went out to get a chocolate phosphate, and when we came back—" Birdie stopped, her mouth pursing into a knot, before gasping. "The door was open. Wide open and unlocked. She was by the door and sprawled out on the floor. She wasn't breathing."

"Good God. Did you call the police?" Uncle Fred asked.

"Yes. We were at the station for three hours, and Holly's been in hysterics the whole time. They finally let me go so I could get Holly out of there."

"Of course." Allene turned to Jasper. "Do you have a telephone? I'll ring Lucy and Dawlish to pick up Holly from here and take care of her until things have settled."

Birdie's body sagged as tension dropped from her shoulders. "Are you sure?"

"Absolutely. Lucy will ply her with tea cake and hot chocolate until she can't see straight."

Uncle Fred had heard everything. He waved Allene to the front door. "Come. Our landlady has the only telephone in the building."

Within the hour, Dawlish had driven up to the curb, and Birdie had placed Holly in Lucy's capable arms. There was a basket with one of Allene's old dolls, three small strawberry tarts, and a wooden peg-and-stick game. Holly went willingly to the Cutter house, after Birdie promised she'd be there by dinnertime. She thanked Lucy with a trembling lip, and Lucy smiled.

"It's been a while since I've taken care of little ones this age. It will be a pleasure," she said. She started to croon a lullaby in Italian, and

Holly sagged a little in her arms. Within a moment, the doors were shut and Dawlish had driven them away.

Allene watched the retreating vehicle. "I always forget that Lucy has children. Why, I don't even know how old they are." Her face was a blank canvas of revelation. "Why didn't I ever ask?"

"Because you're a hopeless narcissist?" Jasper offered.

Allene glared at him. Birdie was too busy waving as the motorcar disappeared into traffic. When it was no longer in sight, she turned to Jasper and Allene, her tears dry. A grim focus brought gravity to her face, as if she'd been carved out of cold marble, when she'd only just been made of cloud and mist.

Jasper put his jacket around Birdie's stiff and unmoving shoulders and went to the curb to wave down a taxi. Uncle Fred stood in the doorway of the building, refusing to step out under that yawning, open midday sky. He waved Allene closer, probably to say good-bye.

He spoke low, so Jasper would not hear him. Jasper turned his back but listened hard and heard it all anyway.

"Don't come back here, miss," his uncle told her. "Jasper ain't yours to play with anymore. He was doing fine before you come back in his life. Leave him be. You and that pretty blonde friend of yours. I beg you."

Silence met his ears. He imagined Allene frowning, confused. A Cutter unwelcome in anyone's home? Unthinkable. A few feet away, Birdie turned her head toward Jasper, eyes large and sad. She, too, had heard his uncle's words.

Allene put her arm around Birdie as a taxicab wheeled around the corner. Jasper hailed the cab as if he'd heard nothing. As if nothing mattered, because it was too late to step outside of the world they'd all sunk into.

It was time to find out what had killed Hazel Dreyer.

The police were still at Birdie's apartment but in paltry numbers and with little seriousness, compared to when Florence had died. They seemed irritated when Birdie, Jasper, and Allene arrived. Birdie wrung her hands and walked up to one, who was scribbling notes.

"Do you have any more questions for me?" she asked.

"No, miss."

"But—"

"Who are they?" He jabbed his pencil in the direction of Allene and Jasper. The three of them looked at each other, and for a moment none of them spoke. What were they, really, to each other? There wasn't one word that could explain the truth. It was a language that Jasper was relearning, and he hadn't yet mastered it. He'd spent so much of the last years thinking about himself and his uncle, but mostly about himself. He thought of his kiss with Allene only an hour ago, and the way he had difficulty taking his eyes off of Birdie when she entered a room. He thought of how all of this was interrupting his climb up the ladder at work. But a word must be chosen for this simpleminded officer in front of him who demanded a label. So be it.

"We're family," Jasper said firmly.

"Well. We think we've got an answer here." The officer led them to the kitchen, where a bottle sat on the tiny table next to a small glass that had dram measurements on the side. Jasper peered at the label: "Tincture of Opium."

"It's laudanum," the officer remarked. "Did you know she took it?"

"Of course," Birdie answered. "Mother has been taking opium for almost two years now. She had a lot of pain. But she took it regularly, three times a day. It's nothing new."

"Were you responsible for giving her doses?"

"No. I didn't want to touch her medicine. I stopped letting Holly pour it for her too. She could have tasted it by accident."

"Well, we also found this. Follow me." He walked toward Hazel's bedroom, but Birdie froze and covered her face. Allene was still staring at the bottle of laudanum. Jasper went to Birdie's side.

"Please don't make me go in there," Birdie said.

"I'm sorry, ma'am," he said, but walked in anyway.

Birdie was miserable and stiff as a board as Jasper led her to the adjoining apartment, where Hazel entertained her customers. He cringed at the knowledge of what took place in here. There was a bedstead draped in cheap fabric to simulate a nonexistent opulence. A chaise with snags in the cushions lay against a wall. Satin slips hung over a screen in the corner, and a tray filled to overflowing with spirit bottles and dirty whiskey tumblers lay next to the door. Some were still wet.

In the middle of everything was Hazel.

She lay on the floor, her eyes closed, with one arm folded neatly beneath her head. Her satin robe covered her body, but it was clear that she was naked beneath the thin fabric. Her blonde hair didn't have the golden sheen that Birdie's had. Nothing marred her skin—not a bruise or a cut—only a smudge of eye makeup that hadn't been washed off since the previous night.

Allene stepped into the room and took Birdie's other side, while she sobbed anew at the sight of her mother. Jasper walked toward the bathroom, wanting to escape from their despair. It wasn't that he didn't care, but he had no idea what to do. Even Allene looked helpless, patting Birdie's back through the hiccups and hyperventilating breaths, all the while staring out the window as if counting the minutes until the sadness would be over and done.

The only bathroom on this floor of the apartment building was shared, but there was an enamel bucket in the corner hung with a used towel. There wasn't a drop of blood anywhere or suspicious smudges. A large, cylindrical syringe and tubing—a woman's douche—were coiled inside the bucket along with a worn cake of soap, a bottle of Palmolive shampoo, and a brush. Nothing looked amiss.

Back in Hazel's bedroom, Birdie had composed herself enough to watch the officer peruse the contents of Hazel's medicine cabinet. It held bottles and pills for all manner of female ailments and to prevent her from being in the family way. Nothing, to Jasper's eye, looked deadly.

"We found lots of empty bottles of medicine. We'll take some for evidence. No foul play in the apartment that's obvious. This was an accidental overdose, no question," the officer announced, before leaving the room. Another officer had to ask Birdie more questions, so Allene and Jasper retreated to the corner.

"Look what I got." Allene opened her palm and showed a scrap of torn label from the laudanum bottle.

"Don't steal evidence!" Jasper whispered. He tried to keep his tone calm. "What do you think this is, a vacation where you get to bring souvenirs home?"

Allene pouted. "I thought it might be useful."

"Not muddied up with your paws, it's not. Put it back, or put it away. Now."

Allene took out a handkerchief and stuffed the scrap of label into it and into her purse, without the police noticing. What a piece of work Allene was.

Within the hour, Hazel's body was covered with a sheet and removed from the apartment on a stretcher. Birdie kept her back to the procession as they inched the body out the door and down the stairs. Jasper tried to console her as best as he could.

"I'll be in the morgue tomorrow, after I register. I'll find out if there's any more information. I promise."

Birdie's eyes were glassy, unfocused. "Register for what?"

"The draft."

"Oh, Jasper. Not you too." Tears welled up again. Her eyelids were growing puffier with every passing minute. "There are so many other young men. Can't you pretend you forgot?"

"I won't be one of those slackers. Dr. Norris might get an exemption for his staff, but it's out of my hands." There wasn't anything else to say.

When the last officer had left, Birdie stood in the kitchen, staring at the center of her parlor, arms hanging down as if boneless. Jasper went to find Allene, who was standing in the doorway to the parlor with two small suitcases.

"What's that?"

"Clothes for Holly and Birdie. They can't stay here."

He knew what it was to have orphan status thrust upon you. Like someone had pushed you through a door, locked it, and left you in a new land with no map. All comforts were gone, unreachable. It seemed, at times, you had to relearn how to speak again. When you were grieving and in despair, basic things were different, like actually responding to yes and no questions. How to eat. How to sleep. How to smile. That one had taken him over a year to relearn.

At his parents' funeral, he had closed his eyes—only for moments at a time—and seen them in his mind's eye. Vital. Real. The creases on either side of his father's firm mouth; the way his mother had a vertical crease on her earlobes from wearing heavy earrings. He could reach out and know their hands were warm. And then he'd open his eyes, and it would be all gone. Instead, he'd see their death, and the open, staring eyes, and he wanted to back through that damned door.

And here was Birdie with that same look on her face, as if she expected to blink and realize it was all a joke or dream. She looked lost and elegant and empty. Her hair was coming undone in ropy locks around her swan neck. She smoothed her dress and began to sift through a pile of newspapers and mail that needed to be discarded. Because doing something was better than thinking.

"I can't believe it. It's just the two of them now. She'll have to take care of Holly by herself," Allene murmured. "I can't imagine being a mother when you were just a child yesterday."

Birdie was holding an envelope in her hand when she walked to Jasper.

"What's this?" Jasper pointed to the envelope.

"I've no idea. The other letters were bills and advertisements. This is so odd. Look."

She handed Jasper the plain slip of paper, words written in beautiful script.

You're welcome.

"Strange," Jasper said, studying the writing. "It's not signed."

"Maybe it's from Andrew," Birdie said absently, before covering her mouth, mortified.

"What did you say?" Allene's voice had suddenly gone cold.

She and Jasper both stared at Birdie, whose eyes flicked between them, guilt flooding her features and shame staining her cheeks fuchsia. She yanked out a kitchen chair and sat down with a thump. The action made her wince with pain.

"That day that you asked Andrew to escort me home? Well, he saw Mother and Holly." She sighed, a long one. "The reason why we have more food in the cupboards and enough medicine these days is because Andrew's been helping me."

"I never asked him to do such a thing," Allene said, all astonishment.

Jasper thought, If I'd had the cash, I'd have done the same thing to get in beautiful Birdie's good graces. She was the kind of gal that men threw money at just in case she felt benevolent enough to return the favor with a kiss, or more. Andrew wasn't stupid. He wasn't noble either, but Jasper wanted to laugh. Andrew buying opium for Birdie's mother? A brilliant play. He wondered how many caring, crooning, meaningful looks he'd practiced on her before she ended up in his bed.

Birdie kept her eyes on the floor. "He was just being nice."

"Why on earth would he be nice to you?" Allene asked, without thinking. She must have caught Jasper's smirk, because her eyes narrowed immediately. "Oh, be quiet!" she spat.

Her anger was so contrary to the teasing, lighthearted Allene who had everything she wanted and not a care in the world. Good Lord, Jasper thought. Who was this woman?

He put his hands out in a placating gesture. "Look. This isn't helping to figure out why Hazel died. Let's all calm down a little, shall we?"

Allene and Birdie gave each other quiet glances. There was an uneasy détente, at least for now. Jasper tossed the note onto the table, and Allene snatched it up. Suddenly, her features morphed into recognition. She gasped.

"What is it?" Jasper asked.

"Oh. I've seen this before. I have!" She pointed to the lettering. "The morning after Florence died, I was in the library reading a chemistry book and"—she poked at the letter—"inside, there was a letter. Like this. I didn't know what to think of it. It must be the very same person. The handwriting, the paper—identical."

Jasper took the paper and scrutinized the ink. "Do you recognize who it belongs to?"

"No. It's perfect handwriting, though. Almost copperplate."

"What does it mean?" Birdie asked. Exhaustion shrouded the poor girl.

"I . . . I don't know," Allene admitted. "It can't be a coincidence. But I don't know what it means. Right now, it all just seems like an accident. Maybe Hazel just took too much medicine. But if it's not an accident, will the coroner be able to find out?" she asked Jasper.

"Yes. They'll measure the levels in her blood. But since she used morphine all the time, how would they know if it was too much or too little without a comparison?"

"But she never took too much," Birdie told them. "She was so careful because she wanted a bottle to last as long as possible."

Allene thought for a second, then went directly to the kitchen and began opening and shutting cabinets quickly.

"What are you doing?" Jasper asked.

"Wait . . . maybe . . . yes. Here. Look."

She withdrew three empty brown bottles from beneath the sink. She set them on the table.

"So? We knew she took it regularly. Empty bottles are no surprise," Jasper noted.

"It's not that." Allene pointed. "Look at the labels."

Jasper peered at the paper on the bottles.

Paregoric

Two grams of opium per ounce
And on the back, he read:
Five Days Old, Five Drops
Two Weeks Old, Eight Drops
Five Years Old, Twenty-Five Drops
Adult, One Teaspoon
Smith & Walley Druggists, Brooklyn, New York
Guaranteed Pure

"Something's not right," Jasper said. "That bottle in the bedroom? It didn't say paregoric. It said laudanum."

"Aren't they the same?" Birdie asked, confused.

"No. They're both tinctures of opium but different. I know because I had to review pharmaceutical dosages for Dr. Gettler two weeks ago. There was an opium overdose in a baby that had colic. Laudanum is at least twenty times stronger than paregoric. Babies get overdosed all the time because of the mistake."

"She gets her medicines from the same pharmacist all the time. How could she make that mistake?"

"Maybe it wasn't Hazel who made the mistake." Jasper picked up the letter again and handed it to Allene.

You're welcome.

A dreadful realization wove its way into his thoughts.

"That letter came to me the day after Florence died. And now after Hazel," Allene said slowly. "Which means . . ."

"Someone is killing people around us," Birdie finished her sentence, before covering her mouth with horror.

"Just us," Allene added.

"The question is why," Jasper asked. He stared at them both. "And who's next?"

CHAPTER 16

Birdie stood up, the color drained from her face.

"Now, let's not panic," Jasper said. "I was hasty when I spoke. Hazel's death could easily have been an accident. I can find out more soon, I'm sure."

"Of course. And none of this is anything but a guess. You and Holly will be safe at our home." Allene showed her the two suitcases. "Both of you must stay with me for a long while. I insist. Maybe I can help you out for a change, instead of Andrew. You're *my* friend, after all. We can keep an eye on each other, figure out what's going on with these blasted letters."

Birdie took the letter from Jasper's hand. "I know a handwriting specialist. An analyst, or some such. Well, Mother did." She colored, and Allene and Jasper graciously said nothing. "He's very kind. I think if I asked, he would look at the two letters and see if they were written by the same hand. Maybe with the same ink." She looked up at Jasper. "Or we could turn them in to the police."

"Not yet," he said, with a little more haste than expected.

"Yes, not just yet. I'll give you the other letter, Birdie," Allene said. "Let's get you to the Cutter house first. We'll have loads of fun keeping you and Holly occupied."

"But my job—" Birdie began.

"When the time comes, Dawlish will take you," Allene assured her.

"What about your father?"

"Leave him to me." Allene didn't look so brave about this point, but Birdie didn't push it.

Birdie asked, "And what about your mother?"

Allene was silent. Birdie didn't want to say aloud that Mrs. Cutter would be quietly thrilled at her mother's death. Being banished to Brooklyn was one thing, but surely she'd have some satisfaction that the Dreyers were moving into permanent obscurity, one by one.

"Don't worry about Mother," Allene told her. "It's Father we have to maneuver around, and I have an idea." A glint shone in Allene's eye. She loved this, being at the center of a bustle of chaos. "Stay until you can get your feet on the ground again. Steady like. It would be absolutely outrageous for you two to live here alone after what's happened. I won't stand for it."

"Very well. Just for a short while," Birdie conceded. Allene smiled and picked up the small case. Jasper picked up the larger one.

Birdie took one last look at her silent apartment. That old carpet. The misshapen sofa. If she listened hard enough, she could hear faint sounds of bedsprings from the next room, the encouraging moans of her mother, the grunts of the men whose faces she refused to remember. She closed her eyes. That part of her life was over, but she would never be able to wash away her memories of this place.

Still, there was no loss without some small gain. Her mother would no longer suffer. And now Holly would be in the Cutter house. Oh God, but what a cost.

She remembered the feeling of her mother's spindly arms hugging her. *Better times are coming, Birdie,* she had told her. *You're so beautiful. I know you were not born so beautiful for nothing.* Birdie was homesick for the time when hope was a bright thing. It was dimming for her, but hope still burnt brightly for Holly. She opened her eyes again.

"Ready?" Jasper repeated, touching her elbow as she paused outside the locked door.

"Yes," Birdie said. "I am." She took the key from the lock and went downstairs for the last time.

⟞⟝

Dawlish had returned to Brooklyn and waited at the curb. Next thing, Birdie was inside the back of the motorcar with Allene. Everything felt unreal—the sounds of the engine, the buildings speeding past. At some point before they crossed the bridge into Manhattan, Allene patted her lap, and Birdie put her head down obediently. She fell fast asleep into a respite of darkness and silence and safety, rocked by the hum of the motorcar, with Allene's hand resting warmly on her back.

Before long, Allene roused her, and Birdie followed her into the front entrance of the Cutter house. Andrew and Ernie were in the foyer, and memories of the years lived here assailed her, but she ignored them, ignored it all. From here on out, under this roof, she would have room in her heart only for what she needed to survive. She needed to take care of Holly at all costs. She made a beeline for Lucy.

"Where is Holly?" she asked.

Lucy put her finger to her lips, then smiled. "Your sister is sleeping upstairs in the guest room."

"May I see her?" Birdie asked.

"Of course!" Lucy seemed surprised by the question, but the Cutter house always had this effect on her. Birdie would probably ask permission to sneeze if the opportunity arose. "You'll be sharing the room." Lucy took the two suitcases in hand and began to climb the stairs. Birdie started to follow when a hand touched her shoulder.

She turned and saw Andrew, with Ernie as a bright shadow behind him. She couldn't have been less happy to see them. Andrew glanced at her with meaning, while Allene watched with narrowed eyes. A dram of rage seemed to simmer under her skin.

God, Allene must see that hangdog look when he was so near. She wished she could run away. Ernie was speaking to her now. What was he saying? She didn't have the energy for simple decorum right now.

"I'm so sorry," Ernie began, even though Andrew was closer (and touching her elbow. Why wouldn't he let go? Was he unconcerned that Allene was just a breath away?).

"What . . . I'm sorry?" Birdie mumbled back.

"About your mother. I came to pay a visit—I've left my card for your father, Allene—we had some business matters to discuss and . . . oh dear. Birdie, I am so sorry. What a terrible situation. How unfortunate. How can I be of help?"

Birdie stared. Her tongue was numb, and she couldn't bring her mouth to speak anything worth saying.

Allene swept up beside him. "Ah, Ernie. Always here to help. You are a dear. Poor Birdie's quite spent."

"I'm sure! What an awful accident. Birdie, you must be devastated. I know I would be. I'd be in such a state! Such a state, I tell you," Ernie rattled on.

Birdie shut her eyes. Andrew let go of her elbow to draw Ernie aside, pointing him in the direction of the refreshments that had arrived in the parlor. She was both grateful and troubled by this. What more could she possibly add to the list of what she owed Andrew?

Allene took Birdie's arm and motioned to Lucy, who'd returned from delivering the suitcases upstairs.

"Lucy, have the servants draw a bath, and lay out one of my clean nightgowns for her. Birdie needs to go right to bed and rest. Poor thing is exhausted."

Birdie wasn't in a state to resist. And yet she couldn't help but feel as if Allene's first order of the afternoon was to eliminate, as best as possible, the traces of Birdie's previous life. Hazel and her death had left a taint, and it was time to scour it away.

Upstairs, they peeked into the guest bedroom. Holly was wearing a new dress—Birdie recognized it as one of her own from years ago. It was a mite too large, and she swam in it. Her head was ensconced in a down pillow, and the coverlet draped across her legs. Her eyes were puffy, as Birdie's must be, but she was deep asleep. She had been sucking her thumb, but it had popped out and lay, ready to relaunch, where her loose fist rested on the pillow.

Birdie exhaled with relief. She was all right for now.

Lucy ushered her to the bathroom, where she left her in the care of several maids. One was running the bath and sprinkling lavender salts into the steaming water, followed by rose oil. A robe was folded and ready on a stool, along with plush, soft towels. Another maid curtsied before coming to Birdie. Her small hand reached for the buttons on Birdie's dress.

Birdie took a step back. "I can do it," she said.

"Miss Allene sent us to help you," the maid explained.

"I don't need help." She was so used to doing everything by herself. Any extra hands on her person felt like she'd owe someone, somehow. And she wasn't wanting to pay what she couldn't give.

"This is how things are done for the ladies of the house. Do you not remember, miss?"

She didn't remember this maid. Many of the servants were strangers to her. And she'd forgotten how things were. Just a few years, and already she had more in common with the cook than with this lady's maid.

This is what you wanted. This is where you wished to be, wasn't it? Birdie asked herself.

She nodded. "Of course. You may proceed." She cleared her throat before adding, "Thank you."

Relief stole over the faces of the maids. It was far easier for them to do their job when their mistresses were docile. First, they unpinned her tight, white-gold braids and laced their fingers through her scalp to loosen the knots. Then they unbuttoned Birdie's dress, taking off her chemise and stockings, her loosely laced corset, brassiere, and drawers. Sinking into the heat of the bathwater, Birdie unconsciously sighed. She was buffed from toes to head and shampooed within an inch of her life, and all the traces of the clock factory were removed from under her fingernails with an orangewood stick.

The scent of Hazel's favorite magnolia perfume—smudged onto Birdie's chest when she held her unconscious mother—was soaped off. So were Holly's tears. All things inconvenient and embarrassing, humiliating and tragic, all the mistakes and unsaid words would whirl down the drain soon enough.

From beyond the door and elsewhere downstairs, she heard Andrew's voice.

Oh, God help me, Birdie thought. God help me survive this house and these people.

If only the maids would use nails and knives to scrape away her shame and leave nothing but her bones. They were so busy polishing Birdie into a bright and pretty thing that they never noticed that her face was wet from tears, not bathwater.

When she was buffed dry and robed, the maids brought her back to her room, where Holly still slept soundly. For the sake of her sleeping sister, she shooed away the maids and insisted that she could dress herself.

She stood in a place that was slipping and slipping fast. Lately, it was her shinbone that hurt. She noticed a bump that shouldn't be there along the razor's edge of bone. It had grown within the last week, and she was trying to ignore the pain that went with it. Her jaw still caused her trouble. She'd lost another molar. Thankfully, no one could see her missing teeth when she smiled.

Holly stirred in her sleep. Birdie forgot herself and went to the bedside. Holly blinked drowsily, looking about her, before poking her thumb across her cheek and finding her mouth. The pale green eyes found Birdie and smiled, then saw the milk-glass lamp next to the bed and the canopy and the window with the costly damask curtain. Confusion filled her face.

"Darling, we're at Miss Allene's home now. You took a nap. Remember?"

Holly nodded. "She said I can call her Auntie Ally."

"Yes. You may."

Memory stirred behind Holly's eyes. "Where's Mama?" she whined.

"She's been taken away."

"I want to see her."

"No, Holly. We can't do that. Mama's gone and they'll take care of her until we can say good-bye at the funeral."

The funeral. She would have to find an undertaker. Buy a plot somewhere—nothing grand like the Evergreens. Where to even look? No one had prepared Birdie for the fact that she ought to have shopped for cemetery plots when it was more convenient, when everyone who counted was still alive. Mother would need a dress. It would cost money, and all that she had was still sewn into the mattress at the apartment. She'd been too dazed to even consider retrieving it earlier.

The door cracked open, and Allene quietly entered. As always, she didn't ask permission or knock.

"I want to see Mama," Holly begged into Birdie's neck, and clung harder.

"Oh, Holly Berry. We can't. Mother has gone to heaven, and she's happy there."

"But we're not there. How could she be happy?"

"It's God's way." When everything in life went well, it was God's way. When everything went to hell, it was God's way too.

Holly sobbed in Birdie's arms for some time. Allene stayed a quiet witness to this, raising her hand once or twice to wipe tears from her own face.

"It's going to be all right. You'll be safe here. And for this, we have . . . Auntie Ally to thank."

Holly sniffled and lifted her head. She saw Allene by the door. Allene smiled and fidgeted with her hands. The little girl extended a plump, tiny arm and stepped forward to accept Allene's small embrace. Allene allowed a flicker of a smile, a few rapid blinks. If all went well, in time Holly's embraces would smite Allene with far better aim and consequence than a German bullet ever could.

There would be no question now: Holly would never, ever be groomed to follow in Hazel's steps. But that comfort didn't displace the fissuring within Birdie herself. This house had broken her, ruined her family, and here she was again. Birdie's heart was a mosaic of cracks, and there was abundant room for more breaking if she wasn't careful.

"Thank you," she whispered, letting her tears fall, "for letting us come home."

CHAPTER 17

Allene left Birdie and Holly in their room, away from prying eyes. Namely, Father's. He would be livid that they were here without his consent. But the maids were almost gleeful. There was an adorable child to look after. There was new gossip. It was heaven.

Downstairs, Andrew and Ernie were having a heated discussion with Jasper. It was odd to see the three of them talking. Ernie's usual sanguine words were wilting in a peacekeeping attempt between Jasper and Andrew, who were exchanging barbs.

"If you were helping her order the medicines," Jasper reasoned, "you had an obligation to make sure they were correct. You're not an idiot, you can read a label."

"I'm not a medical man. But you are. Or I hear you will be. Why didn't you take some responsibility for your friend and check on them? Or were you too busy to care?"

"Some of us don't have money handed to us on a silver platter. I have to actually work."

Ernie looked more upset than either of them. "Ah, maybe we should all take a moment? Get some fresh air. Might we remember that there's a war, and we're all on the same side?"

"Fresh air would be welcome. I'd kill for a cigarette," Jasper muttered.

Andrew coughed and took a tin of fine mint pastilles from his pocket. He helped himself before snapping the tin closed without offering one. Jasper shook his head at Ernie, ever so slightly, as if to say, What a greedy little rat.

"You're looking a little pale, Andrew," Jasper noted. "Maybe you need a stint in the country. Get some fresh air for a while."

Andrew looked pointedly away. If anything, it made Jasper look even merrier. He seemed to delight in irritating Andrew.

Allene strode forward and flashed a brilliant smile, a special one that tended to dazzle when wrought properly. "Are you boys fighting over me again? Aren't you sweet," she said, trying to keep her voice playful. "I'm not Uncle Sam. I can at least enforce some peace under my own roof."

"I wish you were Uncle Sam. Or at least President Wilson. Then none of us would have to register tomorrow," Andrew said.

"Be careful what you say," Ernie warned him. "You could go to jail for that kind of talk."

"Wait a moment." Allene's smile disintegrated. "What, are you all registering?"

"Ugh, I wish to God I might. My birthday isn't until November," Ernie said. He seemed disgusted with his own youth.

Andrew nodded but without a mite of enthusiasm. Oh, that damned draft, dropping the age so all her boys would have to register. Next thing, they'd be drafting little twelve-year-olds.

Andrew reached for his hat. "It's getting late. Walk me to the door?" he asked Allene, who assented. He pulled out a cigarette, searching his pocket for a match. Without thinking, Allene retrieved the Wonderliter from her pocket. She realized her mistake when she saw a brief expression of disgust pass over his face. He used it to light his cigarette but kept the lighter in his palm.

When they were far enough away from Jasper, Allene tugged at his sleeve. "Andrew. May I ask a favor?"

"Of course. Anything."

She dropped her gaze to her polished shoes. "I would like for you to be paying Birdie a little less of your kind attention. I know about the groceries."

Andrew's face clouded over. "I don't see an issue. I was simply generous to a family in need. A family, I might add, that you find dear yourself."

Allene's lips were a grim, tight line. "And Birdie—did she thank you?"

"Birdie Dreyer is, and will always be, a lady," Andrew answered, with a hard edge to his voice. He clasped her wrist in his hand, hard enough to emphasize his point but not hard enough to leave a mark. He lowered his voice to a growl. "And we won't speak of this again. I won't have my future wife question me in this manner, not now and not when we are married. Do you understand?"

Allene responded with silence, but it was enough. Andrew bent forward and kissed her cheek, leaving a moist mark. She felt smeared and soiled, and she stepped aside as Andrew opened the door to leave.

"Oh, and this." He lifted the Wonderliter, pinched in his fingers. "A woman doesn't need a cigarette lighter. I suppose you've been lacking a lady's influence in your life for too many years, but Mother will remedy that."

He pocketed the lighter just as Allene's father arrived—they said rushed hellos and good-byes before Mr. Cutter entered the house. Allene was still seething with fury.

"Allene? Why on earth are there so many guests at the house?"

Ernie stood up at attention—he was army ready, for sure. Ernie would swallow a grenade if his superior demanded it. Jasper stood in the presence of Allene's father too, but without the snap-to-attention deference. His spine curved as he crossed his arms, and his mouth pulled into a defiant frown.

"Allene? What is going on?" he demanded again.

Allene regained her composure. "Oh. Ernest and Andrew were here to pay a call. Jasper came to assist with Birdie and Holly Dreyer. They're staying over for a while."

Slowly, he spoke. "Birdie Dreyer. And who? Why on earth, may I ask?"

"May I speak to you in the study, Father?"

Mr. Cutter nearly threw his coat and hat at the old butler before leading Allene down the hallway. She turned at the last moment to give Jasper a panicked look; a toss of her head told him to leave immediately and to take Ernie with him. She caught up with her father in the study and heard the front door shut.

"What's the meaning of all of this? You know how your mother feels about that girl and her mother."

"Birdie's mother has died."

"Hazel Dreyer?" The news froze Father; he seemed to lose focus for a moment as he remembered something that Allene couldn't reach. "Hazel," he repeated. "Hazel is dead?" For someone who hadn't seen her in years, he seemed startlingly affected by the news.

"Yes. She had health problems and was on medication. She died this morning in their apartment. I just couldn't stand the idea of little Holly and her sister staying there alone, especially with the police buzzing about."

"Who is Holly?"

"Hazel's daughter. She's only about four years old. I guess you never met her."

"No, indeed," Mr. Cutter replied, cold as ice. "Allene. Your mother made it clear that Hazel and her children were no longer to be supported by this family."

"Mother isn't here anymore," Allene retorted.

Mr. Cutter went livid. He swept past her, ignoring Lucy's inquisitive face as she passed in the hallway, and shut the office door. It took him a full minute of pacing before he could string together the words to speak.

"How dare you speak so disrespectfully of your mother? As long as she's ill, we'll respect her wishes."

"Is she ill?" Allene gathered a modicum of bravery. "Is she, Father? She won't let me visit. She won't let you visit. She hardly writes to us anymore. And she never looked sick." Allene laughed ruefully. "A few times, she's had her maids write to us for her! And there's never any correspondence from a doctor!"

Allene knew she risked being slapped, but she didn't back down. She thought of Holly's arms around her, and the memory of Hazel's body lying on that threadbare carpet. It was Allene's doing, because she'd let her mother take them out of her life. She'd allowed it all to happen. She'd been too afraid to defy her parents. And inwardly, an oily dark thought—she'd been jealous of Birdie's beauty. At the blossoming age of thirteen, Allene had silently agreed with her mother—she'd been happy to not have such a girl with her all the time.

Allene tried not to let her voice waver. "Mother had some sort of falling-out with Hazel, didn't she?"

"I won't speak ill of your mother," Father said, doggedly repeating himself. But he wouldn't look her in the eye.

"Mother is not here, and I am. And I say Birdie and Holly will remain under this roof. At least until they can find a safer place to stay. It's the Christian thing to do, and you know it. Mother doesn't even need to know. And I will make absolutely sure that they don't inconvenience the staff. You'll barely see them."

Father had turned away to lean heavily on his mahogany desk. Anger had gotten her only so far, so she attempted a different tactic. She put her hand on her father's large one and squeezed.

"Father," Allene said softly, "this—this will make me happy. Truly, it shall. They won't cause a ruffle at all. Birdie is so dear to me. And

Holly needs our help. Birdie's almost like a sister." She added, "Holly, I suppose, too."

At the word *sister*, Mr. Cutter finally turned around. He blinked several times and stared at Allene, as if waiting for her to speak further. He smiled faintly, the effort aging him by a decade. He coughed and rearranged his expression—order, once lost, was back in his mien.

"They may stay until before the wedding. That gives them two months. That is all, do you hear? And then I want them gone. I'll do my best to conceal this from your mother."

Allene dashed forward, grabbed the lapels of his day suit, and tiptoed to kiss his grizzled beard. "Thank you, Father. Thank you so much."

"Very well. Be gone with you."

Allene didn't wait to be told twice. She spun around and exited the room, closing the doors behind her. Jasper was still in the parlor, but Ernie was nowhere to be seen.

"Oh. I thought you left!"

"Nah. I'm harder to get rid of than a cherry stain. Say, I was thinking. About Hazel."

"Aren't we all. It's hard not to," Allene said. "Especially when you consider that someone might have killed her. We should tell the police. Shouldn't we?"

"I can find out if she truly took too much opium or not. Let's not panic before we have information. Maybe she just had a heart attack. The letters could be completely meaningless. Just a prank. But if Hazel's death is no accident, then they've got to be tied to each other."

Allene bit her lip, thinking. Jasper watched her appreciatively. There was something about these moments—thinking, thinking, thinking. He seemed to like her this way, rather than when she put on her coquettish airs. Odd, this boy.

She snapped her fingers. "Let's find out where the medicine came from. Before anyone assumes this is an accidental overdose, we should be sure, right? Maybe something else was mixed in. Shouldn't the druggist have a dispensary record?"

"Yes. Do you remember what was on the label?"

"Smith . . ." Allene tried to dig the name from her memory.

"And Walley. In Brooklyn." He stood up. "She said that Andrew ordered the medicine, but maybe he ordered it wrong? We should check directly, though. I know Smith Walley. It's about five blocks from Birdie's home. Can you leave her for a while?"

"I can't! I've only just come home."

"What about tomorrow? We have to get some answers."

"Tomorrow you're registering for the draft," Allene reminded him.

The color left Jasper's face. He looked awfully lonely, and fear crept into his eyes. "That's right, I am."

From down the corridor, Lucy came by in her polished black shoes. "Miss Allene, I've drawn a bath for you as well." She started when she saw Jasper. "I didn't realize you were still here, Mr. Jones."

"Oh, I'm leaving now."

Lucy withdrew slowly. She seemed reluctant to leave them alone. She was always protective of Allene in a way her mother never had been, nor even Birdie, who was more a friend. As Allene led Jasper to the door, she squeezed his hand and leaned in to whisper, "Tomorrow at three o'clock. I won't let you be alone on such a day. We'll go after you've done your paperwork. I'll meet you at the druggist shop."

"All right," he agreed. The lonely look in his eyes abated. "Thank you."

With that, he was pushed out the door, and he disappeared into the late-afternoon September warmth. As the door closed before her, Allene smiled. Another promised day spent with Jasper or Birdie would always be a good day, even if the apocalypse descended. She knew Jasper would meet her tomorrow, no matter what the consequences.

But before another day went by, there was one other thing she knew for sure.

She would be purchasing another Wonderliter first thing tomorrow.

CHAPTER 18

Jasper had been absent from work since his lunch break nearly six hours before. The laboratories would be locked up soon. It was rush hour now as he made his way home, and the trolleys and trains were packed. Men around him spoke excitedly about registering for the draft tomorrow; Jasper wished he could stuff cotton in his ears. The war was getting in his way. Someone mentioned influenza hitting Camp Devens, near Boston. Too early in the year, Jasper thought. It irked him that everything moved too quickly or too slowly for his taste.

He thought of Hazel lying inside the city morgue. Her eyes would no longer be pinpoints from the morphine. He itched to run his fingers over her file. It would read of how she was found, the wheres, whys that were dull details for the police but not for Jasper. There would be information on Birdie and Holly, and the bottle of laudanum used. Somewhere in that building was that killer bottle of opium.

The memory of Florence's autopsy was fading fast. But now there was Hazel. He was enamored by what Hazel could do for him, even lifeless on that marble table. He could almost smell the caustic soaps and the inescapable essence of human fat gone rancid. He thought of what he needed to do: get paid, apologize to his boss, pay his uncle's mounting bills, snip pieces from Hazel Dreyer's dead body (this time, the autopsy would be official, and he would be there no matter what), climb another rung of the ladder in his department. Not necessarily in that order.

Once inside Bellevue's gate, he jogged to the pathology building and took the stairs two at a time. By the time he reached the laboratories, he was fully winded, and intention sparked and snapped in his eyes. He pulled on the door to Gettler's lab, but it was locked. He shook the door to be sure.

"Damn," Jasper muttered.

"Your mother teach ya to talk like that?"

He turned to see Dr. Gettler in his overcoat, cigar clamped in his mouth and a recent copy of the *Daily Racing Form* in his hand. The man loved to gamble.

"Uh, no sir."

He pointed his cigar at Jasper's head. "That was one helluva lunch hour you took. I've been working longer than you, and I ain't played hooky once yet."

"Well, you see, someone died," Jasper began to explain.

"And the sun rises and sets, what else is new? We had ten bodies come in today to be processed. Two drug out from the East River." He pointed rudely again with that cigar. "And you weren't here."

"Hazel Dreyer came in today."

"To take you out to your extravagant six-hour lunch?"

"No sir. She's my friend's mother. She died earlier today. We think she took too much laudanum."

Gettler's face clouded over. "I see. Accident?"

"I don't think so."

"Suicide?"

Jasper shook his head. "Doubtful."

Dr. Getter fumbled with some keys in his pocket. He walked toward Jasper and pushed him aside to unlock the lab. Dr. Gettler flicked on the suspended lights that cast a bright, warm light over the central table loaded with shelves and laboratory equipment. The faint buzz from one of the bulbs was a comforting welcome.

"Wasn't there another lady who came through here a few weeks ago, one you thought was murdered?" Gettler asked.

Jasper nodded.

"You, boy, need to stop spending so much time with these people. If your friends all end up dead, the police start wondering what's the matter with you." Gettler's tan overcoat was off now, hung lifelessly on a peg. He yanked on his stained lab coat.

"But I'm not guilty," Jasper blurted out, far too swiftly to sound innocent.

"In this business, words don't matter much. You got enough money, you can pay anyone to pipe up an alibi. But this"—he swept his arm around the lab—"tells the truth like nobody can." Gettler stared at him, his eyes bulging out a bit. "Well?"

"Sir?" Jasper hated to look like a fool, but he was too tired to be clever.

"Are you going to get your coat off and get to work? That lady friend of yours is waiting in the morgue, and you're gapin' like a trout catching flies."

Jasper shed his coat and put on a heavy apron he used around the lab. "Thank you, sir! I don't know how to repay you."

Gettler snorted. "Buy me a doughnut tomorrow. Three, actually. The twisty ones with sugar glaze. I like them the best."

Jasper grinned. They rolled up their sleeves and went to work.

Dr. Gettler went painfully by the book. Before they could autopsy, they had to telephone the police station to bring over the paperwork. But now, Jasper could read about the details of the crime scene from another perspective.

> *Found lying on bedroom floor. No signs of trauma to body. No bruising. Apartment in same order as before,*

no signs of forced entry, though door left open. No signs
of burglary or struggle. Daughter corroborates the above.
Empty bottles and glasses of whiskey but appear to be over
twelve hours old. Habitual opium ingestion. Question of
overdose. Medicine bottles taken as evidence for testing.

There were lists of witnesses, mostly the landlady, Birdie, and Holly. Gettler thumbed through the pages. "Hmm. They almost didn't call the ME." He closed the files and put them on the table in front of Jasper, then headed for the door. When Jasper still stood there, staring at the file, Gettler spoke to him more gently (as gently as that ungentle Brooklyn accent could deliver).

"Son. It's one thing to do an autopsy on a Jane Doe. It's another to cut into someone you know. You sure you can handle this?"

Jasper didn't look up. He was thinking of Florence and the sight of his scalpel pressing against her milky-white abdomen. He remembered the sensation in his hands when the violation of metal on flesh occurred, the precise moment when the tip of the blade sliced into her, like an oar in calm water. It had bothered him. He just hadn't known it until right now.

Jasper betrayed nothing. "I can handle it. Let's go."

It was odd to be in the building at night. Not that Jasper wasn't used to it. He used to stay after hours and scrub the dirtied corners of this very building. But he'd felt like a peasant then, someone who was smaller and less consequential than even the wastepaper baskets.

Now, all was different. Over a few short weeks, he'd become an essential member of the medical examiner's department. The sound of Dr. Norris's shoes pacing his office was a comforting heartbeat. Dr. Gettler's curses were poetry. The laboratory fumes and the scent of the Bunsen burners blended into a perfume, repellent and improbably enjoyable. The other chemists and pathologists worked at a feverish pace, and they yelled at Jasper to order this, answer that, fetch those, catalogue these, and cook something down to a syrup of human and chemical sludge that just might reveal how the person had died. Here, he revealed the souls behind the crimes—the real ones, not hidden by suits and smirks and rolls of cash. Here, money and names didn't matter. Right and wrong were dictated by chemical truths.

The city morgue had become intensely alluring, and he couldn't get enough of it.

He was also becoming increasingly rattled by the same things that attracted him. He didn't yet possess the ability to unpack and understand the center of his discomfort. He wanted this, after all. He knew certain details repelled him—like the chewed hangnails and fingernails on a corpse, bitten to the quick just like his own. Or a child's curled eyelashes that reminded him of a porcelain doll of Allene's. Consciously, these things shouldn't matter. He could handle them. He *should* handle them.

He pushed it aside as he always did and followed Dr. Gettler down to the morgue. There, they found Hazel's body on the third table near the door. One of the other bodies, recently fished out of the East River but not recently dead, inhabited the table next to hers. It was putrefying. The odor was worse than dead fish stuffed with feces and fermented amongst garbage on the most humid day of summer. What was worse was an unexpected hint of sweetness. Jasper swallowed hard and put on a poker face.

They looked at Hazel's medicine bottles, which the charge officer had been careful to procure and label. Jasper studied the nearly full bottle that Hazel had likely last drunk from, the same one whose label Allene had torn a corner from.

"Tincture of opium. Usually about a hundred grams of opium per liter." Gettler pointed to Hazel's old, empty bottles. "These are paregoric. Camphorated tincture of opium, four grams per liter. Straight off, she probably mistook one for the other and overdosed. Seen a lot of babies dead this way. They start off colicky, and Ma kills 'em with stomach medicine because they're wailing too much."

Jasper nodded in agreement. Dr. Gettler rolled the tray of autopsy instruments next to Jasper and stepped back. Neither of them moved. Finally, after too long of an uncomfortable moment, Dr. Gettler pointed.

"I want every specimen labeled. Every step of the process documented in her file. We'll need her entire stomach, ligated at both ends to save the contents. Blood samples, urine . . . make special note of the state of her brain." When Jasper still didn't move, he asked, "Haven't you been assisting the staff here on the autopsies?"

"Yes."

"Have you done one yourself?"

"Well." Jasper scratched his head. "Altogether, no. But I've done every step a handful of times with Dr. Samuels on his shifts—"

"But have you done one entirely by yourself?"

"No," Jasper admitted. Only the fully fledged pathologists were responsible for the autopsies, beginning to end, head to toe, dermis to marrow.

"Well. Time to start." Dr. Gettler walked to the door and left Jasper there, agog.

"Sir? But I thought you—"

"I'm a toxicologist, not a pathologist. I'm going to go place my bets. Hopefully it ain't too late. Get the samples. In a few hours, we can really work."

The door shut behind him, and Jasper was alone with what was left of Hazel Dreyer. She was looking, though dead, more like Birdie than he had ever noticed. The same fine, straight nose; the same rosebud lips, though slightly thinner than Birdie's. He swallowed hard and took a deep breath. His hands shook, though he touched nothing but the reeking air about him. He stared at Hazel, and Hazel stared at nothing.

"Hello, Mrs. Dreyer. How did we get here, you and I?" Jasper asked, somewhat politely. He couldn't bear to say anything further in the cavernous morgue, as if his words might insult the corpse. Well, he thought, you're just a body now. You might as well help my career. I'm sorry, but it's my time now.

Hazel didn't respond to his words or his thoughts. So Jasper picked up a scalpel to seek out the answers imprisoned beneath her cold skin. His nose began to run, and he wiped it off on his sleeve. And all the while he worked, he apologized in the silence of his own mind, over and over and over again.

Jasper had tried. He had been able to perform the incisions and inspections of the body organs, but he had failed when it came to sawing the skullcap off. This was how Dr. Gettler (who was rather merry now that his bets were safely placed) found Jasper, past midnight. Sweating, quietly frantic, overwhelmed, and not so delicately traumatized. Gettler stared at him hard and then sighed in sympathy.

Jasper knew what he was thinking: that he had talked the talk, but when it came down to it, he was too young, too inexperienced, and too close to the victim. It had been a mistake to think he could do an autopsy alone, despite his enthusiasm and Gettler's willingness to let him try. Gettler put a sheet over Hazel, then shooed him back upstairs to the lab. Gettler followed, carrying the enameled tray heavily burdened with specimens and numerous glass bottles containing body fluids.

Once he was upstairs, he barked at Jasper, "Go home. Tomorrow's draft registration, ain't it? You don't need to come in."

"No," Jasper said doggedly. He began setting up the usual extraction apparatus in the lab for the samples.

"It was my mistake. You're just a kid. You don't know enough."

"Then teach me," Jasper said, trying not to clink the glassware as he screwed a round-bottom flask into place with a clamp.

"What's the damn rush?"

Jasper wouldn't look at him. He felt the circling of a tighter noose around him as the minutes ticked by. The letters. Florence and Hazel. The bills that were stacked so high on his uncle's desk that they were starting to fall to the floor like inglorious confetti. General Pershing, ever hungry for more doughboys.

He didn't answer Gettler, instead continuing to construct the extraction apparatus. He could feel Gettler staring at him hard. Jasper knew they had something in common. Not on the surface. Jasper was far more handsome, and he knew it. He was taller, with that well-born upbringing he couldn't hide, even when his shoes were so worn the stitching had come undone around the toes. It was something so familiar that he didn't see it until it was painfully obvious. Gettler said it before he could mold it inside his mind.

"Be careful, boy. When you're this thirsty, you can reach for water, or you can reach for gasoline. One will kill ya, but you won't know the difference until it's too late."

A thrum of energy was back inside Jasper's heart; he'd gotten a second wind. Oh, he heard everything that Gettler was saying, but there was nothing like a warning—a locked door, or a restraining arm—that made him feel like pushing harder and lighting some TNT.

"Morphine extraction," Jasper said, as if they'd been discussing it for hours. "We can use the Marmé-Warnecke method or Tauber's. I'm good with either." He looked grimly at Gettler, who sighed. Cut from the same cloth, Jasper thought. Gettler returned his appraisal but instead of appreciation, there was a small dose of awe and fear. Gettler pushed away from the table.

"Fine. Let's get started." He strode toward the chemical supply room, stretching his stiff neck. The last thing Jasper heard him say before disappearing: "Those better be some damn good doughnuts you bring me."

Jasper woke up the next morning, the scent of laboratory chemicals in his hair, visions of Hazel's sliced skin in his mind, and a drumbeat in his ears: morphine, morphine, morphine.

Hazel Dreyer had died of a laudanum overdose. After a long extraction process and the delicate addition of sodium bicarbonate to neutralize the aqueous acid, the white morphine crystals precipitated immediately and in large quantity. The answer was definitive but dragged along the other question: Was it an accident or a poisoning? He would go to work to see what the next step would be with the police—but then he remembered: today was the third draft. No work.

He rubbed his temples. All the comfort in his usual routine—a path to assuaging his ambition—was in limbo today. He felt an odd disconnect from the war and from those who talked incessantly of the Champagne-Marne and the Hundred Days Offensive. It wasn't that he didn't want America to win. He wasn't stupid enough to be unpatriotic out loud; the Espionage Act was a very real threat. But in his heart, fighting on the front was an end with some rather brutal means. Oscar had taught him that much.

He read the casualty list every day, as he'd done since Oscar was first drafted. Even after his brother died, he kept reading them, as if the dead were owed at least that much from him. Thousands of soldiers died every day from sickness, more from combat. Taking a few Krauts down before his own demise was not in his plans.

Uncle Fred was puttering around the kitchen as usual. When Jasper twisted the doorknob to leave, Fred cleared his throat.

"I'm proud of what you're doing," he said.

Jasper grunted. "That assumes I have a choice."

"You do."

"Look. I'm no coward. I can't dodge what's coming to get me." He left and locked the door behind him.

The city was in celebration mode. Banks and shops were closed. Public schools were closed, most being used for registering men. Several shops opened late and closed early to allow their employees to register. Jasper walked a few blocks to his local board office, where a line of men waited. A boy no older than ten handed out flyers to men passing by. Jasper took one. It read "Learn to Kill Huns." He folded it and put it in his pocket without reading another word. Already, dozens of others had lined up behind Jasper.

Most of the men were merry and spoke of heading afterward to one of the nearby hotels, which were providing free drinks for registrants. Mercifully, the wait to the front of the line was short.

A uniformed man standing at a desk glanced at Jasper before picking up a new registration card.

"Are you a citizen of the United States?"

"Yes," Jasper answered.

"Age?"

"Eighteen, sir."

His address, eye color, build, and Uncle Fred's name were written down in curly script.

"Sign here." The registrar pointed.

Jasper did. And then it was over.

"When will we know?" Jasper asked.

"General Crowder will announce the new draftees in the next two weeks. But they'll likely draw leftovers from the June draft first, and the gents nineteen and up from this one. They're still holding off on the youngest ones yet. Sorry, kid. You may have to wait a few more months."

Relief flooded Jasper before dark guilt replaced it. He hardly enjoyed the lighthearted patriotism that surrounded him as he wandered the streets all afternoon. He even went back to Bellevue, only to be told the pathology department had closed early. At some point, he ate a sandwich. And then it was three o'clock, and he was in front of Smith & Walley. The druggist was closed for the day. A waste. But Allene was there, standing wide eyed, watching men clap each other on the back as they walked down the street.

"Well. Is the deed done?" Allene asked. She wasn't smiling as she usually would.

"Yes. I signed my card. I've done my bit."

She threaded her fingers into Jasper's and squeezed. He squeezed back, surprised that his dark feeling receded a touch.

"I can't imagine what it's like, losing a brother to the war," Allene said.

"Then don't."

"Oscar wanted to fight, didn't he?"

"I don't know. I think if someone told him it was proper to jump off the Brooklyn Bridge, he would have done that too. He wasn't too keen on the future."

"So you're not Oscar," she said simply. She looked at the locked door of the drugstore. "They're closed. I guess everyone thinks it a holiday." She shivered. "Keep me company before I go back home?"

Jasper gratefully offered her arm, and they began to walk down the street. They turned left, then right, aimlessly walking the streets of Brooklyn.

"Hazel definitively died of a laudanum overdose. I found out last night," Jasper said, apropos of nothing.

Allene nodded and frowned. She looked around at the celebrating young men and shivered again. Like Jasper, perhaps she saw the walking dead. Which was perhaps why she refused to look him in the eye.

"I don't want to talk about that. Not today. Tell me about something else."

"Like what?" Jasper asked.

"Tell me what your favorite acid is, and I'll tell you my favorite base."

For two hours, they talked about mercury and sulfuric acid, beautiful benzene and basic aldehydes. They spoke of planets and gases and pieces of the universe they would never, ever touch but longed to.

Jasper enjoyed having Allene's arm leaning on him all afternoon. It gave him purpose, at least for now.

CHAPTER 19

Thank goodness Allene had stopped coming to her bedroom.

There was a routine to things, once Birdie settled into the Cutter house. She took off a decadent whole week from work to mourn. It would give her enough time to decide and act on what to do next for her and Holly. Allene told her that her father was giving them two months. "But I'll change that to forever," she'd said firmly. But Birdie wouldn't assume their welcome would last indefinitely. Self-preservation and survival told her to prepare to leave.

But hope told her maybe, just maybe, they might stay.

For the time being, she and Holly were situated in the all-white guest room. Holly decorated it with a piece of broken brick turned into an automobile with chalk-drawn wheels. New copies of *The Theatre* magazine and *Metropolitan* magazine gathered cozily on the nightstand.

During the daytime, Birdie dabbed her eyes while she and Allene whispered about Hazel, about the results from the autopsy, the letters, Florence. They nervously waited for news from Jasper. Birdie verified that lately, Andrew had always done the opium syrup ordering. Birdie's sadness was assuaged by Allene's comfortable chatter.

But at night, the talk would cease. Holly slept like a wrestling monkey, and often Allene volunteered her own bed to the little girl, with

Lucy at the ready in a corner rocking chair. Lucy said she didn't mind at all, and Birdie once again felt the creeping sensation that Lucy enjoyed becoming indispensable to Holly, her, and Allene.

But it couldn't be helped. Birdie slept terribly too. Perhaps it was the oppressive silence of the Upper East Side; perhaps it was sleeping in a house filled with people who knew she didn't belong here. When she and Allene awoke, like the night after the engagement party, their legs were often tangled skin to skin beneath the covers. Birdie would disentangle herself, Allene allowing it reluctantly, and the day would begin.

It became a habit, until it wasn't.

One morning, only a few days after Hazel's death, Birdie opened her heavy lids to see Allene staring at her. Not with concern but something halfway between curiosity and nausea.

"Are you all right, Allene?" Birdie whispered. "Did you sleep badly?"

Allene nodded. "No." She seemed unaware of her idiosyncratic answer. That nauseated expression worsened. Allene's eyes fell to Birdie's chest. She glanced down to see her nightgown drooping over her collarbone and a crescent of upper breast peeking out from beyond the eyelet. Birdie shifted to cover herself. Allene's legs slid like satin on warm marble, one thigh rising ever so slightly higher against Birdie's inner leg. Allene pinched her lips together and then unpinched them, crimson blood filling them to a rosy glow. She moved her head slightly closer to Birdie's, until the oppressive scent of her lavender shampoo was all around.

Birdie hesitated for only seconds, but it seemed a century. She pulled away and sat up. Allene froze and frowned and went pink in the face.

"You don't know what you're doing," Birdie told her. She untangled her legs and withdrew from the covers. "You simply don't." She put on her robe and went to the door. "I'll call for Lucy. Holly will be wanting breakfast."

They didn't speak of it, for there was nothing, really, to speak of. Birdie regretted leaving her with such haste. She couldn't afford to push Allene away, but these were the types of waters that she did not know how to navigate. Allene packaged away the discomfort and twittered on like her usual self. When she paused between quips, Birdie would see it. A momentary expression of panic, as if Allene had become utterly lost within herself. And in a snap, a brilliant smile would replace the dropped-open bottom lip.

On Sunday morning, Birdie woke up alone. Relieved.

Still in bed, she picked up the newspaper. The Saint-Mihiel salient had been taken from the Germans. Two U-boats had been sunk. Thousands of soldiers had been struck with influenza in a camp near Boston. Thousands? It was an unbelievable number, but Boston seemed yet too far away to be of any worry. A new motor bus had been introduced on Fifth Avenue. Pershing had let out the updated list of casualties and dead soldiers.

Killed in action. Killed by accident. Died of disease. Lost at sea. Wounded. Captured. Missing.

There were grand totals that were not so grand. But it was the number of *missing*—3,990—that gave Birdie pause. The idea of being lost to the world, to everyone . . . this haunted her the most of all the sad tidings. She wondered what it would feel like to be a blur. To have the official title of being neither here nor there, alive nor dead.

And then she laughed. She was already neither here nor there, alive nor dead. She had already descended to become a smudge in history, soon to be forgotten. She flipped the pages of the newspaper, ignoring the available rental apartments. Her mother's death had barely earned a single line in the obituaries, squeezed between the Gimbels advert and the business section.

The finality of those few, worthless words unsettled her more than death itself.

Birdie folded the newspaper and tucked it under the plate on her nearly empty breakfast tray. Lucy had brought the tray to her room, expecting that she would prefer to eat with Holly in private this morning.

Lucy was good at her job. Too good. She watched Birdie with careful eyes. For what? Classless remarks or other proof that she didn't belong here? For evidence of the kernel of deep unhappiness that smoldered always within Birdie's heart, that had singed hotter since she'd stepped back into the Cutter house, despite her quiet mien and softly spoken words? At a glance, the maid was compliant, tidy, and deferential. Lucy couldn't change her bronzed skin and dark hair, but she had trimmed away anything else that made her unlike the other hoity-toity maids here. And yet Birdie knew keen intelligence when she saw it. Lucy observed everything and, according to some universal order within her discerning mind, put everything in its rightful place. Including Birdie.

Holly had already washed and dressed, gobbled down her poached egg on toast (Holly's appetite tripled in the presence of grief; Birdie's vanished), and been taken outside by Allene to feed the pigeons. The bag of crumbs went untouched as Holly spent the morning watching motorcars rumble down Fifth Avenue instead. The endless rolling of automobiles was a balm for her little soul.

Birdie dressed slowly before any of the maids could offer to help. The lump on her shin was aching something horrible. Laudanum would be helpful, but Birdie had refused it. Pain washed her vision of all the softness in life and allowed her to see all in distinct detail. Sometimes the details hurt, but reality was something she clung to. No wistful dreams and half-awake longings for her. Not anymore.

Someone knocked on the door.

"Miss Dreyer? There is someone here to see you."

Birdie frowned. "Who is it?" she asked.

"It's Mr. Ernest Fielding, miss."

"I'll be down in a minute." Why on earth would Ernie want to see her? Ernie had never before appeared at the Cutter house asking for Birdie. When they used to play blindman's bluff, Ernie always let the searching fingers of Allene and Jasper find him, and they'd whoop in satisfaction. When Birdie was blindfolded, he never let himself be caught. Despite her beauty, her quietness placed her in the shadows of the quick-tongued and quick-witted Jasper and Allene. In this case, like did not attract like. Ernie needed their brightness to see his own self in better relief.

She dressed herself carefully, arranging her hair in a simple bun. No jewelry, not even appropriate jet, was worn in her mourning. Which was convenient since she owned no jewelry worth wearing.

Downstairs, Ernie sat on an ottoman, staring out the window and watching the few birds flitting around the Cutter garden. In the distance, Esther was picking the ripe peaches from the heavily laden tree. Esther had been enthusiastically collecting cherry, apricot, and peach pits that would be donated to the war effort to make more gas masks. A basket of victory garden corn at her side would likely be cooked down with cream for dinner.

Birdie was at his side before he noticed her.

"Oh!" He stood up. "Hello, Birdie. How are you?"

She smiled. He was so sincere, so kind. Times like this, he earned his name. "Thank you, Ernie." She sat down, and he mirrored her descent to the sofa.

"I heard it was an accident. Is that true?"

"Yes, I believe so. I think Allene and Jasper were going to see if they could find out why it happened."

"Don't the police do that?" He looked worried. The boy cared too much.

"They do, but I think it's become a sort of game to them. Find out why Florence died; find out why Mother died. It keeps them entertained." She gave an insouciant shrug. The truth was the truth. Whether they cared as much about her, she would never be sure.

"They're looking into Florence's death? I thought it was an accident."

"Well—" Oh dear. Had she said too much? She waved her hand. "It's come to nothing, really. Anyway, it was kind of you to come by. You didn't need to."

"I don't mind." For a while he stared out again at the garden. When Birdie began to wonder how long he planned to sit in silence, he turned to say, "You're not wearing black."

Birdie blushed, then wondered: Did he seem . . . disappointed that there wasn't more fanfare surrounding her mother's death? "I don't own any black dresses. My mother had one, but I left it in the apartment." She hesitated. The idea of wearing her mother's black dress to mourn her mother was altogether wrong.

"I see. Well, that's sort of why I'm here."

Birdie cocked her head. "Pardon me?"

"I know you and your sister are staying here with the Cutters. And now you say Jasper's helping to figure out what happened. Well, I want to help too."

"That's kind of you, Ernie, but it's really not—"

"I've talked to my father, and he's granted me permission to help pay for the funeral costs and burial. I spoke to Jasper on the telephone, and he said your mother would be released from the morgue in a day or two. So the services are planned for Wednesday afternoon."

Birdie was speechless. Ernie took the silence as an opportunity to continue.

"I picked out a nice spot in the Evergreens Cemetery. I figure if it's good enough for Florence Waxworth, it's good enough for your family."

"Oh, Ernie—"

"It'll be a graveside service," he interrupted her, as if afraid he wouldn't get all his words out in time. "I . . . I wasn't sure what church you attended, but I figured you would rather have a small affair at the

Evergreens. Oh, and there's this." He pushed a small envelope into her hands. Dumbstruck, she opened it and found several twenty-dollar bills.

"Oh my goodness. What on earth is this for?"

"For a black dress. Don't worry, it's not much. Father and I made a killing on selling some copper-mining stock I was watching." Birdie tried not to frown. Ernie always talked of money and investing at the most unfortunate times. "Anyways, Franklin Simon's store is right down the street on Fifth, and you could pick up outfits there for you and Holly. Maybe even order some mourning rings. It's only proper."

She was used to being the person watching every single penny, buying the three-day-old bread at a discount, working a surfeit of factory hours on weekends to afford the dual apartment. Even with Andrew's help, the survival of her family had stayed on her mind constantly. Her dreams were filled with worn-out shoes and screaming landlords and overpriced tinned beef. And now she was back in the Cutter house, in a room that smelled not of overflowing hallway toilets and dirty bedsheets, but of clean linen and violet water, and all her worries about the funeral had vanished. She bowed her head and began to cry.

"Oh! I'm—golly, no, don't cry!" Ernie patted her back inexpertly, a little too hard. It actually hurt Birdie's tender spine to the point where she had to hold a hand up to stop his jarring comfort.

It took a while for her to control herself. She took Erie's offer of his handkerchief and blotted her eyes. "Thank you. Oh, Ernie. God bless you!"

Ernie smiled back and stood up. "It's the least I could do after—" He stopped talking abruptly, then seemed to compose himself after clearing his throat. She remembered how he'd wept, secret and surreptitious, at Florence's grave. Maybe he felt guilt at having everything, after she had lost so much. Or maybe he was just nice. That made Birdie the most suspicious of all. In her world, all gifts became payments for something, sooner or later.

"It's the least I could do," he repeated with finality.

She purchased the garments that day. Two sober black dresses with simple lace trim were had for only ten and twelve dollars for Holly and her. Hats and gloves were added. It didn't seem right to wear her old clothes for her mother's funeral or at the Cutter house. So Birdie made use of the money and purchased two other dresses for them—day dresses in printed lawn and plain sateen ones for evenings and Sundays. It was still a woefully inadequate wardrobe, but it was a start. For practicality's sake, she purchased new shoes, stockings, corsets, and other undergarments as well.

Under Allene's watchful eye, she didn't dare consider meeting Andrew at the hotel, where an armoire full of lacy underwear awaited her. How funny that yet another gentleman had just bought her underwear. Birdie tried not to think about it. Sometime next week, she should go back to the apartment to fetch the rest of their things. She didn't want to think about that either.

No doubt Allene would be merry teasing her about Ernie's generosity. She didn't bother to order mourning rings. She never liked the idea of wearing a death memorial as jewelry.

On Wednesday, Birdie felt numb dressing in her new, soot-colored finery as they prepared for the funeral. Holly found everything stiff and strange and formal, for she had never been to a funeral before. Countless times, Holly took off her gloves and slid them back on again. Every few minutes, she squeezed Birdie's hand and looked up at her with a questioning expression, as if to say, Am I properly sad? And Birdie would squeeze her hand back and nod.

The Evergreens Cemetery was lush with verdant leaves and deep-green grass trimmed carefully by the caretakers. Fall had yet to turn any trees gold and scarlet. But to Birdie, after being in the city all her life, the green was almost suffocating. Nature was fierce in her efforts to cover the dead with life, rooting them down without mercy and preventing them from haunting the living.

The afternoon was crisp and lovely. It was the kind of afternoon on which her mother used to take her on outings to the menagerie in Central Park, where they'd gawk at the giraffes and bears, never tiring of their exoticism. She swallowed a sniffle and blinked away tears. It would not do to be a puddle of grief next to Holly.

They were flanked by Allene, Jasper, and Andrew. There were no others. When the priest began the simple graveside service, Allene held Birdie's other hand firmly in her own and never wavered in her strength. Tears pooled in her eyes, and she bent forward so they would drop to the grass instead of rolling down her cheeks. She didn't seem to want to leave track marks down her carefully powdered and rouged face. Andrew stood emotionless, paler than usual, with the proper stoicism. He hadn't set his eye on Birdie all day. What a relief. And finally, there was Jasper to his right, beyond Holly. He kept his eyes fixed on the casket, which was a handsome, polished oak with brass and wood handles. Ernie had spared no expense.

Ernie was nowhere to be seen.

She would remember these moments for the rest of her short life, down to the words spoken by the priest. He was an older man of the cloth and had chosen a piece of scripture from Job. His face was dutifully serious, crepe-crinkled eyes half drawn, his gravelly voice scratching over the aphorisms of life and death.

"For I know," he said, "that my Redeemer lives, and at the last he will stand upon the earth. And after my skin has been thus destroyed . . ."

Here he paused to cough a consumptive pebble from his elderly throat, and she could sense that Holly hung on that last word. *Destroyed.*

Her left hand squeezed Birdie's harder, but it wasn't enough. Her other empty hand pawed the void in front of her and to the side, fingertips scraping against Jasper's pant leg. He looked down, ready to swipe away a passing dragonfly or errant gnat, but found Holly's gloved hand instead just as the priest reclaimed his voice.

"And after my skin has been thus destroyed, yet in my flesh I shall see God."

When Holly lifted her face to find the one that matched the strong hand over hers, she saw Jasper. And Jasper, being Jasper, doused her with a brilliant, irreverent grin. She stared artlessly in wonder. It reminded Birdie of when she would stare at the elephants in the park menagerie, wondering how she could scheme to own such a creature and have it all to herself.

Soon, they laid flowers on Hazel's coffin and turned back to the motorcars that would bring them back to Fifth Avenue. Allene took Birdie's arm in hers, so she could lean on her. She felt strong, so much stronger. It was comforting. When they were younger, it was always Allene leaning her well-fed arm on Birdie's lithe one. They walked too slowly for Holly, whose idle legs yearned for a good shaking out. She tugged at Birdie's hand, and it pained her.

"I'll go ahead with her. Take your time," Jasper said.

Birdie nodded. "Thank you."

"Of course." He and Holly swung their hands back and forth, a lopsided jumping rope with no jumper. Once at the top of the hill, Holly squatted to examine the spokes on the car tires. When Birdie caught up to them, she rested by Jasper. The hill was steep, and she was out of breath. Allene went to thank the priest.

"She's a rare girl, Holly is." He smiled down at her, and Holly beamed back a grin.

"Can I have an egg cream?" she asked. Holly was so good at twisting people around her fingers, particularly where sugar was involved.

"Whatever you want, my girl. Anytime, anywhere." When Birdie closed her eyes to try to calm her fluttering heart after the tiring walk, Jasper leaned closer and dropped the timbre of his voice. "You know, Birdie, you really are one of the most beautiful orphans I've ever laid eyes on."

She smiled at the compliment, but it was a smile born of granite and ice.

"Yes," she replied. She swelled her breath. "I am lovely. And tragic. But the truth is, Jasper Jones, it's terribly inconvenient to be me, and somehow I doubt you tolerate inconveniences in your life." She opened her eyes and stared at Jasper. "And one more thing. You're a young man, and there's a war across the ocean ready to eat you alive any day now. Don't you dare make promises to my sister you can't keep. Lie to me all you want. I'm used to it. But not to Holly. Never to Holly."

Jasper was speechless. Allene sent the priest off, then wiped her hands on her dress, as if to banish the last vestiges of funerary sadness. Holly clapped with glee when Dawlish turned the crank to start the car.

"Shall we go?" Allene said in a voice a mite too chipper for the day.

As they drew away in the rumbling vehicle, the priest raised his hand in a mortal good-bye and sober blessing. Birdie looked backward through the rear window of the Daimler. It would be a long time before she and Holly would be able to come back to the Evergreens and pay homage to her mother here. So she printed the image in her memory as best as she could.

Only one thing marred Birdie's last view of the rolling greens and stately tombstones and obelisks. In the distance, by the mound of soil and staring into the six-foot-deep resting place of Hazel Dreyer—beautiful, elegant, guiltless, and used—stood Ernie, who had emerged out of the shadows of poplars to stand at the grave alone.

CHAPTER 20

It was a lovely funeral. As lovely as they get, mused Allene.

None of that business with hordes of people who hardly knew the dearly departed or maybe were even secretly happy to be rid of them. Funerals should be between a single person (dead) and a single person (alive) and ought to involve a discussion that no one else should hear. Should she ever be granted the permission, Allene would certainly vote on that.

But sad as it was, she was thankful Hazel was dead. After all, her death had brought Birdie firmly back into her life. Now, Allene had more purpose than ever. Of course she would be married soon enough, and Andrew would never tolerate her traipsing about looking for murderers and spending time with such inferior friends. But for now it was manna and nectar, and she was still starving for it all.

It was Friday morning, two days after the funeral, and she and Jasper had made a pact to return to the Brooklyn druggist to find out how Hazel had ended up with laudanum instead of paregoric. Allene walked hurriedly from the elevated train down Flatbush Avenue toward the shop. For bravery she clutched a nugget of cold iron in her hand. It was a souvenir from a thermite reaction she'd done yesterday behind the kitchen, when Father had been out for business. She'd craved a little experiment, particularly after her father's disapproving look when she'd returned from the funeral.

Iron released from an oxide and ignited by pure aluminum. A simple reaction, but soothing nonetheless. The iron left a tang of molecular coating on her fingertips that she almost preferred to perfume. She put the nugget back in her pocket, where it clanked against her new Wonderliter.

Telephone lines marred the sky above her, following the path of the avenue. People walked so much faster than Allene, but she endeavored to keep up. There was an urgency here that was missing on Fifth Avenue. It was the pace of the working. These people had a purpose in their lives, hurrying them along. Allene couldn't remember the last time she'd hurried for anything or anybody. Today was a marked change.

She was early for her meeting with Jasper. On the train, she'd listened to passengers talking of the Germans being slaughtered in counterattacks. Influenza had taken hundreds in Boston. The Spanish grippe was rumored to also be sinking its claws in parts of Brooklyn and the Bronx. Someone had coughed, and Allene had turned her shoulder away. Surely it wouldn't get that bad. Before long it would all blow over, and the city's worry would evaporate with it. In the meantime, she was planning on using the trolley and subway soon, to explore parts of Manhattan beyond the confines of Dawlish's chauffeuring. She planned to make the most of the two months until the wedding.

Smith & Walley was soon before her. Jasper leaned next to the door, smoking a cigarette. His shirt and jacket were crumpled, and his hair was mussed under his newsboy cap. He resembled none of the fine-bred Joneses of yore, and she wondered if hard living could sour blue bloods after only four years.

She glanced inside the store window. A man in an apron behind the counter eyed Jasper suspiciously.

"Well. Good morning," Allene said.

"Maybe for you," he said. There was a waspish tone to his voice. His eyes were bloodshot and lids puffy, as if he'd been out drinking all night long. "I was working a night shift so I could get off to be here." But he seemed more off key than just tired. And then she remembered the other chatter on the El about the morning's headlines—Crowder had summoned more men from the draft.

"Oh, Jasper. Please tell me you're not heading for the cantonments."

He exhaled and dropped his cigarette, crushing it viciously under his heel. "I'm not." He seemed relieved, yet he didn't seem happy. "They're sending mostly boys nineteen and older and the leftover boys from the two earlier drafts. Lucky me."

"I'm so glad!" Allene ignored decorum and embraced Jasper quickly. Oh, but if only his youthful, slim frame could stay in one piece after all. "I wouldn't want you to have Oscar's fate."

"Oscar and I would never have had the same fate. He was lost before the army, and if he were alive, he'd still be lost."

"And you have everything figured out."

"If I did, would I be here?" He squinted at her. The morning sun was in his eyes. "What about Andrew and Ernie?"

"Andrew had a medical release. One of his legs is slightly shorter than the other."

"Adonis is imperfect? Stop the presses."

Allene ignored him. "And Ernie isn't quite eighteen yet. So, if the peace talks don't go anywhere, you both may be up again in a few months."

Jasper stared past her head at a Red Cross volunteer heading their way with a sheaf of flyers. "Well. Are we going in or talking all morning about Pershing's never-ending appetite for soldiers?"

Allene sighed. He was pushing away the conversation the way he always pushed away anything having to do with Oscar. She remembered him from so many years ago. He had been taller than Jasper, but a thin and watered-down version of his younger, stronger, vivid brother. His limpid mood had repelled Allene—she'd found him utterly unattract-ive. Jasper seemed to have enough ambition for the both of them—even though Oscar was buried somewhere in Suffolk County courtesy of the army.

Jasper reached for the door, but Allene held him back.

"Wait." She drew him away toward her and shook his lapels out, ironing them down with her hands. She yanked off his cap and raked her fingers through his hair, settling it down until the waves were some-what more tamed. It gave her an excuse to touch his soft hair.

"You're grooming me? Am I a dog?" Jasper said.

"Don't be silly." She straightened his collar and gave him a peck on the cheek, which made Jasper's eyes sparkle. "There. Now you look more alive."

"Nothing like a pretty girl to wake a boy from the dead." He tried on a smile, and it seemed to fit well. "How are Birdie and Holly getting along?"

"All right. They had a quiet day after the funeral. Birdie went back to work at the factory this morning, though I told her not to. I couldn't believe it. She wouldn't listen." She had told Birdie not to trouble herself about expenses, but off she went at seven o'clock anyway. It would be such a long commute, but she wouldn't listen to reason. When Allene had pressed her again, she said with practicality, "Allene, there's a war going on."

Jasper said, "Well, some people have to make their own way in the world, Allene." He thought for a minute. "Whether they want to or not."

It was a stab at her and her family, she knew. Allene chose to tuck away the comment and consider it later when she could pout in privacy.

"Anyway," Allene said, sweeping away her dismay, "let's go in."

Jasper held the door for Allene. Once inside, her posture changed. She threw her shoulders back, lifted her chin, arched her eyebrows just so. The clerk behind the counter straightened up at attention. He was young, only a few years older than she. His hair was very dark, almost black, but he had that pale Irish skin that made the few freckles on his cheeks look like he'd been sprayed with a mist of brown ink.

Behind him, nostrums lined the shelves. There were rows of blue and brown bottles, lidded jars, and paper packages with tight printing and scrolls with the proprietary Smith & Walley script on each one.

"May I help you?" the clerk asked.

"Yes. I'm looking into a prescription for a friend. Apparently, she received the wrong one, and I'd like to see the records so we may find out where the mistake happened."

The boy's eyes went round, and he clamped his lips shut. Allene and Jasper exchanged looks.

"It's Hazel Dreyer," Allene said. "A dear friend of mine."

"But she's dead," the boy blurted. Once again his eyes bulged, and he put his hand over his mouth before adding, "Oh, I'm sorry. You did know that, didn't you? She's the one who got the wrong prescription and died. The dosage was off, apparently. A terrible mistake. The police asked us all about it."

"Yes, that's the one. Terrible tragedy." Allene leaned over. Her rose perfume scented the air about her like a floral halo, and the boy's nose flared in the presence of so much femininity. "May we see your records? We've been sent by Mrs. Dreyer's daughter to find out how this happened."

"Well—we have one ledger, where we write down the prescriptions— it was misplaced."

"Misplaced?" Jasper asked incredulously. "It's your only one. How could you lose it?"

"I don't know what happened to it. Mr. Walley is going to get a new book with carbon copies, so we have a duplicate from now on."

The missing ledger certainly sounded suspicious. "So all your recent records are gone."

"Yes ma'am."

Two gentlemen and a woman with her baby soon came into the store. The clerk left Allene and Jasper to wait on them.

"Whatever happened to the bottles the police collected?" Allene whispered. "Did they test them?"

"Yes. The bottle of laudanum was certainly too strong for Hazel, even if she was a habitual user of paregoric."

"Didn't her body look . . . sick? Was there anything else?"

The questions seemed to flood Jasper at once; a distinct expression of discomfort filled his face. "She . . . her brain was engorged with blood." He blinked a few times, as if trying to remove a vision from his head. "It was classic for an opium poisoning, but . . ." He seemed unsure.

"What is it?"

"I don't know. After all, it's one thing to give a high dose of opium to someone like you or me. It'd knock us flat," he said, snapping his fingers for emphasis. "But Birdie's mother used it for years. I'm sure there were times when she took a little extra, you know, to sleep or for a particularly bad day. A wrong dose, even of the concentrated kind, should have maybe knocked her out for a day or two, but killed her? Doubtful. Which means she took a huge dose of the laudanum. Far too much."

"Was anyone else in your office suspicious?" Allene asked.

"Yes and no. It's a pretty straightforward case. No one obvious wanted Hazel dead. She has dependent children and no life-insurance policy. But then again, there's the letter. 'You're welcome'? It seems like someone might be killing people but covering their tracks so they're not implicated—and at the same time telling us, as if they've done us a favor. But who could that be? I'm afraid we've hit another dead end here."

"Not entirely dead." Allene sidled up to the clerk, who was helping the patrons. He seemed nervous and annoyed that Jasper and Allene were still in the store. "Say, who was the pharmacist who filled the bottle for Hazel Dreyer? Do you know?"

"No," he said, and turned back to the customers. His *no* was clipped and abrupt. He was a horrible liar.

"We need to know," Jasper insisted.

"I am busy helping these customers. I believe I've answered all your questions. And you are not the police." His neatly shaven upper lip was shiny. He was sweating now.

Allene circled around the desk to where the clerk was standing. The customers raised their eyebrows and watched, while the clerk pointed and babbled.

"You're not allowed—ma'am, you need to go—I'm busy—"

Allene smiled sweetly and marched right up to him. She spoke loud enough for only the clerk to hear.

"I don't think the other customers would like to know that one of your regulars died of an accidental poisoning because of your store's carelessness. Tell us who the pharmacist was, and we'll leave." She smiled again. "Please."

The clerk went positively sheet white. "I can't."

"Why not?"

"Because I'm not to tell."

"Or you'll lose your job?"

"No."

"You don't want this person to get in trouble. Is that it?" Allene cooed.

The clerk nodded mutely. The customers drained out through the door, no longer interested in the drama that couldn't be heard and wasn't as entertaining as a Charlie Chaplin movie.

"Is he family?" Jasper asked him. The clerk shook his head. "Friend?" he tried again.

"Yes. No. Yes," the poor clerk babbled.

Allene crossed her arms, a tiny smile on her lips. She understood. There was no other explanation for trying to protect someone who didn't fit into any proper category.

"It's all right," Allene whispered. Sympathy transformed her face. A useful look. "Truly, we aren't looking to have your . . . *special friend* fired. We only want to speak to him."

After a stare down of only ten seconds, misery suffused his features. "Charles Sweeney. He lives south of Prospect Park. But he already got fired by Mr. Smith. He'd only been a pharmacist for a year. I think he was glad to leave," the clerk admitted, before imploring Allene, "Please, ma'am. He's a good person. It was an honest mistake. There are so many opium tinctures, and so many recipes for compounding. He said he thinks he dispensed the wrong one. He meant no harm, honest!"

Jasper touched Allene's arm, and she backed away. They came together and nodded to each other. Perhaps it was his look of desperation and wrung hands, but she felt like they'd squeezed every ounce of truth out of this poor boy.

"Very well. And have the police already questioned him?"

"Thoroughly, ma'am. But they don't know about . . . me and him. Please leave him be. He never even liked working as a pharmacist. His pa made him do it. He oughtn't go to jail over a mistake."

"I understand," Allene said. She turned to Jasper. "Let's go."

<hr>

Pretending that Dr. Norris requested it from the charge officer, Jasper was able to obtain the interview notes on a certain Charles M. Sweeney, former pharmacist and now unemployed inhabitant of Kensington, south of Prospect Park. The next day, Allene went alone because Jasper could no longer take daytime hours off for their intrepid investigations. She made sure Dawlish dropped off Birdie at the factory doors first (the commute was far longer now, and Allene insisted). Birdie had taken the mysterious letters with her, packaged carefully in an envelope by Allene. She said she'd try to stop by the handwriting specialist during her lunch hour. Allene was irritated that Birdie didn't want to bring her along for the analysis, but Birdie put her foot down.

"Be reasonable. He's a shy and private man, and he'll be embarrassed that I'm even there. If I bring a stranger, he may refuse to help us." So Allene agreed.

When Dawlish parked on the corner of Flatbush and Church, he reached for his door.

"No," Allene said. "I'm not getting out. Just watching."

"Excuse me, miss?"

"Hold on—there." She peered from the shadows of the motorcar. A young man with a perfectly waxed mustache exited a building. He was wearing a crisp plaid jacket, pearl-gray gloves, and perfectly tailored trousers that were becoming to his tall frame. Allene popped her head out the motorcar window and yelled "Sweeney!" before ducking back inside.

The young man spun around, startled, searching for the origin of the exclamation. In comparison, others on the sidewalk looked benignly around. That must be him, Allen thought. Hand on a mother-of-pearl-topped cane, he shrugged after a few moments and strode down the street with a slight limp. Probably escaped the draft, this one. He whistled, ignoring the newsies on the corner with their bound newspapers, trying to hawk the day's headlines.

Hmm. For an out-of-work, young pharmacist, he sure seemed happy and well dressed, especially for this part of Brooklyn. She didn't even have to question him to know that someone had paid him handsomely. Perhaps to make a purposeful mistake?

Dawlish seemed nearly apoplectic at her brazenness. "Miss? Are you well?"

"Very. Let's go home," she told him. "I've seen plenty."

Allene would ask Jasper in the ensuing days and comb the newspapers, but the police seemed to have no intention of arresting anybody over Hazel's death. She would have discussed it with Birdie, but of course Birdie wanted nothing to do with the subject. Birdie came to her after a late day of work at the factory and pushed the letters back into Allene's hands.

"It's what we thought," she said. "The letters are all written by the same person. Right-handed, and someone with a good education. Same ink, same paper, same writing instrument."

"You're sure he's sure?" Allene asked.

"Yes. He was a handwriting analyst for the police department. Used a special magnifying glass and everything."

"What was his name?"

"He made me promise I wouldn't tell anyone his name. He was also rather shaken up about Mother's death." By now, Birdie was fully red in the face from shame. The whole encounter must have been humiliating for both of them.

Allene rubbed her chin. "Who? Who would have killed your mother? Did she have enemies?"

"Oh, Allene. You're really asking me that question?" Birdie said, her red face now white.

Allene stared for a moment, not understanding. "Oh."

Birdie's shoulders slumped. "I suppose one of Mother's clients could have done it. Maybe they got jealous or something."

"Can you find out if she wrote down a schedule of her clients? Maybe there's a pattern worth poring over."

"Yes. She did, but the police have her diary. Maybe Jasper can procure it for us. But how would any of that tie to Florence's death?"

"I don't know."

Allene couldn't help but feel she was skipping stones on a lake, and the lake was this living, sleeping, vicious creature lying in wait to rise up and swallow them one by one. And somewhere beyond the very real, very earthly world she stood in, she got the distinct sensation that Florence was laughing at them all.

CHAPTER 21

October 4, 1918

The air in October was different. In the evenings, it haunted Jasper as he walked home from the city morgue. Sometimes it swept over his head like a scythe missing its mark. Sometimes it skimmed his collar, touching his neck where the blood pulsed, as if checking that he was still alive.

He strode through the October day that hadn't yet decided whether to be a preview of fall or a bit of tired, leftover summer. He, however, was tired. So tired. As he walked past the tenements and stores, there were posters everywhere that pleaded with citizens to cover their mouths when sneezing and coughing. Signs on every street corner in Yiddish, English, and Italian begged people not to spit and warned they would be fined if they did. The scent of cooked onions, reportedly an influenza repellent, oozed out of kitchen windows. Spanish influenza had landed in New York City, and what had started as a small ripple of people falling ill toward the end of September had swelled to a thousand new cases per day.

It was like no other influenza he'd seen in his short life. This one could kill in a matter of hours, only just after symptoms appeared. The sheer numbers had been overwhelming Boston and Philadelphia to the point where mass graves were becoming the norm. The Bellevue morgue was overrun, and bodies were being shunted directly to cemeteries in the outer boroughs with a swiftness that revealed the terror of infection. He himself was either lucky or not susceptible despite being around so many of the sick. He'd gotten over a bout of the grippe in the spring, just after his graduation. He wondered if it had protected him somehow. But it didn't halt his fear.

Something was different. This scourge was an insatiable monster, hungrier and more lethal than anyone was prepared for, and especially deadly for young adults. Jasper saw white gauze masks on passersby. There were rumors that a few of the nurses in the hospital had been kidnapped by families to care for their sick. When he left the entrance gate of Bellevue, women would flock to him, begging him for a house call for a sick family member. They'd let go once he explained he wasn't a doctor.

It troubled Jasper. After all, it might be another year before he began medical school, and even then, he would only be able to do things like point out the difference between the sartorius muscle and the gracilis. It troubled him because he preferred to be around corpses, who asked nothing of him but the truth, and yet their reminder of time's finality made him want to peel his skin off and flee. In the morgue, he found peace and torture.

In his apartment, the kitchen light was on, as it was wont to be. Three letters sat on the brown bureau by the front door. Two had Allene's fancy script, and a small one was from Birdie. He didn't know how long they'd been there. There had been a time in his life when he had eagerly waited for mail. Then he had stopped looking for reasons of self-preservation. Now he glanced at the envelopes, unaware that he was smiling for the first time that day. He would read them later tonight.

His uncle came out of the kitchen, foggy eyed and smelling like a brewery. He'd been testing the results of his experiments today, as always. Jasper noticed that his uncle's hands were controlled in their movements. Nothing oiled away his shakes like alcohol. Only in the mornings was he sober, and then his hands would tremble so much that it wasn't long before he reached for wine, rum, gin, or one of his more potent distillates.

"You'rrrrre back early," his uncle slurred.

"Not really. It's almost seven o'clock."

"Is it?" He reached over and poked the letters on the bureau. "You shouldn't read them. You should stay out of those girls' lives. Love letters are bad for the heart." Though the word sounded like *harrrrr*. He sat down on two cases of whiskey and reached for one of the bottles nestled in the straw.

"You know, you don't need to hoard so much liquor," Jasper snapped. "One match and this whole apartment goes up in flames."

"Then stop smoking," his uncle said, prying the cap off the new bottle. He struggled on, but Jasper made no move to help him. He might give up and just go to sleep.

"The Volstead Act is going to die," Jasper said, exasperated. "They won't outlaw liquor. Only fourteen states have ratified the amendment. They'll never get the thirty-six they need."

"You're a pessimist. I'm a preparer." Tiny globules of spit flew off his lower lip with every *p*. He got up off the liquor cases, his arthritic knee making a crunchy sound as it unbent. Jasper took the three letters but stopped before opening them. The bureau was uncharacteristically clean. Usually it was littered with bills, but now the brass receipt holder was empty, a lone spire in the middle of the desk.

"Uncle Fred, where are all the bills?"

The old man paused in the doorway. Without turning around, he said, "They've been paid."

"With what? We already spent my last paycheck on groceries. We had at least four others I was going to try to get extensions on."

"I had money put by."

Jasper went to the kitchen, where a pail of trash was heavy with glass containers. He pulled out bottle after bottle before he spied the wadded-up bills buried beneath them. Fist full, he marched back to the front room, where his uncle was leaning against the wall, eyes closed.

"Uncle Fred, throwing them away won't make them go away. We'll get evicted. We've already lost credit at half a dozen stores."

"I tell you, I've paid them!" The vehemence of his words made him cough and shudder, but Jasper didn't stop.

"I don't believe you. I know for a fact that your bank account was empty two weeks ago."

"Now, son . . ."

"Don't call me that!" Jasper snapped. "I got a better job, and most of it goes to you drinking all the hours away and squirreling away booze so you can sell it on the black market or just stay drunk. I can't afford to have you get me arrested. You throw away unpaid bills like they're cigarette butts, and you're an embarrassment."

"What about you? You're no angel either." He waggled his finger at Jasper. "Oh, I see you. So hell-bent on getting ahead, you'd step on anyone to do it. Even those pretty girls you're so keen on. You can't have everything you want!" His eyes were wide, and red crept into the edges of his eyes, whether from emotion or spirits, Jasper didn't know. His hands were shaking, but this time it wasn't from lack of drink.

Jasper could barely speak anymore. He thought of how much money he tried to save, and how it was always getting spent on rent and food. It was never enough. He'd never rise up higher in the medical examiner's department without a proper degree and training. What was more, Fred had made it clear he didn't want Jasper anywhere near Birdie and Allene.

When he was newly orphaned, his uncle had meant family and shelter. He had meant belonging somewhere when his friends would no longer have him. But now, his uncle's feckless existence ate away at Jasper's own future, like rain corroding a thinning iron roof.

He reached for the door and stuffed the letters in his pocket. "I'm going out for supper." He slammed the door behind him, hoping it didn't break like everything else in the apartment. The dishes were chipped, the bedspread had a worn hole, sweaters were moth eaten, buttons were missing from jackets. He remembered a time when his clothes were carefully pressed, his meals plated on Wedgwood china and water drunk from Hawkes crystal goblets. God, that was a thousand years ago.

The landlady would come out looking for the rent and find none, so he hurried down the stairwell as silently as possible to bypass her listening ear.

On second thought, maybe he shouldn't. He stopped off at the first apartment nearest to the entrance and knocked. The landlady answered—a shrewd Polish lady with puckered, thin lips. Her blue eyes were bright and watchful. A few wisps of tired blonde hair had escaped the mercilessly tight bun on her head.

"*Tak?* What is it?"

"Can you give my uncle a message? I have to go to a friend's house, and I'll be back tomorrow night."

"*Dlaczego?* Go to tell him yourself. I am not messenger! You haf good legs."

"I'm in a big hurry. *Proszę?*" Jasper smiled. He knew very little of the language, but it worked magic on the lady of the house, particularly when they were late with the rent. When he had first moved in, Jasper earned pennies by running errands for her. He had a quick ear, and her Polish chatter stuck. She reached up to grab Jasper's ear and lightly slap his cheek. She murmured something endearing and garbled in her mother tongue. It sounded like she was calling him a baby frog or some such.

"*Dziękuję,*" he thanked her. For good measure, he added, "I'll pay rent when I get next week's paycheck. I promise."

The landlady raised her hand and swept it through the air. "Your uncle paid. But bring next month early. Goot, goot!"

Wait a moment. He *had* paid? With what money? His uncle had some set by when they first began living together, before he'd lost his old job at the hospital. That cache of money was long since dry. Perhaps liquor prices were already going up, and Fred was making a profit on his kitchen experiments? Impossible. His uncle never left the apartment, not without the disastrous consequence of an incapacitating nervous fit. And they'd had no visitors. The landlady remarked on every person that came by—including that fateful day when Allene and Birdie had visited. *Ach, ładna dziewczyna i bogata pani,* she'd said admiringly. *Ah, the pretty girl and the rich lady.* But all week and just now, she'd mentioned no visitors.

Jasper didn't understand how Fred was paying, but he wasn't ready to go back upstairs and unravel the truth. His temper still flared too hot.

He exited into the night air, hungry and exhausted, with guilt nipping at that soft area of his belly beneath his ribs. In his pocket were the three letters. He drew them out, feeling the crispness under his fingers and anticipating Allene's wit and Birdie's quiet, sweet reflections.

It had been weeks since Hazel Dreyer's death. He'd managed to borrow Hazel's small diary from the police, but the names of her clients were scribbled in code—*G-S, S-R, P-A*. No addresses, no angry cross outs or torn-out pages. Useless. Birdie had recalled that Hazel had never acted as if she'd had jealous lovers, never seemed to fear for her life. But one revelation was hard to unsee—Birdie's and Holly's lives were infinitely better now that Hazel was buried in the Evergreens.

He tucked the letters away, opting instead for the real thing.

Perhaps it was time for a visit.

⟶

It was too late for a social call, but Jasper didn't consider this until he stood shivering before the Cutter house. The lights were bright inside and illuminated the street with rectangles of gold, luring him closer.

Well, he'd spent a fare to get here, so he reached for the great brass knocker anyway. As soon as the elderly butler opened the door, he smelled a fire burning in the hearth and something sweeter, like taffy. He was led into the main sitting room, where Holly sat by the fire, playing with a doll and a wooden truck. Allene, Birdie, and Andrew were at a small Queen Anne table playing a card game. Allene had hooked Birdie's arm in her own, so that their heads were touching while they played cards.

Only Holly saw him at first. She jumped up from her station near the fire and shouted, "It's Jasper!"

The others looked up, and Andrew stood to receive him. Birdie and Allene both smiled, but blandly, as if dampening their true sentiments in Andrew's presence.

"Hello, Holly. I thought it was time to come by for a visit."

Her hand quickly found his, and he couldn't help but notice Birdie's strained expression. Holly didn't notice, only stamping the floor in complaint.

"You said you would visit sooner, and it's been days and days and days and—"

"Holly." Birdie cut her off. "Jasper has been very busy, I'm sure."

"I have." He strode over to the card table, gently extricating his hand from Holly's sticky one. Andrew stood to shake his hand. He was looking a touch thinner than before, which, unfortunately for Jasper, made him seem inches taller and more lordly. "Andrew. How are you?"

"Been better."

Allene tsked. "Andrew had to fire their cook after she made a marvelously bad roast beef. Poor Andrew was quite wrung out."

"I'm fine," Andrew said, irritated. He gestured to the empty fourth seat. "Please, join us. We're playing pinochle."

"Isn't that a Kraut game? How terribly unpatriotic of you all."

"Sit," Allene ordered, eyes sparkling. "So what brings you here on a Friday evening?"

He smiled, feeling foolish, and had nothing to say. Birdie and Allene were dressed in frocks of gauzy femininity, Andrew in a simple but polished suit. Even Holly was wearing a Cutter classic, a white dress with a blue sash around her waist. The only person who didn't belong was him. Jasper knew his trousers were frayed at the hem because they were Oscar's old pair, and they were too long and got caught under his muddy heels. His shirt needed a darning at the elbows.

He thought of his uncle and didn't wish to return to that mess, and realized that this was the only other place he could go. And of course, he shouldn't be here either.

"Where's your pop?" he asked Allene.

"Resting upstairs. He has a cold, but we won't take any chances that it might turn into influenza or pneumonia. He's to stay in bed for a few days."

Jasper's eyes flicked upward, as if he could espy the microbial truth through the ceiling. He slipped his hands into his pockets, fingering the wad of envelopes. "I received your letters, but I figured I might as well skip the reading and slip you an earful in person. It saves me the postage, doesn't it?"

"My letter!" Holly rushed over and grabbed the three envelopes that Jasper was now holding in his hands. She dragged Jasper to sit on a sofa next to her and riffled through them. "I read it."

"This isn't how the mail works, you know," Birdie commented. Even when she was scolding, she was exquisite. But like Andrew, she seemed thinner. Allene must be getting some swell eats off her companions' gilded china. Her figure was as fine as ever.

"It's also from ten days ago. You ought to have *replied* by now," Allene added.

"So much fuss over a few letters. Maybe I should read them aloud?" Andrew asked, standing and heading toward Jasper.

Allene stood abruptly. "Now, don't be silly, Andrew. They're tiresome tirades on a bunch of busy nothings."

"Like I said, so much fuss." He bent to kiss Allene on the cheek. "I ought to be going anyway. I have to wake up early tomorrow for the committee chair meeting. Maybe you could send a few letters to your devoted fiancé once in a while, hmm?"

"Oh, stuff and nonsense, Andrew. You visit every evening!"

"And to think, in one month we'll be in our own house. You can leave me letters by my breakfast silverware."

"As you wish, dear," she said, but the playfulness had crept out of her voice.

"Which reminds me. Mother tells me that you've been late in speaking to the band and florist."

"I'll get to it soon," Allene said. She strode out of the room to accompany Andrew to the door.

When she returned, Holly was still busy reading her letter to Jasper, who was pleasantly lost in the charm of her lisps and mispronunciations.

"I am . . . looming . . . leaning . . . *learning* . . . how to call-tie-vate . . . a rosebush . . . but it pricks me every day."

"Cultivate," Birdie corrected her.

Holly put the letter down, flummoxed. "I said that."

"Of course you did," Jasper agreed, before hiding a smile.

"Holly, it's bedtime," Birdie announced, gathering Holly's toys and tucking them under her arm.

"Do you have to be up early for work too?" Jasper asked.

"But tomorrow is Saturday," Allene complained.

"I work on Saturdays," Jasper said defensively.

Birdie exchanged glances with Allene. Allene answered for her.

"Well, Birdie is taking some time off from work."

"No, Allene, I'm not," Birdie began.

"But you don't need the money. You're here."

"Not forever. I'm not here forever." She was staring into the darkness out the window, but when Jasper followed her glance, he saw nothing. He thought of his uncle, alone in his apartment, feeling misused

209

and abandoned. He ought to go back home, but the magnetic charm of Birdie and Allene kept his feet in place. Why was it that when he was in their presence, he eventually felt all the imperfections and tarnishes in his life buffed away?

Allene was still arguing with Birdie. "You shouldn't. All those women working together? You'll catch the grippe! It isn't safe."

Birdie laughed. "I'm not going to die from influenza."

As if on point, Jasper coughed. They all stared at him.

"It's a tickle! It's nothing. I feel fine. I already had the flu last spring. Anyway, it's time to read Allene's letter—"

"Which is the oddest reason to call on your friends, Jasper." But Allene seemed pleased that he wanted to read it, even in her presence. "Here, I'll do you the favor and read it myself. It'll be like you're inside my head."

"Now there's a place I've never been. Add that to Paris, Belgium, Japan, and Coney Island."

She whacked his sleeve, and Holly trotted over with the envelopes. When Allene looked at them, she said, "Why, Jasper, this one isn't mine." She handed him the extra envelope.

He studied it curiously. It was addressed in an elegant script, which he'd thought was Allene's but, in fact, was different. There was no return address. His skin flushed with anticipation as he tore the envelope open and unfolded the single sheet inside. His mouth went dry, and his hand shook.

Birdie and Allene asked him, almost simultaneously, "What's the matter?"

He said nothing, only showed them the words on the page.

You're welcome.

CHAPTER 22

The look on Jasper's face was more than just fear. It was regret, so deeply etched that he seemed ravaged by time in an instant. Birdie had never witnessed anything like it, and it frightened her.

"It arrived today," Jasper said. "I should . . . I've got to go home."

"Lucy," Birdie called. The maid was at the ready in the hallway. "Please put Holly to bed." She stooped down to hug her. "I'll be back later. Be a good girl?"

Holly looked at Jasper's contorted face with wonder and shock, and obeyed Birdie without a word.

"Allene, I need to borrow your driver," Jasper finally managed to say. "It'll be the fastest way to get there."

"You think your uncle is in danger?"

He waved the letter. "One was found when Florence died. One showed up when Hazel died. This one was sent to me." He wiped his mouth with the back of his hand. "Who else do I have in my life anymore?"

Allene and Birdie reeled from the acid in his voice. They both stepped forward, where human nature said that they should flee, and quickly.

"No, you've got us," Allene said. She snapped her finger at George, who was staring at them with wide eyes. "Call for the motor. Immediately." She looked at Jasper. "Should we telephone the police?"

"God, and say what? We got a letter that says 'You're welcome'? They'll think we're mad!"

In two minutes, Dawlish had pulled up, and they climbed into the back of the motorcar together, with Jasper sandwiched between the two women. Dawlish drove swiftly without a word, but from the puffs around his eyes, it was obvious he'd been awoken from sleep.

"I shouldn't have left him alone," Jasper let out.

"What do you mean?" Birdie asked.

"We had a row. About . . . about money. I yelled at him. God almighty, I was cruel. And I was wrong."

Birdie squeezed his arm. She understood the frustration of parenting your own parent—or uncle—and having to watch over and take care of them. She understood having no security in the future, even if that meant the next five minutes. You swayed on a little trapeze of fate, waiting for the slightest breeze to knock you off. A lost job, a broken bone that might bring expensive doctor's visits. Or something worse.

"Did you know," Birdie confessed, "that in the last month before Mother died, she made it clear that I needed to quit the clock factory and join her?"

"Join her," Allene repeated.

They all knew what she meant. Hazel's work had been far more lucrative than any factory job, and the hours weren't as bad.

"She'd always hinted at it before, but this was different. Our expenses were growing because of the war. She thought that with my face, I'd make so much money and—"

"But that isn't fair!" Allene cut her off.

"No," Birdie said. "It's not fair. But I'm busy enough, trying to survive. Who am I to change what's fair and isn't in this world?"

Birdie had never said out loud how she'd felt about being thrust out of Allene's life. But in moments like this, Allene seemed to understand. She asked to be forgiven with small gestures, like sliding closer and slipping her hand around Birdie's waist. Her hand was warm and possessive. Too warm.

She'd seen that look in Allene's eye with less and less frequency, thank goodness. Oh, Allene had tried to hide it, but it was obvious to her. The men wore it like a second skin when visiting her mother. An expression of fleeting hunger. Sometimes Allene could hide it. Sometimes she couldn't. And Birdie would tolerate it because she didn't want to upset her. But it was tiring, so tiring to never be in full possession of yourself. She was a woman, after all. It was their lot in life, wasn't it? Never to own yourself completely.

The motorcar sped downtown, across Canal and to Eldridge before they could speak of anything else. Jasper opened the car door, not waiting for Dawlish. He shoved the building's door open and tore up the stairs. Allene followed him just as swiftly. Birdie wasn't able to manage their speed with her aching limbs. She was able to catch the front door just before it closed, when something caught her eye. She turned to look down the dark, quiet street. A shadowed figure halfway down the block had watched them exit the motorcar.

They had made a scene, bursting out of the car all at once. But the figure—it looked like a tall man—just stood there, watching Birdie.

She nodded her head in acknowledgment, her heart thumping. It was a bold movement, but Dawlish was behind her. She knew that sometimes the anonymous would disappear, fading to something more benign, when forced to show themselves as real flesh-and-blood beings. It worked. The man receded into the darkness, turning the corner onto Delancey.

She climbed the stairs with effort, her hip joints aching with each step. But she would do this for Jasper. Whatever they found, she needed to be at his side. A dumpy old woman—possibly the landlady—had come out of her ground-floor apartment to chatter in some European language, but she ignored her.

Finally, on the fourth floor, Jasper's apartment door was wide open. Inside, the main room was empty and quiet. A few small pieces of paper lay strewn on the floor. The furniture was worn and bore concave shapes from overuse. There were no sounds inside, no gasps of relief, no cries of grief. She didn't know what that meant.

Birdie walked slowly to the hallway, which led to the kitchen. Allene stood there, her hands covering her mouth as she stared at the kitchen floor. Birdie prepared herself, clutching her chest as she approached.

At first, she saw the kitchen with its countless bottles lined up on one of the counters and the stacked cases of alcoholic tonics. But as she passed into full view of the room, the table in the center came into view—covered in an explosion of broken glass and brownish liquid. The glass had fallen onto the floor, and Jasper kneeled within the mess of it, clutching his uncle, who lay wide eyed, arms spread as if beseeching heaven. There were cuts across the man's face and wrists, and his skin was a waxy pale that Birdie, from tragic familiarity, understood.

Jasper didn't howl or cry or apologize. He held his uncle soundlessly.

Allene backed out of the room. "He was already dead when we found him," she whispered. "It looks like he fell over onto his equipment."

"Fell? Or was thrown?" Birdie asked.

She shook her head. "Maybe he had a fit? Or maybe he was too drunk and tripped?"

"This is sounding too much like what happened when Florence died."

Allene sniffed the air delicately, but this time there was no almond odor. Instead, the kitchen reeked of spirits. Shattered bottles and liquid marred the floor.

Most of the broken glass was thin and clear, from the kitchen-table chemistry setup. But thick pieces of wet amber glass were near to his body—a bottle once filled, now broken and conspicuous amongst the clear glass. Allene took a handkerchief out of her pocket and used it to pick up a shard. Birdie gave her a disapproving look as she bundled up the broken bit and put it in her purse. Then they drew together in their thoughts, standing behind the only boy they both had ever truly loved, before Birdie finally broke the silence.

"We have to call the police. The landlady is downstairs and has a telephone." When Allene didn't move, Birdie's face went hot from embarrassment. "Allene, going up and down those stairs really takes the wind out of me. Could you—would you be so kind as . . ."

Her request jerked Allene out of her trance. Fetching help always existed in someone else's station in life, and for so long, Birdie had been that *someone else*.

"Oh. Of course." Allene turned to the door before stopping. "Since when have you been so fatigued, Birdie?"

It was just like Allene to never look beyond the surface of everything. Birdie had been climbing the staircase at the Cutter house ever so slowly, but Allene had complained that there was no need for such graceful propriety around *her*. Birdie let Lucy take Holly on walks (actually, Holly requested rides on the trollies), and Allene had agreed that it must be a tiresome burden to care for such a person (though she herself took Holly on outings at least as often as Lucy). And when Birdie came home from the watch factory—she was probably the only girl in the world who came and went from her factory work by a chauffeur—Allene chided her for spending all her energy on her job and saving none of it for a jolly evening with her.

Of course, Birdie didn't tell her that half those days, she was at the hotel with Andrew. Andrew had been patient with her mourning her mother, but even patience had its limits. There were still too many uncertainties in Birdie's world, and she needed all that Andrew had to offer. Especially lately, as her weakness grew worse and worse.

At that moment, Allene seemed to see her all anew—the sunken temples, the pale skin growing thin like cigarette paper, the hollows under her eyes, the hint of pain that pulled the corners of her mouth down. Her complexion, once fair and delicate, was now, she knew, the faint premonition of a death mask, and her inability to smile—for a front tooth ached horribly and the gum above it was swollen—had been taken for worry over this never-ending war.

"Of course. I'll go immediately." Allene pointed to the couch. "Sit and rest."

"But—"

"I shouldn't have let you come. You ought to have stayed home with Holly." Allene left, but not before Birdie caught an expression of frustration on her face. Ah, she was angry at herself for not noticing. Tears of relief smarted Birdie's eyes. It was hard not to complain, and now she wouldn't have to.

She didn't sit down, instead walking to the kitchen, where Jasper still embraced his uncle. Birdie went to him, dodging the chunks of dazzling glass littering half the floor. She put a single, tentative hand on his back and waited.

After an eternity that was only a minute, Jasper gently released his uncle, leaving him Christlike, as he'd originally fallen. The front of his undershirt was damp from spilled liquid, and it reeked. There were blotchy reddish spots on his neck too. Birdie didn't know what to say. Her eyes welled with tears, because there was nothing more heartbreaking than seeing someone else shattering in front of you. It was all too familiar a feeling.

"Oh, Jasper" was all she could manage to say. Jasper stood and turned, only to collapse into Birdie's delicate arms, weeping like a child.

Jasper stayed on the couch, between Allene and Birdie, as the police asked countless questions. They grilled him on when he'd been in the apartment, when he'd left, about the argument with his uncle. The landlady came to tell them that she thought Jasper had returned before the subsequent violent commotion, which apparently everyone in the building had been privy to.

The police went from asking questions to pressuring Jasper for answers he couldn't give. They riffled through all the bills on the floor, asked about his job in the medical examiner's office and his access to strange chemicals and poisons, and even went so far as to question him about his parents. After all, one man's only four relatives suffering early deaths in a span of a few years was anything but normal. Oscar had died of an infection, true, but the others? They were far from natural.

It was clear Jasper was shocked. Allene and Birdie were witnesses to his presence at the Cutter house during the past hour, and Allene offered further references from the servants at the house. Jasper bore no signs of injuries or recent fighting, only streaks of blood from when he'd held his uncle's dead body. When they carried Frank out of the apartment, Allene turned away, and Jasper hid his face in his hands.

Birdie pitied him. It wouldn't be the last he'd see of his uncle. After all, the body was going to his place of work. Jasper would not be able to escape his death.

The officer in charge—a big, burly specimen with a lilt of an Irish accent and a double chin like a choice pork rind—held a sheaf of beige-colored papers, all attached together at the top with a binding clip. He thrust it in front of Jasper's face.

"Have you seen this before?"

Jasper took the papers, flipping them over one by one.

"It's a life-insurance policy," he said, before handing the pages back. "And no, I haven't seen it before." He looked up. "Where did you find this?"

"It was in his bedroom, beneath the mattress. So you don't know who the beneficiary is?"

Jasper shook his head. For a moment, Birdie's heart flipped with fleeting happiness. So silver linings really did happen. Jasper's uncle wasn't unintelligent or unkind, and having a policy would have protected Jasper in case anything happened to him. Maybe now he'd have the tuition he'd been working so hard for.

All three of them held their breaths as the officer pointed to the front page. "Didn't you read it? Right here."

Jasper read the document and went white. Wordlessly, he handed it to Allene, which was odd. Allene's hands shook as she read it, and the officer snatched it back.

"What's the matter?" Birdie asked. Allene looked faint.

"I . . . don't understand," Jasper muttered.

"You know this person?" the officer pressed.

"Yes," Allene said in a small voice, a thing so small you could place it in a box and hide it away from the world. "It's my father."

⟞⟝

The police finally left after gathering as much evidence as possible and instructing Jasper to report to the station in the morning for more questions. Jasper's face was wire tight. He waited until they had left the building before turning on Allene.

"What was that all about? Your father took out an insurance policy on my uncle?"

"I don't know! I swear, Jasper. I'm as surprised as you. I have no idea why he would do such a thing."

He marched closer to her, and she stiffened on the sofa where she sat. "It would certainly give him incentive to see Frank dead, wouldn't it?"

"Lord, Jasper! Unlike your parents, my father is financially sound and in no rush to kill anyone, let alone himself." Jasper went white in the face, and Allene clamped her hand over her mouth. "Oh, I didn't mean it." She stood up. "I didn't mean it!"

"Of course you did. That's the great thing about you, Allene. You say whatever's inside that shallow little head of yours!"

"Stop it!" Birdie shouted. They both stared at her. Birdie hardly raised her voice, ever, and the sound of it jarred them like crackling thunder. "This isn't helping! For goodness' sake, his uncle is dead. Dead! We need more information, not accusations. You two aren't here to hurt each other, so just stop."

Jasper cooled himself down by pacing, and Allene fanned her face. By God, it was difficult keeping them from throttling each other sometimes.

After a long, deep breath, Allene asked, "Where will you go, Jasper? Surely you're not going to stay here. You could stay with us."

"Two reasons why I can't stay there. One, your father. Two, your fiancé. We're not kids anymore, Allene." They could no longer hide behind innocence. Especially after tonight. Especially after that fight.

So she and Birdie went downstairs at two o'clock in the morning, letting Dawlish drive them home. Allene's head drooped before they even left the Bowery; before long, she was asleep on Birdie's thin shoulder, a poor excuse for a pillow, though an unconscious Allene didn't seem to care.

Florence, Hazel, and now Jasper's uncle. Who will be next? she asked herself. Who? Birdie felt a vise closing tighter and tighter, and she would have gasped for air if she wasn't worried about waking Allene on her shoulder. This was how it happened. Life and death growing so much bigger than their mere, tiny existences could handle. They were walking on a fault line, waiting for it to open up and swallow them all. Waiting, perhaps, to lose their footing while someone else pushed them in.

She closed her eyes but did not sleep. She saw Jasper's uncle spread out amongst the shattered glass, but instead of pity, she felt a slight longing. Yesterday he had lived, loved, and perhaps watched his last sunset through a dirty window. Elsewhere, men were dying in sodden trenches in Flanders, and the hospitals were transferring those stricken with Spanish flu to the cemeteries as quickly as could be to prevent the spread of contagion. Everywhere there were the dead, and at the center, Birdie watched them through a veil that was growing more transparent by the day.

Soon, soon, she thought. But not yet. Oh dear God, I'm not ready. Not yet.

She envied their peace now. Tears began to fall, and Allene didn't once question why her hair was damp when she awoke from Birdie's shoulder.

CHAPTER 23

The police came by late in the afternoon the next day to question Allene's father. His cold had morphed into a bona fide case of influenza, and his personal physician had been immediately called. The servants whispered about whether or not the Cutter constitution was strong enough to keep him alive. They blamed it on being indoors too much, and his bedroom windows were kept open to speed a cure and allow in the chilly October air.

The officers donned cotton masks to ask questions at a distance. Father wasn't all too pleased to see them or to hear about Jasper's uncle's death. He had lost a little weight, and his cheeks sagged as if he'd been pricked with a pin and deflated. He looked pointedly at Allene.

"You can leave us now, Allene. I'll ring for the maid when we're done."

Allene dropped her jaw in surprise. "Why can't I stay?"

The officers looked at Father, then at Allene, and one of the younger men snickered, as if she were a petulant child being refused a shaved ice.

"Do as you're told," Father said.

"But the insurance policy—"

"It's none of your concern. That's enough, Allene. Leave."

"But—"

"Allene!" her father roared, before coughing so violently that tiny droplets of rust-colored phlegm lightly sprayed the white coverlet. The officers veered away, and Allene was very nearly pushed out of the room by Lucy.

"Oh, Miss Allene. Come. Let him be."

Allene shook. She heard her father cough some more before settling down. She smashed her ear against the finely grained wood to eavesdrop. It was a fruitless endeavor; the door was too thick and the officers too quiet to hear. Lucy sighed and beckoned Allene away yet again, and she finally relented, accompanying Lucy to the laundry room.

Usually Lucy spent her time at Allene's beck and call, but with the evils of infection in the household, the servants were paralyzed with worry. So Allene watched Lucy order about the servants and rattle on about good, thick onion broths. She told them to tackle the dirty towels by rinsing them out with Lysol and doses of calomel. She heard Lucy's words, but her attention was elsewhere. One ear was cocked for the turning of her father's bedroom doorknob.

The interview was done in a matter of half an hour, and the officers left the house without a word to Allene. She went immediately back to the room, but Lucy barred her, closing the door. She leaned on the doorknob, as if she were either resting or ready to plant herself there for days to bar Allene from entering.

"May I see him now?" Allene asked.

Lucy pulled the gauze down from her face to speak. "I have it on his authority that he is not to be disturbed."

"But—"

"He said—very strongly, I might add—that under no circumstances are you to enter his room until he is completely recovered. He was angry that you came in earlier, especially without a mask. He doesn't want you to catch his germs."

"If—"

"No ifs, ands, or buts, Miss Allene. And no more of this insurance nonsense. He said that if you ask one more question about insurance, he will find a finishing school in Iceland and put you on a steamer there, wedding or no." Lucy straightened her spine and nodded. "You leave your papa alone. I put my foot down because Mr. Cutter says I may. It's for your own good."

"So is castor oil. That horrible stuff never did a thing but make me sicker!"

Lucy smiled, but her dark eyes looked tired. "It's almost time for Dawlish to fetch Miss Birdie. Why don't you go with him, get some good, fresh air?"

She nodded. It was getting late now, almost six. On order of the city, Birdie's factory had changed its hours to lessen the commuting burden and risk of spreading influenza during peak hours. For the last week, she had started work late but left late too.

When Dawlish pulled up in front of the factory, a few workers were leaving, most still wearing the masks that factories were now demanding. A small group of women were gathered on the corner wearing aprons and handing out flyers. Likely it was yet another recommendation from the city about influenza. Commissioner Copeland had become rather heavy handed with the warnings, but it seemed necessary. One of the women saw Allene waiting on the sidewalk and boldly drew right up to her, offering a narrow slip of paper.

"I'm aware of the regulations. I know not to spit on the sidewalks," Allene said, refusing. She knew plenty about what to do or not, after listening to Lucy chatter on about it the last few days.

"Would you like to help the city with the influenza scourge? We are looking for volunteers to help with the most needy and sick. Our ladies have—"

"Oh." Allene cut her off. "I don't think that's a good idea. My own father is sick," she added, knowing it was a slight fib. Her father was ill, but the physician said it was not a terrible case. The woman pressed on, though Allene stepped back two paces.

"But we could use every hand! With so many of our doctors and nurses serving in the war, we are in dire need—"

"My cousin is serving in the war," Allene interrupted, as if that were payment enough. Though she never thought of him unless someone asked. Clarence was redheaded, a scamp who'd always stolen her candy when they were little. And now he was fighting in the trenches, and she didn't even know where anymore. It shamed her. "I'm sorry, I can't help you." Allene opened her reticule, took out what money she had, and stuffed it into the hands of the volunteer. "Take this. It's all I have. Surely that can help."

Allene quickly turned away and walked toward the clock factory entrance. She was afraid to turn her head, but then she saw Jasper.

"Oh, Jasper!" She embraced him. She could still hardly believe his uncle was dead. And those letters! She released him before anyone could stare and organized her thoughts. "What are you doing here?"

"What are *you* doing here?" Jasper asked.

"I'm here with Dawlish to pick up Birdie. How did your talk with the police go? Did they find out anything about how your uncle died yet? Who—"

Jasper put his hands up. "You ask more questions than the police and talk twice as fast." Her barrage had seemed to squeeze out any leftover energy he had. Purple shadows hung beneath his eyes, and his lids were puffy again. Grief hunched his shoulders. He paused before glancing at the doors to the factory. The sun was setting now, and the exodus of workers had ended. He sighed and spoke like every word was exhausting. "I'll tell you everything, but let's find Birdie first. Shouldn't she be out by now?"

"Yes," Allene said, concern creeping into her voice. "Maybe we should go in and see if she's all right."

"Will they let us?"

"Might as well try."

Inside the entrance was a tall young guard, his nose and mouth smothered by a mask. The air smelled of wood varnish, and one wall was covered with clipboards where the workers signed in.

"I'm sorry, we're closing," the guard said.

"I know. Our friend is still inside, and we're worried. She hasn't left yet," explained Jasper.

"I can't let you in." The guard started to walk forward, shooing them toward the door. He had the door almost shut when Allene pressed close to the small opening.

"Wait. Can't you look for her?"

"I have to lock up—"

"Her name is Birdie Dreyer. Can't you tell her that Allene Cutter is waiting downstairs?"

The guard abruptly stopped closing the door. "Allene Cutter . . . oh! Are you Mrs. Andrew Biddle?"

"I . . . well, not yet, but soon to be." Who knew plain factory folk cared about the engagement announcements?

He opened the door and waved them in. "You have ten minutes. Go in and have a look, but I'm locking the doors then."

"Thank you!" Allene grabbed Jasper's hand and strode past the guard into the darkened hallway. She tried to orient herself and remember where Birdie's dial-painting room was.

"Do you know where you're going?" Jasper asked, holding her hand firmly. He was warm and strong. She wished they were in a never-ending tunnel and only she knew its secrets.

"I do." Soon, she found the staircase. They walked past the clock assembly and electroplating rooms, the latter leaving their chemical perfume lingering in the hallway. It was odd to see them so desolate and empty. "Ah, here we go."

She led Jasper into the room she remembered. Inside, there was the long table sectioned off into work spaces for each painter. The stools were tucked beneath the stations, and the glass-walled office was there, door open. Faintly, a green-yellow light glowed—at the painter's stations, on the floor, on the stools. The radium dust was everywhere. Allene swiped her hand on the dusty wall and smiled at her luminescent fingertips.

"Where on earth is Birdie?" she asked, after breaking the spell of the glowing dust.

"I don't know," Jasper said. "Does she always come out on time?"

"Yes. Dawlish picks her up and brings her home like clockwork."

Allene walked to Birdie's work space in the far corner. Her paintbrushes were propped inside a small glass jar. The pots of radium dust and glue were capped and lined up neatly. Goose bumps rose and spread along Allene's arms, and her heart sank.

"What if . . . what if . . ." she began, but couldn't bear to finish the sentence.

"By God, I've not been murdered," Birdie intoned from behind them.

Allene spun around at the same time as Jasper. She would have screamed or cried out in surprise, except she was too much in awe to make a noise.

Birdie stood crookedly in the back of the room, near the far end of the office where a second door was shut. Her hair was half down, waves tumbling over her left shoulder. Her dress was mussed as well, as if she'd rolled down a hill. And her entire body glowed with a luster only belonging to fireflies and summer stars. Despite the disarray of her hair and dress, Jasper audibly sighed at the sight of her, and Allene's heart ached just to see something so exquisite.

"What happened, Birdie? Why didn't you leave when everyone else did?" Allene asked.

Birdie didn't approach them, and Allene was almost afraid to go near her, she seemed so unearthly and ethereal. Perhaps if she touched her, Birdie would disappear forever in a shimmer of magic.

"I'm not well . . ."

"Is it influenza? Oh, we have to get you home . . ."

"No. It's not that." Birdie attempted a step forward but stumbled. Jasper ran to her and put an arm around her waist, and she cried out sharply in pain. "Oh God," she moaned.

Allene summoned up her courage and went to her side. Birdie could no longer stand up, and Jasper supported her with his arms so she wouldn't collapse. They helped lower her to the floor, where she sat propped up in Jasper's arms. Now they could see her complexion. It had a greenish cast, and her face was shiny with perspiration.

"I fainted in the bathroom," Birdie mumbled. "I . . . I don't know how long I've been unconscious. And my leg, God, it hurts so much. Like someone sawed it in half." She grimaced and looked out the window. "What time is it? Is Holly all right?"

"Holly is fine. She's at home." Allene touched Birdie's face, but it wasn't feverish. Clammy, if anything.

"Why are you two here?" Birdie asked weakly.

"To find you. I have news about my uncle," Jasper said.

"And I have news . . . that is, no news . . . about my father," Allene added, disappointment coating her words with iciness. "But that's for later. What happened to you?"

She stared at her leg and clenched her jaw for a moment. "I . . . I think it's broken," Birdie admitted.

"Goodness, well, that would make me faint too. How on earth did such a thing happen? Did you fall?"

"No. I didn't do a thing. Only walked to the bathroom."

Allene shook her head. It didn't make sense.

"Come, let's get her home," Jasper said, and he bent to help her up, but she gasped in pain again. He gingerly lifted the hem of her dress. Her shin had a sharp bend where it shouldn't, and darkness discolored her skin beneath her stocking.

"Oh God. I can't bear to move it," she said, clutching at Allene's hand. "What shall I do?"

"We'll need a splint," Jasper said. "She's right, this leg is busted."

"Or we could call an ambulance," Allene suggested.

"No, no ambulance. Please! I want to go home to Holly," Birdie pleaded.

"And we'll never get one anyway. They're all too busy picking up the . . ." He paused, and added, "The people with influenza." Allene was sure he had almost said, Too busy picking up the dead, but checked himself in time.

Jasper and Allene nodded to each other. The electricity had been shut off, but luckily the low moon had risen and flowed through the windows with enough illumination to work by. Jasper found a piece of wood used as a divider between painting stations, and Allene searched for something to tie Birdie's leg to the splint.

She went to the office, trying the doorknob, but it was locked. She heard a creak from inside the room. She held her breath, listening intently, but heard nothing except for Jasper's soothing murmurs as he fitted the splint under her leg and Birdie's whimpers of discomfort. The room, with all its eerie preternatural luminescence, seemed to watch her.

Finally, she decided to tear the lining of her dress but couldn't after several tugs. Jasper took the skirt hem in his hands and lifted it to his teeth to tear the fabric, which it did with a satisfying zipping noise. With one strip, he helped Allene tie the splint firmly to Birdie's leg, as Birdie cried out in agony.

"Talk to me," Birdie said between gasps as Allene struggled to tear off another piece. "Tell me about what you found. Anything to take my mind off this."

Jasper stopped fiddling with her splint and pressed his lips together in a grim line. "My uncle wasn't drunk—well, not that drunk. And none of the cuts from the glass killed him. He was poisoned."

Birdie's whimpers were silenced, and Allene stared at him. Neither looked surprised. They were beyond that now.

"How?" Allene asked. "What was it?"

"Wood spirits. His stomach was full of it. He'd been distilling it for some time and was hoping to use it as an additive in bottles he was going to sell, so they would seem stronger than they were. But it's poisonous."

"Did he know how poisonous it was?" Birdie asked.

"Yes, he knew. I did too," Allene admitted. Birdie and Jasper stared at her, and she explained. "I almost drank some by accident at your apartment. Your uncle told me what it was. Methyl alcohol. With the right apparatus it's easy as pie to distill it from wood chips."

"You're right," Jasper said. He seemed relieved that Allene would understand such things. "He hoarded wood."

"Why would your uncle drink the stuff, if he knew it was poison?" Birdie wondered aloud.

"That's the thing. He wouldn't. He drank some of it once, and he was sick as a dog." He closed his eyes. "That's why the glassware was broken. Someone must have forced him to drink it against his will."

"Oh, goodness gracious." Allene covered her mouth and went silent for a minute. It took effort for her to speak again. "I wish I could say I had information to help. I couldn't speak to my father about the insurance policy. He's isolated himself and won't let me in his room because of his influenza."

"Good. You should stay away from him," Jasper warned.

"That's uncharacteristically caring of you," Allene teased. When Jasper shot her a look, she sobered. "Well. I can definitely go into his office files and see if the insurance paperwork shows anything strange."

"Good idea. Of course, there are those letters," Birdie added. She winced as Allene tied another sash around her knee. "They've got to be linked. We've all received letters now."

"Yes, and they've made me an orphan. Again," Jasper noted grimly.

"Me too," Birdie said. "And Holly."

Allene was silent for a moment. Her eyebrows shrugged closer together. "I don't understand. Florence didn't mean anything to me." She added hastily, "I'm sorry she's dead, of course, but I didn't care for her."

Jasper and Birdie were silent when Allene spoke her realization aloud.

"I'm not an orphan. Not yet."

CHAPTER 24

"What did you say?" Jasper asked Allene.

Suddenly, her face blanched in the pale moonlight of the room. Jasper figured her father was at home, convalescing and safe. Or was he?

"We have to go back home," she said, panic contorting her features. "Now."

Dawlish couldn't drive home fast enough. Birdie sat with her broken leg cradled gently on Jasper's lap, but every bump in the road made her gasp in pain. Jasper had never seen her like this, so utterly unraveled, biting her lip so viciously it puffed out dark pink and bruised by the time they crossed the Brooklyn Bridge.

"Father won't be expecting callers," she muttered. "No one in the house would have any reason to hurt him—he pays their wages, for goodness' sake!"

"Money doesn't guarantee love or fidelity, does it?" Birdie commented. Allene shot her a murderous look, and Jasper leaned forward.

"Dawlish, you need to drive faster. Much faster."

He did, and the three of them felt the tug of the engine dragging them through the streets. As soon as they arrived at the Cutter house, Jasper expected Allene to bolt to the door and run upstairs, but he was surprised to see her making painstaking efforts to help Birdie out of the automobile without hurting her further. Maybe she'd forgiven Birdie for her comment about money. Then again, maybe she knew she deserved it.

Once they were on the sidewalk, Jasper carefully picked Birdie up in his arms. She was gossamer light, which shocked him. The electric lights outside the house showed what he hadn't noticed inside the factory. Birdie's collarbones protruded and the bumps of her sternum showed above the neckline of her dress. Slim hollows carved out her temples, which previously had been covered carefully with poufs of blonde hair.

"Don't," Birdie said. Her eyes couldn't meet his, aware he was judging, understanding, realizing. "Don't," she repeated, so low that only Jasper heard. He turned his eyes forward, and Birdie sagged with relief in his arms, now unburdened by his astute eyes. Allene bustled forward to speak to the butler, who held the door ajar.

"How's Father?"

"He's resting," George replied.

"Are you sure?" she asked hurriedly, glancing up the stairs.

"Yes." George was his usual laconic self; everything must be well.

Allene sighed with relief. "Thank goodness! Please call for Lucy, and fetch the doctor. Tell him we'll pay him double for the visit. We need to be absolutely sure Father is all right, and he needs to see Birdie too. Jasper, put her in my bedroom. There's an adjoining bath, and it'll be easier to care for her there."

"Of course." The elderly butler nodded. "But I shall have to send Josephine. We cannot find Lucy at the moment."

Allene froze at the doorway, and her face paled. "What on earth do you mean, you can't find Lucy?"

"We haven't seen her for over an hour. We've called for her several times."

"I don't understand," Allene said. "I didn't send Lucy anywhere. Where could she be?"

She turned and looked up the wide staircase, left to the parlor and the garden, right toward her father's study. Before anyone could utter another word, she gathered her skirts in her fists and bolted up the stairs.

Jasper couldn't follow her, not with Birdie in his arms. Instead, he followed Josephine, the Irish maid with the dumpling chin, up the grand staircase. Allene's room was just as he remembered it from the fateful night of the engagement party—stuffed with frills and furbelows. He gingerly laid Birdie on the bed, and Josephine went to run the water in the adjoining bath. She returned with a severe expression on her face and made a shooing motion with her thick hands.

"I'll take care of Miss Birdie now. You go wait for the surgeon."

"I'll be fine, Jasper. Go," Birdie whispered.

He nodded and stepped out of the bedroom, shutting the door. He wanted to talk to the doctor about Birdie's leg break—and why on earth she looked so sickly. His heart sank at the possibility that she was being poisoned as well. Were he and Allene next in line? All around him, people were falling sick and disappearing. He called out to the other rooms.

"Where are you, Allene?"

Allene came running out of a hallway door. Her face was awful— contorted and shocked. She suddenly looked both very young and very old—too old for her eighteen years.

"Oh God, I've found her, Jasper! Come!" She darted into the room, and Jasper followed her swiftly.

Inside was a bathroom finer than even his own from years ago uptown. Hidden behind the claw-foot porcelain bathtub, Lucy lay flat on her back. She wore her usual livery of crisp white apron, snowy cap, and black stuff dress on her slim frame. But her eyes were closed and she breathed rapidly, as if she'd just run a mile. Sweat beaded her face. Her usually smooth cheeks of golden tan were far darker than usual, as if ink had seeped beneath her skin.

"What is it? Do you think she's been poisoned too?" Allene asked, as she lifted Lucy's limp hand.

Jasper kneeled beside Lucy and put his ear to her bosom. He heard a wet, crackling noise with every rise and fall of her chest. Her lungs were drowning in liquid. He felt her pulse, nothing but a thin trill under his fingertips. Her nail beds were bluish. He pulled down her lower lip. Instead of the pink color he'd hoped for, he saw a dusky purplish hue.

"I don't think she's been poisoned," Jasper said slowly.

"Oh, thank God!" Allene gasped. But Jasper shook his head.

"Allene, it's worse. She's got influenza. One of the bad cases." He began to lift Lucy's unconscious body. Dark blood, almost black, dripped from Lucy's nostrils. "This is bad, Allene. Very bad. She must have contracted it from your father."

"But he wasn't that ill. He had a mild case! He's doing fine now!"

"I've seen what comes through the morgue. A good number of the dead are young, like us. Lucy is how old? About thirty-five or so, right? For some reason, people your father's age aren't getting hit as hard. It's picking off our healthiest men and women, and I haven't the faintest idea why." He hoisted her in his arms; they were tired from carrying Birdie too, light as she was. A reddish froth, bubbling up from her lungs, seeped out of Lucy's mouth and stained his jacket, but he ignored it. Blood smeared her face in too many places now. "Where can we put her?"

Allene didn't answer him. She stood unmoving in the bathroom, staring at Lucy but not seeing her. Jasper grew irritated—there was no time for her to reflect on how she'd lose the convenience of her own maid or her own room. It was times like this that he truly despised Allene; she was always thinking of how everything affected her own sphere and never looking beyond it.

"Allene!" he barked.

She jerked out of her reverie. "The second guest bedroom," she said. She looked up at Jasper, who was surprised by her words—he'd expected a string of complaints and whines. "Put her there, away from the other servants. We can't have them get sick too. I'd rather nurse her than send her to the hospitals. She'll get better care with us, don't you think?"

This time, it was his turn to be jarred out of silence. "Yes. The hospitals are overrun. And since she's—" He stopped in midthought. There was no question that a certain class of patients in the city weren't receiving the care they needed. "You're right. She won't get the proper attention. But I could help. I've overheard some of the doctors talking about treatments that no one else has tried, perhaps blood transfusions—"

"Does it work?" Allene asked hurriedly.

"I don't know. I'm just guessing—"

"I need what works, Jasper. No newfangled ideas of yours."

Considering the numbers of dead showing up at the morgue, Jasper didn't have the heart to tell her that nothing really worked. Just then, Josephine exited her bedroom, and Allene marched up to her. "I want everyone in the household wearing a double gauze mask, including Birdie. No excuses. Have Esther cook up another thick onion broth—everyone gets a serving daily, no matter what. Every surface of this house will get wiped down with Lysol, and the bedding gets a Lysol soaking too. Air all the rooms out. I don't care how cold it is; we can't keep the air trapped inside the house. There will be no visitors except the physicians."

"Yes, miss!" Josephine bobbled away to delegate the tasks. Allene helped Jasper settle Lucy onto the snowy-white guest bed, and she opened the window to let in the cold October air. When one of the maids came to the door with a handful of cloth masks, Allene waved her away.

"I'll take care of her." She snatched masks from the maid and tied them on, covering her nose and mouth. She turned to Jasper, handing him two. Her voice was muffled as she caught his eye. "Surely my father's physician can direct me how to nurse her. And I want Holly sent away and Birdie too, as soon as she's fit to be moved."

"I can take her," Jasper volunteered. As soon as he said it, he realized he meant it—even though the idea of having a child in his dingy apartment, just cleared of his uncle's corpse so recently—was somewhat abhorrent.

"No, that won't work," Allene said. "Birdie needs round-the-clock help, and the hospital needs you." She seemed to notice his disappointment. He always thought of children as irritating creatures, though he himself had been one less than a decade ago. His reaction surprised him.

"Maybe I can visit Holly," Jasper offered.

"I'm sure that would make it easier on her."

All at once, the chaos hit a fever pitch. The physician, Dr. Hanover, arrived to check on Mr. Cutter but was instead shuttled to see Lucy first, then Birdie. Allene took copious notes on what to do. The maids came to Allene asking for further orders. Nostrums from the drugstore were ordered for a poultice to help with Lucy's breathing and medicines were fetched for Birdie too.

Mr. Cutter's demands were ignored—particularly the order that Lucy be immediately removed from the house. He was still too weak to battle Allene's new and unrelenting hand in household matters, but he was strong enough that his health was less of a worry. Allene also sent word to Lucy's family in East Harlem that she would be caring for Lucy directly, with their own doctor, and not to visit for risk of infecting Lucy's other family members.

Jasper accompanied the physician to see Birdie after he had finished with Lucy. He was an older gentleman with white hair, round brass spectacles, and a grim mouth that didn't waste a single word. When they entered the bedroom, Birdie didn't stir. It looked as if one of the maids had already given her a dose of laudanum, and Birdie slept, but not contentedly. Even in her drugged stupor, her eyebrows pulled together, as if her dreams were stitched together with razor wire. Gently, Jasper raised the hem of her nightgown to show the surgeon her leg. The shin area was deeply purpled from bruising and blood spilled from the broken marrow of the bone. Her limb was at an angle instead of being straight as an arrow.

"There was no trauma," Jasper explained. "She paints watches, no heavy work. She'd gone to relieve herself in the ladies' room—she couldn't remember anything after that."

Dr. Hanover observed the leg without touching it. He leaned closer to Birdie's lovely face, her cheekbones like a knife edge under her translucent skin. Dr. Hanover threw Jasper an accusing glance.

"Why, this girl is positively skeletal." He pointed to the hollows at her temples and cheeks. "She's cachectic." He cradled his generous hands around her face and used his thumbs to pull down her lower eyelids. Instead of the healthy pink color, they were more a yellowish pink. "She's terribly anemic. I would guess her hemoglobin levels to be seven grams per deciliter or lower." He let his hand slide down to her jaw and raised her upper lips. "Tooth decay. No, it's worse. Look." He exposed more of her teeth and touched her upper left canine. It was loose in its socket, with a large growth protruding from the gum above. "There's a destructive tumor in her maxillary bone."

"A tumor? Are you sure?" Jasper's throat was so dry he could barely get the questions out.

"I know a tumor when I see one."

Jasper stayed silent as the doctor bent to examine Birdie's leg. She moaned in pain but remained in deep slumber. Josephine must have dosed her with enough laudanum to take down an elephant. Dr. Hanover's fingertips traveled over her thin, milky thigh down to the broken bone of her lower leg.

"Look here." His finger pointed to a mound on either side of the break. "There's a bone tumor here too. She didn't fall. It snapped on its own accord. Gravity broke her. Pathologic fracture."

Jasper's mind whirred over the information he already knew and what Dr. Hanover was telling him. Anemia. Fractures. Bone tumors. Her thin body wasting like a starvation victim's. Something was eating Birdie alive from the inside out. Oh God.

Birdie.

She was leaving him. She was leaving everyone.

He was so goddamned sick of being left behind.

"What . . . what . . ." Jasper couldn't manage to get the question out.

"What's causing it? She has a malignancy, boy. Clear as day. This girl won't be alive in a month, if she even has that long. How tragic. She's a lovely young thing."

Jasper left him in the company of one of the chambermaids to help properly splint Birdie's leg for comfort. They chattered on about when and if she would walk again. How utterly pointless to talk about walking when her life was to be snuffed out. And here he was, walking healthy as could be, not even having been drafted. Perhaps God wanted him to stay alive and be the last damned man standing.

Jasper escaped straight to the bathroom to compose himself. His eyes stung and his throat was scorched. He stuffed his fists into his eye sockets, willing them to stop oozing wetness. How on earth would he deliver the information to Holly? She'd already lost her mother. Jasper knew exactly what it was to lose a sibling after being orphaned. There were only so many pieces of your heart that could be damaged before it irrevocably changed you. But he was powerless to stop it, just as he had been powerless to save his parents or Oscar.

"Jasper?" a male voice called from the hallway.

"Be a minute." He wiped his face one last time, glanced at the mirror to make sure the redness wasn't bad around his eyes. He looked tired instead of crushed. Small mercies.

In the hallway, Ernie was pacing. "Jasper. I heard there was a to-do. I came as soon as I could. How can I help?"

For a change, Jasper felt relief at his overabundant enthusiasm. Within the hour, they decided to move Holly and Birdie to Ernie's home. They'd had little interaction with Mr. Cutter or Lucy in the last few days, so no one felt it necessary to quarantine them. Andrew had been phoned, but he'd balked at having them both in his home—strangers to the rest of his family. Furthermore, he himself had a touch of the influenza and was weakened from head to toe. His bowels had become a torment, and he could do little himself to help. But Ernie could barely contain his enthusiasm to help.

"Won't your folks mind?" Jasper asked.

"They might. But it doesn't matter."

Jasper watched him as he spoke to his driver and went to use the candlestick telephone in Mr. Cutter's office. Ernie was taller than Jasper but had always given the impression of being smaller. Impish almost, and blurred at the edges from the constant need to please and attend to all. But suddenly having a purpose, he was centered. Authority crept into his voice. Jasper hardly recognized him.

Before long, a second chauffeur stopped in front of the Cutter house. Josephine accompanied Birdie in one car, where she was able to lie down in the backseat, and Ernie himself entertained Holly in the other car as they drove toward the Fieldings' residence farther uptown.

Jasper took the next day off from work so he could visit Holly. He promised Dr. Gettler he'd work double shifts the next few days. At the large marble entrance on Park Avenue, he lifted the great brass lion knocker. One of the Fieldings' maids answered.

"I'm here to see Holly Dreyer. How's the pipsqueak settling in?"

"Oh, like a dream!" the maid said, unable to hide her rapture as she let Jasper in. "Such a clever thing. We haven't had a little girl in this house for two generations! Mr. Fielding himself had a Raggedy Ann doll sent for, and he unearthed a whole trunkful of dolls in the attic. But she won't touch them. She keeps asking for rides in the motorcar instead. What a duck!"

Holly ran straight into Jasper's arms. She was wrapped in an oversized brown jacket, and a pair of old, gigantic driving goggles at least ten years old hung from her neck. "Look!" she intoned. "Goggles!"

"Yes, I see! Where is Ernie?" He turned to ask both the maid and Holly.

"He went back to the Cutter house this morning," the maid reported.

"Ah. And how is Birdie?"

"She's sleeping," Holly told him. "She sleeps ever so much. I didn't know that broken bones made you sleepy." She settled onto an ottoman and explored the paper bag of candy that she'd cleverly fished out of Jasper's left jacket pocket.

"It's . . . very tiring," Jasper explained warily.

Holly was silent. She counted the swirls and knots of colorful hard candy on her lap. Red, green, and yellow twisted within curls of white, like sculpted glass. It was hard to find sugar, let alone candy, during wartime, and Jasper had paid from the bottom of his trouser pockets for the treats. Holly chose a peppermint to share with him, but he shook his head, and she popped the confection into her mouth.

He loved how she was a plainer, brown version of the Dreyer women, with her dark hair in slightly dampened curls around her forehead, cheeks dusted with that satiny rose that boasted of health. She was pretty, no doubt, but held none of that ethereal exquisiteness that defined her sister. Jasper relaxed in Holly's presence. They were made of the same earthly stuff, clay and dirt and such. Birdie was all cobwebs and moonbeams, and Allene . . . well, she was always poufed and rouged and covered in costly lace. Untouchable in another way.

"If she dies, will you marry me?" Holly asked him matter-of-factly. Jasper blanched before reddening. Holly's face was all sincerity, and she stared up at Jasper with eyes prepared to wait an eternity for an answer. He suddenly remembered why children made him so uncomfortable.

"What makes you think she's going to die, Holly?" he asked quietly.

"I know things," she said.

He shuddered at her words. Afraid to ask more, he kept his mouth shut and pushed the bag of candy closer to her.

"Do you have a sister?" she asked, crunching.

"No. I had a brother once. He . . . died in the war," he said. His eyes tingled with warning.

"Oh." She swung her legs, and they knocked the chair legs. "Maybe you shouldn't marry me, then."

"Oh?"

"You can be my brother instead."

Lord, this girl. He was getting the feeling that if she asked him for the world, he'd give it to her in a striped candy bag, whatever the cost.

"I accept." Jasper leaned over to kiss her on the head. He'd never kissed anyone on the head in his whole life. He liked it. "But in the meantime, Birdie needs you. I promise to visit later, all right?"

She nodded. He left Holly in the care of the maids, who supplied her with glossy books and dress-up clothes pillaged from an old cedar chest in the attic, likely belonging to English countesses from years gone by. It felt too improper for him to visit Birdie, so he took the maid's word that she was comfortable for the time being.

When he returned to the Cutter house, he was surprised to see Ernie leaving, white mask sagging just under his nose. His clothes gave off a stink of raw onion.

"Off to get more calomel and Vicks VapoRub and aspirin and Seidlitz powders and Epsom salts . . . Say, are you feeling all right?" he asked. Ernie had enough energy for a thousand electric lights and then some, but it exhausted Jasper just to exchange a few words. His tiredness must show.

"I'm well, Ernie. How are you?"

"Busy! Allene keeps trying to send me away, but I need to help. I've emptied out the druggist store on Madison of their influenza medicines." He waved a list on a piece of paper. "Anyhoo—good-bye!" he chirped. Jasper could manage only to touch his cap.

Apparently, Ernie had been a stubborn fixture at the Cutter house in the last twenty-four hours. He'd visited multiple times a day and begged for an occupation, even after taking Birdie and Holly away—anything to help. So the maids sent him on constant errands to the druggist to keep him out of the house. It was hard enough to care for patients and entertain guests simultaneously.

At the Cutter house, the butler welcomed Jasper with a sedate, clouded expression. He motioned upstairs before he even had a chance to remove his cap.

"Miss Allene was giving Lucy a sponge bath—"

"Really?" He could hardly believe it.

"She won't let anyone else touch her," George admitted. "She ought to be done by now."

"How is Mr. Cutter?"

"Well. He keeps to his bed. Miss Allene gives him an earful every time he attempts to leave."

"Ah."

"I believe the doctor is examining Lucy. If you wish to speak to him, now would be the time."

Jasper loped up the stairs. Dr. Hanover was closing the door behind him. He gave Jasper one look, shook his head, and put his hat on his head before passing by.

So Lucy was dying. He was not surprised. He himself had been lucky—too lucky—with his own mild case in the spring. It was sad when servants left a household, no matter the method. Marriage, death, scandal.

Jasper calmed himself before quietly opening the door. Inside, Lucy lay moribund, eyes closed and her breath rattling in her chest like a wet marble trying to wend its way out of a swampy maze. Allene kneeled at the edge of the bed, apron tied about her waist and her hair messily escaping the knot on her head. She clutched the maid's limp hand. Balled-up towels darkened with blood littered the bedside table. Nearby on the floor, there was a makeshift bed of quilts and pillows, but it seemed hardly touched. The idea that Allene would sleep on the floor startled Jasper; the further thought that she'd stayed awake all night was shocking.

"Lucy," Allene whispered. "Lucy."

Jasper hesitated and said nothing. His hand gripped the edge of the door; he was unable to move, unable to do anything but watch and listen.

"Lucia," Allene whispered, a choking sound coming from her throat that was half sob, half growl. Jasper had never heard Allene call the maid by her real name. "Won't you please wake up?" She shook the flaccid hand with surprising aggression, but nothing happened. Allene dropped her head to the bed. "My Lucia."

It was only two minutes while Jasper watched. He wished to see that unbeautiful, transcendent moment when a soul ceased to reside in its container, weak as it was. There was something to be gleaned in that thin second—a lesson learned, a secret passed to the living that he was greedy to know. So he watched and found he was holding his breath as if suffocation might give him clarity.

The rasping in Lucy's chest slowed and then, like an unwound watch, simply stopped, never to reach the next second. Allene raised her eyes. Her face was swollen with despair.

What followed was a sound that he hoped never to hear again. He didn't know it, but a softened version of it had been residing with tarry blackness in his heart since the day his uncle had died. There had been echoes of it when he found his parents dead in their bedroom, a knock of it against the walls of his heart when Oscar passed away. Death had always hit Jasper with a concrete wave that forced him to think of survival, not of sorrow; of next steps and of wanting to claw beyond the audacity of hurt.

But with Allene, the sound was altogether different. It was savage and vicious, and it terrified Jasper. He ought to make a mental note never to love anyone in such a way as to lay himself open to such a wound. He thought of Allene and Birdie and now of Holly. He realized he would likely fail, and that gave him a dark comfort.

He pushed the door open wider, and the hinge gave a telltale squeak. Allene turned and saw him, and she rose to bury herself in his arms.

He would comfort her while she wept. Forever, if necessary. There wasn't much else one could do when surrounded by so much death.

CHAPTER 25

The dream itself was a sticky treacle that pulled Birdie down over and over again, despite her attempts to fight her way back to consciousness. She needed to protect Holly. Harm was encroaching on Jasper and Allene with an unstoppable momentum. She needed to be awake.

But the dream slipped up her legs, sucked her into a mire of darkness that held her fast in its viscous core. When she tried to yank herself free, she'd find that she'd snapped her leg off above the knee or at the ankle. The darkened ooze pulled at the bony shards of her stump before she could run away, before claiming her arms, her hair, her screams.

Somewhere in her consciousness, she was able to refuse another draught of the bitter liquid that trapped her in this nightmare world. After what felt like years had gone by, she began to wake. The torment in her jaw and the white-lightning pain in her broken leg pushed her out of the numbed cloud and into wakefulness.

Birdie blinked, rubbing the crust from her heavy eyelids. She lay on a soft bed, dampened by her own sweat. Pain from the broken bone lanced up to her hip and down to her foot. She wiggled her toes, happy to find that she could wiggle them, but one leg was firmly tethered to a clothbound splint beneath her. Broad afternoon light flooded in through the window. She saw the ruddy treetops of Central Park out the window, leaves burnished by the beginnings of autumn. In the distance, sparkling water shone from the Conservatory Water.

"You're awake."

Birdie turned her head and saw Andrew sitting in a chair at her bedside. His collar was undone, his jacket slung on the chair back. His face was gaunt, as if he hadn't eaten anything in a week. In his eyes glittered a starved eagerness. Whether it was for food or for her, Birdie didn't know.

"Where's Holly?" Birdie croaked.

"She's with the maids. Having a ball, I might add."

"How long have I been asleep?"

"Almost two days."

"Where am I?" She managed to push herself up to a sitting position, but not without soul-sapping pain. Andrew helped prop her up with some feather pillows that were stuffed within an inch of their lives. He settled back into his chair, took out a tin box of pastilles, and popped one into his mouth. He offered one to Birdie, but she declined. Her appetite was nonexistent, anyway.

"So many questions," he said, snapping the tin closed. "And not one about me." Birdie said nothing. She watched Andrew watch her. "You're in Ernie Fielding's home. I would have taken you both in, but Mother was afraid of bringing in influenza." He reached for a silver case in his jacket pocket, pulling out a cigarette. His casual words repelled Birdie. Of course he'd never allow his mistress into his parents' home. The least he could do was not lie to her about an excuse. "Anyway, I think I had a touch of influenza myself, but nothing horrible. Allene had you and Holly removed when her maid got it. Pretty bad too."

"Lucy?" Birdie asked, her eyebrows rising on her face.

"She's dead." Andrew tapped the end of the cigarette against the case before lighting it. He blew a single puff of smoke away from Birdie. "Died yesterday morning. Bloody awful mess, I hear."

Lucy. She'd had what Birdie had wanted, that nestled place of receiving Allene's trust and confidence during those years while Birdie was gone. She'd been jealous of Lucy, and Lucy's suspicion of her had always made her feel like a street rat. Birdie looked down at the bumps of her splinted leg beneath the bedsheets. In the winning position, she felt nothing but emptiness. Lucy was a good woman, and she was dead from a stroke of fate.

"Well, maybe I'll join her soon. I'm not doing so swell myself." She would have laughed aloud if she weren't in so much damn pain.

"Don't say that." Andrew stole one of her hands in his, ever so gently. His was almost as cold as her own. "The doctor came by today already. He won't be able to do much besides keep it in a splint. He said . . . he said . . ." Andrew paused. The cigarette was now burning low in his other hand. It almost burnt the skin of his hand before he crushed it in an ashtray.

"I know I don't have very long. Does Allene know? Does Jasper?"

"Why are you asking about *them*? I'm right here."

"Because, Andrew, I believe you'd lie with me in the grave if I asked it of you. And I don't have to ask." She opened her eyes and smiled. She knew what she looked like. Lately, in the mirror, her angelic face had become beauty corrupted, a grinning skull behind the thin veil of life. And just like that, her energy seemed to deflate to nothing, and she sagged back onto the bed. "I would like very much to go home now."

"Home?" Andrew asked. "I thought you already retrieved your things. Do you mean the hotel?"

"No. I mean back to the Cutter house. It's where I was born, and it's where I ought to die."

"Why won't you stay here? Ernie is happy to have you and Holly stay for as long as necessary."

"Oh, Andrew. Nowhere is safe for me anymore. Don't you see?" She raised her hand from his, and it fell limply at her side.

Even when Andrew waited inside his car by the entrance to the Ansonia Clock factory all those mornings after Birdie had been dropped off by Dawlish, he hadn't seen. Oh, Birdie felt guilty about it, leaving the Cutter house with Allene merrily waving good-bye. To Allene, Birdie was a garnish, a game, a posy to hold. To Andrew, she was a life necessity. Even once she was gone, he would placate her while she lay in her grave, for she had insinuated herself like a cancer into his soul, and he would never stop being a willing victim.

This way, she had the power to make Andrew promise her things, in case her hopes of keeping Holly in the Cutter house disappeared. Andrew would make sure Holly was always cared for. One of his loyal servants, a good and kind lady, was barren and might adopt Holly. Birdie had to keep planning, planning incessantly.

So Andrew had continued to take her to the Hotel Martinique, always made over cleanly with crisp new bedsheets and fresh glasses beside a bottle of Andrew's favorite brandy. And Birdie had allowed it. Lately, she'd insisted on making love to him astride, so as not to put undue stress on her bones. Andrew would lie, nearly unmoving, watching her in rapture as she rode him at her own pace, never looking at his face, ignoring the large hands cupping her diminishing breasts. Before, it had been impossible for her body to respond to his. But lately, with eyes closed and her mind in a fantasy that had nothing to do with Andrew or anything real in her own life, she had been able to bring herself to an apex of pleasure. Birdie would shudder and cry out, tears at the edges of her squeezed-shut eyes. Andrew understood that her gasps were in spite of rather than because of him.

He knew. He always knew. And still, he was ravenous for her.

They blinked at each other, thinking their own thoughts, before Birdie rang the bell.

"I have to go home," she repeated.

She had been asleep too long. She was fading fast, and sleeping was a waste of time when she could be spending more time with Holly and the brilliancy that was Allene and Jasper. Unlike Andrew, they made her feel more alive than she was, and that, too, was seductive. There was more information to be had, more clues. What had they learned while she slept? Drat this influenza. It was such a careless killer and a distraction. It was the careful killers they had to focus their attention on.

"What's the rush, darling?" he murmured.

Birdie shivered whenever he said the word *darling*. "Florence is dead," Birdie said. "Mother is dead. Frederick Jones is dead." She inhaled. "It's my turn soon. Very, very soon."

⎯⎯✦⎯⎯

The Cutter house was fumigated and cleaned from top to bottom before she and Holly were allowed to return. Ernie was disappointed she was leaving. But he would find other ways of helping Allene and, by extension, Birdie too.

Allene wore a black band around her arm when she received them. Crepe hung on the grand front doors, like so many others in the city. A morose, dark mood had pervaded every occupant, and even the floorboards of the house creaked with an ominous sigh.

"You can stay with me in my room," Allene said. Dawlish and George carried Birdie upstairs as if she weighed no more than the crepe paper on the front door.

Birdie nodded, secretly terrified that she might lie in the same bed in which Lucy had died. It seemed that Allene's old room was going to be the official gateway for exiting the land of the living, but of course she said nothing.

Once Holly was settled downstairs with milk and gingersnaps, her wooden truck tucked happily in her lap, Allene sat at Birdie's bedside, mirroring her exhaustion.

"Will Jasper be here soon?" Birdie asked.

"I think so. He promised to visit today after work." Allene stared at the window absently, as if someone else had answered beside herself.

"I'm very sorry," Birdie began, "about Lucy. I know she meant a lot to you."

Allene didn't answer, didn't move. Her face seemed carved of stone. October light shone from the window against her skin. She looked so much like her mother from the photographs. Birdie herself had completely forgotten what it was like to look upon Dorothy Cutter's face. They shared the same elegant nose, those same deep-set brown eyes that sparkled with whimsy more times than not. They didn't sparkle now.

"It's not your fault, you know. That she died." Birdie tried to console her.

"What?" Allene shook herself from her distracted thoughts.

"I said, it's not your fault that she died. Influenza is just a terrible blight. We're lucky we haven't been afflicted ourselves. It could have been us, not her."

"Yes, it could have been us. It could have been me." Allene went back to staring out the window. She was sinking into a dark territory, so Birdie attempted to pull her into a different sea altogether.

"I had a visit from the doctor. About my broken leg."

It worked. Allene's eyes went straight to Birdie. "What did he say?"

"That I shall never walk again."

"Oh, Birdie!" She reached for Birdie's hand. Allene's fingers were strong, her hand broad without being coarse. Strength simmered beneath the skin there, and Birdie wondered at it. Since Birdie had been banished, she had always thought of herself as the strong one— her life had been taken away, yet she provided for her sister and looked after a mother who had been willing to descend into moral decay in exchange for numbness. When Birdie reentered the Cutter house, she had kept that inner part of herself taut, knowing what was at stake and what Holly had to lose.

But now, looking at Allene, she felt unsure, and it was her own bones crumbling to dust before she was ready. How had this happened? Why should Allene always, *always* be so fortunate? But then her old, passive ways won, and Birdie sank back into the cushions, ready for the inevitable.

There was a quiet knock at the door. Jasper entered, nodded at both of them, and drew a chair to Birdie's bedside next to Allene.

"Well, what did I miss?"

"That I'm dying?" Birdie quipped, but no one laughed.

"Why?" Jasper asked with the appropriate gravitas. What a good boy.

"Don't play dumb, Jasper. The doctor told you. There are tumors in my bones," Birdie explained patiently. "It's why my leg broke. And he doesn't know why I have a cancer. Bad luck, I suppose."

"Is it possible," Allene began, "that you've been poisoned as well?"

No one spoke for a moment.

"Perhaps. The truth is, I've been feeling sick for a long while. What could it be, though? Something I've eaten? Then Mother would have suffered from it, and Holly as well. But they were—are—"

"No, it can't be that," Jasper thought aloud.

"But what if I have been poisoned? I don't care about me anymore. It's too late. Maybe that's the answer to this sick game we've been immersed in. Maybe we're the final players. Maybe I'm simply the first of us three."

"What can we do?" Jasper said. "Stop eating for fear that every morsel is going to kill us? Stop living?"

"Or we could get out of the game completely," Allene commented. "Forget the policy my father had on your uncle, forget the methyl alcohol, forget everything."

They both looked at her. She had an untouchable, faraway expression. Something had profoundly untied Allene from the world they were living in. Her friend was falling beyond her grasp, and it terrified Birdie.

"No. Not yet," Jasper said. He leaned closer to them both. "What do we know? Florence was poisoned with cyanide. We don't know who put it in her wineglass, but we're sure it wasn't an accident. Hazel died of a laudanum overdose, but it looked like an accident. A simple switch of one bottle for another by an inexperienced pharmacist who lost his job over it. And my uncle died because he drank one of his fake alcohols."

"Violently," Birdie added. "More like he was attacked and someone poured wood alcohol down his throat."

"Then there were the letters," Allene said, seeming to wake up from her torpor. "It's as if someone is making them all look like accidents but letting us, and only us, know that it was on purpose."

"And there was that man I saw," Birdie began. "I never did tell you because I wasn't sure. But he was standing at the end of the block, watching us all as we ran into the apartment the night Jasper's uncle died."

"How do you know it wasn't just a bystander watching?" Jasper asked.

"I don't know. It was just a feeling. When I stared at him, he practically ran away from me."

Allene frowned. "That isn't enough information for anyone to use."

"Well, I know it was a man," Birdie insisted. "He was tall, nearly six feet. Slim. And he didn't walk like an old man. He was youngish, I'm sure."

"That narrows it down to, oh, at least a million possibilities," Jasper mused.

"But a million possibilities are all fighting in France," Birdie reminded him.

"What about Lucy?" Allene added.

"Lucy was just bad luck," Birdie noted. "It was the flu."

"How can we be sure? You could easily hide a murder in all the influenza deaths," Allene retorted.

Jasper tilted his head thoughtfully. "But Lucy was just household help. She wasn't important like the other people dying around us."

Allene stared at Jasper coldly. "Are you saying that Florence Waxworth meant more to me than Lucy?"

"Did she?" Jasper asked, less of a challenge and more an honest question. Allene went quiet, and she stared at the carpet for a long time. She sniffled.

"No. Lucia was so much more important. I think she was a better mother to me than my own mother."

Birdie felt a prickle of jealousy. Stop it, she thought. You're here now. "She's right," Birdie admitted. "Lucy was special to Allene."

"But no one knew that. Even you didn't, until it was too late," Jasper said.

For several seconds, none of them could speak. Birdie seemed too frightened to correct him, and it was Allene who finally broke the silence.

"Jasper Jones, that is the coldest thing I've ever heard you say. Are you just fussed that Lucy doesn't fit into this neat, dramatic string of murders you're keeping track of, trying to prove you're a star at your new job?"

He reddened. "I'm just trying to help!"

"Are you? Because it sure seems like everything is going your way. Just swimmingly! Florence dies and you get a new job. And you get your feet wet trying to solve a case that wasn't even a case to begin with. Your uncle dies of something *you knew* was poison. You were running out of money; I saw the bills. Maybe you didn't know about that insurance policy, and you just wanted to get him out of your life."

"Oh, so now *I'm* a murderer? And I killed Birdie's mother because I woke up and felt like it?" he yelled, standing up so he could use the full force of his lungs. "Let me slip you an earful. You're just fussed that I've got a life, though you kicked me out of yours four years ago, aren't you? And we all know you're trying so damned hard to lie to everyone and yourself!"

"What are you talking about?" Allene practically spat.

"Andrew!" Jasper pointed out the window, as if the offending gentleman were standing on Fifth Avenue, watching the whole argument. "By God, he's having an affair with Birdie under your nose. He smells of her perfume all the damn time. Are you blind? It's obvious to everyone in all of New York and in this house! And you won't break it off because you like the name Biddle better than Cutter, and I won't marry you, and you want to make me jealous. You don't want Birdie to have me, or to have Andrew."

"Be quiet!" Allene hissed.

"That's why you never called Birdie all these years you spent shopping for new clothes and a new husband, because you were so bloody jealous. That's why you brought us back into your life, because you couldn't bear the thought that we went on living without you, and you had to show that you're faring so much better than we are. And it wasn't just a party either. Of course it had to be dramatic. Of course there had to be a scandal with Florence—"

"Stop it, Jasper!" Allene yelled, standing up.

"—And you want to pretend that you've got this perfect life, while your mother is drunk and having parties of her own in Saratoga—"

"*Stop!*"

"—And she couldn't stand that your own father wanted Hazel Dreyer more than her. Birdie's mother was pregnant when she left this house! God, it was so obvious!" Jasper wiped the spittle from his mouth and swelled his chest. "You're so blind. Even *I* saw that Hazel's dresses were let out around the time she left. Holly is probably your sister, Allene. You never guessed, did you? Did you, Allene?"

Allene jumped out of her chair, eyes shot with red and hands shaking. "Shut up, shut up, *shut up!*" she screamed. She stormed to the bedroom door and opened it so violently it slammed against the wall on rebound. Two maids and the butler had come running to the upstairs hallway and stared at the three of them through the opened door. "Get out, Jasper," Allene ordered him, her voice shaking and face furious with tears. "Get out, and don't you dare come back."

"Finally something we agree on!"

He stormed out. They heard him flying down the stairs and out into the hazy October day. Allene finally composed herself, wiping her face with a handkerchief. She dismissed the servants with a wave of her hand. Tears streaming down her face, she clicked the door shut and faced the invalid in her bed.

Allene whispered, "Oh God. Is it true? Is my father . . . Holly's father?"

Birdie stared at her lap miserably. God. Her family was nothing but a tangle of shame, but now Allene could make it better. She had to.

"Yes. He is." Her eyes lifted to meet Allene's. But soon, her heartache transcended to hope. "Oh, Allene. I beg you. You will take care of her, won't you? She's family. Promise me you won't hold it against her—she didn't choose her mother and father. They're not her sins. She deserves a better life than she has."

"Of course she does. But what will Father think?" She looked at Birdie. "She is family. Of course I'll help her. I will."

Birdie deflated against the pillows. Relief filled her. She already felt light as a sunrise knowing Allene would try to help Holly. Now she could concentrate on other things. There were tasks yet unfulfilled.

"And the rest—it's true, isn't it?" Allene finally managed to say, without meeting Birdie's eyes. "You are having an affair with my fiancé, aren't you? He wasn't just helping you with groceries, was he?"

Birdie wanted to crumple inside of herself and disavow the truth. But she would not lie. Not now.

"Yes."

Allene's face curdled into something ugly and petulant, morphing into a despair that Birdie recognized as her own mirrored reflection.

"Oh, Birdie." Allene sat down limply. "Oh, Birdie," she repeated. This was not the behavior of a girl who was angry about being cheated on. It was the face of a girl who'd been left behind. Allene touched her lips the way she had after the girls had kissed that night at the engagement party. It was true what Birdie had said all those weeks back. Allene didn't know what she wanted, but she knew what it felt like to lose it. "How long has it been going on?"

Birdie took a deep breath. "It started the day after Florence died. When—"

"When I asked you to keep Andrew out of my hair and get more information from him, because I couldn't be bothered." She laughed without smiling. "You said he was just helping you out with groceries. And I was too stupid to see the truth." She flopped her hands onto her lap. "So this is my doing. I put you two together in that motorcar, didn't I?"

Birdie nodded.

"Do you love him?" Allene whispered.

Birdie dropped her head into her hands. "No. He helped take care of me and Holly. He made sure I wouldn't get fired from the factory. He paid extra wages so I could spend more time with Holly and Mother."

"The factory?" Allene said, confused.

"He owns part of Ansonia. Didn't you know? He's my boss. I didn't have much of a choice, Allene."

Allene was silent for a while. No, she couldn't have known. Her expression grew murky, and she whispered, "Oh, Birdie. Did Andrew . . . did he force you to . . ."

"No," Birdie admitted, before adding, "yes."

"I don't understand."

"I never pushed him away. I never said no. But it didn't matter, did it? Because I had no choice." The flat tone of her voice underscored the fact that Andrew wasn't a pleasure in her life. Her shoulders drooped like she could barely tolerate the weight of the air.

"But I could have helped you," Allene said, trying not to pout. "Why didn't you ask me?"

"Because you never offered, and I was too proud. At least with Andrew, he . . . he needed me."

Allene's eyes went red with tears. Her faced aged a decade in seconds. She looked more like her mother than ever before—knowing all, wishing none of it were true. "I need you too, Birdie."

Birdie frowned. "Allene, you need the *idea* of me. So does Jasper."

Allene laughed, the laugh of someone giving up. "Is that what this feels like? Losing an idea?" She stared at Birdie. "I'd tell you that you mean more to me than that, Birdie Dreyer, but I'm not sure you would ever believe me. And what about Jasper?"

"Lord, no. Jasper will never love anyone more than himself, and I think we both know it. Only one day, he'll find that's a lonely business. And then what will he do?" Birdie laughed, then winced from the pain. She brought her hands to her face, gingerly touching her left jaw, which was swollen worse than the day before. "This hurts so much I'd take a gallon of laudanum if I didn't need to be awake right now."

"Then take it and go to sleep," Allene urged. Of course, quieting Birdie's suffering meant quieting Allene's as well. But enough was enough. Her body was failing, and soon, more teeth would fall out, and Allene's book of revelation needed to happen sooner rather than later. So when Allene reached for the glass bottle at the bedside, Birdie did not stay her hand.

She took the draught and shut her eyes. If she were to die now, it would be a relief. But she knew somehow she wasn't that lucky. Not yet.

CHAPTER 26

Allene leaned against the closed door, beyond which Birdie was falling into a drugged slumber. If only Andrew had drawn a bead on any other girl. She wouldn't have cared nearly so much. But Birdie was hers. She was tempted to crawl into bed with Birdie, to slip her hands around that waist again, nothing but the thin fabric of their nightgowns between them. But there was no point. Birdie never reached for Allene; her hands never crept upward on her bodice, under her bodice, under anything.

Birdie had never belonged to her. She never could. And now Allene had all but handed her over to Andrew. Andrew! Of all people.

And what was more, her mind couldn't fathom what she was coming to understand, with shame and anger. She thought of herself and Birdie just over four years ago. They were still busy playing in the garden all the lovely summer days, when her mother had come down with consumption. Mother hadn't looked ill, but she coughed once in a while. In retrospect, it was a hollow, fake cough. An act.

The Dreyers had packed up and left without any fanfare. She tried to remember Hazel Dreyer's clothing at the time. For certain, it was morbid, gloomy stuff and shapeless, as if trying to hide her beauty.

Allene hadn't realized that she was hiding something else. She'd been too naive to see the obvious.

And there were other uncomfortable visions in her mind. Those nights when Birdie, who usually shared her bed with her mother, would sneak into Allene's bedroom. She would seem upset but wouldn't say anything. Allene had assumed it was nightmares, but now she understood that the nightmare was usurping Birdie's place in the welcoming warmth of Hazel's bed.

The vision of her father coupling with anyone—particularly Hazel Dreyer—drew acid up her throat. And there was Holly, who was no replica of Hazel or Birdie. She looked more like a Cutter, and Allene hadn't even realized it.

Allene inhaled sharply.

Why, Holly was her sister! She was no longer an only child. It warmed her cheeks—a tiny morsel of goodness in all this atrocious news.

How could she have been so blind?

Allene let the coolness of the door temper the warmth rising in her face. Josephine approached with a pile of clean linens. A slight gust of air wafted by, as well as a familiar scent of cigars. Blue Ribbon. Her father's favorite. He was somewhere nearby, his health improved to the point where he'd lit a cigar for the first time in weeks.

Suddenly, the walls were intolerably close. Birdie was too near, as was Josephine, the air stifling. She backed away from the door.

"Miss Allene? May I get you something?" Josephine asked.

She had to leave. Holly laughed somewhere downstairs, and the sweet brown scent of tobacco brought on a wave of nausea. The sick threatened to overtake her, but she forced it down.

This was not a home to her. This banister, these polished stairs, this golden-scrolled wallpaper—none of it belonged to her, none of it familiar. They had long concealed truths, and it had made her a stranger.

She descended the stairs, dizzy from her thoughts. She didn't wait for George to dig out her coat from the closet.

"Shall I ring Dawlish for you, miss?" George asked, startled.

"No, no."

"Indeed, you look very ill! At least wear your mask if you venture outside," he urged, and pushed a clean gauze mask into her hand. With her other hand, she snatched her reticule from the marble-topped table in the foyer.

The sun was halfway to the western city skyline, and peach-colored light fell on the quieting streets. Without knowing where her destination was, she walked eastward. A few times, her thoughts tumbled around and her feet forgot to move. And when she stopped, she heard footsteps also halt nearby. Allene twisted around, only to see other pedestrians walking and too busy to notice her. So she continued.

Before she knew what she was doing, she mounted the iron steps of the Second Avenue elevated train station, paid her fare, and stepped onto the uptown platform. She'd welcome dissolving into the crowd of quotidian commuters, but that became impossible when a familiar face turned to her with surprise.

"Why, Miss Allene!" Esther, the wizened cook, stood on the platform. She was dressed smartly in a woolen coat and polished black shoes, and her salt-and-pepper hair was coiled beneath a dark hat. She was standing only feet away, and Allene had hardly noticed. "Where are you going, miss?"

"I hardly know," she said in truth. She blinked at Esther. "Where are you going?"

"Why, I am on my way to poor Lucy's funeral."

The funeral. She'd completely forgotten. She had known it would happen—these things do, after all—but as soon as the coroner had whisked away Lucy's lifeless body, Allene had moved on to grieving over her inward loss and worrying about Birdie.

"Oh. Of course. I am too," Allene replied quickly.

"It's a mercy we're allowed to attend," Esther said. "I heard that in Boston, their health commissioner won't allow any church gatherings. My, couldn't Dawlish drive you, Miss Allene?"

"Oh. No, he couldn't," she said, not having any other explanation. Esther's hooded eyes glanced over Allene's clothing. Besides the black armband, she wore a regular dress of pale-blue bombazine with lace edging. Not exactly funeral attire. But Esther knew her place and said nothing.

As the train rolled into the station, Allene once again had the uncomfortable sensation that eyes were on her or someone was too close behind, hovering. She and Esther took adjoining seats. Esther's substantial hips touched Allene's, and their elbows were but an inch from each other. She didn't think they'd ever been so close before.

"Will your father be attending?" Esther asked.

"No." Allene dropped her chin and stared into her lap. Funny how one question could fill her with shame. Would someone like Esther know that her father had been intimate with Hazel in his home? That he'd fathered a child under his wife's nose? The flashing emotions on Allene's face must have made her look unstable, because concern overtook Esther's expression.

"Are you all right, miss? Where is your coat? You'll catch your death."

"Oh, it's warm for me . . . I'm just worried because I'm not wearing black." Allene felt frayed and had to bring herself to calm, even if it meant fibbing. "You see, my one black dress was ruined yesterday."

"Ah. I'm sure everyone will understand. After all, you were Lucy's favorite at the Cutter house. It's so kind of you to come, Miss Allene. Very kind, indeed."

The warm words ricocheted off Allene's frigid demeanor. Today would end up being a memorial to a servant, and Allene had no place in receiving praise of any sort. Normally, she enjoyed a bit of lamplight on herself, but she wished to be made of shadow and ash and disappear into the background.

She thought of how Lucy's death had stolen momentum from Jasper's loss. They still didn't understand who had killed his uncle or who had killed Florence and Hazel. Why, they knew nothing, really. And then their discussion had devolved into the most poisonous shouting match she'd ever had. Jasper would never forgive Allene. Nausea lurched in her stomach, but she took a deep breath to keep it at bay.

The elevated train went deep into East Harlem, and the landscape of stately houses and marble fronts changed to drab tenements, row houses, and storefronts. A hand-painted sign outside a fountain shop read, "Support our Harlem Hellfighters!" Allene had no idea what it meant.

The two women got off at the 117th Street station and walked south and eastward to 115th Street, just by Pleasant Avenue. The landscape of faces had changed to mostly Italian immigrants like Lucy, with pale-skinned Europeans and more dark complexions than she was used to seeing. This was Lucy's home, Allene thought. Not the Cutter house. Not with me.

They finally reached the gray-bricked church nestled between apartment buildings, its simple bell tower on the side. "Our Lady of Mt. Carmel" was carved into the stone above the double doors. Allene felt small and mortal beneath it.

There was a very small crowd of people in front of the iron church gates, all dressed in black under a constellation of felt and woolen hats. Most wore gauze masks. Allene felt completely out of place, an invader. If only she had a mask to hide behind, but she had dropped it somewhere along the way.

Esther noticed her reticence and gently led her inside. There was a schedule of services written on a placard inside the vestibule. Too many for a single day, Allene thought. Thousands were succumbing every day, she'd heard. They were just in time for the mass for Lucy and three others. There were so many dying that the services had to be grouped together.

The priest stood tall and unbreakable and began the mass. He spoke a few kind words about Lucy and the three other women who had died. Soon, he switched to Latin and Italian, shutting her out completely. Allene stole a glance around at the community and wondered who the strangers were. The priest spoke on, his voice creaking from tiredness. He must have been speaking all day about the dead, and such work couldn't be kind on his voice box. They stood and kneeled and stood again, and Allene, who was Presbyterian, lagged behind, lost amongst the Catholic rituals. Finally, the priest switched back to English.

"And as Mary loved her child, so did our good sister Lucy. Never was there a more devoted mother to her children." He went on, but Allene was lost again.

"Children!" Allene said aloud. It sounded like a sneeze in the dark.

Several faces turned and stared at her rudeness. Allene knew her face went crimson, and her heart ran like rain on a dry roof. She clutched at Esther's arm, feeling faint.

"Are you well, Miss Allene?" Esther whispered. "What is the matter?"

"Oh, I forgot. I forgot! How many children does she have? Oh, how old are they?"

"Shhh!"

She didn't know who shushed her, but she deserved it. Allene bent her head, her forehead swimming in new perspiration that began to trickle down her neck. What on earth was happening? Everything she knew to be true was tilting and sliding off, crashing into the chaos of her painfully inaccurate memory. After Birdie and her mother left her home, Lucy had always been there for her. She'd tended to her every need, listened to every complaint, reassured her when she wasn't fully sure of her own brilliance. Lucy's life had been Allene's to order about. The comfort and care had always been given in a single direction, and arrow-like, it thrust into Allene's center. Her very lungs ached.

Her Lucy was dead. And Lucy had children, and Allene hadn't ever bothered to ask about them all these years. She remembered hearing about them once in a while—Lucy had been absent when one had the measles—but outside of those inconveniences, Allene knew nothing. Lucy never volunteered information about birthdays or celebrations or those little proud things mothers might say about their children. It wasn't her place.

And there was Holly. Oh God. Had Lucy known who Holly's father was all this time? If only she could ask her now. Had she pitied Allene for her idiotic stupidity in not seeing the obvious? Perhaps everyone had known except her.

The mourners began to leak out of the aisles and the church. Allene stood up dizzily. Her chest felt heavy, and her breath came with effort. The darkened apse with its painted walls and statues and staring saints and gods suffocated her. Esther nodded with apology to the others in the church as they filed out of their pew.

As they entered the dimming afternoon light outside, Allene stumbled slightly against Esther. Allene's feet felt heavier than ice blocks.

"Miss Allene? Are you well?"

"I'm fine. I'm just . . . oh, Esther. What's become of her children?"

"Well, they are twins, you know. I went to their last birthday party. They just turned ten." She paused to study Allene's face, which was moist with perspiration.

"I didn't even know how old they were," Allene murmured. She knotted her hands, wishing she had worn gloves to absorb the dampness. She didn't know where to put her eyes or her hands. "I didn't know. She never said anything."

And the worst was—oh God. Allene had never asked. Not once.

Esther patted her back awkwardly. A man in a suit approached her with two children, each holding one of his hands. He was in his forties, with a dusting of curly gray hair at his temples, large eyes like Lucy's, but a thinner smile with a mustache. The two children had dry, wary eyes. One wore a crisp sailor dress and the other a neat brown suit that nearly matched the man's. Someone loved them enough to iron the garments into painful stiffness. The children stared at Allene with bland curiosity, from her dusty shoes to her face, which was surely melting her makeup onto her dress collar. They held that same expression she'd seen so many times on Lucy—patient, thoughtful, slightly exasperated. It said they knew the truth behind it all but were too wise to say so aloud. Allene wanted, simultaneously, to embrace them and bolt away.

"You are Miss Allene Cutter, yes?" the man asked. His Italian accent was thick, much thicker than Lucy's.

Allene nodded. She searched for a handkerchief in her reticule, but all it had was a powder compact and jangling coins.

"*Prego.*" He offered a folded handkerchief, and Allene took it gratefully. He smiled. "I lose many to women these days."

"I'm sorry," Allene said. She wished she could expand the words to mean more. They were woefully inadequate.

"I am Alessandro Rossi, the brother of Lucia." His voice was warm and rich, like good brandy. "We hear so much of you, Miss Allene. She know you so long, since you were . . ." He held his hand at the height of the two children next to him. "*Piccola ragazza.* She say you are good at, what do they call it? *Chimica?*"

Allene smiled in spite of herself. "Chemistry. Did Lucy . . . Lucia say that?"

"*Sì.* She was proud. Very proud. But she is afraid you going to set house on fire!" He chuckled, before sobering. "Miss Allene. Her family and I . . . we thank you for being her nurse." He put his hands together as if in prayer. "*La ringrazio tanto.*"

"I wish I could have done more," Allene said, rushing her words. "I wish . . . I wish . . ." She stopped and burst into tears. Everything that came from her mouth was empty and useless. Esther flushed ruddily with embarrassment, and Allene released her arm, which she'd been leaning on. "I have to go. I'm so sorry."

"Miss Allene!" she called as Allene trotted away in her heels as quickly as she could.

She needed fresh air, to be away from those staring, sympathetic eyes that made her wretched. Her buckled shoes were too tight, and she slowed to a walk. Her legs felt stuck in tar, every step more arduous than the last. The bad feeling inside coated her lungs, and her breathing became labored.

Was she going east or west? How would she find the train to get back home? Her reticule was still hanging from her wrist, and faintly she heard the jangling of a few coins inside. It wasn't enough for a cab. Her blurred eyes searched the streets, but there were no livery cabs anywhere, anyway. Harlem was an altogether alien landscape to her. Passersby stared at her and gave her a wide berth—she must have looked a fright, with tears still pooling in her red eyes. Her nose began to run, and she blotted the back of her hand to her face. Blood smeared on her skin. Somewhere in her milky consciousness, Allene thought, This is very bad. But she was too driven to keep walking, walking, walking. Go home, she told herself. You must get home.

Her breath came in wheezes, and her hands flailed out, pawing the air as if it were water drowning her. Darkness nipped at the edges of her vision—the sun was setting, but darkness had never come so quickly before.

The muscles of her legs spasmed, and she felt herself falling. It would be a relief to lie on the dirty sidewalk, just to rest. Rest. If she could only rest, and sleep, and leave all these terrible thoughts behind. If only—

"Whoops! I've got you."

Strong arms caught her before her knees could slam against the hard ground. She felt another arm scoop her legs up below the knees, and her head knocked against a broad shoulder. Unconsciousness began to close like an aperture over her vision and thoughts. Before she fell into a dead faint, she was able to see a bit of blond hair and brown eyes full of concern.

It was Ernie.

CHAPTER 27

Jasper had been watching over Allene for almost a week now.

She had shown up at the Cutter house after Ernie Fielding had miraculously found her insensate. What a champ. He'd followed her on foot like a pet on a long leash, taking his usual hovering habits a bit far this time but with good effect. He'd caught up to Allene the moment she'd swooned and had carried her for an exhausting twenty blocks before he managed to get a cab. Ernie was far stronger than Jasper gave him credit for.

Once she was at home, it was clear that Allene's body had become an estuary of blood. It poured from her nose, her mouth, at times even her ears. It curdled into the edge of her scalp and turned her lovely, cushioned bedroom into a scene of muted violence. Sometimes the torrent would stop and her breathing would settle, become less frothy; at other times, death hovered too close.

The sickness exhaled its inevitable fog over the whole household as more servants grew sick and fell to the floor—sometimes dying before they could even speak for help. George, the elderly butler, had succumbed that very night. Two of the youngest maids, barely in their twenties, went by the same dark path later that week.

Allene's body was being devoured by sickness. Mr. Cutter was paralyzed by the blood that caked his daughter's waxy, white face and lips. The same night that she was rescued by Ernie, Jasper demanded that she be brought to the hospital.

"Is there no other way?" was all Mr. Cutter managed to say.

"She can't be nursed back to health. It didn't work with Lucy. I don't understand why, but this influenza is like none the doctors have seen. I can ask them to administer oxygen, maybe some transfusions. It's a stretch, but there's nothing to lose but Allene. We have to do something."

With the help of Dawlish—eyes wide with fear and suffocating under the three layers of gauze masks—Jasper had carried Allene into the car. Within the next few hours, Jasper secured Allene a rare open bed at the hospital, surrounded by an entire long, windowed room filled with the dying. The exhausted doctors and nurses, scant in number, shook their heads at him.

"It's useless. Calomel is all we can do—and aspirin."

"We've been doing that already."

"Then she's done for. An oxygen mask and blood can't help, boy. You're trying to outrun a waterfall. Call her priest if you want to do something useful."

"Damn the priest," Jasper muttered. "I'll treat her myself if you won't."

The doctor was older, too old for the draft. He watched Jasper as he rolled up his sleeves and barked orders at the nurses.

"Are you one of the medical residents?"

"No sir. I'm entering medical school next year."

The doctor clucked at him, wiping his bloody hands on a cloth, before tossing it onto a pile of rust-colored, stained linens in the corner. "There's a war going on."

"I already registered. I didn't get called yet," Jasper said defensively.

"Not that war. This one." He pointed at the forty or so other patients lying on the cots in the gigantic ward. "You have to prepare."

"For what?"

"For the next bloody war, and I don't mean the next kaiser. They never stop getting sick. Don't burn yourself out for one person. Steel your heart. Save it for your future patients."

Jasper turned away, ignoring him. He was sick of people being plucked haphazardly out of his life and tossed into his memories. Allene's breath came shallow and quick, black liquid staining her chin. Steel his heart? He didn't want to save it for anyone, not anymore. He'd rather use it, and then some. It was no good to Jasper anymore.

It took hours and hours to arrange the blood donation. He managed to pin down the only available physician familiar with the apparatus and practically dragged him to Allene's bedside. The copper cannula was a wide bore, and it hurt like hell to tunnel into his arm vein, but it was worth it. Thank goodness he was a match. And the second he had a chance, he phoned Mr. Cutter and Andrew. Andrew wasn't a match, but Mr. Cutter and Ernie had type O and were universal donors, and they were more than willing to give to Allene.

Jasper prayed that the blood wouldn't simply go into her vein and pour out of her lungs. He procured some oxygen too. The tank rolled to her bedside was a behemoth. He fashioned a tent of oilcloth about her upper body and let the oxygen issue around her. Every few minutes, he'd duck beneath the tent to sponge away the bubbling, frothy liquid emanating from her lungs so she wouldn't aspirate her own secretions. It was a constant struggle to bathe her, keep the tent on, force-feed her calomel, and clean up the ensuing bedpan mess from the potent cathartic.

The nurses didn't offer to help. The staff was too busy wrapping up the dead and comforting the dying.

One minute went by, then an hour, then a day. Allene should have died. Most people their age did, especially when they bled the way

Allene did, from her eyes, her nose, her throat. Actually, *bled* was too calm a word for what was occurring. *Gushed* was more the truth.

But at some point—was it three days after she'd fainted in Harlem? Five?—the deluge slowed to a trickle. Allene's eyes opened. Jasper was asleep when it happened. He'd been so sleep deprived he thought he was hallucinating when he felt her bony hand rest on his forearm. For a moment, in his half-asleep state, he thought death was tapping him politely, asking him for a slow waltz.

Allene moaned and blinked, her eyes sunken into purplish sockets. "Jasper" was all she was able to say. Jasper ducked beneath the oxygen tent, ignoring the hissing from the nearby tank.

"I figured you'd do something pigheaded like get influenza," Jasper chided her, his voice muffled beneath the gauze masks. Allene rested for another five minutes before she could attempt to speak again.

"Only you . . . would . . . yell at a sick woman," she rasped.

"Teasing is a service I'm always happy to provide," he said, smiling. His eyes, however, prickled. He'd cry if he wasn't careful.

She was so dehydrated that her eyes stayed glassily dry. "Thank you," she whispered. "So much."

Jasper patted her hand and blinked before withdrawing his hand and reaching for a stethoscope. Relief filled him. The sun had risen somewhere behind his leaden heart. He carefully uncovered her arms, examined her legs, listened to her heart (though all he understood was that it was beating slower than a hummingbird's, and that was good). Allene was as pale as the fresh sheets he laid over her body. But her color had gone from blue to white, and he nearly wept from relief.

By the next morning, she was able to sit up in bed for a few minutes and sip some broth. Exhaustion had wrung out Jasper. His hands trembled, and he stuttered when he spoke. Dr. Gettler had heard about his bedside vigil and marched over to the main building from his lab to tell Jasper to go home.

"Don't return for twelve hours," he ordered. "Your girl will be fine."

Jasper bristled at his words. "She's not my girl. But the lab—I should be getting back to work."

Gettler pulled him toward the main door to the ward. Coughs and wheezes filled the background with a pulmonary symphony of saturated alveoli. "Dr. Norris and I have been reviewing your work. You're very good at what you do."

"Thank you."

"It's not a compliment." Gettler squinted at him. "We have eyes, you know. Our job is to observe things that others miss. Anytime a case comes in that's related to you, your work gets messy. And we're too busy to be messy."

"But I helped get information on Hazel Dreyer's death!"

"At what cost?" Gettler said. "You didn't notice, but your focus was off. Messages were lost, items got ordered wrong that week. Small mistakes in any other office don't matter. Here, they could mean a sample going bad before we can analyze it. It can mean someone getting away with murder." He shifted uncomfortably. "You're fired, Jasper."

"What? Sir, I can . . . I promise that in future cases, I'll—"

"Future cases? Son, how many friends of yours are you expecting to die soon?"

At this, Jasper was silenced. How could he explain the letters? The creeping darkness closing upon Allene and Birdie and him? But the lure of solving the puzzle in order to polish a shining career had dimmed. Jasper used to care about Jasper's best, and now he didn't care much at all, which was both liberating and terrifying.

"You should be proud. I hear you saved that girl's life." Gettler began to walk away, then turned. He shook his finger at Jasper. "Forget pathology. Go live with the living. It suits you better."

Jasper slept for nearly fourteen hours. He awoke in the same position he'd fallen asleep in, as if weighed down by concrete. When he sought out Allene at Bellevue, she'd improved enough to go back home. A few days later, Mr. Cutter greeted him at the door, looking paler (he'd given a pint of blood recently, after all), thinner, and about a hundred years old.

"Jasper." He had never called him by his Christian name before. "Thank you for taking such care of Allene. I'm in your debt."

"It was nothing," Jasper said. He itched to loosen his hand from Mr. Cutter's grasp, particularly when he heard feminine voices arising from the sitting room.

Allene. Birdie.

It always came back to the three of them. Together, the girls gave him direction, like the triangular point of an arrow telling him where to be.

Mr. Cutter finally let go but seemed to struggle for a moment before speaking again. "I never explained to Allene or to you about your uncle's insurance policy. I'm sorry he never told you, but let me be clear. It was brought to my attention that he needed help. So I paid his rather substantial debts, and in return the policy was put in place to guarantee his debt release if he were ever unable to repay me."

Jasper was wordless.

"I am sorry about his passing. It was all just an investment of sorts, to be quite honest. And in fact, the insurance money will be coming my way shortly—and there was no appropriate time to mention it, but—it's yours. Minus the debt, of course. It doesn't feel right to hold on to it."

Jasper stood there, stock still, trying to understand. In his last conversation with his uncle, he had accused him of neglecting the mounting bills, when in fact they'd been taken care of. He felt wretched.

"I can't touch that money." He straightened up and stared at Mr. Cutter evenly. "But I thank you for helping my uncle. For helping me. If you keep that money, I won't feel like I owe you anything."

Mr. Cutter nodded, and a small gleam of appreciation lit his eye—and pity. Jasper would truly make his own fate now. With no Bellevue in his future.

Ernie walked into the foyer. His face lit up. "Jasper! What a saint you are!" He shook his hand a little too hard. It actually hurt. "You should go rest, Mr. Cutter. We'll watch over the girls."

Like an obedient child, Mr. Cutter nodded and took his maid's firm arm as they mounted the staircase.

Jealousy crept across Jasper's skin. Ernie was looking well, dressed as usual in pressed trousers and tailored shirt. He wasn't fidgeting anymore. It was as if he had grown from a simpering boy into a man overnight. Perhaps rescuing damsels was all it took for a transformation. But what was more, a shrewd look lit his eyes as he glanced over Jasper's threadbare elbows and shifting glance.

There was a knock on the door. Josephine came scurrying down the stairs to welcome Andrew into the foyer.

"Andrew! How are you?" Ernie strode forward as if he were the host, extending a hand. But Andrew dodged the gesture, instead rubbing his palms together. He wore a dark suit, and he looked like he hadn't slept in a year. He was a tarnished penny compared to the gleaming gold piece that was Ernie.

As the maid removed Andrew's coat, Jasper casually examined his hands. Dark spots colored Andrew's palms. Had he been writing letters and spilled an ink pot somewhere? The skin seemed thickened too, as if recently calloused from heavy labor.

"Did you get struck down with the flu as well?" Ernie asked.

"Yes. I'm just about over it, though." Andrew gestured beyond the silken screens. "How are the ladies?"

"Allene is better," Ernie said. "Thank goodness she had a good constitution to begin with. She's been able to walk without assistance, and her appetite has returned. Her color is good, but she's still coughing. I made sure the doctor paid a visit this morning. Birdie still can't walk. She's . . . advancing."

Jasper and Andrew stared at him, surprised that he was the owner of such intimate details.

"Advancing?" Andrew said. What color he had possessed drained away.

"Yes. The cancer in her leg is growing. She's in a lot of pain, but I've been making sure the maids keep it at bay with her medicine. It's terrible, but sometimes these things happen."

Andrew grabbed Ernie's shirt collar with a violence that astonished Jasper. "These things don't just *happen*! She's only just eighteen, for God's sake!"

Ernie pulled his hands together, drove them between Andrew's, and broke his hold too easily. His face reddened with anger, not cowardice.

"And how would you know? So self-involved, you never even saw that your fiancée's best friend was dying in front of your eyes!"

"All right, that's enough," Jasper said, stepping between them and raising his hands. "This isn't helping them."

The maid in the hallway cleared her throat and curtsied. "I am sorry for the delay, but they've asked for you, sir."

All three men turned on their heels but exchanged glances. The maid had said *sir*, not *sirs*.

"I'm sorry, for who?" Jasper asked.

"For Mr. Fielding. I'll let the ladies know you two gentlemen have also arrived," she said.

"Well, I'll be," Andrew huffed when Ernie picked up his coat. Several magazines and papers were stuffed into his coat pocket and nearly fell out when he followed the maid.

"Humph," Jasper murmured, after a long silence. "I feel like a coat hanger with no coat."

"I understand that metaphor," Andrew said. He hid his spotted hands in his trouser pockets and pulled out a tin of lavender pastilles. As usual, he didn't offer one to Jasper. Selfish prig. Soon, the maid returned and ushered the other two men into the salon.

Allene lay on a chaise, covered by a damask coverlet. She looked pale and thin, but color once again ignited her cheeks. She donned a brilliant smile at their entrance and reached for Jasper's hand.

"Oh, Jasper. What would I have done without you? If only you could have helped Lucia too." Jasper blinked at the pronunciation of the maid's name. "You've heard about George and the others . . ." She dabbed at her eyes.

"Well, I didn't know any of it would help. You're lucky."

Allene nodded. "Very lucky." Holly emerged from behind the sofa and sat on Allene's lap.

He pointed. "Is that a good idea? Having Holly here?"

"No, it's not," Birdie agreed, reclining on a chaise opposite Allene's. "But we think she caught the flu last week, though it was the smallest trifle. Can you believe it? Anyway, we can't keep her away from Allene." Allene seemed in a sort of bliss with Holly on her lap. Matching cups of tea sat at the ladies' elbows on three-legged marble tables. Allene and Birdie were once again two peas in a pod. Ernie sat between them, studying them for any signs of discomfort.

"Jasper, did you know what you are?" Holly asked aloud to everyone. "You're a rock. You're in a book too. Want to see?" She lisped her words. *Want to thee?* A book was open on the table by Allene. While she and Birdie spoke to Andrew and Ernie, Jasper strode to the open book. Their faces were now all turned away, and for all he knew they'd already forgotten he was here. He disliked being excluded from their conversation, but they were talking about the stalled peace talks in Europe, and he disliked that subject too.

Holly pointed a chubby finger at an open page in *American Gems and Precious Stones*. A pencil had marked a chapter on jasper.

275

"Oh. Of course." He'd assumed she thought he was a mighty, unmovable tower of mountainous strength, but here she was telling him he was a shiny, pretty thing. "Can you read this?"

Holly shook her head. "No. But Auntie Ally reads it to me at bedtime."

"Let's see what it says." He peered closer and read aloud. "'Jasper is found at many localities and in a great variety of colors. Jasper is very little used in the arts, and for so common a stone, the entire annual sales would not be more than one thousand dollars.'" He hooted out loud.

"What's funny?" Holly asked.

"I'm common and cheap, and I'm a dime a dozen." He grimaced. "My parents named me well." He patted her on the head, and Holly pulled him back over toward Allene's chaise. Andrew had suddenly gone to crouch by Birdie's side. He hid nothing, that one.

"It's just a few things I left at the factory. Would one of you be able to get them?" Birdie asked.

"Ernie can fetch those things for you. Won't you, Ernie?" Allene interjected.

Birdie gave Andrew a single look, and he rose to his feet and stepped closer to Allene.

"Actually, I did promise to pick up a few more things for the girls anyway. Why don't we go together?" Ernie suggested.

"Fine idea," Andrew replied, though his face showed no enthusiasm for company. He bent down to dutifully kiss Allene and squeeze her hand, but he grimaced in discomfort. Her sapphire engagement ring had become loose on her thin finger, and the large stone had twirled downward inside her palm, where it poked its giver.

Andrew soon left with Ernie. Minutes later, Birdie exclaimed, "Oh! Ernie left his coat." She patted the garment draped over the end of her chaise. The paper contents of his overstuffed pockets tumbled out.

"My magazines! He brought them for us to read. Jasper, would you mind?"

Jasper picked up the pile of papers, removing the curled magazines to give to Allene. "Ugh, what a pack rat he is. Look." There were three crumpled Mary Jane candy wrappers and a creased envelope as well. He flipped it over and stared at it.

"What is it?" Allene asked.

Jasper was silent as he stared at the script on the front. "It's for you," he said to Allene, but ice had crept into his voice.

Allene picked up the cream-colored envelope and opened it, withdrawing a sheet of folded paper. No stamps, no date, yet again. Her lips barely moved as she read it.

"No," she whispered. "No, it can't be." She handed it to Birdie, who read it aloud.

"'You're welcome.'" Birdie paused, and handed the letter to Jasper. "I don't understand. What was it doing in Ernie's pocket?"

"You're joking, right?" Allene said, staring at Birdie like she was a simpleton. "It's so obvious. How could we not have seen? It's Ernie. Ernie has been giving us those damned letters."

Jasper dropped the letter to the floor. "What? Ernie Fielding? The kid who let us tie him to a chair for hours and thanked us for letting him play with us? Ernie couldn't hurt a fly, much less orchestrate a murder."

"Or several," Birdie added. She frowned. "Then again, he's been coming to all these funerals lately. He was at Florence's graveside. And he was at Mother's too."

"And Lucy's," Allene added. "He had no business being there."

"His business was to follow you, Allene," Jasper noted. "He's always had the rottenest kind of crush. Even now, even with Andrew being one foot away. He moons over you like nobody else. And that night that my uncle died. You said there was a man on the street watching us when we went inside. Was he Ernie's height and breadth?"

"Yes, it could have been. Ernie's so tall now," Birdie said. "But why? Why would he do such a thing?"

"He wanted to be close to us. Maybe he's just trying to get our attention."

"By murdering the people around us? What lunatic of a person would do that?" Allene cried out. Jasper shushed her, and she calmed. "And what about Lucy? She died from the flu. Was that murder?"

"No. That must have been bad luck," Jasper said. "But look. Every one of us has had someone . . . removed . . . from our life who was making our lives harder in some way." They all stared at the floor, and Jasper went on. "I'll admit that I might have been able to save money better if my uncle hadn't drunk down our savings. Life for me is easier without him."

Birdie looked at her lap. "And I was terrified that my mother would make me and Holly follow in her footsteps. You know."

"Florence could have tried to heave some nasty gossip about you, Allene." He rubbed his chin. "God, is it your turn again? Is Ernie going to keep at it until we stop him? Who would you be thankful was gone, Allene? That Ernie would be welcomed to kill off?"

Allene stared at her lap hard. The glistening Ceylon sapphire on her engagement ring shone like a tiny ocean in her hand.

"Oh God." She looked at them both, eyes full of panic. "Andrew!"

CHAPTER 28

Allene stared as Jasper paced about the salon. "You really think that Ernie could want to kill Andrew?" Jasper inquired. "Really? I just can't see it."

"Forget what you can and can't see," Allene said. "Our vision hasn't been so sharp lately. Especially mine." She slipped her legs over the edge of the chaise and slowly pushed herself to her feet. It was hard, but not so hard as yesterday. Her eyes blinked in dizziness, and dark spots twinkled in her field of vision before dissipating. "Ernie was too eager to go off with Andrew. We have to tell Andrew or telephone the police."

"Have Josephine call," Jasper said quickly. "But we should go now. By the time they get there, it might be too late. Did Dawlish take them to the factory?"

They rang the bell for a motorcar. It turned out Andrew's chauffeur had taken them. Allene spoke to Josephine and asked for her coat.

"And my good boots, the sturdy ones without the heels," Allene instructed, coughing a little. "And I need a cane."

"You are *not* going!" Jasper told her.

She balked at the order. "Yes, I am."

"I'll get your father and make him forbid it."

Allene stopped struggling with her coat to stare at him. "Jasper Jones. Are you my friend or not?"

"I am. But you're still convalescing, Allene. You shouldn't—"

"Think about it. Ernie adores me. If anyone can make him stop, it's me. And you're not going to stop me anyway."

"I should come too," Birdie said. Allene and Jasper half spun around to shout at her.

"*No!*"

Birdie shrank on her divan.

"Your leg is broken. You can barely stand! Stay here, and we'll tell you everything when we get back."

Birdie's lower lip wavered, and her eyes began to fill with tears. "What if you don't come back?"

"We'll be back. We promise," Allene said.

Birdie nodded meekly, and Allene left with Jasper. Walking those fifteen feet to the curb, even with his arm to lean on, was exhausting. She huffed and puffed, trying to catch her breath.

Jasper stared at her anxiously. "I shouldn't have let you come."

"I don't have the breath," she gasped, "to argue with you. So be quiet, please."

Dawlish drove as quickly as he could downtown toward the Brooklyn Bridge, occasionally stealing furtive glances at the two. Jasper kept his arm protectively around Allene's shoulders, and Allene allowed it. She had a sense that somehow Jasper was dangerously close to breaking away from her orbit. She missed him already. So she sank into his shoulder, grateful for someone to lean against, even if he was borrowed for the time being.

As they pulled up to the front of the factory, Andrew's chauffeured car was nowhere to be seen.

"What if they're not here?" Jasper wondered.

"One way to find out. Help me out?" She extended her hand as Dawlish opened the door, and once again leaned heavily on Jasper's arm.

The doors to the factory were closed. It was Sunday, after all. And as expected, the police weren't there yet. The door was securely locked, and no one answered when Jasper pounded on it.

"There must be another way in. This building takes up an entire block. Surely there's another door somewhere."

They snaked around the west side of the building, and lo and behold, Andrew's shining automobile was waiting beneath the line of trees. The chauffeur was inside reading a weekly. The sight of Allene and Jasper walking up to his window startled him.

"Miss Cutter! What . . . What . . ." he sputtered.

"Are they inside? Mr. Fielding and my fiancé?" Allene demanded. The young man began sweating and couldn't put together a coherent sentence. Clearly, he'd become accustomed to bringing Andrew here to visit Birdie. The sight of Allene had turned him into a simpleton. "Never mind. They're here."

"Of course they are," Jasper told her. They walked past the motorcar to the only door on the side of the building. It looked securely closed, but Jasper tried the doorknob and, wonder of wonders, it turned in his palm.

"He's part owner. Of course he'd have a key to the factory," Allene said. She pushed it open, and it was very dark inside. The corridor led to a hallway that circumscribed the entire building. The faint noise of a machine whirring sounded from somewhere above, giving her the impression that the building was awake and breathing, its industrial heart beating somewhere. A loud knock and a shout echoed from the ceiling above them.

"What was that?" Jasper asked for the both of them. Their eyes grew accustomed to the darkness, and they pressed forward past the administrative offices, the case and finishing rooms. A narrow stairway emerged from the gloom, and they began to climb, slowly because of Allene's fatigue.

"I don't know why I let you come," Jasper growled.

"Because I would have killed you if you hadn't."

"Oh. Of course."

Upstairs, it was dark. Jasper tried a light switch but it didn't work. The whirring sound was closer, and a metallic scent pervaded the air. A muffled grunt came from down the hallway. Jasper clasped Allene's hand and led her quickly down the corridor, past a room filled with half-finished mantel clocks and another containing nothing but metalwork.

They approached the last room. Inside, the electric overhead lamps were off, but light from the row of windows shone on rows and rows of black drills and machines for buffing and sanding clock parts. Electric cords twisted to the ceiling, and belted rotors coiled in figure eights every few feet. Several of the drills had been turned on, accounting for the hum in their ears.

Allene peered down the aisle between the rows of worktables and machines, all covered in fine metal dust. Two sets of feet tangled and kicked on the dusty floor twenty feet away.

"Andrew!" Allene cried out.

A choking, gargling sound came from the struggling figures. Jasper broke free of Allene's hand and bolted down the aisle. Despite her weakness, she gathered her skirts in her hands and scurried after him, barely able to catch her breath.

Between two machine tables, Ernie and Andrew lay locked in battle. Ernie was sitting astride Andrew, who was struggling with one hand to choke Ernie and with the other to prevent the descent of the jeweler's screwdriver in Ernie's fist.

Andrew half screamed, half shouted, "Get him off me! He's trying to kill me!"

Jasper lunged forward, but Ernie turned to him and yelled savagely, "Stay back! He's lying!"

Never had they heard such a voice come from the complacent and obedient Ernie. Allene held on to a table, the violence of the scene making her flush. Blood streaked down Ernie's back, and his shirt was torn where something had pierced his right shoulder. And Andrew's face was like a skull, his skin like yellowed vellum. He kicked and screamed again, trying to buck Ernie off him, but Ernie was a vigorous six feet of well-fed youth.

Jasper and Allene froze.

It was obvious who the aggressor was—Ernie's screwdriver inched its way closer to Andrew's face, and that was sufficient information. Jasper dashed forward and yanked Ernie's shoulders from behind, and grabbed the wrist holding the screwdriver. They both flailed backward. Ernie swallowed a protest as Jasper pulled his arm back hard. It looked like it would dislocate with one more tug.

Ernie howled in pain, and Jasper wrestled the screwdriver out of his hand, tossing it behind him, but not before Ernie kicked Jasper in the gut so hard, he crumpled to the ground. Andrew scrambled back, distancing himself from Ernie. Allene darted to Andrew's side and cradled his shoulders. He trembled from head to toe, and his pale face had a sickly green tint. Ernie stumbled away from Jasper and rubbed his sore shoulder.

Allene thought, He's going to attack again. And I'm too weak to do anything. It was up to Jasper to catch his breath and stop him, but Jasper was still moaning and clutching his abdomen.

The air sparkled with the faint dust of powdery metal shavings. She looked quickly at the table nearest to her. A pile of clock faces had been sanded down so their surfaces were etched with a pattern. Piles of silvery metal dust covered the table. But it wasn't silver. It was like the face of the clock she had at home—a zinc disc, a touch cloudier than silver with a matte finish.

Ernie gathered himself to renew his attack on Andrew. Without hesitating, Allene drew her beloved lighter from the hidden pocket of her dress, pulled the strike out, and quickly ran it against the ferrocerium on the bottom. It lit, and she puffed forcefully on the table, sending a cloud of zinc dust into the air. Ernie ran forward.

Allene threw the lit striker into the cloud.

The zinc combusted with a flash and a bang. The explosion was big, enough to slam Allene back onto the floor and on top of Andrew. Ernie fell too, his hair singed and shirt smoldering. The blast didn't kill him, but it dazed him enough to give Jasper the momentum he needed. He managed to plant his feet, lift Ernie by the collar, and slam his fist against Ernie's right temple. Ernie's body jerked at the impact. Andrew pushed Allene away and scrambled on hands and knees until he found the screwdriver on the floor. He plunged it into the center of Ernie's belly and pulled it out.

Ernie couldn't speak, either from having the wind pummeled out of him or from being impaled. He curled his fists into the bleeding wound of his belly and rolled over. His body jerked once before sagging against the dust- and soot-covered floor.

"Good God!" Andrew wheezed.

"Allene, are you all right?" Jasper asked.

She nodded. She was still sprawled on the ground, skirts askew and petticoats in a tangle around her calves. She panted with exertion, unable to utter a word. Andrew lay flat on his back, taking rasping breaths, rubbing his recently choked neck. Finally, Allene composed herself and stood with Jasper's aid.

"We ought to call the police. And an ambulance." Jasper looked over at Andrew and offered a hand to help him up, but Andrew ignored him, still rubbing his throat. Slowly, he got to his knees and then stood, leaning against one of the drill machines. His usually slicked-back hair was in a tumbled disarray, his shirt untucked and stained with industrial grease and blood.

"No. Not that." Andrew shook his head. "I don't need an ambulance."

"He tried to kill you!" Allene's voice trembled and tears gathered at her eyelashes. "You almost died, Andrew!"

Andrew smiled, which was odd and unexpected. "Eh, that is true. That is true. But I'm already a dead man, anyway."

"What are you talking about?" Jasper took a step closer.

He laughed again and took out a folded handkerchief and rubbed the perspiration away from his forehead. "Lord, you have poor eyes. Can't ever see what's in front of you."

Allene glanced uncertainly at Jasper, who took a careful sideways step just as Andrew lifted his fist.

He was still holding the bloody screwdriver.

He held it in his thickened palms, transferring it from one hand to the other, testing its weight.

"Ernie tried to kill me, it's true," Andrew said. "Because I was trying to kill him first."

Allene swallowed, taking a cautious step back to lean against one of the drill tables.

"No, Andrew." She shook her head. "We found the letter in Ernie's pocket! The one that foretold of someone about to die. He was about to give it to me, I know it."

"Oh, that. The letter was waiting for you in the foyer. It was from me. Ernie simply picked it up to give you, along with the other magazines he was delivering. He's so good at scurrying after anything you want, isn't he?" He chuckled and frowned simultaneously. It turned his visage into a gruesome mask.

"You? You put the letter there for me?" Allene asked, her voice cracking. "Oh my God, Ernie!" She rushed to his side, where he was still unconscious, but thankfully breathing. Ernie, who was only trying to help. Oh, God in heaven. How could she have been so wrong? As her hand rested on his cold, sweaty forehead, a million scenes played out in her mind, a kaleidoscope of images. Hazel Dreyer dead on the floor of a laudanum overdose. Jasper's uncle splayed out on a floor of broken glass, with too much wood alcohol drowning his mind. Florence.

"Yes. I put it there. And yes, I killed Hazel and your drunk uncle."

"You goddamned bastard!" Jasper hollered with a viciousness that sent spittle to the factory floor. Jasper took two rushing steps to attack Andrew, but Andrew's legs shuddered, and he collapsed to his knees in weakness before Jasper could even touch him.

"I am. I am. I own that I'm a monster." He began to laugh and slowly sat down to rest his arms on his knees. "Oh, this business. It's killing me. I need a breather. I need a bracer too. Got any whiskey?" he asked Jasper, chuckling.

Jasper gathered Andrew's shirtfront in his fist. He didn't even try to resist. He even dropped the screwdriver, as if thankful that Jasper was keeping him from falling over. "Why?" Jasper growled. "Why would you kill my uncle? He did nothing to you."

"Ah, but he did plenty to you. Look at you, all indignant and playing the victim. He was a drunk, in debt, and an embarrassment. He wanted you to stay away from Allene and Birdie. Didn't you ever listen to him?" Allene and Jasper exchanged glances. "Oh, it was easy enough to overpower him and pour the wood alcohol down his throat. Allene gave me the idea. She told me that she'd almost poisoned herself by accident. I bought a bottle, but no one would know it was mine, not his. All too easy."

Allene's stomach curled into a knot. She remembered the remark and remembered Andrew had waved it off as a minor accident. She thought Andrew had forgotten it. She hadn't wanted him to be jealous of her being in Jasper's apartment, but the whole time, he'd been thinking of murder instead.

"But Hazel Dreyer? So you did get the wrong prescription?"

"I did. And I didn't." He shrugged.

Allene remembered the young pharmacist wearing far too fine a wardrobe after he'd been fired. "The pharmacist. You paid him off, didn't you?"

"Eh, he hated the job anyway."

"Why, why? Why would you do these things? They didn't deserve any of it! Why would you kill Florence? What did she do to you?"

"Florence?" Andrew rested his head in his hand, scratching his head. A few strands of his hair fell loose to the floor, revealing small balding patches beneath the dull-brown hair. "Oh, Florence. Well, I didn't kill her."

"And we're to believe that?" Allene said. She stood, placing herself between Ernie's unconscious form and Andrew. "After you've confessed to killing our dearest . . . you killed Birdie's *mother*. I thought you loved Birdie!"

Andrew's head snapped up at Birdie's name. "I do." He held an apology in his eyes. "I'm sorry, Allene. So sorry. But you won't miss me. You never loved me, and perhaps I never loved you. But now Birdie won't have anything to do with me." He dropped his head, and Jasper let go of his shirt, not wanting to touch Andrew's face. He collapsed to the factory floor and began to weep. "She despises me for giving her everything she wanted."

Jasper and Allene stared at him, this grand, six-foot-tall man crying like a left-behind child on the playground.

"What, did you do these things to get her attention? Why, why would you?" Allene asked, incredulous. What a way to woo a girl! None of it made sense. But Andrew was still sobbing into his arms. Soon, the weeping began to abate. He seemed to be meditating on his sins in silence. They waited to hear more.

"Andrew," Jasper said, but Andrew stayed silent. His story was finished and unraveled, for the time being. The police wouldn't be so patient. "Allene, see if you can send Dawlish to bring the police. I'll watch Andrew and Ernie," Jasper said. Behind Allene, Ernie was starting to moan and regain consciousness.

"No. Wait." Allene was watching Andrew acutely. There was something strange and still about the way his head sagged into his folded arms, the way his fingers hung loosely over his elbows. She took a deliberate step closer, letting her boot clack hard on the floor, yet Andrew stayed frozen still. Two more steps, and she gathered her skirts to crouch at his side, observing him down to the factory dust in his hair. She lifted her fingers, readying herself to touch his shoulder.

Jasper raised a hand of warning. "Allene, don't—"

With a small grunt of effort, she pushed Andrew's shoulder hard. He fell over, eyes open to the ceiling, the mask of death already finding a home on his grimacing face.

CHAPTER 29

This is becoming a habit, Jasper thought.

This has to stop.

Another crime scene was laid out before him, and once again, he was threaded into the story inextricably, irreversibly.

An ambulance arrived to whisk away Ernie, who had awoken in excruciating pain from the stab wound. While Jasper spoke to the police, Allene stayed with Andrew's unmoving body, as if guarding him. Yet he'd seen her eyes. It was the same expression she'd have when experimenting with one of her new parlor tricks. Which proportion of alcohol and water do I need to infuse and light up a dollar bill without burning it to a crisp?

What he didn't see was sadness or regret. For Allene, Andrew was a mystery to be solved, even in death. The coroners placed Andrew's body on a stretcher and covered him decently with a sheet. They asked Jasper what the devil he was doing at yet another crime scene, but he didn't respond.

With no corpse to watch over now, Allene hugged herself as she turned to stare out one of the smoke-stained windows. The police had already exhausted their list of questions and promised to ask more after she revealed the letters they'd been receiving and why she, Jasper Jones, and their friend Birdie Dreyer seemed to be involved in non-influenza New York City deaths with alarming regularity.

"I should go," Jasper told Allene. "Dawlish can take you home."

"Where are you going? To the morgue?" Allene asked, without breaking her stare out the window.

"Well," he began. He no longer had a job there, but it wouldn't stop him from trying to find out more about Andrew's death. "Yes."

"You're always going to the morgue." She turned to Jasper, and he realized now that her dry eyes were red and her eyelids and nose were swollen. She was a quiet crier, he now knew. "Why is it, Jasper, that you prefer to spend time with the dead and not with the people who love you?"

"I had a job," Jasper began. "I had to work. I've no money. You do. It's that simple."

She stared at him. "*Had* a job?"

Embarrassment suffused his cheeks. "I got fired."

Allene's shoulders fell in exhaustion. "Oh Lord, Jasper. When?"

"Around the time that you got sick. I was becoming unfocused and messy. And I seemed to coincidentally know too many corpses that came though the morgue." He waved his hand. "But that's not important. Not now. I think we should find out what killed Andrew."

Allene sobered further. "The police think it's a suicide. They don't believe the fight with Ernie killed him."

"Well, we see it all the time. Murderers don't want to go to Sing Sing or fry in the electric chair or deal with the circus of the courts. Death is easier. Murder and suicide go together like peaches and cream."

Allene shuddered. "I don't believe Andrew wanted to die."

"Neither do I. And what's more—Andrew said he had nothing to do with Florence's death, and you and I both know that she was murdered too. So let's find out the truth. The pathology laboratory is probably closed, but I can still get in."

"But you've been fired!"

"I still have my keys," he said thoughtfully. "And you have money, which opens all sorts of doors." At Allene's silence, he added, "Or I could just ask nicely. Want to visit the morgue with me? I could use the company." He reached for her hand, but she shied away.

"Don't. It gives me hope where I don't have a right to feel it."

Jasper took his hand back. He'd been so used to toying with Allene and her affections. She was a chum, a rare gal, and he was used to playing her any way he wanted, whatever was convenient to him. But there was pain in her eyes. There were consequences to his actions, and he hadn't cared before.

"I'm sorry," he said.

"It's all right. I'm getting used to not getting what I want." She gave an empty laugh before hugging her arms to her chest. "Jasper, if Florence hadn't died, I believe you never would have stayed in my life after that party. Why are dead people the only things that bring you closer to me?"

They stared at each other. Neither of them truly wanted to hear the answer.

⟨⟩

"This will be the last time you're to set foot in this department, ya understand?" Dr. Gettler barked at Jasper. It was early evening. The rest of Manhattan was sitting at their tables, digging into their wheatless, meatless wartime suppers, caring for their sick, while Allene and Jasper were in the coroner's office at Bellevue. They'd called Dr. Gettler for an emergency toxicological consultation ("I'm eating my dinner!" he'd yelled at Jasper on the telephone), and now the Bellevue campus was dark, save for the lit lamps in the hospital and a single one in the pathology building where they stood.

"Yes sir."

"And why on earth did you bring your girl? This ain't the theater."

"I'm not his girl," Allene said. Bitterness didn't suit her, and it was time to discard it. "I'm . . . we're . . ." Her eyes rolled to the ceiling, searching for the word. "We're family."

They'd used the word when speaking to the police after Hazel died. It felt more and more right this time. Jasper took her hand and curled it around his arm. Funny how he didn't realize he'd been lonely until he wasn't.

"Please, sir. She can handle it. She's a whiz at chemistry."

"Really?" Dr. Gettler looked at her suspiciously, a challenge lighting up his eyes. "What's your favorite molecule?"

"Ozone," she replied, without missing a beat. "It's so delicate, so ephemeral. And what could be more beautiful than something created by light and energy?"

"Humph." Dr. Gettler shrugged. "You're one of those poet chemists. I'm more of a bricklayer chemist."

"So what's your favorite molecule?" Allene countered.

"One three seven trimethylxanthine."

Allene nodded in acknowledgment. Jasper waited for the punch line, but neither said a word. The parts of the formula were familiar to him, but Allene had always outshone him in her pure love of the subject.

"What is it?" Jasper finally asked. They both looked at him like he was a simpleton.

Allene whispered, "Caffeine. The man likes his coffee."

The door opened. Allene and Jasper turned around and saw Charles Norris, the chief medical examiner, staring down at them with his fierce eyes beneath those bushy salt-and-pepper eyebrows.

"Alexander, what is this boy doing here? I thought we fired him."

"We did, sir. He came back anyway. Brought a chemist too. A pretty one, at that."

Dr. Norris stared at Allene, who, to her credit, stood up straighter and met his eye, before he turned back to Jasper.

"We're not a charity organization," Dr. Norris told him. "You have no job here. Go home."

"But sir. See, there's a problem."

"Not doing your job? Using our lab as your personal playground? You know, we fired Barston too. He told us you tampered with that socialite's corpse before it went to the undertaker."

"I'm sorry. It was wrong of us. But I swear to God, we had the best intentions." Jasper put out his hands in supplication. "Sir, I believe that my friend Allene . . . and I . . . and our friend Birdie Dreyer . . . well, someone is killing the people we love. All of them have come through the morgue, and each one has shown evidence of foul play."

Dr. Norris frowned. "So you—"

"And my fiancé just died," Allene blurted out.

"Your fiancé?"

"He says he killed everyone," she added. "But we think he was poisoned. He may have even poisoned himself."

"And we need to find out immediately, because these letters of warning—or declaration, rather—keep coming," Jasper added. "And our friend Birdie—you remember her mother; she's the one who died from a laudanum overdose? Well, she's dying from some sort of cancer, and . . ." He let out his suspicions because there was no point in hiding them. "I think she's being poisoned too."

Allene nodded in agreement.

Dr. Norris took this all in stoically, without one trace of confusion. He peered at Jasper. "What letters?"

"Ones that said 'You're welcome.' Presumably for murdering someone we know," Jasper said. Allene opened her mouth to add more when Dr. Norris held out both hands, silencing them.

He worked his fingers into his beard, thinking. Meanwhile, Dr. Gettler leaned back against a countertop and waited, studying them both. Norris pointed at Jasper, then Allene. They had the feeling that the judgment of

God and all the apostles was coming down on them. Allene shrank a little as he waggled the mighty finger in their faces.

"You have some nerve."

"We know, sir." Jasper and Allene spoke simultaneously.

"Alexander!" he barked.

Dr. Gettler rolled his eyes. "I'm right behind ya. No need to scream, Charles."

"Oh. My apologies. Please brew us a pot of tea on the Bunsen burner." He pulled out a chair from the nearest desk and sat down before pointing at Allene and Jasper. "You two. *Sit*. And tell me everything you know."

⟶

After an hour of anxious explaining passed, with Norris and Gettler interjecting to ask thorough—and uncomfortable—questions, Jasper felt himself in an uneasy equipoise. Once the details and facts were curated by those two discerning minds, Norris ended the session by staring at Jasper. The staring continued for nearly a full two minutes.

Finally, Norris stood abruptly, as did the rest of the party. "Well. There is one piece of information missing. It's time to get back to our trenches, so to speak."

"Sir?" Jasper was still waiting for the verdict, and Allene glanced at him uneasily.

"You've both surmised that this young lady's fiancé has been poisoned, but it's still only a hypothesis. And our work doesn't end with hypotheses." He plucked a laboratory apron from a wall hook and tied it on. He turned to Allene. "Have you a strong stomach, young lady?"

"Yes."

"Good. We've no alienist here to revive you with smelling salts. You, boy"—he pointed at Jasper—"what on earth are you waiting for?"

Jasper jerked out of his chair, feeling unmoored and unsure. Did this mean there was a chance he'd have his job back? It didn't matter. And, oddly, he realized he didn't care. He only wanted answers now. He almost laughed at how hungrily he'd wanted fame and glory, while now the simple truth would suffice to keep him satisfied. He was positively soft boiled these days.

Gettler stayed in the lab while the others followed Norris down to the autopsy room. The glittering pendulum lights cast a yellow glow on the tables. The copper basins and spigots at the end of each table had been polished cleanly. Norris wheeled over a tray of instruments—the bone saws of various sizes; the picks, scissors, and knives of different shapes and curvatures. Jasper was both impressed by and relieved at the preternatural calm that had overtaken Allene. Even in the presence of the many bodies laid out on the dissecting tables, and the stench (one of the bodies had apparently decomposed in a cellar for two weeks—slightly suspicious but more likely an influenza victim who went to fetch a bottle of medicinal whiskey and never returned), Allene remained stoic. After all, this wasn't her first trip to the morgue, but Jasper knew she wouldn't admit this aloud.

Well. Until they uncovered Andrew.

Jasper stared too. Andrew lay on the cold marble table, eyes closed, his body stiffened with his arms at his side. In death, the gauntness of his frame was more marked, and his skin had a papery-thin quality to it. What was more, it was a deep brown color, as if he'd been pickled in brine and set out to dry under a desert sun.

Norris picked up the tablet and began taking notes in silence. Somewhere in the room, a tap was dripping water at the rate of a slow heartbeat. Norris nodded to Jasper, who lifted a short blade with a thick handle and held it poised over Andrew's bare chest. Then, only then, did Allene step back.

She covered her mouth with both hands before finally bursting out, "I can't. God knows I didn't love him but . . . still. He was my fiancé. I cannot do this." She turned to the two of them. "Thank you, Dr. Norris.

Jasper—" She couldn't say another word but instead gave him a look that said, Oh, Jasper. How on earth did we get here? She turned on her heels and swiftly left the room.

Jasper stood at the side of the table, and Andrew waited for the truth to be diced out of him. Dr. Norris must have sensed Jasper's discomfort and shame at feeling exactly the same way as Allene, the same horror and disgust at Andrew's shrunken, browned body, the same avoidance of that familiar face that would grin at him no longer. Jasper put down the blade. Norris simply handed him a tablet to take the notes and made the first cut himself.

Later on, Jasper would recall the dissection only in parts, as if bits of his memory had been cut and preserved in jars for another time and place. He remembered the bloody trail of macerated stomach lining; the yellowed, fatty deposits in the liver and kidneys, which should have been a healthy burgundy color. He would remember the tap, tap, tapping sound of body liquids falling into the collection containers beneath the marble table, but not Andrew's face during the actual autopsy. He recalled being in the laboratory afterward with Gettler, but not taking the stairs to get there. Dr. Gettler had scowled over their discourse on the matter.

"Reinsch's test for heavy metals. We'll start there."

"No, Marsh's method is better," Jasper replied.

Gettler furrowed his eyebrows. "Are you stupid or tired, or both? Reinsch's test is more sensitive—"

"And it'll take all night, and I need an answer now." Jasper didn't balk at Gettler's reddening face, which was gearing up for a Brooklynese tirade. "Look, I'm already fired. You can do what you want, but you'll have to double check the results anyway, right? Marsh's test will take less than two hours."

"You think it's—"

"I know it is," Jasper finished his thought. He put on his lab coat and rolled up his sleeves. "I'll get the hydrochloric acid."

Jasper was right; the answer did come in less than two hours. Somewhere around three in the morning, he knew. It was one hour before the dockworkers would be heading for the piers, before the rest of New York would be waking up to the paralyzing fear that another loved one had died in the night from the Spanish grippe. More men would be drawn into the war if the armistice talks stalled. Even now, Pershing was stalwart in pledging to send 250,000 American boys a month to the front lines. On both sides of the vast, uncaring Atlantic Ocean, everyone was hoping desperately for a cease-fire.

So was Jasper, in their own little circle.

He had his answer in the form of a gleaming, shiny residue of darkness coating the inside of a test tube. He didn't need to say what he and Norris had already guessed from the autopsy. Dr. Gettler announced the answer with that pride he always had when he'd pulled the truth, one atom at a time, from a silenced corpse.

"It makes sense. The skin color, the thickened palms."

"You mean . . ."

"Yes. Say hello to arsenic, young man."

CHAPTER 30

Birdie had been staying in Allene's room and welcomed her back after Allene's influenza symptoms had finally dissipated. Holly stayed in the guest room, banned from sleeping with Birdie because a simple leg jerk in the middle of the night would break another of Birdie's fragile bones.

The laudanum had reluctantly become a friend, but it nauseated her terribly. She watched the tumorous mass on her leg grow week by week, sometimes day by day, and wondered about her death. Like the menu at Delmonico's, there were so many options. Would it be a gentle passing in the night or a tumorous stricture somehow choking her to death? Would her bones simply stop holding together and splinter into a million pieces?

The end was drawing near, and she had what she wanted. Holly was in the Cutter house; Allene doted on her, and her sisterly love grew daily. They had yet to discuss Holly's status with Mr. Cutter, but Birdie didn't doubt how strongly Allene would fight for her when the time came.

Allene had arrived over an hour ago from the morgue. She'd changed her clothes without waking the maids and crept into bed. She told Birdie everything that had happened, between sobs.

Andrew was gone. Gone! It was too difficult to believe. Andrew, who'd given so much to her family, who'd spent his heart on Birdie all these last months. Gone! Ernie would be having surgery tonight and would hopefully recover. But it was too difficult to understand.

"I still don't understand why Andrew wanted to hurt him. Ernie is harmless."

"No, he's not. Not exactly. He was always in everyone's business. He was a nuisance, always showing up uninvited."

"Was he?" Allene's voice quieted. "I would rather have Ernie be an alive, sweet nuisance than dead."

"Well. I'm surprised," Birdie began, then shut her mouth. "I guess it's not the same unless Ernie's around somewhere. He'll be back to doting on you before you know it."

Birdie waited for the usual quip about Ernie, about how even a stabbing wouldn't keep him from returning to the Cutter house like a magnet. Her previous words were meant to cheer, but Allene shivered and frowned.

"I would never have dreamed that all this would happen. And . . . I know you must be upset," Allene began bravely. "Oh God. Andrew! To think he killed your mother! And all the while, he was so sweet on you."

"Allene—"

"No. It's all right. But though I'm sad, you must be devastated."

Was she? He'd been her benefactor and lover. He would have died for her. And now here he was, departed. Blamed for a string of deaths that changed everyone's lives. It didn't seem real. She would have felt it deeper in her heart if Allene had told her he'd boarded a train to California and planned never to return.

"I'll be all right," Birdie said truthfully. She allowed Allene to snuggle closer to her side (her ribs didn't hurt so much as her legs and jaw) and sighed. "I have you and I have Holly, for now."

"Don't say that!" Allene dampened Birdie's gown with her tears. "Don't say *for now*."

"But you know it's true. I might only have another few hours, or days, or weeks. But we both know that before Christmas, I'll be in the Evergreens like my mother."

Allene sat up abruptly. In the darkness, only a tiny sliver of moonlight illuminated the room through the gauzy white curtains, which looked more like sentry ghosts than window coverings. "I miss those days when you used to glow in the dark at night."

"Yes. It's been a while since I was covered in radium dust," she said, laughing. That was one of the most magical things about her factory work. No, it was the only magical thing, actually.

Allene reached over to flick on the bedside lamp, with its milky pendulum beads around the shade. They always reminded Birdie of drops of pure sugar. When she was a child, she'd actually licked one, disappointed to find it was tasteless and cool. The amber light flooded half the room.

"Let's talk about something else. I can't bear it," Allene said, kicking off her bedcovers.

Birdie sat up straighter and bit her lip from the movement. Lately, the laudanum had not been working. Her body was in a flux of varying, violent states of torment, seemingly filled with shards of glass, needling her with lacerating, fiery jabs every second. Sleep was no respite, because sleep was impossible and she no longer wished to dose herself into a stupor.

Time was ticking, and she wanted to keep a clear mind while she could. "What would you like to talk about?"

"Let's talk about the murders," Allene suggested.

"Oh! And this is going to cheer you up? It's ever so morbid, Allene!"

"But it helps to think, rather than to feel. If that makes any sense."

Birdie nodded. Of course she understood. She would do anything to stop feeling so damned much, particularly when it came to her memories, which begged for attention at night. There were a lot of reasons why Birdie never slept any longer.

"Let me show you something." Allene hopped off the bed and padded to her vanity table, the one Allene always kept locked. From her reticule, she pulled a scrolled, copper key and unlocked the drawer with a snick. She removed a large cigar box, cradling it carefully with both hands, and set it on the bed next to Birdie.

"What is it?" Birdie asked.

"Look." She lifted the pasteboard box lid and took out a sheaf of papers. "These are the letters. I have four of them. One after Florence died; the one you got when Hazel died; the one Jasper received before his uncle died; and this one, before Andrew died."

They laid them out on the bed. The script was perfectly written.

"But Andrew never said he killed Florence," Allene said, confused. She rubbed her temples. "I still don't understand."

"What's that?" Birdie pointed to a small handkerchief bundled in a ball.

Allene unwrapped it in her hand, as if peeling the petals off a lotus flower. Nestled in the center was a broken piece of glass.

"It's part of the champagne glass, the one Florence drank from." Allene reached for a tattered piece of printed paper. Birdie recognized it as a piece of the label from Hazel's medicine, the one that was laudanum instead of the usual paregoric concentration. "You remember this, of course."

Birdie nodded, but goose pimples ran up her arms and spine. There was no denying that Allene seemed to enjoy perusing and gathering the artifacts of death. "It's quite a collection you have," she said quietly.

"And there's more. Here's a piece of broken glass from Jasper's apartment. It was near his uncle when he died. And this too." She pointed to a small tin of pastilles. "This was the only thing Andrew carried in his pocket. He left one of his tins at our home last week." Birdie reached for them, but Allene stayed her hand. "Don't touch them. We don't know for sure yet, but they might be poisonous."

Birdie didn't know what to say. Would the items speak out loud and scream the truth? Would the answer to all their questions strike Allene's mind with a bolt of brilliance? She waited as Allene touched one item, then another, before finally puzzling it out aloud. "Andrew said he killed everyone but Florence. And now he's dead. I don't understand. Maybe Jasper will tell us more once he's done with Andrew's autopsy." She pursed her lips like a duck. "It's like there are two loose ends on a story that barely makes sense. The beginning . . ."

"And the end," Birdie finished, before yawning. "I'm so tired, Allene dear. Maybe we could talk about this more tomorrow? Or you could bring all these things to the police? Surely they'll help you. But right now, you've had such a fright with Andrew and the morgue—you've had so much excitement. You need to rest."

Allene smiled, but disappointment drew the corners of her mouth down. "Of course. And I'm keeping you awake. I'm so sorry."

Allene carefully packed all the evidence back into the box and sat it on her vanity. She tucked Birdie into bed, offering her some medicine, but Birdie refused.

Clear mind, Birdie thought. For whatever time I have left, I want a clear mind.

When Allene switched off the light, Birdie pretended to sleep, if only to make her friend feel better. But in the darkness, Allene tossed and turned. From beneath her almost-closed eyelids, Birdie watched Allene carefully peel away her covers and silently leave the bedroom with the cigar box in her hand.

CHAPTER 31

Allene stole downstairs with her treasures carefully in hand. The Cutter house was sound asleep, and it seemed an altogether different country in the dark. She went to the sitting room and inhaled the quiet, waiting. For what, she didn't know.

Sleep was impossible. The puzzle gnawed at her insides. Dawn had yet to break its peachy gold onto the city's horizon, and the stars outside the salon room window twinkled merrily despite the violence and sickness spread over the world.

Allene took inventory of the fallen. Hazel. Jasper's Uncle Frederick. Andrew. Florence.

And then there were the other casualties. Lucia. Oscar. George. The two young maids whose names she'd only just learned—Ellen and Dora. Father's previous butler, Stephen, who was in Belgium and thankfully still alive, but for how much longer? Her cousin, Clarence, somewhere south of Soissons. He'd been hospitalized for influenza too, but so far, alive. It hurt her, the details.

"Too many. There are too many," Allene said to herself. It had to stop. Why wouldn't it stop? As she sat on the divan by the window, there was a sharp rap on the window glass.

"Mercy me!" she yelped, and jumped up, nearly dropping the box. She peered out the window and saw Jasper standing before the polished window with one hand in his trouser pocket. It was so dark, she could hardly make out his expression. He motioned to the iron door that led to the enclosed garden.

Allene scurried over to open the french doors and stepped into the night air. The paved paths were partially obscured with fallen leaves, and the moss tickled her toes. Carefully pruned boxwoods stood sedately against the walls, and the creeping vines held their ivy leaves stubbornly, not quite ready to relinquish the waxy green to the coming winter. The dahlias had faded and died. The peach tree had browned, with all its sweet fruit plucked, preserved in the kitchen pantry. The peach pits within had probably been burnt into charcoal to filter out mustard gas at some disputed barricade.

Allene quietly unlocked the black gates where Jasper was waiting.

"What are you doing here?" She wished she'd brought a shawl; her robe was whisper thin.

"Can't sleep. I have news."

"Let's go inside and talk. It's so cold."

"Let's stay out here. I can't stand being indoors right now. After the morgue, I need to smell nothing but fresh air for a while." Jasper shrugged off his coat and draped it over Allene's shoulders. His tobacco-warm scent curled around her neck, and they sat down on a cast-iron bench. Dead leaves swirled about their feet, and the faint light of the moon illuminated their skin. "Why are you awake?"

"How could I sleep?" she responded simply. She hugged his coat closed around her chest but still hung on to the cigar box. "Birdie just fell asleep, but we were talking too."

"How is she?"

Allene didn't answer. There wasn't anything good to report, and Jasper understood her silence.

Finally, he said, "I can't believe she's gotten so sick. Doesn't seem right that you could dodge influenza by being lucky and the war by being a woman, and still have no chance."

"Nothing we do is guaranteed, is it? What if there is no armistice? You'll get called to Camp Upton soon enough, Jasper. And then you'll be gone too."

"Maybe. Maybe not." He took out a cigarette.

"I'd light it for you, but I left my Wonderliter at the factory. I'll probably never get it again."

"You saved my hide with that trick." He reached into his pocket for a match. Before he lit it, Allene sniffed the air.

"Do you smell smoke?"

Jasper's hand holding the match paused in the air. "Are you trying to get me to stop smoking?"

Allene shook her head. "Never mind."

He struck the match, and the flame warmed Allene's face. He shivered. "Living isn't always such a hoot. Have you ever been jealous of the dead? That they have no worries anymore?"

"Stop it, Jasper." She put her hand on his. They were both cold now. He put his arm around her shoulders, trying to warm her.

"What's this?" He pointed to the cigar box.

"I'll show you in a second. First, tell me what happened at the morgue after I left."

Jasper leaned back and stared up at the sky. It was inky black, and the stars were crisp and shining. The sickle moon was sharp enough to draw blood.

"Arsenic," Jasper said.

"So it's true." She blinked, but tears still came. They warmed the skin of her face as they rolled down. It wasn't right for them to feel so good. "Did they test the pastilles they took out of the tin?"

"Yes. That took a little longer, but after we found it in his tissues, we found it in the candies too."

"Couldn't he taste it?"

"I don't think so. The amount in the pastilles wasn't actually very high. And the results of the autopsy showed his kidneys and liver were affected."

Allene shook her head. "I'm no doctor. What does that mean?"

"It means he was poisoned over a period of time, not just recently."

"That's obvious. He always blamed it on something else. First it was bad beef, and then the flu . . ." She covered her mouth.

"What?"

"What if Birdie is being poisoned by arsenic too?"

Jasper shook his head. "Arsenic doesn't cause these sorts of cancers in the victims. And it turns the skin this odd brown color, thick and peeling in places. Birdie's skin is like bleached paper."

"Well, she's being poisoned. I know it. I just don't know how." Allene curled her fists so hard, her nails dug into her palms. "I wish I knew more than just chemistry. It's like having one key to one room in a house, and I need ten other keys to open the other rooms."

Jasper nodded. "So are you going to tell me what's in that cigar box? It's not cigars, is it?"

"No. I've had this ever since Florence died. You know I kept a piece of broken glass from her champagne glass, right? Well, I kept other things as well."

"Let me guess," Jasper said, pushing the box closed with his hand when she tried to open it. "The letters."

Allene nodded.

"The laudanum label?"

Allene nodded again.

"Something belonging to my uncle."

"A piece of broken bottle from the night he died," Allene admitted.

"Ah. And . . . something from Andrew. Oh, a pastille tin, right?"

"I had one of his other tins he left at my house. Yes." She looked down at the closed box. "I just feel if I can piece them together somehow, we'll figure it all out. This box—these murders, they feel like they're so much larger than the life we've living, yet . . . I can't live at all without knowing why."

"You know the answer is not in this box," Jasper said gently. "The police have had their say. In fact"—he tapped the box—"you should probably hand this over, so we can be done with it all."

"I thought you always wanted to be the hero to figure this all out. The thing that would make you famous," Allene said.

"Did I ever say that out loud?"

"No. But I know you."

"You know, it's funny growing up and realizing that you—and the circle of friends and family and your life—aren't this big, bright, enormous thing that eclipses everything. It's the opposite, isn't it?"

"It is." Allene sighed.

"And you know what? It's a relief. To be nothing but me, and not this idea of me I wanted."

"Come on. Let's do some sleuthing, shall we? What else would we do on a cold, pretty night like this?"

He cracked an uncertain grin. "All right. Let's solve the mystery." Jasper reached to carefully lift the lid on the box. The contents were all there, but viewing them in the dim light, they both gasped with astonishment. There was, of course, the folded letter, the glass shards, the tin, the peeled corner of laudanum label. Everything was there that was expected to be there, but something was different.

In the darkness of the garden, the items were luminescent. A green, powdery radiance covered each object.

Radium dust. It was on everything.

That was when the maids started screaming.

CHAPTER 32

After Allene had disappeared from the bedroom with the box, Birdie left too. She would only have a little while. Hours before, she had listened for the telltale sounds of Mr. Cutter heading for his bedroom, the knock of his slippers hitting the floor, and the steady, sawlike buzz of his snores.

He'd entirely ignored her existence since she'd come into the house. After all, what wasn't acknowledged could be not believed. Birdie had said nothing, so he had honored her silence. A gentleman to the end! She wanted to laugh bitterly. He remained content to stay in the background, playing the perpetually convalescent father.

Good thing too. Because like an unstoppable, insidious heartbeat, she could feel the presence of *him* in the house. Sleeping in his room, working in his office. She could still feel his meaty hands on her delicate skin after all these years. He was the taint that made every moment of her existence here an ongoing persecution.

Everywhere she turned, there were bad memories. The second-floor corner by the guest bedroom, the place where she'd once run into him before bedtime. She'd been eleven years old, and without a word, Mr. Cutter had slipped a large, possessive hand down the top of her nightgown. There was the library downstairs, where a kiss was stolen from her, an indecent tongue forced into her throat. A warning that if she told anyone, her mother would be taken away from her. His bedroom, of course, where she was told to deliver his newly mended slippers one evening when she had only just turned thirteen. That was the evening when the last of her innocence had been violently rent.

It was the night Holly had been conceived.

But he chose not to remember such things. Everyone thought Hazel was the pregnant one, disguising her form with loose dresses. There had always been rumors and murmurings that Allene's father had been having an affair with Hazel. It was all too common a scenario. The lady's companion both was friend to the wife and kept the husband occupied at night. Convenient for everyone, so long as the money and power stayed with the rightful lady of the house. But in those last months before they'd left, Hazel had been trying to protect Birdie's chastity, to take the focus off her stunning young daughter. It hadn't worked.

Tonight, Mr. Cutter would not notice her yet again. He was a sound sleeper. Memory had taught her that small lesson. Only a week ago she'd calmly asked Dr. Hanover for a soporific to help with her pain-ridden nights. Chloroform made her sick; laudanum was too nauseating. Ernie himself had picked up the bottle of ether at the druggist.

"Only three drops in a glass of water, my dear. That should be plenty," the doctor had warned. She picked up the bottle—labeled neatly with brown printing ("Poison! Anesthetic!" it yelled)—and quietly hobbled with excruciating slowness out of the bedroom. Walking on broken bones was no easy task. She paused at the top of the stairs. A puff of cold air told her that Allene had opened a door somewhere. No matter. She didn't need much time.

The door to Mr. Cutter's room was well oiled and quiet as she pushed it open. She nudged a chair to his bedside. He was a picture of health despite the recent influenza. Pity that it hadn't killed him. Influenza irritatingly lacked sympathy for Birdie's plight, but she knew—she'd always known—she'd never leave Holly in the Cutter house with Mr. Cutter alive. From her robe pocket, she drew forth one of her favorite embroidered handkerchiefs, folded it in fourths, then soaked it with the sweetish, cloying liquid. She laid it carefully over his mouth and nose.

He didn't stir, only sank into a deeper sleep. She trickled more ether onto the handkerchief every few minutes, keeping it saturated, until the room stank of the stuff and she herself grew dizzy from the fumes. How much time had gone by? She wasn't sure.

She'd used only half the bottle. There were at least another thirty drams left. She cocked her head at the unconscious man. How unconscious?

She leaned over the bed and slapped his bearded face hard. The ether was so potently volatile that the handkerchief was already half dry as it tumbled off his face. The strike hurt her more than it hurt him, though. Mr. Cutter turned his face. His breathing had become shallower, but he breathed still.

"Well. Best be safe, I suppose."

She grasped his face and righted it so he faced the ceiling again. His mouth was slightly open, his graying beard obscuring his lips. She ignored her disgust at being so close and carefully tipped the bottle over his open maw until a slip of liquid poured in. The ether made him gag and sputter but not quite wake up. It reddened his lips and tongue, bubbled and rattled in the back of his throat. She repeated the act three more times until the bottle was empty and she was sure the liquid was scorching the insides of his lungs and stomach.

She remembered the lesson that Allene had given her years ago. On and on, she'd prattled about this molecule or that element. It was both adorable and tiresome at the same time.

"Ethyl ether. It's like a bird, like you, Birdie!" she'd said. "Two carbons attached to an oxygen in the middle. It has wings."

"What's it for?"

"Oh, in chemistry, for so many things. It's a wonderful solvent. And they use it to put people to sleep, but . . ." She had scanned a page of an open book before her. "It's too flammable. They use chloroform now, which is safer in that respect. Oh, chloroform! What a tidy little bugger, it has three chlorines . . ."

But Birdie had not forgotten the lesson.

She stared at Mr. Cutter's insensate body, went to the water pitcher in the corner, and carefully rinsed her hands, leaving them wet. And from her other robe pocket, she took a small box of matches.

An arm's breadth away, she lit the match.

"You're welcome," Birdie whispered, and dropped the lit match into Mr. Cutter's fume-filled throat.

There was a brilliant flash of fire as the ether quickly ignited inside his throat and lungs, his face, his beard, the bed linens. It was the most beautiful thing Birdie had ever seen, even more beautiful than Holly. She shielded her face and backed away from the searing heat. Leaving the roar of fire behind her, she hobbled to the guest room, gritting her teeth, tears running down her face from the pain.

The room had become Holly's entirely. Tiny books were tidily arranged on a little white shelf, and a toddler's crib was covered in a fairylike tenting that the maids had created out of a bolt of old organdy fabric found in the attic.

Birdie was careful not to gasp in discomfort when she bent over the crib. She kissed Holly's warm cheek and tucked a curl behind her ear. It was hard to look at Holly. In that sleeping, innocent face, she saw her own nightmares.

"Good night," she murmured. "Sweet Holly Berry."

There was a pitcher of water and a glass on a stand near the bed, as Holly always woke up thirsty. Birdie soaked a tiny blanket, left the room, shut the door, and wadded the wet fabric in the crack by the floor. Holly would be saved. The maids adored her and would rescue her first.

Plumes of black smoke now boiled out of Mr. Cutter's bedroom. A yell sounded from the stairs below. Good. The servants must have heard the explosion. With great difficulty, Birdie maneuvered to Allene's room, locked the door, and climbed into the bed. More cries of horror came from downstairs. Feet thumped up the stairs, then downward; a telephone call was being made. And yet no one sought her out. It didn't matter; they knew where she was.

The worst was over, and now she was free. Free, yet unable to move without excruciating pain. Free, but with the coming hatred of the people she most loved. Free and penniless. Homeless too, for that matter. Free, and revolted by her own memories. Revolted by herself.

A paroxysm of agony once again lacerated her leg and throbbed deep within her malformed bone. She shifted on the bed, trying to find a more comfortable position, but searing pain spread through the center of her chest. It quite took her breath away. She panted for more air, feeling like she was inhaling nothingness, devoid of oxygen. The pain spread rapidly, and she felt her heart race, skip a beat, race on, skip two more. It did a frenzied jig in her chest. Her face and neck felt oddly engorged with blood, as if a ligature were being tightened irrevocably. Relentlessly. The breathlessness became suffocation.

Sometime in the next minute, she flitted in and out of consciousness. Surely she would go to hell, but at least Andrew would be there, mooning over her, grasping her so hard in his effort to possess her that her joints would loosen. Her limbs would give way, twisting off like an overcooked chicken leg. He would hoard these bits, and Birdie would look at the leftover pieces of her fairy self. Mr. Cutter would be there too, strung up on razor wire and charred to a crisp, his glittering eyes still able to watch with enjoyment.

And Birdie would laugh through the torment because at least she had this one grace—Holly wasn't there. Holly would never belong in such a place. Just as Birdie had never deserved the poisons that touched her life, neither did Holly. But Birdie had sacrificed enough to keep her daughter protected. This one good, pure thing she would cling to. The darkness in the Dreyer family would end, once and for all, with Birdie.

She awoke for one last moment, convulsing, and then she shrieked, the terrorized cry of a child in the dark, just before her heart beat its final pulse.

CHAPTER 33

They found her in bed, dark as the room, her preternatural glow winked out. Her eyes were open, staring up at the ceiling, her mouth slightly agape as if in surprise that death had finally come for its truant visit. Allene and Jasper saw her at the same time, after the police had broken open the door; the key was nowhere to be found.

And there was a letter.

Always, there was a letter.

Jasper held Allene by the shoulders. The police had not let her see the charred remains of her father's corpse, but Allene knew that it was horrific. She imagined blackened flesh, a wide-open jaw with burnt lips adhered to teeth, the ungodly scent of cooked human flesh. So when she saw Birdie's corpse, it was too much. She promptly vomited on the pristine carpet underfoot.

Once recovered, she read the letter with the police. She and Jasper hadn't recognized the handwriting, but on closer inspection, they saw flourishes that resembled Birdie's. She'd disguised it enough to throw them off. And of course Birdie had volunteered to have the killer's notes examined by a "professional," because she had been driving the game all along.

There was no anger in the words on the page. Every cursive letter was written with care, almost lovingly. How Andrew had, out of infatuation and love, performed her killing deeds by proxy. How she had laced his pastilles with arsenic almost as soon as they'd begun their affair. Months ago, he was a dead man walking.

And the start of it all. Florence.

When Birdie had arrived at the Cutter house the night of the engagement party, she had gone to the kitchens to say hello to the staff that still remembered her. And there she had taken a single champagne glass and smeared the inside with a barely visible layer of poisonous silver polish. She'd held it all night, hoping to switch it with someone else's.

Remember what Florence said? "Trying so damn hard not to be yourselves." Even she saw what you couldn't. Jasper trying to rise out of obscurity. Me wanting a life I couldn't have. And you! You were the worst. You pretended you had all you wanted when you had nothing.

I didn't suggest solving Florence's murder. You did. It was easy to choose her as the first to die. Did you know I overheard her planning on ruining your party? On spreading a vicious lie that you were having an affair with Jasper and me at the same time? Oh, it was so dark that it would ruin your reputation. Well before I arrived, I planned to give you the ultimate engagement gift— something to bring you and your old chums together and liven up your dull life. And in time, Holly would enter your life and you might find her worth fighting for, when I couldn't anymore.

So before we all went upstairs, I gave Florence my champagne glass. She treated me like a servant and took it without thinking. And when she was dead, I gave you the spark, and you breathed on the ember, like I knew you would. I put the note in your book on cyanide when no one was looking. I was good at leaving bread crumbs for you to follow.

With Andrew's help, I started removing the obstacles to Holly's path to a better life and the obstacles for all three of us. The atrocity that is your father. Jasper's drunkard uncle and my mother, the whore. And Andrew. He'd never have let Holly stay in your home. Sweet Andrew, so gluttonous for my soul, he was all too willing to kill for me. He would have eaten me alive if I'd let him.

I deserve their companionship in hell.

But there is one good thing that has come from all this horror: Holly, now in the home she deserves. I shall cling to that one redemption for eternity.

Allene had to put the letter down to her lap several times while reading it. It was all so much, and there was no Birdie to scream at, to plead with. She missed Birdie, and yet that sentiment was altogether at odds with the truth. What was more, Allene felt responsible. If Birdie and Hazel hadn't been thrust out of their home years ago, their circumstances wouldn't have become so dire. She should have fought to keep them here. She could have protected Birdie.

And then there was the truth about Holly. Birdie's daughter. Birdie didn't hold back in the letter. She spoke of dates, and hospital records in the women's ward, and details about Allene's father that were altogether obscene. Allene didn't want to believe any of it, but Holly's face told the truth. The little girl had Allene's own indefatigable inquisitiveness and the coloring of a Cutter woman. A brown-haired shadow at the foot of Birdie's brilliance, just like Allene had always been. She was astonished at how lies had entirely filtered her vision for the last several weeks. Years, even.

"I've been living with monsters," Allene said, looking at Jasper with a feeling that was half disgust, half profound emptiness.

"We both have."

"Oh, Jasper. How am I to tell Holly the truth someday?"

"I don't know." He put his hand into Allene's. "Good God, I don't know."

CHAPTER 34

November 21, 1918

Allene had spent far too much time at cemeteries this year, but there was hope that this would be her last graveyard visit for a long while.

Holly's tiny, gloved hand hugged Allene's skirted leg. A crow cawed in the distance, an oddly fitting avian farewell from a consummate trickster and harbinger of death. The fall leaves had made their descent, and the trees stood in stark emptiness, a contrast to the crisp blue sky overhead.

Before them, the newly turned soil rested over Birdie's casket. No priest or pastor had accompanied the farewell. A small stone had been placed at the head of the plot. Carved into it was simply:

Birdie Abigail Dreyer
1900–1918

There was no epitaph. There wasn't room on the small stone, and it would have been too difficult to write the proper words. Allene had thought of several but didn't disclose her thoughts to anyone.

Holly tugged at her arm. "Does it hurt to be buried?" she asked.

"No, dear. Birdie is sleeping away for eternity. She can't suffer anymore."

"Sleeping is nice," Holly said, before going quiet.

Allene was glad of the silence. In the distance, she spotted her father's stately obelisk, and over the next hill, unseen to her, was the Biddle mausoleum. Somehow, it seemed fitting that her father, Andrew, and Birdie would share that same plane together, perhaps yelling ghostly complaints over each other's early demise.

It would take a while before she could even think of her father in any way but with roiling disgust. Forgiveness for him was not in her repertoire right now. She didn't spend time wondering if it ever would be. After all, the murmurings in her small world were now all about the ignominy of the Cutter family. It had been in the papers everywhere for a week or two. There were others to do the wondering for her; she had to spend her time more wisely.

Jasper had declined to attend their visit today. Birdie's body had been kept at the coroner's office for over a month because they still couldn't understand why her body had fallen apart in such a dizzying variety of pathologies. She had been released for burial only yesterday. Father's funeral had been a month ago. Hundreds of mourners had attended and gawked at Allene, Holly, and Mrs. Cutter, who'd dragged herself down from Saratoga to attend. She and Allene had tea, then met with the lawyers. She kissed Allene on the cheek, shuddered at the sight of Holly at her side, and took the next train back to Saratoga. If there was any chance that Allene's mother would reenter her life, it died the moment Allene announced she was using a substantial portion of her inheritance to create a trust fund for Holly and was legally adopting her.

"I knew he'd never touch you," Mrs. Cutter said, waving her gloved hand dismissively at Allene. "He's not interested in Cutter women in that way. He did his duty and then never laid a finger on me again." Duty. She meant Allene, didn't she? Which made Allene's own conception sound like a dull moment in a tiresome factory.

But Allene was inured to her mother's distance and disgust. When she told her mother of her plans, her mother gave her a look of shock and opened her mouth to argue, but Allene shut her down.

"My life. My money. My decision."

And with that, her mother had picked up her purse, motioned to her attendant, and headed to the train station without a word of good-bye.

The cold November wind pushed hard at Allene, and she stepped backward to catch herself.

"Whoa now." A warm, strong hand steadied her shoulder. Maybe Jasper had decided to come after all. But when she turned with a sad smile to greet him, she saw that Ernie was standing behind her.

"Oh. Hello, Ernie. I thought you were Jasper."

"I went to his apartment to convince him to come, but he . . . had another engagement."

Allene nodded. Jasper was faring far worse at dealing with Birdie's actions than she was. He hadn't attended her father's funeral but had sent a note of support to her and to Holly. She was glad of Ernie's company now. Since leaving the hospital after recovering from the wound to his stomach, Ernie had lost much of his youthful plumpness. He'd left other things behind too—his puppylike eagerness and his ability to see only good in everyone around him. The change wasn't the kind brought about by illness. It was the transformation seen when someone relentlessly attends to the business of sad things. His cheeks had become carved, bequeathing him a masculine serenity she'd never noticed before. He smelled of aftershave and pine.

He smiled mildly back at her. What a handsome smile. He could have been a film star. Funny how she'd never noticed.

"Have you forgiven me for singeing your eyebrows?"

"Of course! Truly, it was a stroke of chemical brilliance, that zinc-dust explosion. I would have applauded you if I wasn't so damn scared for my life."

They laughed together. Holly was growing restless, though. It was time to go. Two motorcars waited at the curve atop the hill, engines ticking idly at the road.

"Thank you for coming," Allene said as they walked to meet their respective chauffeurs.

"If you have the energy," Ernie said, "I'd like to show you something." When she hesitated, he added, "Holly can come, of course. In fact, I'd rather she did. It will only be an hour or so."

Allene assented, telling Dawlish to go home without her. They entered Ernie's motorcar, and Holly was placated with a wax-paper-wrapped Danish and a cloth bag full of tiny circus finger puppets. Allene gave Ernie a look of thanks. He had planned this outing in advance, it seemed. He stayed quiet as the motor turned onto Atlantic Avenue and then toward the Brooklyn Bridge.

They passed the usual turns she'd grown accustomed too—Vanderbilt Avenue, the way to the Ansonia Clock factory by Prospect Park, and, once they were in Manhattan, the Twenty-Sixth Street turn toward Bellevue. She gave Ernie a sideways glance when they passed Sixty-Eighth Street, where the Cutter house was.

Onward north they drove. It wasn't until they were far uptown, within a few streets of the church where Lucy had been memorialized, that the car slowed to a stop in front of a neatly swept brick row house on One-Hundredth Street, near First Avenue. The door was freshly painted in a glossy nut brown. The polished brass numbers were new. She could see plaid curtains hanging inside the window.

"Are we stopping here?" Allene asked as Holly scooted over to peer out the window.

"We are." Ernie waved away his chauffeur and opened the door for them. He led them up the stairs and knocked the small brass knocker on the front door.

"Do you know who lives here?" Allene whispered.

"Yes. And so do you." He turned toward the door just as it opened. A middle-aged man wearing a shirt with rolled-up sleeves and dusty trousers opened it, and Allene immediately recognized him.

Alessandro, Lucia's brother. He smiled gently at them. Behind him, several opened boxes were spread around the floor, and a chair covered in a bedsheet and twine sat before a fireplace. A whoop sounded from upstairs, and two children raced down the stairs and bumped abruptly into him from behind.

"*Bambini! Calmatevi*, eh? Miss Cutter, you remember Catarina, and this is Rafaele."

Allene let their names turn about in her heart. There was a beauty and steadiness to Catarina that seemed to match the little girl's wide eyes. Rafaele was calm and intelligent, but a ripple of nervousness hid there. Fittingly, the boy stood just behind his sister, hands clasped behind his back. Otherwise, they were just as Allene remembered them but no longer in stiff formal wear. The little girl wore a soft woolen dress of blue, with her brown hair braided into two long plaits. The boy pulled at the neck of his shirt collar. It must have been itchy. Both looked at the visitors with curiosity.

"*Bambini*, this is Miss Allene and Mr. Fielding."

The children murmured hello.

Ernie shook Alessandro's hand warmly. "Hello, Mr. Rossi. So sorry for dropping in unannounced, but—"

"Not at all. We hope you would come by." He stepped back to let them into the parlor. A fire crackled in the fireplace, a perfect antidote to the chilly fall day. Boxes, both open and unopened, were piled here and there. But there was a comfortable, uncovered sofa facing the fire and an open box spilling with toys. When Mr. Rossi spied Holly, he flashed a warm smile. "Now, who is this little one?"

"This is Holly," Allene explained. She had yet to decide what her last name would be. It would be at least another week or so before the adoption paperwork would be complete.

"*Ciao!* That is how we say hello in Italian. Catarina, Rafaele— come, come." He gestured and chattered rapidly in Italian, and the boy, Rafaele, fetched a brightly painted wooden train car from a pile at the back of the room.

"Trains!" Holly blurted. Her fistful of finger puppets dropped to the ground.

Wordlessly, Catarina took Holly's plump hand in hers and, with a calm authority, led her to the back of the room. The two older children murmured while Holly made exclamations of ecstasy over the brightly colored vehicles.

Mr. Rossi ushered Allene and Ernie to the sofa by the fire. They declined his offer of tea or coffee. Allene was too nervous to drink or eat a thing. She was too busy watching the three children playing together in the corner. It made her think of Lucia, and she dabbed at the corners of her eyes with her gloved fingertips. Now that Allene's life had stopped churning with violent sadness, she missed her more than ever. And then she silently berated herself. Here she was again thinking of her own needs, when these children were motherless. Motherless! She blinked away her tears.

"I am glad you come, Miss Allene," Mr. Rossi began. "You are so kind to the children of my poor Lucia."

Allene stared at Mr. Rossi blankly. "I'm sorry, to what do you refer?"

"He's speaking of the trust you set up for Catarina and Rafaele, and the new deed," Ernie reminded her with a slight crinkle to his left eye that Mr. Rossi could not have seen. "You know, to compensate for her lost wages, since she died."

"The trust," Allene said slowly. What a wonderful idea.

Mr. Rossi nodded. "Yes. We signed papers last week. And we move in only two days ago! Close to family. Close to my shop."

"Mr. Rossi was a classics professor in northern Italy," Ernie explained. "But there were no jobs. Lucy came over with him when she was only ten and studied while he worked as a tailor. Her husband died just after the twins were born, and the tailoring work didn't bring in much money. Most of it came from Lucy. After she died, they were considering going back home."

"*Ritornati*," Mr. Rossi said, nodding.

"But now they can stay. The children can get a good American education. And Mr. Rossi's hours are better, so he can care for Lucy's children."

Allene went silent. For a long while, she let Ernie and Mr. Rossi chat, their conversation flowing between Italian and Latin. Latin, of all languages! At one point, Mr. Rossi switched back to English to say something to Allene about murder.

She flushed red. "Pardon me?"

"I say, I knew you did not hurt anybody. In the newspapers. About your friend, the girl? Lucia says, not my Miss Allene."

"Lucia? What did she say?"

"One day she come home with silver polish. A big can. She says she did not want police to think you did it. Because you like the *chimica* so much, and because she knew you not like that girl who died."

Allene dropped her mouth in surprise. She remembered. Even then, Lucia protected her, even when she didn't know the truth. Even when Allene thought her actions were suspicious.

She hung her head. "I don't think I ever did a single thing to deserve having your sister in my life," she said. "Everything she did for me—I can't ever be thankful enough."

"*Acceptissima semper, munera sunt, auctor quae pretiosa facit.*" Mr. Rossi turned to Ernie for a translation.

"It's Ovid. The most acceptable gifts . . . are the ones made precious by our love of the giver."

Allene nodded and dabbed at her eyes again. She could feel Mr. Rossi smiling at her with pity. Her heart ached for Lucia, and she wondered if the ache would ever abate. Ernie stood up, and Allene did too.

"It's getting late. And you'll be wanting dinner," Ernie said. Allene looked longingly at the three children, who were chattering in English and laughing over a jumping jack of Catarina's. Considering the age difference, they got along splendidly. And Holly hadn't played with any children at all in months. Allene had to refrain from sweeping the twins into her arms somehow.

"Ah, please stay for dinner," Mr. Rossi offered. "It's too much for three people. Come, eat." He waved toward the kitchen, from which came the savory scents of chicken and sauces bubbling.

"Oh, but . . . won't it be too much trouble?" Allene asked.

"No, no. You two, sit." Mr. Rossi left them to go to the kitchen. Allene turned quickly and pinned Ernie's hand with her own.

"What is going on here? A trust? Did you set it up?"

"Yes."

"And you told him I did it?"

"Yes."

"Ernie Fielding? What are you up to?"

Ernie stood up and leaned against the mantel. The fire flickered and glowed against his skin. He frowned and clenched a fist as thoughts flitted across his forehead. "You know, I'm really terrible at this."

"At what? Making secret financial plans and giving other people the credit?"

"Oh, at that I'm a whiz, no doubt." He grinned, then frowned again. "But, ah, I'm terrible at . . . courting."

Allene dropped her lower lip and stopped breathing for several seconds. "What?"

"I know. It's awful to even bring this up, after everything with Andrew and . . . everything. See, I knew what Lucy meant to you. Lucia, I mean." He fiddled with the andiron by the fireplace. Poor Ernie was talking so fast Allene could hardly keep up. "I just . . . wanted to help. I don't want it to seem like I'm buying you favors. I swear that isn't my intention. I would never disrespect her family in such a way. I just figured you'd have done the same thing, but you had so much on your hands these past few weeks. So I just made it happen a little faster."

"How did you do it? Did you speak with my lawyers?"

"Oh, I used my own money." He waved his hand like he was shooing away a fly. He cautiously stole a glance at Allene. "I'm good at money. And you can pay me back, of course."

"Wait a second." Allene stood up. She heard dishes clanking in the dining room but ignored them. Holly gave a whoop as she chased Catarina and Rafaele upstairs. Good. She needed to say this without a witness. "Ernest Fielding. What else have you done?" Allene whispered. When Ernie stayed silent, she took another step closer. "What else?"

"I . . . I was the one who helped out Jasper's uncle. I was the one who approached your father and Fred Jones about the insurance policy. I made it seem like an investment, a five hundred percent return."

"Why didn't you do it yourself?"

"Well, my parents are very particular about *my* money. At least until my trust fund came to fruition, when I turned eighteen. Which I just did. They didn't let me touch any of it before." He shrugged. "But I knew how important your friends are. I remembered you mentioning Jasper's suit, how he wasn't so well off. So I tried to help him and his uncle, for you. I didn't realize that at the time it made me—or rather, your father—look like a murderer."

"All right. I can understand that, but was there something else?"

"Yes, but you won't be happy about it."

"I can take it." She took another step closer and slipped her hand into Ernie's. It was surprising how large and strong it was.

"I urged Andrew and his father to purchase a large share in the Ansonia Clock factory last year. I did some digging and found out that was where Birdie worked. I knew how close you two had been. It was so her job would never be in jeopardy. My father drew the line at an investment that large for his own money. So I asked Andrew, whose family was looking to expand their portfolio anyway. But I didn't realize that they . . . if I had known that Andrew and Birdie would . . ."

"Ah. That explains a lot. So much, actually." She tightened her hand on Ernie's and smiled. "You know, that wasn't your fault. That was an inevitability no one could have prevented."

"Perhaps."

"And all those times you showed up at the funerals . . . I didn't know you even liked Florence."

"I didn't. But having someone our age, in our circle, just die like that—it was hard for me. I've no family in the war, no friends. My parents have never been ill or died. And then to have it happen over and over again—I just—" He shook his head. And Allene felt burning shame. For a while, they'd thought Ernie was the killer. He'd been mourning. *Mourning*, for God's sake.

Lately when she saw him, she recognized this new expression on his face. He'd been sobered by the cold truth of mortality. Oddly, it suited him. He was actually more handsome now, with a quiet thoughtfulness about him and a penetrating eye that made Allene blush when they caught each other's glance. She found that she wanted to touch his chin, capture it in her hands, and bring it closer.

"So," Allene said, clearing her throat. "You do have a funny way of courting a girl. A girl who was engaged!"

"Apparently."

"Well, I'm a funny girl, so it fits."

Just then, Mr. Rossi reentered. "Dinner is ready. *Per favore, mangia.*" He saw Allene's hand in Ernie's and smiled. "Oh! What is this?"

"Oh. I suppose you're the first to know, Mr. Rossi," Allene said.

"Know what, exactly?" Ernie asked nervously.

Allene gave him a shy smile. "That I'm being wooed."

"Well. If you court Miss Allene, she will be happier with a full stomach. *Mangia*," Mr. Rossi said brightly. He went to the stairs to call the children down.

Allene grinned. They called the children, who were ecstatic at being together for dinner. They sat as children ought, seen and not heard, while the adults continued their conversation in choppy English, Italian, and Latin. There were memories of Lucia, more tears, and even a little laugher. The pasta and braised chicken were consumed with the hearty appetites that accompany the happy and, for the moment, the fearless.

All in all, it was one of the best dinners Allene had ever had. The only thing missing was Lucia, and somehow, she felt as if Lucia were with them. On the way home in the deepening twilight, Holly fell asleep in Allene's lap. Allene wrapped a protective arm around her and leaned into Ernie.

"Ernie," Allene began, "what would you think if I told you I was applying for medical school?"

"Since when do you want to be a doctor? I always pegged you as a chemistry professor. All those fun parlor tricks of yours and all."

"I don't know. I think it was . . . because of Lucia. Taking care of her was something I'd never experienced. I find that I like to take care of people. I feel like there are a lot of Lucias out there that I could have saved if I'd been trained properly."

"You'd probably be the only woman in your classes."

"True."

"It'll be a lot of work."

"True."

"And the other students would probably flirt with you endlessly."

"It would be easy to ignore their advances if I were married," said Allene. It was an effort not to make her voice shake.

Ernie abruptly stopped talking. This time, it was he who commented, with excruciating slowness, "True."

They'd arrived at the Cutter house. The driver opened the doors, and Allene asked Josephine to put Holly to bed while she said good-bye to Ernie. She shut the door for privacy as they stood, chilled, on the street outside.

"I won't be an ordinary wife, you know," Allene warned him.

"If I wanted ordinary, I wouldn't be standing here with you, would I?"

"And Holly must be with me. She's my sister, see, and I'll not—"

"Holly would have to be safe," he said firmly. "With you. And us."

"Say that again."

Ernie took a step closer and stared down at Allene. She felt tiny next to him but held his hand as firmly as he held hers.

"Us," he murmured.

She stood on her tiptoes and took his face in her hands as she'd wanted to before. Ernie took her waist in his firm hands and pulled her ever closer.

Somewhere in the world at that moment, there was a birth, a death, a sunrise, and a sunset. There was despair, and a burst of laughter, a promise broken, and a vow made.

And there was this kiss.

It was far from disappointing.

CHAPTER 35

In November, Christmas came early. Twice.

An armistice was signed, and all the terrible killing overseas ceased. And then, for reasons unknown to the scientists in and around the city, influenza somehow loosened its stranglehold on the city in small, blessed increments. All of it was a relief, yet it left behind a bitterness that was impossible to spit out. After all, the dead from both catastrophes would never return.

The war never did consume Jasper, but he didn't feel graced with good luck. Oscar was forever gone. Birdie's actions haunted him. He thought about her every day and cursed himself for his accurate memory. In his mind's eye, he saw her standing in the dark, a luminescent goddess, in Allene's bedroom that night of the engagement party. He saw the swell of her milky breasts below the edge of her silk dress, her wide, elfin eyes staring blandly over her mother's casket.

Why? Why hadn't he understood the darkness already thrumming in her veins? Why had he been so blind to her actions and his own inability to see his future?

The night that Birdie had scribbled down the awful truth in her letter, Jasper dealt with not only his own blindness but his grief too. Theirs had been a magical, tumultuous few months together. Birdie had gotten her wish—they'd spent more time together than ever. But all the memories were laced with bad feelings. The stain would linger until Jasper and Allene themselves turned to dust.

The firemen came to the house and broke down Birdie's door, only to find that there was nothing to save but a corpse. The autopsy happened soon after, but it was one that Jasper refused to attend. The game, in the words of Birdie, was finally over. True, she had achieved a bit of immortality by having her picture and name in the papers the next day, hawked by the newsies on every corner. But the one unknown was still yet to be revealed. He waited, like Allene did, for the medical examiner's report several weeks later.

The day the report arrived, Allene quietly called him to the Cutter house so he could read the results himself. Jasper peered at the familiar script from the coroner's office.

"Blood cancer of the bones. Multiple fractures of the left tibia, right wrist, thoracic vertebrae numbers nine and ten. Advanced osteosarcoma of the leg. Jaw necrosis, bilateral, with abscesses. Saddle embolus of the pulmonary arteries." Jasper sat down and folded the papers. He felt as spent as he looked.

"Does it say anything about poison?" Allene asked.

"No. They couldn't find anything beyond a little ether, but that's no surprise. But it didn't kill her. The embolus did. It was enormous. She had no blood flow to her lungs after that clot hit her."

"So Birdie was right. There is a final mystery, isn't there? Why she had all those cancers?"

"Yes. But I for one won't be searching for the answer. Let the coroner do that. Not my job anymore."

That wasn't strictly true, though. Once the end of the war came, the morgue stopped needing him so desperately, but until then, Dr. Norris couldn't quite fire Jasper. A live body willing to work was something he was unable to reject, especially after he learned about how Jasper was innocent but irrevocably tied to Birdie and her legacy.

So when things began to quiet down a month later, Allene invited Jasper to go ice skating on the Seventy-Second Street Lake in Central Park. This was an exaggeration, of course. Allene all but dragged Jasper out of his uncle's depressing apartment to sit in the cold, on a bench, while they watched the healthier population of New York skate on the pond. Allene had put on her ice skates, but Jasper only kicked his rental skates where they lay unbuckled by his feet.

"What will you do?" Allene asked. She wasn't asking about the skates.

"I don't know." He gave her a sideways glance. "Where's Ernie?" Allene blushed immediately, as expected. "He's a rare old scout, isn't he?" Allene blushed deeper, so he stopped. Clouds of breath framed her auburn hair.

"Don't change the subject. So why don't you go to school?"

"I don't want to be a doctor anymore."

"Why not?"

He shrugged. After taking care of Allene, something inside of him had ignited painfully, burnt, and collapsed into ash. "I think . . . I'm going to apply for graduate school." He took a deep breath. "In chemistry."

Allene stared at him before bursting out in laughter. Hoots and hollers and guffaws most unbecoming of a proper Upper East Side socialite. A few skaters slowed down to stare at her quizzically.

"What on earth is wrong with you?" Jasper asked.

"Oh, Jasper. It's just . . . funny."

"Why?"

She told him about her plans. He stared at her in wonder, but the wonder lasted only a few seconds. This was Allene, after all. "You know," she said, "I always thought between the two of us, *I* was the better chemist."

"You are. For now," he challenged.

She hugged his arm. "Now, I suppose you'll be vying for the Nobel Prize or be a preeminent scholar at the best universities. Am I correct?"

Jasper tried to temper his emotions. He hadn't thought chemistry was his forte, but it had insinuated itself into his life while he'd danced around death and ambition. Like a partner written in last on his dance card, it waited its turn to show its worth. There was a solace in studying the elements that he desperately sought. There was a steadiness to its logic that didn't depend on the whims of people. Chemistry would reward him with alchemic twists and explosions. It told stories that were altogether inhuman. That he could handle. It was the hospital and its inhabitants, dead and alive, that he could no longer bear.

"I have a brilliant, three-step plan. Do you want to hear it?" he began, reaching for his ice skates.

"Of course!"

Jasper buckled them on before hobbling out onto the edge of the ice. He had remarkably weak ankles that bowed inward, and his knees shook. It was an odd thing for him to feel so physically precarious. He offered his hand to Allene.

"The first part of the plan," he announced, "is not to fall on this ice and permanently injure my pride."

"Excellent." She grabbed his hand and joined him on the ice, far more steady than he. "And the second?"

"Buy some candy for Holly."

"Well done. You're a stellar godfather. And the third?"

"Wake up tomorrow morning, and keep going."

Allene nodded her approval, and Jasper attempted to smile. It wasn't much, but it would do. He took a shaky step, feeling the ice beneath the blade of his skate. Allene had released his hand already; his unsteadiness was holding her back. She sped past him with a whoop and swirl of woolen skirt. In the spring, this ice would melt and the lake would reappear. In ten years, these skates would be irreparably rusted. In thirty, his hair would gray, if he were that lucky. How capricious and temporary everything was. He wondered when the feeling would go away, if ever.

He thought of Oscar and how much he must have understood about this blasted world, how he'd refuse to eat breakfast or read the news after their parents died. "What's the point?" he'd say, dead toned, and he was right. Hopelessness had murdered him before he'd ever set foot in Camp Upton. Jasper realized it would be an uphill battle not to become his brother. But he was willing to fight, goddammit.

And then he shrugged, just as Allene circled around him and taunted him to catch up with her.

Step one, he thought to himself, and dug into the ice with his toe.

AUTHOR'S NOTE

All physicians can tell you that medical school and residency leave an indelible mark on their lives. I myself had the privilege and honor to study at New York University School of Medicine and complete my training in primary care internal medicine at NYU as well. For both of these stages in my career, much of my time was spent at Bellevue Hospital. I had heard of Bellevue's both infamy and acclaim, but there was precious little time during those busy years to learn about its long and colorful backstory.

And yet the history was ever present on campus. There were the iron gates on First Avenue; the men's shelter that was once the psychiatric hospital; the original pathology building, a classic McKim, Mead & White design. The office of the chief medical examiner was across the street from my dorm room. When I began writing fiction, I knew I would at some point include Bellevue as an homage to my relationship with the campus and its people.

A second influence in writing this book is thanks to Deborah Blum, who wrote *The Poisoner's Handbook: Murder and the Birth of Forensic Medicine in Jazz Age New York* (Penguin, 2010). Here was a fantastic trip into the origin of modern forensic medicine, and at Bellevue, no less. Dr. Norris and Dr. Gettler are true pioneers in the field, and I did my best to tip my hat to them and maintain their personalities, while having fun bringing them to life in this fictional world. Furthermore, after reading and rereading passages on methanol, chloroform, arsenic, cyanide, and radium, I was entranced. Birdie's, Allene's, and Jasper's characters popped into my head, each with their own identities, each inspired deeply by this nonfiction book that took my love of chemistry and pathology, and urged me to transform it into a story.

Around the same time that I read *The Poisoner's Handbook*, I got my paws on *The Great Influenza: The Story of the Deadliest Pandemic in History* by John M. Barry (Penguin, 2005). Seriously, this book terrified me. On multiple occasions, I found myself yelling at my husband, Bernie (also a doctor, whom I met in medical school and who thus shares my love of Bellevue), "*Oh my God, this is terrifying. You have to read this.*" (Eventually, he did. And he was terrified too.)

Some may read my novel and think I have exaggerated the swiftness and virulence of the 1918 influenza epidemic. After all, it's not like the flu that hits the United States every year, is it? But I attempted to stay as historically accurate as possible. This strain was a beast like no other. It killed the young more often than the old. People indeed died within hours of showing their first symptoms, and yes, their faces turned startling dark shades from hypoxia, and yes, blood poured from their orifices. It was, however, fascinating to incorporate influenza in this murder mystery as its own lone wolf, one that could care less about the whims and plans of all humans but would affect them forever.

I did leave one mystery unanswered at the end of this story, and that is the fate of poor Birdie Dreyer. Birdie died of radium poisoning. It was convenient to consider her being poisoned as a red herring—who could be trying to kill off one of our story's heroines? To be historically accurate, though, I couldn't include closure on this, as radium poisoning in the dial painters of the time wasn't truly understood and discovered until the early 1920s.

The element radium was discovered by Marie Curie in 1898 and later isolated in 1910. It's been said that Curie adored this glowing element so much that she often carried a sample of it in her skirt pocket—a habit that contributed to her death from aplastic anemia. Her personal possessions are said to be so radioactive that they are kept isolated in lead-lined boxes for posterity. Radium's ability to glow in the dark (and energize zinc sulfide to fluoresce in dial paints) made it immediately attractive in clock and watch manufacturing. Unfortunately, the women who painted this radioluminescent substance often "tipped" their camel-hair brushes, twirling them on their wet lips to keep a sharp point. By doing so, they ingested the radioactive element. Some painters would playfully put the paint on their teeth for a Cheshire cat smile in the dark or put it in their hair. They literally glowed in the dark from the dust after a day's work, just as Birdie did.

By the end of the 1920s, many women had been diagnosed with radiation poisoning in the form of severe anemias, jaw necrosis, and debilitating bone cancers. Several dial painters—Grace Fryer, Edna Hussman, Katherine Schaub, Quinta McDonald, and Albina Larice—were dubbed the "Radium Girls" and sued the US Radium Corporation. They settled in 1928, but their work laid the foundation for modern labor safety regulations. For those that wish to learn more, I highly recommend reading Claudia Clark's *Radium Girls: Women and Industrial Health Reform, 1910–1935* (University of North Carolina Press, 1997).

And finally, an answer to the question posed in the book: What's my favorite molecule? It's a tie between water (it's more complicated than many people realize) and isoamyl acetate—the essence of Juicy Fruit. I have fond memories of making the ester in high school organic chemistry lab.

Also, it's my favorite gum.

ACKNOWLEDGMENTS

Authors often speak of a mystical animal called "the book of their heart." In many ways, this was *that* book—one that drew from my own personal history with Bellevue Hospital and my long love affair with science. So, to the colleagues I've worked with at Bellevue, and the thousands who've cared for those very special Bellevue patients in the past, I thank you. And to every science teacher out there, your passion for this beautiful earth, down to the subatomic level—it lives on in all your students.

I also have many people to thank without whose support this book never could have been created. To my husband, Bernie, my biggest fan and best friend. To my children, who are my best inventions of all time. I love you all so dearly. And to my extended family, who always supports me in my creative endeavors. Eric Myers, my agent, has always been a champion of my books, no matter how quirky and odd they are. Sarah Fine, thank you again for your encouragement when this story was but an infant of an idea. Your friendship has meant so much. To my many beta readers—Miriam Forster, Mindy McGinnis, Dushana Yoganathan, Cat Winters, and Maurene Goo—thank you for pointing out the flaws and making it shine that much more. Many people helped with historical details—the staff at the Brooklyn Historical Society, the staff at the Tenement Museum in New York City and especially David Favoloro, and Deb Salisbury—thank you so much. Any inaccuracies in the text are due to my own choices. To Lacey Boldyrev, Matthew Richard Lesinski, and Anna Staniszewski, *dziękuję* for the Polish expertise. To Caitlin Alexander, for her excellent editorial input. You made this project glow! To Sara Addicott, Kirsten Colton, and Katie Allison, who helped make this story absolutely shine. And to Pepe Nymi, who made it pretty!

And finally, to my editor, Jodi Warshaw, and my team at Lake Union Publishing, who fell in love with Jasper, Birdie, and Allene and gave them a chance to find an audience. I am forever grateful for your vision and your support.

ABOUT THE AUTHOR

Photo © 2012 Chelsea Donoho

Lydia Kang is a physician and author of fiction, poetry, and nonfiction. She was born in Baltimore, Maryland, and graduated from Columbia University and New York University School of Medicine. She completed her residency and chief residency at Bellevue Hospital in New York City and currently lives in the Midwest, where she continues to practice internal medicine.